CHILD OF DRACO

CHILD OF DRACO

MELISSA RAKESTRAW

For my mom,
who always told me I was better than everyone and instilled
a sense of unwavering self-confidence within me.
You're my hero.

For my children,
I hope you always believe in dragons,
and know when and how to slay them.

And to all the queer kids growing up in rural, conservative places around
the world;
you are needed and your story isn't over.
I love you all.

Copyright © 2024 by Melissa Rakestraw
All rights reserved. No part of this book may be reproduced in any manner whatsoever without written permission except in the case of brief quotations embodied in critical articles and reviews.
First Printing, 2024

Contents

Dedication   iv

1	Chapter One	1
2	Chapter Two	9
3	Chapter Three	19
4	Chapter Four	31
5	Chapter Five	41
6	Chapter Six	55
7	Chapter Seven	65
8	Chapter Eight	75
9	Chapter Nine	85
10	Chapter Ten	95
11	Chapter Eleven	105
12	Chapter Twelve	119
13	Chapter Thirteen	127
14	Chapter Fourteen	137
15	Chapter Fifteen	145
16	Chapter Sixteen	155
17	Chapter Seventeen	163
18	Chapter Eighteen	173
19	Chapter Nineteen	185

20	Chapter Twenty	201
21	Chapter Twenty-One	209
22	Chapter Twenty-Two	219
23	Chapter Twenty-Three	233
24	Chapter Twenty-Four	243
25	Chapter Twenty-Five	251
26	Chapter Twenty-Six	263
27	Chapter Twenty-Seven	275
28	Chapter Twenty-Eight	285
29	Chapter Twenty-Nine	295
30	Chapter Thirty	303
31	Chapter Thirty-One	311
32	Chapter Thirty-Two	319
33	Chapter Thirty-Three	327
34	Epilogue	337

About the Author   340

1

Chapter One

The forest was a haven, insulated against the vibrating energy of the outside world. A weary traveler could lay there on the thick moss carpet, the musty scent of earth enveloping them as they did so, and the deafening silence would cause their ears to ring. Nora sought this silence on the rare occasions she could slip away from the DuPont Estate. Insects climbed over her out-stretched limbs and she lay still, barely daring to breathe, as she imagined her skin being replaced by rough tree bark and spatterings of mushrooms. Her long brown hair fanned out around her were twisting tendrils of roots creeping through the thick ferns and giving small creatures refuge, her arms and legs submerged below the forest floor as rolling hills of moss broken up only by the steady stream that cut through the forest and connected it to the outside world.

Nora let her hand slide across the moss-covered stones lining the creek and dipped her fingers in, allowing her arm to be tugged along by the current as she felt her eyelids droop. She rested her cheek on the mossy floor and allowed herself to drift into a soft slumber, inhaling the smells of the forest as she drifted.

"Are you sniffing the ground, love?" A voice called from the tree line.

Nora's eyes shot open, and she sat up with a start, relaxing at the sight of the older woman making her way through the thick forest brush.

"You shouldn't sneak up on people like that, Tulee." Nora grumbled as she stood, wiping the dirt from her breeches.

"I wouldn't say I was sneaking." Tulee looked Nora over and brushed off bits of dirt and moss from Nora's back. "Your mother wants you."

Nora frowned. Tulee tried her best to not refer to Lady Adelle DuPont as Nora's mother, but occasionally she slipped and the reminder was a hot iron to Nora's heart. Any motherly love Adelle had within her was reserved only for her oldest daughter, Larissa, the only one of the two daughters who had any magical ability. After years of rigorous testing, Adelle gave up on Nora, sending her entirely to the care of Tulee, the head of staff at the DuPont estate. Adelle might have given birth to Nora, but she was no mother to her.

Nora followed Tulee down the winding forest path until they broke through the tree line and found themselves on a bluff overlooking the estate. The main building stood a proud three stories high boasting ornate wooden balconies dripping with wisteria, and a handful of small courtyards that broke the building up into different sections. They walked the trail down into one of the courtyards, making their way through the small potted herb gardens the kitchen staff kept nearby and the shady seating areas the staff escaped to during rare moments of leisure. Darker slabs of flagstone tucked into the shadows of this particular courtyard signaled the staff entrance, a common theme most lords and ladies requested to keep the help from mingling with their esteemed guests. Nora looked for the dark flagstone patterns at other estates she visited, surprised at the obvious security breach but aware that aside from lowly staff, most people would never notice.

"Hurry and change; she'll want you presentable." Tulee thrust a dress into Nora's arms and nervously shoved her into the washroom.

Nora quickly changed and ran water through her long tangled hair, smoothing out the fly aways that Adelle never failed to comment on and scrubbing the dirt from beneath her fingernails. She inspected her face in the mirror, her blue eyes searching for any signs of dirt or debris that would give away her lazing about in the forest. She turned in the mirror and surveyed herself; at twenty-four, she had shed away all signs of girlhood and was growing into features she had once seen as awkward. Her body was softer, her eyes wiser, her face rounder than it had been years ago when she was all elbows and knees and grime. She stepped out of the washroom to be fussed over by Tulee, who gave Nora's hair the usual look of disapproval.

"This damned hair. If you would just let me braid—"

"It ends up a mess no matter what we do to it," Nora argued as the woman spun her around slowly. "What's the occasion today? A duke? Wizard? A man come to finally whisk her away?"

"Actually, a princess." Tulee smiled when Nora whirled around to meet her gaze. "No smart-ass remarks? Have I finally stunned you into silence?"

"What princess?" Nora looked at the heaps of freshly baked buns cooling on a wire rack and reached for one.

"Hey!" A stout older woman shouted, swatting Nora's hand away. "They aren't for you!"

"Cookie. I'm *starving*."

"Serves you right running off to the forest and not eating with the rest of us!" Cookie scolded, rolling the cooling rack out of Nora's reach. She gave Nora a sharp look and handed her a bun, grumbling as she did so, and returned to her work in the kitchen.

"As I was saying. The princess is the daughter of the King of Madrall; I don't know her name, but she is to be wed to Prince Adrian tomorrow at the Temple of The Faith. Apparently, the princess is devout."

Temples of The Faith littered Troque and were pillars of resources and aid to areas far from the royal city. Ran by women who lived simple lives, it mostly concerned itself with charity and help for those in need. A royal hadn't married outside the castle in ages. But, if they chose a temple, Nora knew the one in Sorudi was the best option. Not only was it closer to Madrall and the largest of all the temples, but, in Nora's opinion, it was the most beautiful. She had gone several times with Tulee, and each time the stunning beauty of the large white stone building with glittering stained-glass windows that cast shimmering rainbows of light across the pews within left Nora speechless. The temple's surrounding gardens, open to all, buzzed with musicians and artists.

"Tomorrow seems kind of sudden."

"Yes, it is. Adelle generously offered the west wing to house the princess and her entourage until her wedding night; it should at least bring some excitement." Tulee stepped back and surveyed Nora one last time. "This will have to do."

"Why does she want to see me? With everything happening, I'm better off hiding away."

"Just don't give her any reason to be unkind." Tulee's voice was steady, but Nora could read the worry in the older woman's eyes.

Nora smiled reassuringly. "I'll be on my best behavior."

Tulee nodded as she took a deep breath and thrust Nora into the great hall before her. Large stone pillars supported the vaulted ceiling, with depictions of celestial beings during the Great War covering the entire ceiling. A platform, where musicians occasionally played, stood at the far end of the room, and a long mahogany table capable of seating twenty sat before it. At the side that Nora and Tulee entered, there was an enormous fireplace and small sitting area with mahogany bookshelves and a marble chess board that Nora had never seen used, but Adelle insisted be polished daily. Between the platform and the fireplace was a large archway that opened up into the main entryway and, as Nora's eyes adjusted to the dim light of the hall, she saw the form of Adelle and Nora's sister, Larissa, standing in the archway.

"Finally. What took you so long?" Adelle demanded, her footsteps echoing through the room as she hurried towards them.

"Sorry, ma'am." Tulee kept her eyes fixed ahead, avoiding the question entirely.

Adelle shot Nora a dark look and returned her attention to Tulee. "I gave Cookie a full order for each meal. Meet with her to get details."

Tulee stood frozen for a long moment before turning.

"Come, Nora—"

"She will stay." Adelle's voice was icy, and Nora saw the delight in her eyes as Tulee pursed her lips.

"Ma'am—"

"She will stay."

Tulee nodded, squeezing Nora's hand gently and walking from the room towards the kitchen. Nora kept her eyes fixed on the wall in front of her, barely daring to breathe as the sound of Tulee's footsteps eventually disappeared. She could see in her peripheral Larissa shuffling awkwardly beside the dining table, and Nora wondered what her sister was thinking. Did she know what Adelle was about to do? Did she care?

"The princess is coming to stay with us, as you know." Adelle glanced around the room. "Her head of staff sent instructions for us to prepare for her arrival. I have added my own chores to the list. These tasks are for you."

Adelle handed Nora a piece of paper that presented a sweeping list of chores that made Nora's eyes widen. Sweeping out fireplaces, cleaning rugs and tapestries, polishing, dusting, lighting fires, preparing a bath—all this work that normally took multiple people several days to complete.

"This is to be done *today*?" Nora was careful to keep her voice devoid of emotion. Adelle enjoyed nothing more than getting a rise from her, and keeping her composure was Nora's one power against her mother.

"Before dinner." Adelle stood beside Larissa, who kept her eyes fixed on the ground, refusing to look at her sister.

"Ma'am, might I have some help? If we want the princess to feel welcome—"

""What's the use of you being here if you can't do simple tasks? Perhaps if you weren't spending your days lazing about in the forest, you would have had much of this done already."

Nora felt heat rise to her face at the mention of the forest. She had been careful to leave when Adelle was sleeping. Someone must have reported her. Her eyes met Adelle's, and she felt like prey caught in the gaze of a predator. A cruel smile spread across Adelle's face.

Nora straightened. "I will do what I can, but this is impossible for one person to achieve on their own. So, when it's not to the princess' standards, it will be a poor reflection of *you*."

"Nora—" Larissa's voice was pleading, but she was cut off by the sound of Adelle's hand striking Nora across the face.

Nora dropped to the ground, her vision spinning from the impact, and blinked her eyes hard as she tried to refocus.

"Don't you ever talk to me like that again." Adelle walked past Nora, digging her heel into Nora's hand and twisting it down hard.

Nora screamed as the heel pierced her skin, and she felt the warmth of blood pouring from the wound. Adelle kept walking, leaving a trail of blood behind her.

Larissa knelt to Nora and inspected her hand as she held Nora upright with her free arm. She murmured an incantation, and warm magic radiated through Nora's hand. She winced as her sister's magic worked to stop the bleeding.

"Larissa! Come, *now!*" Adelle stood near the kitchen door and Nora could see Tulee standing behind her, a hand clasped over her mouth.

"Mother, her hand." Larissa kept her gaze focused on Nora's hand.

"A lesson in manners! Come, I won't say it again."

Larissa looked at their mother and then back into Nora's eyes. Nora nodded, grateful enough to no longer be bleeding, and braced herself against the wall as she stood. She turned and looked at Adelle, allowing one of the rare slips of rage to show across her face.

Larissa furrowed her brow as she inspected her blood-soaked hands, looking up at Nora with a confused expression before hurrying after Adelle.

"You're a mess; let's get you cleaned up." Adelle crooned at her eldest daughter.

Adelle led Larissa from the room, and as she disappeared through the doorway, Larissa stole a glance back at Nora before following their mother. As soon as they were gone, Tulee burst through the kitchen doors and sprinted across the hall to Nora. Resting against the cool stone wall, Nora focused on the paintings above as Tulee examined her hand. She felt her heart race as the familiar attacks that she suffered most of her life took hold of her. Her breathing became shallow and frantic and it was as if a great weight pressed down upon her chest. She inhaled slowly, counting to three and closing her eyes as she released the breath. She continued like that as Tulee wordlessly spread salve over the wound and pulled out a piece of cloth to wrap her hand.

Nora opened her eyes and returned her attention to the painting above. The king of the Gods, Draco, peered down upon her in his magnificent dragon form. Blue and purple scales made of the night sky wove around brightly colored stars that made up the pattern of the constellation, and its bright blue eyes seemed to watch Nora, anticipating her next move. Nora met its gaze, realizing in that moment her entire life was a wait for her to act.

"I shouldn't have left you," Tulee murmured as she led Nora into the kitchen.

Nora felt a calm spread through her and she let out a slow breath as she followed Tulee into the kitchen. Clutched in her uninjured hand was the list of tasks waiting ahead of her, and she knew that the punishment waiting for her if she failed to complete them was much worse than a bloodied hand.

2

Chapter Two

With her hand bandaged up, Nora hurried through her chores before returning to clean out the fireplaces in each of the bedrooms. Tulee was busy in town gathering food and drink for their visitors, but had instructed the staff to assist Nora in any way they could without Adelle being aware. As Nora moved through the rooms, she noticed that someone had removed the curtains from the windows and had them ready to be washed, with some already hung out to dry. The main entryway, polished and spotless, flooded Nora with relief as she noticed more and more tasks being completed as she readied the rooms for their guests.

They had secured five rooms, which was a surprisingly small amount for a princess to be traveling with, but their lands had long been peaceful. Aside from a princess staying at their estate, the servants seemed most excited about the celebrations that would take place sometimes for weeks after the ceremony. Nora vaguely remembered when King Alexander had remarried after his wife had died and even Tulee, who wasn't usually concerned with the affairs of the wealthy, had joined in the celebrations and had taken Nora into town to get some cakes for the staff to share.

Nora, however, was most excited about the prospect of her mother being gone for a few weeks, as she was to take Larissa to the palace to train at the Royal Mage Academy. King Alexander himself had extended the invitation, which was unusual as Larissa at twenty-seven had surpassed the typical first year academy age by almost a decade. They wasted no time in securing an apartment so Adelle could join her daughter as often as possible. Nora hoped for her own sake that this would afford her weeks, perhaps months, where Adelle would be so occupied with reveling with the royals that Nora could figure out a life outside of this world. She knew in her heart she could not stay in this house forever.

The smell of food wafting through the air signaled to Nora that dinner was about to be served, and that their guests had likely already arrived. She hurried to fill the large copper tub with boiling water and Tulee's own special blend of herbs that would promote relaxation, and sprinted down the servants' quarters to change into a more presentable dress and fix her unruly hair. She pinched her cheeks until they reddened and hurried to meet Tulee in the kitchen.

"You look stunning!" Tulee exclaimed proudly as she turned Nora around. "If I could just braid—"

"Let it go," Nora teased, moving to peek into the dining hall. A string quartet played on the platform at the opposite end and Adelle sat perched at the end of the table, busying herself with explaining the paintings that decorated the room.

The princess had long red hair that was braided back from her face and hung past her waist. Her skin was deeply tanned, and she wore plain traveling clothes—not at all what Nora had expected. She raised her eyebrows with interest as Adelle spoke, casting occasional sidelong glances at a guard seated across from her, who did his best to conceal his annoyance. Nora smiled at the way Adelle was so self-involved she couldn't see the way she put people off. It was a slight comfort to Nora that people who spent time with Adelle never truly cared for her.

"Food is ready. Come on, ladies!" Tulee called out to the staff.

Each staff member took a rolling cart and moved across the room towards the table. Nora realized at that moment just how far away the table was and the uncomfortable silence between the music stopping as the musicians prepared a new song and the sound of wheels scraping against the marble floor made Nora's face flush with embarrassment. Adelle surveyed each staff member, her eyes lingering over Nora's bandaged hand before raising her glass to be filled by a staff member carrying a bottle of wine.

Nora stood across from the princess just behind her guard and could see she had thousands of freckles covering her face and her bright green eyes seemed to take in everyone in the room. Her heart pounded hard in her chest as the princess surveyed her, her eyes lingering on her hand for a half a second before moving on to the next staff member. The command of the princess's presence even in such casual attire left her feeling a strange sense of awe.

The servants lifted the lids from the trays and made their way around the table, offering the contents to each person. Princess Gabriella met anyone serving her with kindness, asking them questions about their lives there, if they had children, or what they would recommend from their tray. The staff continued to move around, Adelle watching each one so carefully she didn't notice when Nora served her and Larissa.

"Thank you," Larissa mumbled.

Nora nodded and continued until she stood before the princess herself.

"Your highness." Nora bowed her head slightly.

"Briella." The princess murmured as she surveyed the food.

"It's sweet bread."

The princess froze and looked up at Nora before bursting into laughter. "No, my name! My name is not 'highness', just Briella. But I will take some sweet bread."

Nora flushed and straightened as the eyes of Adelle burned through her back.

"What happened to your hand?" Briella asked as she examined the breads.

"Just an accident earlier today." Nora focused on her breathing, trying to keep her mind blank. She just needed to get through this dinner.

"What kind of accident?" Briella looked up at Nora and cocked her head to the side. "Does it hurt?"

Nora flushed a deeper shade of red, painfully aware that all eyes were on her, and stared back into Briella's face. Her eyes seemed full of mischief, as if she was giving someone a dare, but they softened as moments passed with Nora not speaking. The softening and concern surprised Nora, and she found the princess to be in that moment something entirely unexpected. She had seen nobles have a causal interest in staff before, polite questions here and there, but Briella seemed genuinely concerned and the longer Nora withheld answers, the more interested the princess seemed to be.

"Sorry—I fell while carrying a tray and the glass broke and cut through my hand. Thankfully, the staff here are equipped to deal with these sorts of accidents and I can assure you I am quite pain free." Nora held up her hand and smiled. "Thank you for asking."

Briella smiled. "I am glad to hear Lady Adelle takes such good care of her staff. That is not always the case in some households."

Nora bowed and pushed the cart to the next person at the table. As she moved down the line, she looked back at Briella, who watched Nora as she drank her wine. A chill ran up Nora's spine, something between excitement and fear, and she busied herself with serving the rest of the dinner party before hurrying back into the kitchen.

"She can't be a real princess! She wasn't even wearing a dress!" One maid complained, clearly upset that there wasn't more fanfare.

"There will be plenty of time for gowns and dresses, Lily. She has been on the road for days. You can't blame the girl for wanting to be comfortable." Tulee chided the girl, urging the staff to make their own plates quickly so they could clean up.

Nora made herself a plate and wordlessly left the bustling kitchen to go find a place she could eat in silence. She loved the staff like family, but the work from the day had left her bone-tired and she knew if she had to listen to gossiping maids any longer, she would surely descend into madness. She wandered into the courtyard just outside the dining hall and found a small spot where she could see clearly while being concealed by some of the greenery that surrounded the building.

Briella was sipping her wine, listening to Lord Bennet, an old friend of Adelle's deceased husband, as he likely regaled her with stories from long ago that had progressively become more interesting as time had gone on. Briella's eyes glazed over as she nodded politely, only looking away to take another bite and eye the guard that sat across from her occasionally. The guard was older, his hair mostly gray with darker wisps of black. Tulee had come back out with one other servant with trays of desserts and was now locked in conversation with the man, and Nora smiled as Tulee blushed and shook her head, hurrying off to the next guest. The guard's gaze followed her and Tulee stole a few glances back at him, shaking her head and smiling as she continued to serve everyone. Adelle conversed with a stern-looking older woman who seemed to have authority over everything Briella needed. The woman matched Adelle's own imposing stature, and it looked to Nora like two wolves circling each other as they ironed out details and arrangements.

Nora finished her food slowly and returned her gaze to the princess, who was no longer at her seat. Nora looked around the room lazily before straightening at the sound of a twig breaking behind her. She quickly stood and paled at the sight of the princess before her.

"Your highness!"

"Shhh! It's ok, I just needed some fresh air." Briella smiled and held her hands out in front of her in surrender. "I saw you sitting out here alone and thought this might be a good place to get away from the chatter."

Nora felt a wave of embarrassment wash over her. "I was just—"

"It doesn't matter to me what you were doing, as long as you stop calling me 'highness'. Such a peculiar word 'highness', I'm not tall, and it just makes it seem like I'm on some other plane of existence looking down on everyone."

"If I may be frank, some might argue that members of nobility, particularly royalty, are on another plane of existence." Nora looked back at her Adelle, who was now directing servants with the woman who had escorted Briella.

"It would surprise you to know how similar we are." Briella followed Nora's gaze. "Her name is Alice. She means to marry my father."

"Does that displease you?" Nora moved to a small bench and watched Briella as she continued to watch Alice and Adelle command the servants.

"It would have, once. When I was young, I would've been furious, but my father has changed since my mother passed and this woman seems to suit him. It doesn't matter to me. I am to be sold off to your prince and will never see either of them again."

"You do not love the prince?"

"I do not *know* the prince." She turned to face Nora, her eyes searching Nora's face. "Would you want to marry someone you have only heard vague rumors about?"

Nora shook her head, keeping her eyes on Briella.

Briella smiled and looked out at the fields of heather that surrounded the estate. The sun had set, and fireflies flickered in the distance. She was an imposing figure, but Nora saw a softness within her. She watched as Briella marveled at the lights of the fireflies in the distance, and she smiled as Briella jumped back when one lit up in front of her.

"We don't have fireflies in Madrall." Briella reached her hand out and allowed the tiny insect to land on her hand. "They're beautiful."

Nora watched as Briella brought the bug closer to her face, the blinking light illuminating the wonder in her face.

"There're loads of fireflies in this area, especially in the forest." Nora stood and held her hand out, allowing the firefly to crawl from Briella's hand to hers. "Maybe if you get some reprieve from royal duties, you could come back; I would be happy to show you."

Briella furrowed her brows for a moment, watching the firefly as it crawled across Nora's hand and eventually returned to the field. A great weight seemed to bear down on the princess in their shared silence. Nora wondered for a moment if she said the wrong thing; the anxiety of Briella's sudden change in mood caused the hairs on the back of her neck to rise. She knew what awaited her if she angered such a distinguished guest in her mother's estate.

"My path is uncertain. I don't know what to expect in the coming months–days even. But thank you for your invitation; it is one that under normal circumstances, I would accept unflinchingly." Briella offered Nora a small smile. "Well, I had better head back before Horace comes looking for me. I will see you at the wedding?"

Nora nodded and bowed as Briella returned to the dining hall, relief and frustration flooding her guard's face. Tulee made her way out of the hall and into the courtyard, looking around at the fireflies for a moment before she realized Nora was standing nearby.

"There you are, love." Tulee grabbed Nora's bandaged hand and turned it over as she inspected it. "We'll need to change this tonight."

The trees in the surrounding forest swayed in the steadily increasing summer breeze and the light of the fireflies dissipated as the wind ran through the heather and over the estate into the town below. Unseasonably hot, Nora closed her eyes against the warmth and debris, following Tulee inside through the servants' entrance. Their hair billowed around them and the kitchen door slammed shut with the sudden force of the wind.

"Well, that was unexpected!" Tulee laughed, leading the way to Nora's chambers.

"It's so damn hot lately; I'm ready for autumn." Nora flopped down onto her bed and held her hand out to Tulee, allowing the woman to peel off her bandages.

"Hmm. Let's leave the bandage off tonight and let it breathe. I'll dress it in the morning before the ceremony."

"Tulee? Don't you think this wedding is kind of sudden and, well, strange? I would have expected months of preparations; I would expect the King himself to be here when the princess arrived. It just seems off."

Tulee pursed her lips and nodded. "I agree it's strange, but if I spent my days asking why about all the things I don't understand, I wouldn't accomplish much!" Tulee laughed and kissed the top of Nora's head. "Get some rest. We have a busy day tomorrow."

Tulee shut the door behind her and Nora listened as her footsteps faded down the long, twisting halls. She sat up in her bed and looked out the small window, which sat level with the ground outside, and smiled as she saw Briella standing outside, her guard giving her a respectful distance, her face illuminated by the light of fireflies.

"I wish it could always be like this, Horace." Briella's voice was quiet, and Nora could hear a sort of heartbreak in her words. "That girl invited me back here, you know."

Horace chuckled. "Her eyes never left you all night."

"I would be lying if I didn't admit that mine were on her as well."

Nora reddened slightly and laid back in her bed, looking up at the ceiling. Nora felt mortified to be listening in on a conversation involving her, but the grin on her face betrayed her modesty.

"I'm sure you could find your way to her room." Horace teased.

"She seems like a forever kind of gal, and I have little forever left in me."

"There's still time. You don't have—" Horace went silent and released a long sigh.

"Everything I have done in my entire life has led up to this moment. You know that there is no other way."

Horace grunted indignantly, and Nora could swear she heard a soft sob escape his lips.

"I know." His voice wavered slightly as he spoke.

Nora listened as their footsteps faded into the distance, wondering just how alike she and the princess might be.

Chapter Three

The next morning was full of nervous excitement and high energy as the staff hurried under the instruction of Alice who barked out orders, and Adelle, who seemed to be in a constant state of battle with Alice. Nora was careful to avoid both, keeping to the stables to help prepare the horses. She had just finished Adelle's own carriage when Briella's guard, Horace, came in to ready their own carriage.

"Good morning, sir." Nora smiled at Horace, who beamed back at her.

"Good morning missus!" He said cheerfully, inspecting a basket Tulee had sent up with some fruit, bread, and cheese for her to snack on as she worked. "Do you mind?"

Nora held the basket out to him before grabbing an apple for herself and taking a seat on a stool.

"How is the princess this morning?" Nora pretended to not look interested in the answer, but the truth was that she hadn't been able to stop thinking about the princess all morning. From the moment she woke up, she wondered what she was feeling, what she was thinking. She had even almost gone to her chambers to check on her but decided that would be not only entirely out of place but also extremely off-putting.

"She's nervous, as one would expect." Horace looked back at the estate below and sighed. The same heaviness Nora saw weighing on Briella seemed to plague Horace, and Nora sensed there was more meaning to their words than what they let on. "She is here to do her duty to her father and kingdom, and I am here to help her however I can."

Nora nodded slowly and looked up towards the window of the princesses' room. She could see figures casting shadows from the candlelight inside and returned her attention to Horace, who had followed her gaze.

"I've heard your prince is quite the cad; I never imagined Briella marrying anyone that she didn't love passionately."

Nora had heard the prince was a frequent visitor of brothels, and that he was unkind to the women who he employed to serve his needs. Nora heard once that one of those women had become with child and vanished. She didn't know Briella well, but she wondered how the princess would fare under those circumstances.

"I had spoken with her last night and offered my time if she should want an escape in the future."

Horace smiled. "She told me, and I thank you for that. Her future is uncertain, but she will never forget your offer." He sighed and stood up, inspecting the horses, and smiling at Nora's handiwork. "Well, it looks like you already have things ready to go. I will alert your head of staff that we are ready to set off."

"Her name's Tulee." Nora smiled. "She would rather be called by her name."

Horace grinned and walked down to the estate, whistling as he walked down the dirt path. Nora finished her preparations and, with the help of one of Horace's three guards, brought the carriages out in the particular order Alice had demanded for the wedding procession. The heat was unbearable, and Nora could feel beads of sweat sliding down her back as she hurried along.

"You there!" A voice called out to Nora, and she turned to see the princess, her mouth falling open with the surprise at the sight of her.

Her long crimson curls were held in place with pearls fused to the ends of pins, and a small silver tiara gleamed in the sunlight. Her dress was white lace and had to be making her miserable in the heat, and as Nora approached, she realized Briella's face was covered in thick powder to hide her freckles. Why anyone would want to cover them was beyond Nora; she thought the princess looked beautiful now standing before her in her gown, but she had been radiant the night before, freckles and all.

"What do you think?" Briella asked, holding her arms out and turning before Nora. The gown was fitted tightly in the torso with swirling patterns of lace tendrils up into sleeves, and the bottom half billowed around her with lots of movement and a modest train that followed about a foot or two behind Briella as she walked. Pearls matching the ones woven into her hair glimmered iridescent against the lace and now closer Nora could see Briella's skin shimmering with a body paint that caused her skin to match the pearls' iridescent sheen.

"I think you look beautiful and uncomfortable." Nora smiled when Briella blew out her cheeks and nodded in frustration. "Who put all that powder on you?"

"Alice," Briella grumbled. "She says I look too common."

"I wouldn't say there is anything common about you." Nora blushed as the words left her lips and cleared her throat. "You look beautiful either way."

Briella stared at her for a moment and smiled softly. "Thank you."

They stood there for a moment, looking at each other. Nora felt butterflies rising in her stomach and cleared her throat, nervously kicking the ground.

"I should, uh, probably get going."

"Oh yeah me too. Will you be coming to the–"

"Ceremony. Yes."

"Ah, good. Well, perhaps I will see you there?"

Nora nodded and waved as the princess entered her carriage, stealing one last look at Nora before the carriage door closed behind her. Nora hurried into the courtyard outside of the kitchen entrance and nearly ran into Horace as he exited, falling back onto the ground to avoid plowing him over. Behind him was Tulee, straightening out her skirts anxiously and her face flushed. Nora looked from her to the guard and back to Tulee, raising her eyebrows.

"Get up, you idiot," Tulee hissed, waving a hand dismissively at Nora, who continued to raise her eyebrows.

"I'll see you at the ceremony, then?" Horace grinned at Tulee's flustered expression.

"If you should be so lucky! On with you!"

Horace hurried towards the princess's carriage and disappeared into the crowd of staff rushing to finish last-minute preparations.

"What did I walk into?" Nora grinned sheepishly at Tulee.

"You walked into a man and fell on your ass. Now hurry along." Tulee hurried back into the house and Nora noticed a smile tugging at her lips as she turned away from Nora's gaze.

Adelle rushed out of the house with Larissa in tow, and Nora quickly tucked herself into a corner. She watched as Larissa followed their mother, nodding and murmuring agreeably as Adelle spouted off complaints about Alice and Horace and how inconvenient all of this was for her.

"Mother, I forgot my fan."

"My goodness *hurry*, child, you will melt in this damned heat. Be quick before that bitch Alice makes a fuss over our timeliness."

Larissa hurried from the carriage into the courtyard Nora was hiding in and stood silently for a long moment. She peaked out of the courtyard after Adelle and then returned, looking straight at Nora.

"You can come out; she's gone."

"What are you–"

"I needed to talk to you." Larissa pulled her fan out of her sleeve and grinned sheepishly. "There isn't much time, but I needed to tell you in person. I'm leaving immediately after the ceremony. We were going to leave tomorrow, but the King insisted we come back with him."

Nora allowed the information to sit for a moment before responding. She didn't know how she felt; part of her felt like she should be heartbroken. That this moment with her sister could be her last and she should feel the loss of it all, but as she looked at Larissa before her she saw a stranger. A stranger who had watched as their mother beat Nora her entire life. The lack of emotion was more startling to Nora than the news itself.

"Will you be back?"

"It's very unlikely. Mother thinks I'll be one of Prince Adrian's royal mages, like she was to King Alexander and Brutus is now. It will be an immense honor for our family, and I could help you."

"Help me?"

"Yes. I mentioned to Mother that I would like to bring you with me as a lady-in-waiting. I know it's not the work you're used to, but I–"

"No." Nora's voice was hollow.

"No? But Nora–"

"You are telling me, but you have not asked me if this is what I want and it is not. I will not leave a life of servitude to go serve someone else."

"But Nora, I wouldn't have you serve me."

"But I will not have any right to refuse any command from you. Larissa, you leaving and taking Adelle with you is the most freedom I will ever have. I don't want to spend my life here, and leaving to go live as I do now beneath you is no better. Do you honestly believe that my life will be better?"

Larissa stood there nervously fiddling with her fan. "I thought it might."

Nora shook her head. "Then you are more foolish than I give you credit for."

Larissa let out a laughing breath, her eyes fixed on the stone floor of the courtyard. "I suppose you're right." She looked out at the heather fields that climbed up to the forest tree line behind the estate and released a long sigh. "When she–stepped on your hand. I–"

"You helped me, and I am grateful for it."

"Just–let me finish. I wanted to do more; I wanted to stop it. But I couldn't. I have felt this way all our lives. This desire to help, and this fear that if I do, it will be me that suffers."

Nora straightened, clearing her throat uncomfortably. Larissa was being franker with her than she had ever been, and although she had always wondered what Larissa thought when she watched Nora suffer, hearing it now was more than Nora ever expected. She felt anger, sadness, betrayal rising within her as a swirling tornado of contradictions and pain.

"When I healed you, your blood was on my fingers and I–I sensed something. I am not sure what it was, but I want you to come with me so I can keep an eye on this, perhaps I can help you."

It was Nora's turn to laugh. There was always more to the story; there was always a veiled ulterior motive behind every kindness. She shook her head and looked at a group of servants who were slowly gathering to make their own way separately from the lord's and lady's.

"You know as well as I do if there was anything magical within me, Adelle would have found it through one of her *tests*." She grimaced at the word, recalling a series of cruel and grueling tests Adelle had made her endure when she was very young. Flashes of memories of being locked in cages and left for days without food, of being beaten with chains and left within an inch of her life to provoke some natural defensive magic. Adelle had been unyielding, and it was only when people began refusing to test Nora and claimed she was too old to be considered a late bloomer that Nora was eventually cast out as a servant and mostly forgotten.

"You don't need to worry about me, Larissa, but I worry for you."

"Me? Nora, you have *nothing*."

Nora shrugged. "We all have cages, Larissa. Mine is just not as small as yours. You have a part to play, designed by our mother to give her what she believes is owed. You play it beautifully, but it is not you doing the choosing."

Larissa inspected her fan before looking back at Nora. "I suppose you're right." She looked at Nora for a long moment before pulling her into a tight embrace. "Please promise me you'll stay away from her as much as possible."

"I promise." Nora wrapped her arms around her sister for what might have been the first time in years. She willed herself to cry, to shed tears for a sister she would never know. but her eyes remained dry, and the exchange felt tense and forced. Larissa pulled away from Nora's embrace and was visibly uncomfortable, and Nora knew in that moment Larissa felt the same.

"Larissa, hurry!" Adelle's voice rang out from the caravan and Nora quickly slipped back into her hiding spot.

"I'm coming!" Larissa called back.

Nora could feel Larissa's presence still standing there, waiting for Nora to come back out, but Nora didn't dare risk it. Eventually, Nora heard Larissa make her way down the winding path and released a long breath. Nora was surprised at the relief she felt at the realization that Larissa, although never once laying a finger on Nora, had been the greatest source of Nora's pain. Now at the thought of being free of them both, a weight lifted from Nora's shoulders.

When the caravan had pulled away, Nora hurried to join the staff as they walked down a shorter forest path that would lead them to the sweeping gardens of the temple. When they arrived, Nora was surprised to see that very few noble families were in attendance, and even more surprised to see that the wedding was to take place outside in the gardens where everyone could watch.

She truly wants the people to be part of this union, Nora thought as she found a place beneath the shade of a tree.

Prince Adrian was standing beneath the altar, the church priestesses beside him and king Alexander sitting in a throne at the head of the ceremony, as if he was a god himself casting judgment on the union. Adelle and Larissa were sitting on the other side of the procession, Adelle's eyes fixed on the king and Larissa squirming in her seat awkwardly as the heat bore down upon them.

"Her Royal Highness, Princess Gabriella Velannize of Madrall." Horace's voice rang out and from behind him the princess emerged.

She was like a princess from a storybook, and the people devoured the image of being present for their future queen's wedding. Children stood transfixed by her, their parents crying and tossing magnolia flowers on the ground before Briella, the traditional wedding flower for Sorudi brides. Briella smiled at the people, aware of how important this was for all of them. She never once looked at Adrian, whose eyes were fixed on her as if she was a lamb brought to the slaughter.

Finally, she made eye contact with Nora, and she smiled. It looked painful, and Nora suddenly felt like grabbing Briella's hand and running into the forest with her. She felt her body tense as she kept herself rooted to the spot, fighting against the voice within her that screamed *something isn't right*. The heat bore down upon them and Briella turned her gaze up towards the sky, shielding her eyes as she looked into the sun. She dropped her bouquet just as the sound of screeching boomed from above.

It was as if everything moved in slow motion. Nora watched as the crowds of people followed Briella's gaze; mothers swept their children up in their arms and ran as a hot wind poured down on them. Nora was pushed back against the tree she stood beneath, trying to look up against the wind and brush to see what was making the horrible screeching. She hurried forward as the king's voice cried out around them.

"Dragon!" He bellowed, grabbing his sword and rushing forward with his guards.

Brutus, the king's royal mage, grabbed Prince Adrian and dove beneath a cart as the king rushed forward toward the princess. She ran as talons closed in around her, her dress ripping and blood pouring from her arm as she continued to rush towards the guards. She grabbed a sword and turned around, kicking her heels from her feet.

"Horace!" Briella braced herself, holding the sword out before her as the dragon let out an ear-splitting roar and released a stream of flame at the guards who ran with the king.

Nora sprinted to Briella, dodging people as they ran in the opposite direction and ducking below the tail of the dragon.

"Nora!" Tulee's screams rang through Nora's ears. Nora pressed on, desperate to reach Briella.

"The prince!" Adelle thrusted Larissa over to Brutus and Adrian, and Nora watched as she ran as Larissa raised her arms above them muttering an enchantment until they were completely encased in what looked to be a bubble of green light. Flames engulfed them and Nora stood frozen in terror as the fire obscured her sister. When the flames subsided, Larissa was screaming against the force of the dragon's flame, but it seemed to Nora that the magic had held up and all of those within were unharmed.

Nora returned her attention to Briella, and the two locked eyes just as the dragon rose into the air again, its wings sending a stream of air that pushed Briella to the ground. Nora stayed low, moving as fast as she could to the princess just as Horace stood over Briella, his sword raised above him. He slashed at the beast's extended talons, causing it to roar with pain and rage. It swung its massive claws at the knight, sending him flying away from the princess. He lay on the ground unmoving, and Briella rose with her own sword, her eyes wild with fear.

Briella ran towards the beast, swinging her sword at its face as it lowered to her level, cutting through the skin just above its eyes and sending a spray of dark black liquid all over her once pristine dress. Her hair had loosened from its pins and she looked the picture of a warrior as she reared back to slice at the dragon again.

"*Foolish girl.*" The dragon's voice rang out, its massive claw pinning Briella to the earth as its steaming maw rose above her.

Briella screamed and Nora sprinted towards her, grabbing the sword the princess had dropped and driving it down into the beast's foot. It let out a piercing screech, and rose into the air, closing its injured claw around the princess and bringing her up with it. Nora grabbed Briella's hands, looking into her terrified eyes.

"Don't let go!" Nora shouted, feeling her feet lift from the ground. Heat surrounded her, and she saw the dragon bringing them closer to its mouth, its teeth dripping with fresh blood and the stench of death radiating from its jaws.

Briella smiled at Nora and shook her head, tears streaming down her face and her eyes full of terror.

"Don't–!"

Briella closed her eyes and released Nora's hands, sending her falling back to the ground. A silver bangle with the crest of Madrall made from emeralds and rubies slid off Briella's wrist and Nora clutched it as she fell, looking up in horror as the dragon's jaws snapped where she had just been, and watching the creature fly higher into the air as Nora hit the ground with a sickening thud.

"Nora!" Tulee's voice cut through the screams of the injured, rushing to Nora and pulling her head into her lap.

"*Dragon Slayer!*" The dragon's voice was deafening and Tulee held Nora close, shielding Nora from further harm with her body. "*I can taste your fear. Run, run with your people and crown your king.*"

His chest glowed a blinding fiery red that climbed up his throat and into his mouth, releasing a river of flame that quickly engulfed the temple and most of the garden area. Nora watched in horror as the trees in the surrounding forest erupted into flame, the fire tearing through the canopy toward the city of Sorudi.

"The town!" Larissa screamed down to her mother, who cowered beneath her magic.

"Hold your position!" Adelle commanded.

Tulee helped steady Nora to her feet and they moved towards Horace who was now bracing himself against a pillar that was catching fire, his eyes fixed on the dragon that was quickly moving higher into the sky above.

"Come with us!" Tulee shouted, allowing Horace to drape Nora's other arm around his neck and the two helped Nora through the crowd of rushing people back towards the DuPont estate.

The heat was unbearable and Horace kept his eyes fixed on the dragon which circled the temple, too high to be injured but not yet finished with the people below. Nora could see Briella still in its clutches, fighting for her life as it taunted all of those below. They hurried through the forest, the heat of the fire bearing down on them as the surrounding trees caught flame. When they finally emerged at the edge of the estate, Tulee carefully lowered Nora to the ground, yelling for Horace to stay with her as she ran into the building. Nora's ears had finally stopped ringing, and she followed Horace's gaze towards the dragon, unsure if it was heading towards them or away from them for a long moment.

"Is it–?"

"Coming this way," Horace murmured. "Tulee!"

Just then, Tulee ran out to them, a large pack on her back and another in her arms. Tears were streaming from her eyes as she thrust a pack into Nora's arms.

"Listen. You must go." Tulee's voice had the final tone she would give Nora when she would not be argued with, and she seemed oblivious to the screaming and running staff members or the intensifying heat.

"We *are* going. We need to go now, the dragon—"

"I am going to take the rest of the staff safety." Tulee looked up at the dragon, which had stopped its rush towards the estate to release a stream of flame into the city of Sorudi. She returned her gaze to Nora. "Run away from here, Nora. This is your chance to be free."

"What do you mean? You can't leave me! No, I'm coming with you."

Tulee flinched slightly at her words. "I will tell Adelle I lost you in the fire. You will wither away here, and I can't bear to watch you fade into nothing." Tears fell down her face as she spoke. "I would keep you as mine forever if I could, but that is not the way of things."

Horace pursed his lips, looking back at the estate where the last of the staff members were flooding out into the courtyards.

"I don't want to leave you. I love you." Nora spoke between choking sobs. She could feel her heart breaking; it was a deep ache, a longing for things to be different

"There's no time for this! You must go–*now*." Tulee helped Nora to her feet and pushed her towards the forest edge that climbed away from the town and into the mountains above. "I love you more than you could ever know."

Nora held the bag tight and watched as Tulee and Horace sprinted towards the estate, the sounds of their voices fading as the heat intensified around Nora. She looked up at the dragon one last time before bolting into the forest. The smoke smelled of sulfur and something else that felt both familiar and entirely alien to Nora, and the forest was so thick with it she struggled to navigate through the dense brush.

Nora willed herself to keep going and as she got higher up the mountain, the smoke thinned slightly and the heat no longer felt it would melt her from the inside. She continued as fast as she could manage through the game trails until she came up to a small meadow that jutted out from the mountain miles above the city. She turned to look back and felt the air leave her body. Everything had burned.

The dragon soared above triumphantly, rising straight up into the sky, and letting out a scream so loud it rattled Nora's bones. She watched in horror and dumbfounded wonder as it disappeared into the clouds above, leaving its destruction behind.

It began to rain, and Nora lifted her hood, stealing one last look at the destruction below before disappearing into the mountains.

4

Chapter Four

Nora continued up the mountain for several days, stopping only to rest before pushing on to the hunting outpost she had been searching for. Located on a cliff that overlooked the valley below, the outpost was little more than a resupply checkpoint for long hunting parties. Despite its simplicity, the thinning trees opening to the small landing that jutted from the cliffside sent a wave of relief through Nora. The supply shed sat between the sheer mountainside and a small lake the locals knew as Reflection Lake, named for its crystal-clear water that reflected a mirror image of the mountain's peak. A small grassy meadow extended around the lake towards the cliff's edge; this small meadow on the side of a mountain seemed to have been carved out for the weary traveler. Nora collapsed on the bank of the lake and dipped her hands in scooping mouthfuls of ice-cold water. Tulee had brought her here several times with various hunting parties, hoping that Nora would learn to navigate the forests that surrounded the estate. She remembered how afraid she had been of the creatures that lurked in the dark corners of the forest, and the people in the hunting parties had been patient in their teaching. It was largely from those experiences that Nora now found refuge in the forest.

 Nora stood and looked out over the cliffside overlooking Sorudi and saw the smoke from the town she had grown up in still smoldering all these days later. The fire had extended through the forest towards the lakes and she said a silent prayer to any gods listening for the townspeople who had evacuated there. She didn't see how anyone could have survived, and the realization of what that meant sent a chill up her spine. She pushed the thought from her mind; Tulee was resourceful. She would have figured out what to do.

She returned to the lake and removed her clothes before slipping in, wincing as the scrapes and burns on her body hit the coolness of the water. She closed her eyes and dove in deeper, scrubbing away the ash that coated her skin and hair. When she surfaced, she allowed herself to float and felt her muscles ache in appreciation of the weightlessness. Movement caught her eye, and she adjusted herself so she was between whatever it was and the shore.

It took a moment for Nora to realize what exactly shared this lake with her. At first, Nora believed it to be a person, until she noticed that its skin had a tinge of greens and blues, and its eyes stared back at her, solid black. Its long hair was the color of the algae that bloomed on the water's surface, and it was an unmoving, silent observer.

"Hello?" Nora kept her voice low and made no movements towards the creature.

"Hello?" Nora's voice echoed back from the creature's mouth, its head cocked to the side, and water spilled out as it spoke.

Nora slowly moved towards the shoreline, her heart pounding in her chest. Her foot slipped on the rocks below and she went completely underwater, the full image of this creature finally visible. It was human-like but had a fish tail that extended behind long legs with long, webbed feet.

A nymph, Nora's eyes went wide with the realization. Nymphs were creatures from bedtime stories that had been long gone from this world, but here was one as clear as day treading water before her.

The nymph submerged with her and Nora realized it was hooked on a net, likely one of the magicked ones she used herself several times before, which was wedged between large boulders. She remembered stories told by travelers of people who turned their back on creatures like this and lived a cursed life.

Nora considered for a moment if it was safe for her to approach before coming up for a long breath of air and diving back down towards the net. The nymph's eyes followed her as she moved and it watched as Nora cut the ropes.

Nora felt the need to come up for air and moved towards the surface when the nymph grabbed her arms and held her in place. Panic flooded her body as her lungs screamed for oxygen. The nymph placed its webbed hands-on Nora's ears and cocked its head, its face shifting slightly until it became an almost perfect reflection of Nora.

"Hello?" It asked in her voice again before placing its mouth on hers.

She felt air fill her lungs like an icy balm to a wound and she relaxed at the nymph's touch. It released her slowly and looked over at the netting. Nora nodded and resumed her work, turning to the creature whenever she felt like she needed more air and allowing the air to fill her lungs. The nymph smirked when Nora's heart began racing and its lips lingered a little longer, its hands moving from Nora's face down her shoulders. Nora pulled back, her face flush with embarrassment, and tried to avoid its amused gaze as she pushed herself to cut the last of the netting. Once it was finally free, Nora allowed the nymph to pull her to the surface, and they both took in the fresh air together. They slowly made their way to the shore and Nora bundled the netting up, pulling on her underclothes and tossing the netting into the shed, keenly aware of the creature watching her work.

"It's gone; you're free now." Nora turned to face the creature as she spoke, holding her hands up in silent surrender.

The creature stood there, its face still mirroring Nora's.

"You're free now." The words echoed Nora's own.

Nora smiled. "Yes, we're both free."

The nymph smiled back at her and placed her hand on Nora's chest as it slowly melded back into its true form. It was unsettling to watch the transformation from Nora to nymph; the sight of her own face melting from the creatures made Nora's stomach churn. It ran a long claw down its hand, purple blood pooling up slowly as it did so and indicated for Nora to extend her own hand. Nora allowed the creature to slice through her palm and rub it against the nymph's own bleeding palm, their blood intermingling and the feeling of cool water spreading through Nora's veins. Nora looked at her palm and her eyes widened in astonishment as the cut was replaced with a dark blue line filled with white glimmering flecks that resembled stars.

The creature spoke in a strange language into its palm, and Nora felt the creature's voice in her mind.

I owe you a life debt. Thank you, star-child. The voice reverberated through Nora's mind. They were now linked, and Nora could feel the connection within her body.

Nora lifted her own hand to her mouth and spoke into it softly, her eyes fixed on the creature before her. "What is your name?"

The creature considered her for a long moment before answering.

Phillandra, of the water nymphs. She looked around slowly, taking in the world around them, her eyes lingering on the smoldering forest and town below. *I have been asleep for a long time–this place has changed.*

Nora followed Phillandra's gaze and wondered what this place must have looked like when she had last called the mountain her home. The stories she had heard in her childhood of nymphs painted them as powerful guardians of nature that had been gone from the world for at least a hundred years, perhaps much longer.

Move carefully. Phillandra's voice echoed in her mind.

She pressed a small stone into Nora's hand, bowing deeply before moving to the cliff's edge. She spread her arms like a bird about to take flight and closed her eyes as the sun kissed her face, smiling with a relieved sigh. As she exhaled, the wind lifted her into the air and she gave Nora one last look before disappearing into the air before her.

Nora stood in silent wonder until the heaviness of the past few days washed over her and her stomach rumbled. She looked down at the polished black stone in her hand and tucked it into her pocket before building up a fire, filling a small pot with water and whatever herbs and vegetables she had scavenged on her way up the mountain. While the food simmered, she set up her bed and rubbed some ointment on her aching joints. She ate in silence and, once fed and clean, her situation felt less dire. Her mind raced with legendary creatures long thought to be erased from this world; she saw her forest as being an entirely new world.

Nora lit a small lantern and stepped inside the small outpost shed to pick through the stored supplies, stocking up on arrows and knives and any dried meat that had been stored for later use. She pushed away the sadness that built within her as she saw signs of the villagers, she may never see again all around her. Nora took her supplies out to her campfire and packed them away before laying out on her bedroll and pulling out a map from her bag. She traced a line from the estate to Reflection Lake with a piece of charcoal, placing an 'x' for her campsite.

Theren, the royal city, sat just on the other side of the mountain. Nora had never been there before, but she remembered during the great floods in the valley refugees passing through Sorudi to seek shelter and aid in the royal city. Unsure of where she should go or what to do next, heading for Theren seemed like the logical next step for her.

When she woke the next morning, she lay unmoving for a long while, the smoldering coals the only remnants of her campfire. She stared out from her bedroll at the grassy bluff surrounding the lake and felt hot tears welling in her eyes. Tulee could have come with her. They could have navigated the mountainside together safer than Nora could on her own.

Maybe this is what she wanted, Nora thought. *Not worrying about keeping me safe from my mother; maybe this is how she gets the life she always wanted.*

The thought of her mother sent a chill up Nora's spine, and she wondered if she even noticed Nora's absence yet. Would she celebrate when Tulee told her the tale of her youngest daughter's death? Would she be indifferent? What would Larissa say when she heard the news?

Nora buried her face in her blankets and breathed deeply before pushing herself up on her hands and knees and slowly rising to her feet. She made quick work of packing her things up, pushing the thoughts of Tulee and her mother from her mind as she busied herself with preparing for the next part of her journey. She looked around the bluff for a long moment before picking up a piece of charcoal and writing on the door that covered the supply shed:

I survived and will go on.

Nora stared at the words before her and grabbed her belongings, throwing the last of the water in her pot on the nearly extinguished embers from her fire the night before and making her way down the mountain.

It took two days off the main roads before she reached the junction where she could continue south towards Theren or east towards the fabled Leiney Woods. Nora could see the trees of the old growth forest through a mist that obscured its vastness. There was no official word on who or what lived there, but she had heard tales of ancient cities of elves and magic radiating from every stone. The forest was the gateway to the rival country of Ospas, a land of dragon worshippers who had been warring against the kingdom of Troque since the end of the great celestial war. Beyond the trees, the towering mountain that lay as a boundary between these two warring lands were jagged teeth waiting for a too-curious traveler to get close enough to bite.

Nora grappled with the idea that she had a choice between the two, that she could go where she pleased and forge her own way, made her heart beat faster. Nora, however, was not too-curious, and she continued down the road south towards the royal city of Theren.

She hadn't made it very far before the sound of shouting and a wagon jostling down the path caught her attention. She ducked into the tree line until the shadow of the wagon came into view. Nora took in a sharp breath as she realized it was a cart full of people.

Trafficking had been banned long before Nora was born, but when the people of Ospas ventured too close to the borders of the two countries, this law became flexible in the eyes of the king. That combined with the way different lords could punish their people, however they deemed fit, helped feed a growing human trafficking trade that the citizens of the country turned a blind eye to. Nora felt anger boiling in her stomach as she noticed a mother and three small children huddled together, the mother's eyes wild with rage.

A hand touched Nora's shoulder and she whirled around, her dagger out to the intruder's throat before she had time to take in who they were. A man with deep brown eyes held a finger to his lips to silence her, holding his other hand up in the air in surrender. His eyes darted urgently in the direction of the cart and he jerked his head toward his bow. Nora lowered her dagger.

The man nodded and drew an arrow, notching it into his bow and pointing it at the man who was driving the cart. Nora noticed the slight point to the man's ears, not elongated like the elves she knew but small enough to escape notice, something typically seen on half-elves.

"Jeb, I'm starving. I need to stop and eat!" The heavier set of the two traders complained, throwing a bag full of supplies on the grassy roadside.

"We're nearly to Theren, shut your yap and keep goin' we can eat there!" The taller, leaner one called Jeb snarled, flashing a toothy grin at the prisoners in the cage.

The mother inside kicked the cage bars defiantly, causing both men to jump and curse in frustration.

"You won't be so fiery soon!" Jeb jeered as the kids held tight to their mother and buried their faces in her shirt.

The half-elf man let out a slow breath and Nora watched as the arrow flew and lodged itself into the heavier man's back, causing him to shudder for a second and then topple to the ground.

"Ernest!" Jeb roared, looking around wildly for the source of the arrow.

"I'll take care of him; you go around and let them out. The mom's name is Luna. Tell her you're with Finn or she'll kill you." The half-elf murmured, tearing off away from the cart. Jeb roared in anger and drew his sword, following the sound of the half-elf. Nora moved quietly, watching Jeb as she slid out of the tree cover and motioned for the people inside the cart to be silent. She carefully moved Ernest's body and found a ring of keys attached to his belt.

"I smell ya, Finn!" the trader growled, his voice low and menacing. "I can always smell a traitorous half-elf scum."

"Luna? I'm with Finn." She whispered as she made quick work of the lock. With a final flick of her wrist, the lock sprang open, falling to the ground with a deafening thud.

"Hey, you!" Jeb whirled around; his voice screwed up in rage. He bolted towards the cart and an arrow flew past his ear, lodging itself into the side of the cart.

Finn bolted out from the trees as he pulled out a long sword and slashed at the trader. Jeb met him each time, and Nora hurried to help the prisoners out of their cage.

"Watch out!" Luna shouted.

Nora whirled around and felt the sharp sting of a blade grazing her ribs, cutting through the fabric on her shirt and drawing a thin line of blood. The hulking form of Ernest stood before her, his dagger in hand and his chest heaving with overexertion, the arrow still lodged in his back.

"What the hell?!" Nora screamed, jumping back again as he swiped at her a second time.

Another prisoner threw a blade to her before bolting into the forest and Nora held the blade up as she parried off a third attack. The hits came fast and heavy, and despite some light training with the hunting party, Nora was unfamiliar with the weapon. Each hit pushed her back and down towards the ground. Ernest looked stupid, but he was good with his blade and his eyes shone with a sickening excitement.

A heavy blow landed on Nora's shoulder and she felt hot blood pouring from her wound. She screamed and rolled out of the way of another heavy swing. Nora looked up as the hulking figure raised his sword and brought it down hard and fast upon her. She held her blade up, supported by her free arm, and closed her eyes as a great clang of metal on metal rang through the air. She looked up and saw the half-elf, Finn, standing over her with his sword taking the blow. The force from the hit slid him back into her, and she saw his entire body shake as he struggled to hold the blade back.

Nora reached for her dagger, her vision darkening from the pain and loss of blood, and drove it into Ernest's foot, his scream the last thing she heard as she drifted into unconsciousness.

5

Chapter Five

The smell of lavender brought Nora back to consciousness, and as she opened her eyes, she found herself in a small bedroom. A fire crackled in a hearth at the opposite end of the room and the half-elf leaned against the wall beside her, snoring softly.

"Hold still." A woman's voice called from the doorway. Nora squinted at her and when three other small faces peered out from around her, she realized it was the woman from the cart. "Your wound was deep; I did what I could to keep you alive, but we needed to get off the road. This is a halfway house of sorts. I used to live here in another lifetime–it's safe. I've been dressing your wound these past few days. My name is Luna Wildone."

"Days?!" Nora sat up quickly, a shooting pain in her shoulder sending her falling back into her pillow. She pressed her eyes shut hard against the pain and then, steadying her breathing, inspected her injured shoulder. Fresh clean bandages were wrapped from the base of her neck down to about half-way down her forearm.

Finn opened an eye lazily and looked down at Nora before moving to stand behind Luna as she moved to sit beside Nora.

"You said *days*?" Nora's voice was strained against the pain, and she attempted to sit up again, this time careful not to put pressure on her injured arm.

"A few days. I figured I would stay and see you healed, as I was partly responsible for you being injured in the first place," Finn said dismissively.

"I'd say more than partly," she grumbled. "Where am I?"

"Theren." Finn turned and extended a hand, flashing Nora a dashing smile. "We haven't been introduced. Finn Meadows, a half-elf bastard."

Nora shook his hand. "Nora."

Finn chuckled. "You look like a Nora, all broody and angsty." He turned to look out the window. "Have you ever been to Theren?"

"No, I haven't done much traveling. I worked as a servant in my lady's house."

"That would explain why you're so terrible with a sword." Finn continued looking down at the street, seemingly unaware of Nora's glare. "Sasha, Reid, Beau. Come look, there's a parade!"

The three children squealed with delight and jumped up onto a small bench that sat within a large bay window. They pressed their faces against the glass, fogging it with their breath and shoving each other slightly whenever one got too close.

"Wow." The youngest, Sasha, murmured.

Luna smiled at them and stood to help Nora to her feet, guiding her to the window. Finn pushed the top half of the glass pane open and smiled as Nora leaned forward, her eyes wide at the number of people that filled the streets. Full of color and brimming with flowers, every building seemed to burst with excitement over the event. Adrian, the newly crowned king, followed the procession in a golden chariot pulled by massive black horses. Nora's smile faded as the image of him cowering beneath her sister's magic flashed through her mind. Rage boiled within her belly. He had cowered and watched his father die; when his betrothed took up arms against the dragon, he hid away and allowed his people to fight for him. And despite it all there he was, crowned in glory and buzzing excitement by those who would believe him to be their protector.

"What are they celebrating?" Nora tried to disguise her disgust as she spoke.

"Princess Gabriella was taken by a dragon during her wedding to the prince, the king got fried in the fight and Adrian's first act as king was to offer a reward to anyone who can return the princess to him," Finn's eyes locked on Adrian, "Foolish men and women will sign their lives away for a chance for something better. Never mind that the last dragon killed required some of the most powerful magic in existence to defeat. I'm sure they'll be *fine*. I'm sure the princess is *great* and not dead or *anything*."

"What kind of reward?"

Finn cocked an eyebrow at her, the trace of a smile tugging at the corner of his mouth. "The standard land, title, riches untold. Not worth the price of a life, but maybe others feel differently."

Nora looked back out at the window and she felt something inside her stir with excitement. The king's reward could give Nora agency; a chance to start over. She thought of Briella and looked down at the bangle that fell from the princess's wrist and now rested on her own. Nora was the last person to see the princess alive; she had been determined to hold on to whatever end. Now she was presented with a chance, however small it may be, to bring her home.

"I'm going to sign up," she said, her eyes fixed on Adrian.

"You and what arm?" Finn jeered.

When Nora didn't look at him, he ran his fingers through his hair, shaking his head. "You can't be serious. You'll be dead before you leave the kingdom. There's no way you'll be able to rescue the princess. It's a fool's errand; a way for King Adrian to look good to her family."

Nora turned to face him. "I was fine until I stumbled across *you*. If it hadn't been for you, I would have already signed up and off on my way."

Finn studied her for a moment. "You would've left those people in their cage?" He looked at her injured shoulder. "I don't believe it."

"No," Nora admitted, "I would've been smarter about it. Used my *head*."

"Calm down, children," Luna said, rolling her eyes and shoving Finn playfully. "I don't think I've ever seen the city so busy, it's a little unnerving. We should set out tomorrow morning. These challengers look like a rowdy bunch."

Nora raised her eyebrows. "We?"

Luna nodded. "You're going to need someone to keep an eye on that arm, and I need someone to escort me and the kids to Sue City."

"Sue City—"

"But not until after we finish signing up to die a terrible death!" Finn said in mock excitement, bouncing the squealing children in his arms as he did so.

Nora frowned. "*We?*"

Finn lowered the children and cocked his head at Nora. "We might help each other. Well, I will help you. I think you will be very little help to me. Except possibly regaling my tales to the masses."

Nora opened her mouth to protest but was immediately cut off by Luna, who held a motherly hand out to silence her.

"If you're signing up for the king's quest, we'll have to take the tunnels out of here. The front gates have been the beginning and end of many adventurers who have set off on this quest. The competition just picks them off as soon as they are under the cover of the forest."

"I didn't exactly agree to going with either–"

"Well then, it's decided!" Finn grinned at Nora, his eyes gleaming with a challenge to her resolve.

Nora rolled her eyes before returning her gaze to the parade below as the newly crowned king passed before the house.

"Oh, I almost forgot." Luna pointed to a pile of clean clothes sitting on the edge of Nora's cot and smiled softly. "These were my husbands; might as well have someone get use out of them."

Finn straightened at the sight of the clothes but remained silent.

"Thank you," Nora murmured. The clothes were simple but well made; the dark green breeches sported complex gold stitching embroidering the shapes of leaves on the bottom of the legs and the white cotton shirt was simple but shimmered with signs of magical properties.

"It's magicked against filth. I got tired of scrubbing stains." Luna's eyes betrayed her smile, and she looked for a moment like she might cry before she ushered Nora into a small washroom to change.

The shirt was a little loose but comfortably so in how it afforded Nora free movement. Her bandaged arm was easily concealed beneath the fabric and, although it was stiff, it seemed to cause her less pain. The smell of herbs and oils beneath the bandages assured Nora that this was partly to do with magic healing, and although she hated the accelerated healing caused by magic, she was grateful to have the pain eased.

I guess I could use their help, she thought as she admired herself in the mirror.

If it hadn't been for Finn, she wouldn't be alive right now. And as much as she hated to admit it, he was right. She wouldn't have left those prisoners to their fate. But it was now painfully clear to Nora how ill-equipped she was to survive on her own. She knew how to find food and shelter in the forest; she knew how to survive on her own, but surviving other people was entirely different. As she examined herself in the mirror, she thought of Briella. Was she still alive? If she was alive, what was happening to her? The sound of voices brought Nora from her thoughts and she pressed her ear against the door of the small washroom.

"The prophecy is clear; it *has* to be this." Finn's voice was low and urgent.

"I just don't understand why it has to be *you*." There was a long stretch of silence before Luna continued, "Malachi thought it was his duty as well, and look where it got him."

"That's why I have to go, Luna. Malachi–"

"Don't you dare. If you want to do this, it's because you want to. You will not make this about him. If you die, it will be your own fault, not his."

Finn let out a long sigh and Nora retreated from the wall as she heard footsteps heading towards her. She pretended to be admiring herself in the mirror, doing her best to look surprised when Finn walked in.

"You clean up–erm–decently."

Nora glared at him, resisting the urge to hit him. Luna looked annoyed until her eyes softened at the sight of Nora in her husband's clothes.

"I'm glad someone is getting use out of them," she whispered, smiling down at her oldest boy. "It's a good thing, Beau. It's what daddy would have wanted."

The young boy nodded slowly. He couldn't have been older than four years old, but Nora could see in his eyes that he had seen much in his short life. Luna moved throughout the room, jotting things down on a piece of parchment until she created a detailed list of supplies for Nora and Finn to purchase.

"If you two are going to be so stupid as to sign your lives away, you might as well make yourselves useful." She grumbled, thrusting the list into Finn's hands.

Finn stood in silence salute, winking at the children as they giggled, and beckoned for Nora to follow him out the door. She looked back at Luna, who waved and offered a reassuring smile and allowed Finn to lead her through Theren. The sun had almost set, casting the city in a soft glow that faded into starlight and Nora felt a strange sense that she was exactly where she was supposed to be.

The city was a work of art, with buildings and streets built with mysterious white stone that left a soft glow in the moonlight. Canals weaved through the city like a black ribbon dotted with reflecting starlight. Everything seemed clean and beautiful, even in the lower districts, where laborers were ignored by nobility. Nora had once been told that the people who lived in the city didn't receive pay for their work but in exchange for their labor, their housing and other needs were all taken care of, but they also could never leave or better themselves. So, festivals and other celebrations that brought in outsiders were especially important for disposable income. It seemed to Nora another form of a cage, however gilded it may be.

As they approached the castle, Nora noticed mages dressed in the signature blue robes of the Royal Mage Academy. Larissa would be here soon, if she wasn't already. She would fit in here; she had always been too bright and excited to stay in their small village. Here she would train to guard the royal family and protect the people of Troque, and with enough work, possibly advise the king himself as the high mage Brutus did and their mother before him. It would be a huge opportunity for Larissa, and Adelle would reap the rewards of being so closely associated with the royal family again. They would have all they needed, and if Nora could pull this off, so would she.

Crowds of people became denser and more difficult to navigate, signaling that they were nearing the main courtyard, and as they came around a bend Nora gasped at the impressive sight of the castle before her. Built from the same shimmering stone that could be seen throughout the city, the castle was a marvel to behold. With veins of shimmering gold snaking its way through the masonry, creating a dazzling marbling effect. Nora smirked at the sight of the familiar servants' entrance markers.

The royal family is as careless as the rest of the wealthy, she thought, somewhat comforted by the consistency.

Finn stopped to haggle with vendors as they moved through the crowd and Nora continued without him until she found an empty bench on a landing overlooking the courtyard. She watched the people bustle around, some sparring in a ring at the center of a small arena, others making deals and arrangements for the journey ahead. Finn waved up at her in acknowledgment before disappearing into a group of men surveying weapons.

"Is this seat taken?" A voice asked from behind her.

Nora jumped and reddened with embarrassment. The man standing behind her was tall and handsome with black hair and blue eyes similar to her own shade of ice blue. He smiled as she shook her head and took the seat beside her, surveying the people below.

"Pity most of them will be dead soon." His voice was bitter, and something about it sent a shiver down Nora's spine. He smelled faintly of sulfur.

"You've been near the dragon?" She asked.

"Do I smell that badly?"

Nora reddened, "I didn't mean–"

"It's fine. Yes, I have, most of the country has by now. The path of destruction it's left is hard to miss. I received news of the king's challenge and knew I couldn't pass it up." He returned his attention to her, his eyes seeming to search for something within her own. "And yourself? Have you seen it?"

"Yes. It destroyed my town." Nora returned her attention to the crowd, searching for Finn in the sea of faces.

He raised an eyebrow. "So, you're here for revenge, then."

"Mostly the money." She kept her voice casual and disinterested, careful to not tell this stranger too much.

The man nodded and returned his attention to the crowd below. "Well, at least you're an honest dragon slayer."

"I'm no dragon slayer. I'm just here to save the princess."

His eyes locked with Nora's and a smile spread across his face. Nora felt her stomach drop. There was something about him that felt almost predatory. The hairs on her neck stood on end and a chill ran through her body. She could feel her heart race as a wave of what felt akin to magic washed over her.

"And you think you can do that without killing the beast? I don't know if I would call you brave or stupid, perhaps a mixture of the two." His eyes scanned her face, and Nora straightened uncomfortably as he did so. "Who–?"

"Who's your friend?" Finn's voice cut through the tension of the moment.

"How rude of me, my apologies. My name is Talon." He stood up and extended a hand to Finn.

Finn frowned at his hand and shrugged with disinterest. "A pleasure, I'm sure. Now, if you'll excuse us, we have a book to sign." Finn grabbed Nora's hand and pulled her with him.

"Goodbye, m'lady. Good luck." Talon returned to his seat, his gaze falling back to the people below.

"What the hell was all of that about?" Finn whispered, guiding Nora to a spot near the large stage that connected the castle to the courtyard.

"He just came and started talking to me. Something isn't right about him."

"He's dripping with magic," Finn whispered, looking back up at Talon over his shoulder. "It's probably best we avoid him."

They were pulled away from their conversation when the sound of horns signaled the arrival of the king.

"My people, welcome."

Adrian was handsome, with dark unruly hair tucked beneath a simple crown and deep brown eyes that shone with enticing danger. He was tall and broad-shouldered; an exaggerated picture of what a young king should be–as if he was molded from clay to play this role.

"You have all come here for one purpose, and that is to save my betrothed, Princess Gabriella. I will award groups as large as five with gold, land, and title. Let's show this bastard what happens when you cross the people of Troque!"

The people cheered loudly, some stumbling from too much ale and others raising their fists in solidarity. Nora glanced back at Talon and swore he was looking right at her. She twisted away, her heart racing.

"This book is our contract. Anyone who signs their name will be granted aid throughout this journey." He motioned to a mage behind him who moved to his side with a chest full of gold medallions bearing the king's seal.

Nora's jaw fell open as she realized the mage holding the medallions was Larissa herself. Behind her was a disgruntled-looking Brutus and, to Nora's surprise, the smirking form of Adelle watching her daughter stand beside the newly crowned king. Nora felt rage bubbling within her. How dare they come and stand here in celebration when the people Adelle was charged with caring for dealt with the aftermath of losing their homes and families. Sorudi had to be an absolute disaster still; it had only been a few days since the dragon attack.

"These medallions are marks of the king. They will allow you rooms, food, and supplies throughout the kingdom, and will also be your ticket to board the ships that leave from Balcross and Gaboga in two weeks!"

Nora was barely listening, her eyes fixed on her sister. Her robes were like the other royal mages, but there were symbols she didn't notice on the others embroidered in gold on her collar. Nora glanced again at Brutus and noticed he bore the same markings on his own collar. She realized in that moment what it meant; Larissa was now one of the King's Own, possibly even an advisor. Nora had thought it strange that Adelle had ordered her daughter to protect the prince instead of his father, but she understood now that with a new king came new possibilities and the sickening genius of it all left a bitter taste in Nora's mouth. Even in the face of certain death, Adelle was calculating her next moves.

Finn tapped Nora's shoulder, pulling her from her thoughts.

"You ok?"

"Yes," Nora murmured.

Finn looked from Nora to Larissa and back to Nora. "Do you know her?"

Nora nodded slowly, returning her gaze to her sister.

"Okay...is she friend or foe?" Finn shuffled awkwardly as he waited for an answer.

"Neither." Nora's voice was icy and she could not push the image of the dragon's attack from her mind.

"A lover perhaps?"

"She's not a lover of mine," Nora's voice was quiet.

Finn shrugged, not caring to dig for more information, and urged Nora forward to stand in the now growing line to sign the king's ledger. As they moved up in line, Nora fidgeted uncomfortably. Larissa was still holding the chest of medallions, which never seemed to lessen in number despite the fifty or so people who had already taken some, and Adelle stood surveying everyone who passed before her daughter. Panic flooded her body as she tried to come up with a plan. If she slipped out of the line now, it would be painfully obvious, but she couldn't walk before them. She cried out as she felt Finn's hands grabbing and twisting her hair up off her neck.

"Hey, what–?"

"You don't want her to notice you, right?" He hissed. "Shut up and let me help."

He tied the hair into a tight knot at the back of her head, lifting her hood to conceal her face as much as possible. The line moved closer, and he placed his hands over her ears. Nora could hear him mumbling, and then felt a stinging pain as the skin on her ears stretched. She winced, holding her hands to her ears and noticing immediately they had a slight point to them.

"My ears?"

"You aren't totally unrecognizable, but I'm working with what I've got." He whispered as they stepped up onto the stage.

Nora felt her stomach lurch as they bowed deeply before the king. She kept her eyes fixed on Finn's hand as he signed their names.

Finnigan and Noma Meadows

Noma was the best he could come up with? She pressed her lips together to suppress a smile when he winked at her.

"My lady." He crooned at Larissa, lifting two medallions from the chest. She glared at him, one eyebrow cocked in exasperation, and Finn stared at her for a moment too long.

"Excuse me, sir." Her voice was tinged with annoyance. Her eyes moved from Finn to linger on Nora, her face that of someone who couldn't decide how they knew the person before them.

Nora could feel sweat beading on her brow and thought she might be sick. She looked over at Adelle who had her eyebrows furrowed in the same expression of recognizing someone you shouldn't. Seeing them this close, and having them look at her not as someone beneath them or in Larissa's case someone to pity, was the most uncomfortable Nora had ever been. She had to fight the instinct to apologize, to allow herself to admit to her deception and accept the inevitable punishment.

"My apologies." Finn's voice brought Nora back to herself and he bowed deeply, nudging Nora to join him. The King waved them off the stage and Finn led Nora off, handing her the second medallion and fastening his around his neck.

Nora looked back at Larissa, whose gaze was fixed on her. She saw something in her sister's face; a mixture of confusion and recognition. Nora's heart raced as Larissa opened her mouth and took a step in their direction, freezing for a moment before returning to her post.

"You didn't say she was your sister!" Finn's voice cut through the silence and he glared down at her. "If we're doing this together, I'm going to need you to level with me more. She glared just like you; your mum must've been vicious."

"I'm sorry. I don't really know how to do this."

"Do what? Be a human being who interacts with others?" He jeered, nudging her with his elbow. When Nora was silent, he let out an exasperated sigh. "Don't tell me you were locked away in a dungeon and never allowed to speak to others."

Nora shook her head, her smile breaking through her dark memories. She stopped, the now familiar chill of powerful magic running down her spine. Finn felt it too, his face darkening. Magic was tugging at them–*powerful* magic.

"Let's hurry. We need to get out of here tonight."

6

Chapter Six

When they arrived at the house Luna had packs lying open for Nora and Finn to fill, and food prepared for the journey ahead. They rushed to a table at the center of the room, spilling the items Finn had purchased on its surface and quickly shoving them into bags. Luna watched as Finn and Nora packed, her eyes full of silent concern.

"We have to leave tonight." Finn's voice was low and urgent. "Someone was trying to use magic on us—it's not safe. I'll only ask you once; are you sure you don't want to stay?"

Luna furrowed her brow and looked down at her children. "You aren't leaving us that easily." She lifted the children and wrapped them one at a time around her in a long piece of fabric.

A smile tugged at the edge of Finn's mouth. "I would never *leave* you; I promised—"

"I know." Luna's voice wavered slightly and she looked away from Finn's gaze.

"Let me take one of them for you."

Luna grabbed another piece of fabric and wrapped Sasha to his back, smiling as she squeaked in protest but eventually calmed. Finn turned and handed Nora a sword and scabbard.

"Put this on; we'll work on training later." He winked and made his way towards the back door.

Nora shook her head at the sight of the roguish half-elf with a little girl strapped to his back before following him into the night. They made their way through the streets wordlessly, Nora finding herself thoroughly impressed with Luna as she navigated through the winding side alleys with ease. She wondered how much time Luna had spent in these underground tunnels and what exactly she had used them for. When they reached the city walls, Luna stopped before a drain and lifted it carefully before urging the other two to enter. They hurried through and disappeared into the darkness of the tunnels.

"Finny, I'm scared," Sasha cried out softly.

Finn extended a hand and began muttering an incantation, the space illuminating as five balls of light grew in his palm. One slowly drifted to each adult, and the other two danced around them, putting off a shimmering show of color as they rotated.

"You don't have to be afraid," he crooned. "Look at the pretty pixies!"

The little girl giggled and laid her head against Finn's back. They moved quietly through the tunnel system, which was a maze of interconnected pipes that seemed indistinguishable from each other.

"How do you know you're going the right way?" Finn asked, his voice an echo of Nora's own thoughts.

Luna pointed to runes etched in the shadowy corners of the tunnel walls. "It's all by color. Green is out, red is the castle, purple the upper district, yellow the lower—"

"These tunnels lead beneath the castle?" Finn interrupted. "Quite the security breach."

"The people who use these tunnels have no interest in politics. They are moving goods, mostly on the king's behalf. He might not know about the tunnels, but he sure does use the hell out of them." Her voice was dismissive, and they continued until they saw moonlight streaming in from ahead. Luna raised a finger to silence them and made her way up, scanning the ground outside for a long while before returning to Finn and Nora.

"Guards," she mouthed, pointing out into the darkness.

Nora moved beside her and looked towards the area Luna indicated, straining her eyes to see in the dark. She could faintly make out two figures moving in the distance, and she signaled for Finn to extinguish the lights.

"Sometimes it feels like we're being watched." The guard sounded slightly inebriated as his speech slurred.

"We've been stationed here for years, Borlan. Nothing has ever happened here; we're *fine*. Enjoy the easy money; you wouldn't rather be at the front gates, would ya?"

The men jeered in protest at the very idea and flew into a heated discussion on city politics. Luna nodded to Nora and Finn before creeping out of the tunnel and slipping into the night air. Concealed by overgrowth and a large weeping willow, the tunnel entrance was mostly obscured and afforded them coverage to disappear into the forest undetected.

Out of eyesight but still on alert, the rhythmic breathing of the now sleeping children was deafening to Nora's ears, and she held her breath as they moved. They continued silently for an hour before Luna finally slowed her pace, her stiff shoulders relaxing and the urgency of her movement lessening. She turned and smiled at Finn and Nora.

"We can't stop yet, but we should be clear." She whispered, bouncing slightly as the children on her back stirred. "Puroux should be only an hour further–we should cut across to Sue City before we get too close if we're to avoid challengers. From there you have two options, east to Gabodga or southwest through the mountain passes towards Balcross. Although, I would hardly recommend either path."

"We can decide when we reach the city." Finn whispered, turning to look back at Nora.

She nodded in agreement and they continued through the early hours of the morning until they came into a wide, dusty clearing full of sagebrush and spatterings of pines. They made their way slowly, taking care to stay off the road. The sage brush grew higher than their heads in most places, offering some semblance of cover. Nora couldn't help but keep her eyes training on the skies, knowing that they would have little cover if the dragon saw them. They stopped only to eat, Luna allowing the children to walk as much as possible before strapping them back on to her and Finn's back.

The sun set and as the darkness settled around them, they stopped to set up camp. With a small fire going, Nora examined her map and saw they were less than halfway to Sue City. She let out a long, frustrated groan as Finn worked on skinning some rabbits he managed to catch and Luna tended her children. Nora folded up her map and peeled some of the potatoes and carrots that were stuffed into her bag. She tossed them into a now boiling pot of water, smiling as the children watched with large interested eyes.

"If we hurry, we can have you guys in Sue City by this time tomorrow." Finn said as he dropped the meat into the water. "As long as nothing stupid happens—"

"Hello?" a meek voice called from a short distance off.

"What was that?" Finn hissed, grabbing his sword from his scabbard and standing to address the voice.

Nora stood, drawing her own sword, and realizing for the first time how awkward she was with the weapon. She peered around Finn to see a young woman standing before them, her arms held out before her like a shield.

"Please! Please, I mean no harm. I have nothing—"

"You shouldn't sneak up on people like that!" Finn snapped as he sheathed his sword. "What in god's name are you doing out here alone this late?"

The girl came closer, smiling down at Luna who glared up at her, a dagger in hand and her children tucked behind her.

"Why are you out here alone?" Finn's voice was becoming increasingly impatient and his eyes surveyed the area around them for more intruders.

"My name is Hanna. I was traveling with my father to Askinia, and we were attacked on the road two days ago. I ran off and I've been trying to find my way to Sue City; I'm hoping he's there waiting for me."

"You've been wandering out here for two days?" Nora began ladling the stew into small bowls for the children and handed her own bowl to Hanna. "You must be starving."

"I am, thank you." The girl sniffled, accepting the food.

"If you were headed to Askina, why would you think he'd be in Sue City?" Finn asked.

"I—I don't know." She burst into tears, cradling her head in her hands and shaking as she sobbed.

"Finn!" Nora snapped, wrapping an arm around the young girl. "Can't you see she's exhausted?"

Finn rolled his eyes and sat back down on his sleeping mat.

"This is the kind of stupid I was talking about," he grumbled.

"You can come with us to Sue City. We should be there tomorrow. Perhaps your father is already there." Nora tried to keep her voice calm and kind, surprised at Luna and Finn's harshness. They had been far more welcoming to her and had even less information when they met.

They ate in an uncomfortable silence, Hanna's shaky breathing the only sound aside from the crackling fire. Luna moved her and the children's bedroll behind Finn before signaling for Nora to come speak with her.

"Trusting strangers on the road rarely turns out well." Luna whispered as Hanna made her own spot to lie down.

"You trusted me and it turned out ok." Nora took another bite of her stew.

Luna raised her eyebrows and shook her head before laying down with her children. The three of them rotated their watch throughout the night, Nora keenly aware that Finn stayed awake during their shifts. He would get up occasionally to walk around the perimeter of the firelight, his eyes sweeping across the expanse of sagebrush and stubby juniper trees. Nora felt the tension hanging heavy in the air but eventually found her way to sleep.

The next morning, they cleaned up wordlessly and set off towards Sue City. They stopped very little and talked even less; the tension in the group hanging thick in the air. Sagebrush and juniper trees gave way to spatterings of pines as the landscape shifted into groups of small forests. The shimmering waters of Lake Varen brought greenery to the high desert; an oasis teeming with life and a sign that they were very near Sue City. When Nora could finally see the city before them, she turned to point it out to Hanna and was startled to see she was no longer with them.

"Finn?"

Finn whirled around, his eyes wide, and shouted, "Ambush!"

As the words escaped his lips, an arrow flew past him and lodged into a tree nearby as Hanna stepped out from the tree line followed by a group of six men. Finn grabbed Nora and pulled her down an embankment that tapered towards the lake, looking over and ducking as another arrow flew past him. Luna swore and tucked the children beneath a blanket on the other side of Finn, shushing them as she peered over the embankment.

"Damn it, damn it, *damn* it!" Finn cried, stringing an arrow onto his bow and standing to shoot at the men.

"Hanna!?" Nora stood there in total shock, unable to move or think.

Finn continued firing into the group of men until finally, he looked down at Nora, clearly exasperated. "Are you going to *do* anything?"

Nora felt her heart racing, the familiar panic rushing up from inside her as a heaviness settled in her chest. She looked up at the forest before her, her body willing her to run from the danger. She looked beside her and saw the terrified faces of Luna's children peering from beneath the blanket. Beau watched her, his eyes locked on Nora's in a silent judgment. She stared back at him; the moment stretching out between them as her heart rate sped up.

Are you going to do anything?

Finn's words echoed around her as she quickly turned, grabbing her bow, and laying her quiver full of arrows on the ground beside her. She rose, arrows whizzing past her, and noticed Hanna was standing behind the men and seemed to be focusing magic.

"How many of them *are there?*" Finn shouted in frustration as the arrows he shot hit their marks, but the men seemed undeterred, steadily approaching, and firing as if nothing had happened.

Nora frowned, squinting her eyes. One man shimmered with a strange light, and Nora realized there were two exact copies of him. "Finn, some of them are illusions. She's conjuring them!"

"Magic, eh?" Finn grinned, ducking back down and pulling Nora down with him. "When I stand up, I'm going to need you all to run as fast as you can towards the tree line. Do not look back and do not stop, no matter what."

"And leave you? You're out of your mind!" Luna's voice was sharp and her eyes were wild with rage. "Our best chance is to stay together."

"Can you *ever* listen?" Finn growled.

"Come out, loves! I'm lost and need your help!" Hanna's voice was taunting as it rang out across the landscape.

"Oh, I'll help you alright." Luna drew an arrow and then stopped, her eyes going wide as a wave of hot air hit them.

"Dragon," she whispered.

The familiar burst of heat laced with a faint scent of sulfur, and Nora knew at that moment they needed to get out of there fast. Her mind flashed to the dragon's fire, and how quickly it had leveled the trained soldiers sent to protect the royal family. She scanned the skies for any sign of the beast before peeking up over the embankment. The men were no longer shooting, but they kept their bows at the ready.

"The one in the center behind the largest boulder is definitely real." She whispered. She noticed two more eyeing Hanna while the rest stayed fixed on their position. "And the two on either side of him as well. Those three are real; I can see them listening to her. The others—I'm not sure."

Finn nodded, peeking up with her. "When I stand up, I'm going to release lightning, and I won't have much control over it. It will take all of her focus just to deflect the bolts, so we will know who she doesn't put energy into protecting are likely illusions. While I'm holding her, you need to get behind them. Try to use the tree line for cover and be wary of the lightning. Once you get there, put this on her." Finn grabbed a necklace from his bag and smiled at Nora. "It won't kill her or even hurt her, but she might wish she were dead."

Nora nodded, grabbing the necklace and slipping it into her shirt pocket.

"On my count then. One, two...three!" He jumped up and immediately magic burst from his hands and sparked all around him in long whipping tendrils of white-hot light.

Nora felt the hairs on her arms rise from the electricity and ran as fast as she could around the boulders into a small patch of trees. Dodging lightning was as impossible as it sounded, and she let out a cry as one bolt burned her skin. She saw Hanna waver, looking back to see where the cry had come from and Luna threw a bottle of red liquid into the air that landed in front of Hanna, causing a massive explosion that sent the woman flying backward through the air. Nora limped as fast as she could through the cover of the trees and stopped at the edge of the tree line waiting for Finn's signal and breathing through the burning sting that radiated through her leg.

Wild arcs of lightning snaked through the air and Nora could hear Hanna's sickening screams as the smoke settled, revealing her bloodied form. She quickly used her magic to heal herself as the three men who Nora had identified as not being illusions quickly turned to help her. As they did arcs of lightning struck them and their muscles seized up, their eyes wide with shock as they fell to the ground rigid and paralyzed.

"Nora, now!" Finn roared.

Nora ran towards Hanna as Finn summoned the magic back to him, doubling over slightly at the exertion. Hanna was screaming as she burst healing magic through her leg, desperately trying to heal herself enough that she could stand. The heat was intensifying and Nora could hear Luna shouting, but could not make out her words. She dropped and slid towards Hanna, slipping the necklace over her head and rolling out of the way of the woman's tearing grasp. A half second stretched out like an eternity as Nora waited for something to happen, fear rising inside of her as Hanna stood and turned to face her. Before Nora could draw a weapon, a pulse erupted from the necklace, throwing Nora back and a guttural scream erupted from Hanna. Nora felt the air knock from her lungs as she hit the ground and looked around to see Luna running towards her, her children tucked in her arms.

"Quickly, to the river!" Luna screamed

"What did you do to me?!" Hanna shrieked.

Nora tried to stand and felt a sharp pain stealing her breath. Luna lowered her children for a moment and helped her to her feet before scooping the children up and continuing towards the river that fed into Lake Varen.

Finn stood and returned his attention to Hanna, who was frantically trying to remove the necklace. "Keep trying, dear. I have heard many people struggle with removing a necklace of Elven binding, but maybe you'll be the first."

"Elven binding?! Take it off!" Hanna's voice came out in choking sobs. "Please, I'm dying!"

"You'll be fine; your magic is just draining. Each ounce of magic that pours into the necklace makes the enchantment stronger—you won't be able to remove it from anyone else's hand but my own."

Hanna crawled towards him; her face wet with tears. "Please, please, sir. Please."

Finn looked at the three men who watched in horror, still paralyzed on the ground. "You three will be yourselves in a couple of hours,

I suggest you—" he pointed to the sobbing form of Hanna, "—get them off the road before someone less forgiving comes along."

"Forgiving?!" Hanna shrieked. "You're a monster, you half-breed ingrate!"

"Finn!" Nora cried as she waded into the water with Luna.

"You bastards! Come back!" Hanna shrieked, desperately dragging the men towards the tree line for cover.

The heat became intense and Nora looked up at the form of the beast swooping down from the sky.

This is it, she thought.

Luna's children buried their faces into her chest and clung tightly as she lifted a piece of bloodied metal from her bag, frantically muttering an incantation in a language Nora had never heard before. The metal lengthened until it domed around them, and Nora looked up as Finn lept through the air, diving into the water as the dome closed around them.

"Captivate the serpent's flame, reflect this celestial power!" Luna screamed as the dragon's fire engulfed the metal.

The sound of the dragon's roar rattled their bones and Nora felt heat spreading within her, her mind reeling as a flood of something both alien and familiar seemed to rush through her veins. She pressed her hands against the hot metal, helping Luna and Finn hold the dome over them as her children screamed, each grasping onto their mother and pressing their faces into her body. The metal radiated with a blinding purple light, and Nora closed her eyes against the brightness. She could hear Finn shouting, but his voice was distant.

You're awake, a voice echoed in Nora's mind before a blinding light filled her vision.

Chapter Seven

When the light subsided, Nora regained her vision and was still within the dome, her hands still pressed against the top while Luna held her children close to her, their faces barely above the water.

"We—what—" Nora stammered, her breath catching as a pain shot through her ribs.

Finn lifted the metal slightly, peering out from beneath. The heat was still intense, but there seemed to be no sign of the dragon. He held a finger to his mouth and dipped below the water, disappearing for a minute before returning to them.

"It just—left." Finn's voice was quiet.

Luna let out a sigh of relief and lifted the metal dome, making her way to the shore and placing her children on the sandy bank. She inspected them for injuries, shushing them as they sobbed and kissing their tears away.

"What was that?" Nora asked as she joined her on the shore, laying flat on her back and groaning as her ribs ached.

"Alchemy." Luna's voice was quiet, and she kept her eyes focused on her children.

"Which is forbidden." Finn's voice was stern.

Luna rolled her eyes and gave Nora a grave look. "People would have you believe it is too unpredictable. They would have all of us believe that high magic is reserved for those born with the Gift, but it is not true. The only thing alchemy does is make things fair, and *that's* what is unpredictable."

"People?" Finn rolled his eyes. "I am not trying to take it from you, but you must know it's dangerous. Alchemy is not something you can just haphazardly—"

"I know that it's saved us—more than once." Luna shot him a warning look before she let out a deep sigh. She moved towards the domed piece of metal and drew a series of runes, pressing her hand against the metal until it shrunk down small enough that she could place it in her bag. "I do nothing for my children lightly."

"Thank you." Nora winced as pain radiated through her body, her hands clasped to her side, and the burning feeling returned to her leg. A dark spot was growing on her shoulder as the bandage below her shirt became saturated with blood, and Nora eased herself to sit on the ground.

Finn ran his hands across Nora's shoulder and ribs, scolding her when she protested, and poured healing into her. It felt slower, more deliberate than the magical healing she had received in the past. It didn't hurt even when she felt her ribs slide back into place. When he finished, Finn offered her a hand and helped her to her feet.

"I can't heal the burn, but we can get something in Sue City for that." He turned towards the city, the sounds of people shouting and arming their gates echoing over the surrounding fields. "Shall we?"

Luna stood, wrapping her children around her and raising a hand in refusal when Finn offered to take them.

"I'm sorry, but they need me right now."

Finn nodded and looked at Nora, who couldn't help but notice the tenderness in his eyes.

"Let's go." He pointed towards Sue City.

Nora looked back where Hanna had been and saw her dragging the last of the three men into the forest, her eyes fixed on Nora. A shiver ran through her, and she turned to follow Finn and Luna. They moved silently, Luna only speaking to calm her children as they clung to her desperately. The heat still hung in the air and helped spur them along quicker than previously. As they approached the gates and Finn held up his medallion, signaling through the crowd of people that they were on the king's quest. The guards beckoned them in quickly, their eyes fixed on the sky.

"Someone get Wolfgang!" One guard shouted.

"I'm here! If you'd all just move!" The voice of an older man hidden within the crowd rang out.

The man pushed through the crowd, waving his hand above his head, and shouting for the guards to let him through. His hair was grey and showed signs of thinning on the top, and his blue eyes glistened through his oval-shaped spectacles. He was tall and surprisingly agile for his age, weaving through the crowds of people and jabbing his elbow into ones who refused to move.

"Move aside!" One guard bellowed, causing a ripple of movement as people parted to allow for him to pass.

"Well, you could've done that to begin with." The man grumbled, straightening his glasses. "I'm the owner of the Snowy Scheme, a tavern selected by the king himself to house challengers." The man beamed at the group before his eyes stopped at the burns on Nora's leg. "You get that from the dragon?"

"Well,—"

"My wife will patch that up just fine; don't you worry about it. When you've been around as long as I have, you know how to deal with burns. Dragon burns are no different. People act like they've never heard of a dragon, but it hasn't been *that* long since Adelle slayed 'the last dragon'." He scoffed at the last part, indicating for them to follow him as he made his way from the gates. "I knew it wasn't the last one. You go around killing them all and they hide; it's just common sense. I was there when she killed it, you know. In a pub not too far away, we were having a drink, me and the guys, and then everyone started screaming and carrying on and we went outside and watched it take its last breath. Once you've seen one dragon slain, you've seen them all—"

Nora smiled as they followed the man through the twisting streets, listening to his tales of dragons in silence. He was a talented storyteller, and Nora found herself hanging on his every word.

They stopped before a large inn and tavern with a sign hanging high that said "The Snowy Scheme." Wooden mountains were carved into the background, painted white against the dark wood. The children watched the man with heavy eyelids, lulled to near-sleep by the motion of Luna walking.

"Oh, I haven't introduced myself. The name is Wolfgang Aloysius. My wife and I bought this tavern when I got too old for adventuring, well *she* said I got too old for adventuring. But maybe if she laid off the sauce, she would see I'm as young as ever."

"I've seen many older and less fit than you on the road!" Finn grinned at the man as they walked into the tavern.

"That's what I tell her, but she doesn't listen. All she does is read her books and work at her potions and you can't very well do that on the road, can you?"

The tavern was surprisingly beautiful. The wood was stained dark, with intricate carvings to make them appear like living branches weaving throughout the building. Leaves were carved into the beams and painted a deep shade of green and gold leaf decorated the edges of each leaf. Stained glass lamps that resembled long tendrils of purple and blue wisteria hung from the ceiling and brought brightness that balanced out the room. Sitting in a larger rocking chair was an older woman with soft brown hair punctuated by streaks of gray, a thick book in one hand and a large mug of steaming liquid in the other.

"There's the old ball and chain. Tabantha, we have customers!"

Tabantha looked up from her book, resting the mug on the table beside her, and sitting up in her recliner.

"You're on the king's conquest with young ones? Curious." Her voice was low and her eyes softened as Luna lowered the children to the ground.

"Ah, we're not going farther than Sue City, ma'am. These two brought us this far and we plan to stay for a bit." Luna took a seat in a recliner across from Tabantha, ushering the children to a small wooden dollhouse that sat beside the fireplace.

"Our grandchildren visit occasionally, so we keep this house on hand. Never thought I would have dollies in a tavern, but here we are." Wolfgang urged Nora forward, pointing to her burned leg. "Why don't you put your book down and do some work around here? This young lady is practically burning alive before our eyes and you can't even drop the book."

Tabantha eyed the burn on Nora's leg. "Let me finish this chapter and then I will see to it. She will survive that long."

"Waiting until you finish a chapter; that's all we do around here is wait for another chapter." Wolfgang turned to Finn, shaking his head, and making his way to the bar. "I'll whip you up my famous firewraps; you won't find wraps like mine anywhere else. People don't take *time*, but the trick is the seasoning. You must season everything *individually*."

Wolfgang continued in a flurry of instructions on firewraps to Finn, who helped himself to a bottle of wine, pouring a glass for Nora and Luna when they were ready. Nora moved to sit beside Tabantha, waiting anxiously for the woman to finish her book. The woman seemed unbothered by her presence, sipping at her mug, which at a closer proximity Nora could smell a hint of alcohol, and sighing to herself as she turned the page. Finally, she finished the chapter, set her book down, and turned to inspect Nora's leg.

"Hmph. This is quite the burn."

"It's nothing compared to other burns; why when I was a young man—"

"Do you want to take care of the burn or the food?" Tabantha snapped at her husband.

"Sure, I'll clean the tavern and make the dinner and heal the guests too while I'm at it!" Wolfgang threw his hands in the air and rolled his eyes at Finn.

"Curious." Tabantha murmured, ignoring her husband. "Why haven't you tried healing yourself?"

Nora pursed her lips. "I do not have the Gift."

"You certainly do, child." The woman smiled. "It is–strange. But it's there."

"My mother had me tested," Nora murmured. "*Many* times. I assure you; you are mistaken."

Tabantha said nothing, reaching into a jar labeled 'BURNS' and rubbing the thick ointment vigorously across Nora's leg. The oil burned at first, but the burning melted away and Nora felt her skin tighten, the charred flesh scabbing instantly and falling away to reveal fresh skin. A scar ran the length of Nora's leg and Tabantha smiled.

"I'll let you keep that souvenir. Scars show where we've been; they're special. Now let me check the rest of you." She ran her hands carefully across Nora's injured shoulder, stopping at the ribs that Finn healed, and frowned. "A good patch job, but a patch job nonetheless." She lifted Nora's shirt and rubbed an oil that smelled heavily of lavender and oranges across Nora's ribs and shoulder, pain coursing through Nora's body as familiar magical healing burned through the tissue and bruising.

Nora tensed as the magic worked through her, gritting her teeth and closing her eyes tightly to press out the world around her. Magic healing hurt because it interrupted your body's natural process, and even though it was a common practice, most preferred natural healing.

"There, I have done what I can. Your shoulder won't get better if you don't stop battering it, but the burn should be fine." Tabantha smiled, leaning back in her chair. "I can't help with the magic part, unfortunately. You'll have to figure that out for yourself, although it seems like you are on the cusp of it. Wish I could be there when you unleash it."

Nora ran her hand over the scar on her arm thoughtfully before standing. "Thank you for the healing. What do I owe you?"

The woman was silent for a long moment. "Just make sure you come visit again. That's enough for me; we never get enough visitors."

"Foods almost done, just need to cut up some peppers." Wolfgang pulled out a large knife, running it across a whetstone and looking back at Finn. "Always sharpen your knives. The most dangerous thing in a kitchen is a dull knife."

Finn nodded solemnly, sipping the wine, and listening to Wolfgang intently.

"It's nice to see them playing like normal kids." Luna murmured, watching the kids play by the fireside. "Children are the most resilient of us all."

Nora couldn't imagine being a mother in this world. Only a few weeks ago, even with the trials of her life, she felt like the world was full of beauty and possibility. Now as she traveled, Nora saw from the cities to the edges of society, there was an overwhelming shadow of suffering hanging above it all.

"Alright, dinner is served. You can plate yourselves; I'm an old man after all!" Wolfgang chuckled as she poured himself a beer and moved to sit beside his wife with a plate of hot food.

They got plates for the children and themselves, moving to sit around the fire and listening to more of Wolfgang's tales while Tabantha read, interjecting with facts here and there as he spoke. It seemed as if Wolfgang had been all over the continent, and present for almost every event that Nora had ever heard of. He told them of King Alexander's coronation, of the witches of Goghbuldor who used to teach royal mages long ago, and even stories of Nora's own mother that left her speechless. The scandal that was Adelle, a woman from nowhere who suddenly appeared with untold power, and the way she found her way into the highest circles of society. Nora thought of the woman she had known, stuffy and stiff, wandering the estate to pick things apart and bark orders. It didn't seem possible that the fiery woman full of life in Wolfgang's tales could be her own mother.

When they finished eating, Tabantha gathered the dishes while Wolfgang led them to a suite upstairs. The room had a large common area and two bedrooms; an inviting fire kept out the chill and a pot of hot tea sat beneath the window. Wolfgang closed the door behind them and Nora could hear him and Tabantha chattering as they made their way down the stairs.

Nora took a seat and closed her eyes as exhaustion washed over her. It felt like she had lived a lifetime in the short span she was on the road and she had scars to prove it. She wondered what Tulee would think.

The children piled on top of Nora, their mouths greasy with food and their eyes glossy. Nora let out a slight yelp as they elbowed their way into a comfortable position and settled in to sleep.

"You lot! Into the bath with you, now!" Luna scolded, tugging them off Nora.

The children cried in protest, following their mother into the bathroom and disappearing into a cloud of soapy bubbles. The gleeful cries and splashing signified the change of tune and Finn smiled at Nora who shook her head.

"These kids." She murmured.

"They're pretty great. They kind of grow on you." Finn sat across from Nora and handed her a cup of tea. She sat up to accept it and rested her elbows on her knees. "How did the healing go?"

"It went good, actually." She stretched out her leg to reveal the scar and smiled. "That's all that's left of it. No pain at all."

"I should've controlled it better. I just was so focused on the children—"

"You don't need to explain anything. I'm the one who should be sorry. I didn't trust your instinct and allowed Hanna to put us in that position to begin with." Nora sipped at her tea, closing her eyes as the warm liquid spilled down her throat. "Tabantha mentioned something strange, though. She insisted that I have magic about me."

Finn raised an eyebrow and sipped at his tea. "And?"

Nora shook her head. "Well, I don't. I'm not elvish, and I don't have the Gift. My mother had me tested many times, but there's nothing."

"Normally, the Gift has an aura that signals its power. It's something elves can see. Non-magic people also have an aura; it's dull but present. The Gift is only one source of magic in this world; there are others that are much older." Finn inspected Nora's face. "The thing with you is I can't see your aura. And that wouldn't be so strange, but I *never* see it. They aren't always beaming outwards; sometimes the aura fades or is difficult to see for whatever reason, but I have looked constantly and haven't seen it once. Except—"

Nora set her cup down, waiting for Finn to finish. "Except?"

Finn rubbed at the back of his neck. "I could've sworn I saw your aura when we were in that dome of metal. It was a flash of light. The energy felt like an aura, but I have never seen one so bright. It was a flash and then it was gone."

"What could it mean?" Nora whispered.

"I have theories, but—" Finn sat up as the three children ran out of the bathroom wrapped in towels, their wet feet slapping against the hardwood floor as they ran into the bedroom. Luna followed them, soaking wet and frowning, and Finn let out an uproarious laugh. "Oh, gods be *damned* did they get you!"

"Yes, it's so very *funny*." Luna spat, stomping after the kids and shutting the door behind her.

"How long have you known them?" Nora asked quietly, eager to change the subject.

"I knew Malachi—Luna's husband—since I was a boy. We grew up in an elven village, finding brotherhood in being half-elf outcasts." Finn sipped on his tea before relaxing deeper into his chair. "I met Luna when they were courting; I was there when they wed and then named their children's godfather. Malachi wanted glory and renown;

he hated being an outcast. He went searching for–well, there's a story we were always told as children. It promised power, and the ability to change the world, and he had wanted nothing else all his life. It killed him in the end."

"What was it he was after?" Nora's voice was low, and she kept her eyes on the door Luna had shut.

"A dream, Nora. Not much different from what we are doing now. I promised him I would care for them if anything happened, so Luna joined a refugee caravan and tried to find me. I received word from my—contacts—that they were ambushed on the road and I tracked them for weeks. Then I stumbled into you."

Luna quietly opened the door, easing through the doorway and holding her breath as a floorboard creaked. She shut the door so slowly it felt as if it took an eternity, and she collapsed onto the couch beside Finn.

"I'm *spent*," she exclaimed, accepting a cup of tea.

"It sounded like quite the tussle." Finn winked at Nora. "It would be a shame if they woke up again."

"The way I would end you." Luna gave Finn a playful shove.

Finn grinned and picked at the bread and jam still left on his plate. They sat up for a bit longer, talking about their lives and sharing stories before Nora returned to her room, Finn claiming the couch as his own. Nora noticed how their eyes lingered on each other, and she recognized the attachment formed through their shared grief. Nora shut the door quietly, offering the two of them much needed privacy.

As Nora lay in her bed, she could hear their muffled voices. Her name, power, prophecy. Words she couldn't make out repeated over and over, words that made her want to stand and press her ear to the door, but her body protested the movement and she eventually went to sleep.

Chapter Eight

Nora rarely dreamt, and when she did, it was mostly jumbled moments that were difficult for her to remember. But as the darkness of slumber peeled back in her mind, Nora stood in what could only be described as a forest city built into the surrounding landscape. Homes were built against trees, some built up in the branches, and a towering cliff side where a cathedral was built into the stone itself. Small hills sported doors that led to shops and living spaces beneath the ground, and a small silvered lake with floating homes connected by a series of bridges and canals transporting heaping goods from somewhere further upstream. As she moved through the space, she marveled at the way the people here existed with the surrounding nature, careful to honor what had always been.

No one seemed to notice her as she moved through the space and she realized their faces were shrouded with shadow, as if obscuring their identity from her. She wanted to stop and ask them where she was, but she found herself propelled forward, her feet hovering inches above the ground as some unseen force pulled her towards the stone cathedral. As she approached, a shadow fell over her and the world around her slipped away, replaced by the blackness of the night sky filled with twinkling stars. A face was before her, shrouded in shifting shadows. All Nora could make out was a pair of bright blue eyes and glistening ebony skin with gold-painted designs adorning the face. The eyes were kind but surveyed her with a sense of judgment that made Nora feel naked in the expanse of space.

I see you.

The voice echoed around her, and Nora recognized it from the dragon attack at the lake. A shiver ran up her spine.

"Who are you?" Nora's voice sounded far from herself and echoed around her.

I am waiting for you. Good luck, star child.

A booming eruption of light pulsed towards Nora and sent her flying back through the darkness and the forest city, dragging her away as the face of the being before her slowly became clearer. The shroud of blackness melted away, and the being rose like a giant the further Nora moved away, a dangerous smile spreading across her face until Nora shouted, sitting upright, and finding herself still in her bed.

"What's that?!" Finn rushed into the room, hair a mess and dagger at the ready.

"I—I had a bad dream."

He frowned down at her, raising his middle finger and shutting the door behind him.

When she was alone, she felt the panic rise inside of her again. Nora was used to panic attacks, but that did not make them any less terrifying. She felt the panic rise within her, a pressure on her chest that made her feel as if she would suffocate. What was that being? Was it truly a dream? It felt real–too real. And she had heard the voice before. She stood up and poured a glass of water from a metal pitcher on her windowsill and looked out at the cobblestone street below. Focusing on the street below, she began counting the stones. This was something she found that helped her quiet her mind enough that the panic would pass, and eventually, when she felt like herself again, she opened the window and breathed in the cool night air. She leaned forward and looked out at the darkened homes and empty alleys that dotted the landscape. Tears escaped her eyes freely as she tried to relax her still-tense body, pushing back the thoughts of doubt that inevitably greeted her when she was alone.

She wondered what Briella was doing, if she was even alive, and if so, what state she was in. She looked down at the silver bangle that had slipped from the princess's wrist that Nora kept on her own wrist. The gems gleamed in the moonlight as she fiddled with the crest, frowning as the top seemed to separate from its base. With a small pull, the crest opened, revealing it to be a locket. Inside was a small painting of the princess sitting in a library unlike anything Nora had ever seen. Vines hung from bookshelves and sunlight shined all around the space, revealing the library to be outside. Nora inspected the tiny painting, marveling at the detail in such a small space and the way the artist captured the princesses's challenging smile. She closed the seal and pulled the window shut, returning to her bed, and falling into a deep, uneventful sleep.

The next morning Luna looked over their maps and helped them come up with a plan for going to both Gaboga and Balcross, insisting that Balcross would have fewer contestants to deal with and was safer despite the mountain terrain well known for its dangers.

"There are worse dangers than animals and difficult terrain," Luna argued. "You're going up against desperate people. If I were you, I'd be heading to Balcross."

Finn smiled. "It's almost like you care about us."

Luna chuckled, giving him a soft kiss on the cheek. "Remember us little people when you become lords and ladies of the land." She pulled a scroll out of her pocket and handed it to Nora.

"I worked on this last night—it's instructions for the alchemy I used on the dragon. Very detailed, even this idiot could do it." She nudged Finn, ignoring his wary look. "Be very careful with the runes. One circle not closed enough, one rune drawn incorrectly, and the result can be catastrophic. Alchemy is as beautiful as it is dangerous, but if you are careful, it might save your life."

"Thank you." Nora accepted the scroll and tucked it into her bag.

Luna looked at her for a long moment. "Trust in yourself. Don't let anyone tell you who or what you must do. Destiny is for fools."

Nora bit her lip, confusion written across her face, and nodded slowly. She found she disliked goodbyes more each time she was forced into them. She looked at Finn, whose eyes lingered over Luna and the children, and Luna who carefully kept her gaze from his, as if she might break if she were to look at him. Nora wondered what it felt like to be so connected to someone in that way, where words weren't needed and where you knew them so deeply that you could expect their every move.

"Tabantha has offered me a place here for my children and me and some work in her kitchen. Sue City is well protected and one of the king's favored cities. We're as safe here as anywhere else, and I am not too keen on being on the roads again soon. Please write to me when you can. Let me know you're alive."

"I'll send letters whenever I can," Finn promised.

"Take care of each other." She pulled Finn into a tight embrace before turning her attention to Nora. "Keep an eye on this one for me, ok?"

Nora nodded, and Luna allowed the children to say their goodbyes before following them out into the backyard. Finn watched until she disappeared from sight.

"Should you stay?" Nora asked. "You don't have to come. You could have a whole life here."

Finn said nothing for a moment before turning to face Nora. "I need to do this for Malachi, and those kids have no chance of a life with this beast destroying everything. I'd rather die trying to change things than stay here and hope it doesn't come back. Besides, Luna can take care of herself. She's tough as nails."

"She's an amazing woman, she must have had quite the life before having children." Nora thought back to the way she had navigated the secret tunnels with ease, combined with her ability to use alchemy, Nora couldn't help but wonder who Luna had once been.

Finn grinned. "She has always been something fearsome. Even Malachi didn't know what to do with her." He cleared his throat and flashed Nora a sly grin. "So, you up for a game of chance?"

Nora frowned in response.

"Heads Balcross, tails Gabodga." He winked, holding a coin between his pointer and middle fingers.

"Might as well." Nora shrugged.

He flipped the coin in the air and they watched as it rotated before falling back onto his outstretched palm.

"Tails! Gabodga it is!" He exclaimed excitedly.

"Gaboga was attacked by the dragon two days ago," Tabantha said lazily as she turned the page in the book. "Sorry—I thought I'd wait to see how the coin landed before tellin' ya."

Finn let out an exasperated sigh. "Ok then, Balcross it is!"

Nora laughed as she followed Finn out the door, the old woman grinning sheepishly as they left.

"Come back to visit anytime!" Wolfgang shouted after them. "If you survive!"

Nora could hear him chuckling as they made their way towards the main gate. They followed the main road until the city was no longer in sight and then moved into the forest, chancing animals over people they may encounter.

Around midday, they stopped at a small stream to rest; Nora caught a few fish while Finn worked on building a small fire. Once the fish were cleaned and cooking, Finn drew his sword and pointed it at Nora.

"If you're going to be worth your salt against a dragon, we need to practice."

Nora smiled and stood, drawing her sword. "Oh, you don't think I know how to use this?"

Finn grinned as he crouched into a fighting stance. Nora lunged at him, gasping as he swiftly turned out of the way and sent her tumbling to the ground.

When she turned with a look of bewilderment, he burst out laughing.

"No, I do not!" He returned to his stance and beckoned her to try again.

They sparred for some time, stopping to take the fish out of the pan and eat before resuming their lesson. Finn was merciless with his blade, swinging so hard and fast that Nora struggled to keep up. He pinned her against a large boulder and pushed his sword into hers with all his weight, his eyes flashing with excitement.

Nora's eyes darted around for something to help her. She felt the sweat pouring down her face and struggled to maintain the pressure against his sword. She drove her knee hard into his groin, causing Finn to double over, and kicked him away from her. He reached for his blade, his free hand still holding himself, but couldn't grab it before Nora. She raised it and crossed it with her own against his throat.

"Give?" Nora panted heavily as her heart pounded in her chest.

"Give." Finn dropped to the ground when she lowered the swords.

Nora tossed his blade on the ground beside him and sheathed her own, sitting down on a rock to catch her breath.

"That was a cheap shot," Finn groaned.

"Ya, I figured if someone was trying to kill me, it justifies cheap shots." Her voice remained calm despite her being out of breath. "I think that's enough for today."

Finn nodded in agreement. "You aren't as bad as I thought you would be."

"What's that supposed to mean?"

"Well, when I found you, you didn't even have a weapon. I didn't think it would be something you'd be too familiar with."

"Remember, I escaped my burning village with a dragon at my heels. I wasn't exactly able to run back to the armory." Nora said defensively. "Besides, I had my daggers."

Finn shrugged. "Daggers aren't much help against what we're going to be dealing with."

Nora sat back and watched the fire, her belly full and her mind racing. She couldn't shake the possibility of having magic from her thoughts. She remembered the rigorous testing by mages throughout the kingdom and the way Adelle put her in terrifying situations to provoke the magic out of her.

When Nora was about eight years old, Adelle took Nora out for what she believed to be a picnic. They enjoyed the afternoon together and Nora had allowed herself to let her guard down–a mistake she never made again. Weariness spread through her body, and she fell asleep to the sound of Adelle's crooning above her. When Nora came to, complete darkness surrounded her and her mother was nowhere to be found. She stumbled through the forest, crying out for Adelle to come to her, and eventually hid within the roots of a large tree. The sound of animals moving through the night kept her awake, and it wasn't until the next day when Tulee heard her sobs that she was found.

She remembered Tulee wrapping her arms around her and lifting her, running her hands through her hair, and reassuring her she was safe now. Exhaustion washed over her and she fell asleep in her arms, waking in her bed at the estate with Tulee fussing over her. Tulee never asked what happened. She mentioned nothing about it, but from then on, she followed Nora anytime Adelle tried to take her off of the property. This interference had annoyed Adelle, but she said nothing when the older woman insisted.

Nora remembered feeling Adelle was searching for something within her, something more than a parent who wanted their child to continue their legacy. She would beg Adelle to stop, insisting that Larissa was enough, but Adelle would scour through ancient tomes and come back with more tests until finally, she gave up.

"You'd think the Celestials would have intervened by now." Finn's voice drew Nora from her memories.

"Hm?" She straightened and prodded the fire with a stick.

"It's just—well, you know the stories. The great battle at the beginning of creation, the formation of the celestials who are supposed to look out for us. There are reports of creatures awakening and walking the earth that I thought were long gone. It just seems like this would be the time they would come down to aid us again if they're even watching." Finn carefully placed another log on the fire.

Nora looked up at the stars, turning her head to make out the constellations. She was never good at discerning them, only the ones nearest the Northern Star were easily identifiable to her.

"Maybe this is part of their plan. Why would they intervene if they have decided our time is up?" She ignored Finn's stare and continued to scan the heavens. "I met a nymph right after the dragon attack. I helped her, and she blessed me." Nora held up her hand and allowed Finn to inspect the deep blue starry lines. "Perhaps they're what we need. Maybe this awakening is a good thing."

Finn turned her hand over, inspecting it closely before releasing her. He shrugged and laid out on his mat.

"I don't know, Nora. Seems like quite the gamble to make, but then again, who knows if the old stories are true. So much time has passed, and people have a way of twisting the truth to fit their own needs."

Nora nodded slowly.

"So, what exactly does that mark do?" Finn asked.

"It's some kind of connection to her. When I was with her, it allowed us to communicate. I'm not sure how far it works, but it's a comfort to know there's a connection." Nora looked at her hand and then laid on her own mat.

"It could prove useful. Hopefully, it works no matter the distance." Finn yawned.

"Good night, Finn," Nora muttered as she stared into the fire.

"Good night, Nora. Try to get some rest; we'll get an early start tomorrow."

Nora rolled onto her back and looked back at the stars. The clearest constellation tonight was Draco; it had been the most easily identifiable for the past few weeks.

Perhaps they are watching, Nora thought before drifting to sleep.

They rose early and made quick work of cleaning their camp. Nora poured water over the smoldering remains of their fire and Finn scattered brush to make it seem as if the site hadn't been used in a while before continuing towards the towering mountains ahead.

They spoke little and stopped only when they absolutely had to, the deadline for the ships setting off bearing down on them. When they finally reached the opening for the mountain pass, Nora noticed a large sign that read:

DANGER—TROLLS—PROCEED AT YOUR OWN RISK

Finn scratched the back of his neck as he looked at the pass before them. "If I die, I'm fucking haunting you."

Nora couldn't help but notice large boulders smeared with blood. She heard stories of trolls rolling boulders down to crush unsuspecting travelers; she shuddered at the thought of those people who had been trying to find a safe passage through the mountains.

"I think it's best we stay off the main roads," Finn murmured, moving off the worn path into the dense forest.

Nora followed wordlessly, and they continued that way for a long while, with no signs of life anywhere. No birds chirping in the distance, no lizards or squirrels scurrying from their footsteps. It seemed to Nora that they were the only living things in this part of the forest, and the thought sent a chill up her spine.

Finn stopped and pointed ahead of them, motioning for Nora to remain silent. She followed his gaze and took a long, silent breath as she saw four towering figures sitting a short distance from them. The stench alone would have given them away, but even from this distance, Nora could see clearly that they were trolls. Their gray skin was leather-like, and their torn scraps of cloth barely covered their bodies. They were close enough that Nora could make out their yellow eyes and see that they were feasting on something that bore an uncomfortable resemblance to a human.

Finn motioned for Nora to follow him further into the forest, away from the trolls, every leaf crunching beneath their feet, creating a sick feeling in Nora's stomach. Finn kept his eyes on the trolls, who seemed completely oblivious to their presence. Nora heard trolls were stupid, and they had little in the way of a sense of smell, but their hearing and speed she knew little about. The smell dissipated as they moved further from the trolls and Finn let out a sigh of relief.

"Well at least—"

As Finn spoke, the forest floor seemed to cave in around them. Finn shouted as he plunged into the hole. A sickening thud echoed through the darkness as he hit a hard surface below. Nora barely suppressed a scream as she quickly grabbed one of the exposed roots from the trees around the hole, grunting in frustration as she tried to pull herself up.

Nora looked down below and squinted at a figure that seemed to move within the darkness. As she looked, the root separated from the roof of what Nora could tell now was a cave and she shouted as she slammed up against the cave wall, grabbing the stones to keep herself from falling deeper into the darkness. The light from the hole above illuminated the cave slightly, and as Nora's eyes adjusted, she noticed Finn lying on the ground motionless.

Please don't be dead, she thought. She heard something move below her and squinted at a figure that reared up to look at her. The figure rose and was nearly at Nora's feet. She could make out the head and torso of a woman, but from her hips down was the body of a snake.

Nora felt fear rise within her and closed her eyes to steady herself. She knew what this creature was, and though they were thought to be long extinct, this one was clearly alive and they were in her den. She opened her eyes and stared down at the creature.

A serapin.

Chapter Nine

"I hear you," the creature's voice crooned from the darkness. "I can hear your heart beating. Are you afraid, human? You should be. I am Gilade and I will be your doom."

Gilade, Nora thought, breathing slowly.

She heard about the serapins and their role in the world's creation. In the legends, Draco, king of the Dragons, led an army of creatures against the Titans, creatures whose existence would have led to the ruin of the world. He enlisted the help of Gilade and her army of Serapin, promising them a place in the celestial court if they should succeed. However, when the battle was won, Draco betrayed Gilade and abandoned her with the other creatures of the world. Feared by man, the serapins were hunted to extinction—or so the stories claimed. Nora had once seen one mounted on the side of a traveling caravan that presented oddities and ancient artifacts for a small price at local festivals.

Seeing the creature before her now, she knew that whatever had been on the side of the caravan had not been a Serapin. The face was human-like, but just barely. Scales shimmered where skin would be, her eyes were larger than a human and her nose was two small slits that sat above a wide, fanged mouth. Her tongue flicked through the air and Nora knew she was tasting the air for her.

A wide grin spread across Gilade's face. "I hear your heart beating faster. You know who I am."

Nora watched Gilade silently. Nora could make out the rise and fall of Finn's chest, so why wasn't she attacking him? She studied the creature's face and realized that her eyes had a milky film covering them. Nora had seen the same thing in other cave-dwelling creatures and closed her eyes with relief. Gilade was blind; her hearing was good and likely her smell, but she could not see where Nora was.

Nora's eyes adjusted to the dim light, and she looked around for something to help her. On a small ledge below where she stood was a large boulder that looked like it could be moved with enough force and hopefully distract the creature; however, this would put her near eye-level with Gilade. Even though the serapin could not see her, the thought of being so close to those long, sharp fangs sent a chill up Nora's spine. She looked down at Finn, still unmoving, and knew she had to do something.

Moving at a painfully slow pace, her eyes fixed on the creature before her, Nora made her way toward the ledge. Gilade jerked her head around frantically taking in the sounds around her.

"There has not been a human in this cave in a long time, a few elves and mostly trolls, but no humans wander this far off the mountain paths. Something about you smells–odd. Not like the humans I remember." Gilade sniffed the air, her grin fading as she did so.

Nora still said nothing. Slipping slowly over the edge of the higher ledge and dangling her feet towards the ledge below, she searched for something to put her feet on. When her boots hit stone, she watched as Gilade jerked her head towards her, and seemed to stare directly into her eyes.

Fuck, Nora thought as the creature reared up.

Nora froze as she heard a groan escape Finn's lips. Gilade whipped around, and Nora threw her full weight behind the boulder as quickly as possible. Pushing against the cliff's edge with her feet, she watched in horror as Gilade slowly made her way towards Finn.

"I am not magic born!" Nora shouted.

Gilade stopped and turned, the wide grin menacing. "You're a girl. A young one at that. What is your name?"

"Nora DuPont. I am on a quest on behalf of the king."

Gilade was close enough now that Nora could see her face clearly in the dim light. Wild, feral, and cruel, but Nora could see remnants of the great beauty Gilade once was. In all the ancient texts, serapins were said to possess unparalleled beauty to trick men into following them into their dens. As they were all female, serapins needed human men to continue their line. However, Nora questioned the validity of these stories after looking at the creature before her. Banished to the darkness of these tunnels, forgotten by the celestials and humans she helped, Gilade seemed now a product of what was done to her.

"This stream brings me news from the kingdom." Gilade gestured towards the glowing river. "I have heard much of your noble *king*." Gilade spat at the last word. "And his lost princess. You think you can defeat a dragon? I would like to see that; you first will have to escape me. I think you'll find that *exceedingly* difficult."

Gilade flashed a cruel smile, and Nora knew Gilade knew exactly where she was. With one last shove, the boulder dropped from the edge of the ledge and plummeted to the cave floor below. Nora slid down the cliff side, careful to use her feet to control her descent, and moved towards Finn as Gilade shot after the boulder.

Finn's head was bleeding and he was unconscious, but he was alive and Nora knew she could figure out the rest later. Nora heaved him up onto her back as she heard the serapin let out a scream of rage.

"You think you can play games with me, Nora DuPont? You will beg for the mercy of death when I'm finished with you!" Gilade's voice rang out, echoing off the cave walls and surrounding Nora and Finn.

Nora made her way to the stream slowly, her eyes darting around the room whenever she heard a sound. Finn's weight made her footsteps heavier than she would have liked, and she held her breath through each movement. As she approached the river, Gilade reared up on the other side of the water, her tongue flicking wildly from her mouth, tasting the air for her prey.

Nora slipped into the water slowly, her eyes fixed on Gilade. She slowly moved until the water was up to her chest, relieving some of Finn's weight. The water pulled at her as she ran through the situation quickly, trying to come up with a plan.

She recognized this river from stories traveling merchants would tell; the healing waters of The Nymph's Tears. Legend said that all nymphs were born from it and it stretched through the entire continent; a magical vein cutting through the land. It couldn't *end* in this cave. It had to exit somewhere. If she could follow it, she might get them out wherever it flowed out. She closed her eyes, took a deep breath, and slowly lowered her body until only her nose and eyes were exposed. She used her hands to prop up Finn's head so his face was out of the water, but his body was just beneath. Slowly, Nora moved them forward towards Gilade.

"You can hide, but I will find you, Nora Dupont. I have spent many lifetimes in this darkness. I know the void; the emptiness is my domain. Even now, I feel your heartbeat reverberating off the walls. I can smell your fear; you know you will not get out." Gilade slithered towards the edge of the water as Nora inched closer.

Nora called upon the calming techniques she learned to work through her sudden panics as she drifted closer to the serapin, desperate to slow her racing heart that seemed to thunder all around her. The sickening smell of decay and blood overwhelmed Nora as they passed beneath the creature. Nora watched Gilade, looking directly at the underside of the creature's face as she passed beneath her. Her teeth were exposed and her tongue flicked out rapidly. She seemed unaware of their presence and Nora wondered how much of her senses the creature still had. She didn't want to find out.

Nora turned in the water so she was still facing Gilade, walking backward slowly deeper into the darkness of the cave as the creature stood still as a statue, listening for her. They turned down a bend,

Nora's eyes searching for any sign of an opening. The stones illuminated the path at the bottom of the stream, and as Nora approached the end of the glowing path, she reached out and felt a wall of rocks blocking her from going any further.

A cave-in, she thought helplessly, *how the fuck are we going to get out of here?*

Nora felt the familiar panic rise in her chest and she squeezed her eyes shut against the feeling, cursing herself for not keeping her composure in these situations.

Not now, not now. Please, not now. She felt the heaviness settle in her chest, the feeling that she would suffocate and die here in this cave.

She heard Gilade's terrible chuckle coming closer and closer, and tried to calm herself, knowing now that her panicked breathing was drawing the beast nearer to her.

"I told you there's no way out." Gilade's voice rang out around her.

The panic within her left Nora feeling lightheaded, increasing as her vision blurred and her breaths became shallow gasps. She looked around for a sign of the serapin, moving Finn so his head rested on her shoulder as she tried to think of a way out. Nora reached into the water and lifted one of the glowing stones, hurling it ahead. Gilade lashed out from the darkness, diving into the water, and screaming out curses when she did not find her quarry.

Nora pulled at the rocks that blocked the path, trying desperately to make an opening big enough for her and Finn to pass through. She felt her nails break as she clawed at the wall, looking over her shoulder to keep her eye on the creature, who was quickly exiting the river. She heard Finn groan again. Nora's heart skipped a beat, and she turned to see Gilade rear up towards them. She grabbed Finn, pushing him behind her and shoving him into the wall with her full weight. He let out another groan of pain and Nora closed her eyes, extending her hands to shield her face as Gilade hurled her body towards them, teeth bared and eyes wide with excitement.

Nora felt something hum around her. A purple light burned through her closed eyelids and she heard Gilade scream as the rocks behind her gave way. A loud blast erupted from around them and the impact pushed them out of the cave mouth. They plummeted in a waterfall of stone and debris towards the river below, and as she fell Nora turned just in time to see the serapin turn to stone at the mouth of the cave, frozen in a terrible scream of rage. She gasped and hit the river hard, engulfed by the rushing water below.

Birds chirped in the distance as Nora dragged herself onto a bank, choking and coughing up water from her burning lungs. When she finally caught her breath, she sat up slowly and checked herself for any injuries, surprised to find that, aside from the pounding headache, she was uninjured. She looked further down the river bank and saw the figure of a person lying a short distance away and hurriedly got up, swooning slightly as her vision darkened from standing too abruptly.

"Finn!" she shouted, half crawling, half running through the uneven rocky river bank.

She heard him groan, and she felt her breath release. She dropped to her knees and wrapped her arms tightly around him.

"You're *alive!*" Nora allowed the tears to fall freely from her, burying her face in Finn's neck. She didn't know how either of them survived, but she sent a silent prayer to the gods for sparing them.

"Only as long as you don't suffocate me," Finn whispered before Nora let him go. He took a slow breath and smiled before giving Nora a thumbs up. "I feel like dog shit."

"How did you blow up that cave?" Nora asked as she wiped the tears from her face.

"What?"

"There was a serapin living in that cave—Gilade. I tried to escape with you through the river and at the end was a cave-in. She was about to kill us and then there was this bright light and the rocks seemed to explode away from us and we fell into this river."

"What color was the light?"

"Purple?"

Finn pressed his lips into a straight line and shrugged. "I don't know and I am in no position to muse on it at the moment. Now, you said *Gilade*?"

Nora slowly explained everything that had happened. She told him about the river running through the cave, and Gilade launching at them and turning to stone after they fell. Finn listened wordlessly, considering everything Nora said.

"It's—well, it's hard to believe. Serapins have long been believed to have been extinct, but one so old as Gilade still being alive is even more difficult to fathom. Celestials exist as something separate from us, defying all logic. The rules don't apply to them in the same way they apply to the rest of creation."

"But she isn't a celestial," Nora said flatly, glaring when Finn rolled his eyes.

"You humans think you know everything. She *was* a celestial. She and her generals all were until she was rejected from the heavens. I have heard no tales of their specific deaths; I wonder how many others exist in the shadows of this world."

Nora rolled her eyes. "Very poetic of you."

"You know I *do* try." Finn slowly rose to his feet, stretching his stiff limbs and groaning as his back popped loudly. "I'm too old for this shit."

They moved from the river bank and emptied their packs in a small clearing. Nora smiled when she found everything to be intact and dry; it was almost as if they *hadn't* been catapulted through the air in a magic explosion.

"Luna is a wonder," Finn said absently. "I don't love alchemy, but I saw her working on these bags before we left, and I knew it was right to just allow her to do her thing."

Nora smiled. She knew that, however unbothered Finn tried to appear, he missed Luna and the kids. She pulled out Finn's map, surveying it.

"We're close," she grinned.

Finn frowned at her and snatched the map from her hands to inspect it himself.

"I don't trust your judgment with maps." He murmured as he looked it over. He furrowed his brow and thrust the maps back into Nora's hands. "I would hardly say we're *close*."

Nora glared at him as she folded up the map. "Well, it's not on the other side of a fucking mountain!"

Finn rolled his eyes and leaned back onto a log. The sky was darkening and Nora settled on her bedroll, appreciating the silence to process what happened to them. Finn hadn't spoken on the revelation that the explosion was someone else's magic, and his silence was loud. She found herself torn between the way she had failed her mother by being born without magic, and this sudden emergence of something that seemed to baffle those around her. The thought of something within her that was uncontrollable terrified Nora, and she wondered if Finn was afraid, too.

"Finn?" Her voice cut through the long moment of silence.

"Hmm?"

"Do you think we'll find Briella?"

"Briella?"

"The princess."

Finn was silent for a long moment. "When did you start giving the princess a nickname?"

Nora looked up at the stars peeking through the trees. "I was there when she was married. I met her the night before—"

"You met her the night before, or you *met* her the night before?"

"You idiot." Nora shook her head and suppressed a laugh. "I spoke with her, we—watched fireflies."

"Fireflies. Well, this is a lot more intimate than I would have—"

"*Anyway*, when she was taken by the dragon, I tried to help her. I was taken up with her, and she let me go before we got too high." Nora pulled out the bracelet, opening the locket and handing it to Finn. "This is hers. It came off her wrist when I fell."

Finn inspected it for a moment and returned it to Nora. They sat in silence, Nora eyeing Finn, waiting for him to make another smartass comment. When the silence stretched on, she turned to look at him.

"Nothing? You're going to say nothing."

"I just feel kind of bad that I made that comment about her definitely being dead. I didn't know you had the hots for her."

Nora kicked him and rolled back onto her back.

"You idiot."

Finn let out a soft chuckle as he rolled back onto his back. "You know, I think we have as good of a chance of saving her as anyone else."

Nora frowned.

"Not the answer you *want*, I'm sure." Nora could tell Finn was smiling in the darkness by the slight lilt in his voice. "It's us against a dragon. We have fewer numbers than most, which is good for detection purposes. As long as the thing doesn't see us, I think there's a chance. Then there's Luna's alchemy. If we do it correctly—and that's a *big* if—it might buy us time. But the actual key is being undetected."

Nora considered his words. "Well, technically the real key will be getting to the ship before it takes off."

"Oh, that will be a damned miracle," Finn chuckled. "Go to sleep. I'm exhausted from being saved by you."

Nora looked at the stars above twinkling in the night sky until she finally drifted off to sleep.

10

Chapter Ten

Purple light filled the air, suspending Nora amongst a sea of stars. She looked around for Finn, reaching for her dagger and finding her pockets empty.

"Hello?" Nora tried to use her arms to move through the air as if she were swimming but found that she could not move. Where was she? How did she get here?

"Beneath the stars where ancients sleep..." A man's voice echoed through the surrounding air. *"...A child wakes from shadows deep..."*

"Who are you?" Her voice was distant, and she recognized the same feeling she had when she had dreamed of the woman's bright eyes two nights before.

"...in divergence comes the endless night, their choice shall bear the heavens might..." The voice trailed off into the distance.

Nora felt heat behind her and turned to see a fireball rushing at her; as it neared, it took the shape of a dragon. She screamed, raising her hands in front of her face to shield herself from the fire. The creature ran through her, the sparking fair glittering around her fingers but not burning her as it moved through and past her, bounding off through the stars and disappearing into the darkness.

Shimmering light spread around her fingertips and ran down the lengths of her arms, warmth flooding her body as it moved. It was as if she was melting away into the purple light, and her body felt light and supported in space, as if someone was cradling her. More lights shot through the sky around her and she could see hundreds of dragons tearing through the skies, a trail of flame following them as they wound through the stars. The constellation Draco was directly above her, radiating brighter than all the stars that created the celestial body. She pumped her arms and kicked her legs hard against the denseness of the space around her, slowly moving herself toward the constellation.

Again, the ebony face with gleaming blue eyes appeared in front of her, so close that all she could see were the being's eyes. She gasped, trying to pull back, but was frozen to the spot. The face shook slowly from side to side; the eyes sparkling with wild excitement.

Not yet. A woman's voice rang through her mind. *Wake up.*

She opened her mouth, but no sound came out.

Wake up! This time she heard two voices, the woman's and Finn's frantic voice calling her back to him.

Suddenly she was on her back, trees above her swaying in the breeze, and Finn's face before her, his eyes wild with fear.

"Wake up!" Finn shouted, shaking her hard.

"I'm awake!" She shouted as she blinked against the brightness of the daylight.

Finn sat back, his face pale with fear. "For fuck's sake, Nora, what the hell was that?"

Nora slowly rose to her feet, bracing herself against a nearby tree and taking slow breaths against the rising panic within her chest.

"What happened?" She murmured.

"I should be asking *you* that." Finn's voice was harsh, and when he saw Nora turn away, he took a long breath and softened his tone. "I'm sorry, you just scared me. What happened?"

Nora described the dream and previous dream she had in Sue City to Finn, sparing no details as she recounted the experience. Finn listened patiently; his face unreadable. When she was done, he slowly rose and began packing up their camp.

"You're not going to say anything?" Nora asked, frustrated by his silence.

"There's nothing to say." Finn sounded distant as if his mind was somewhere else.

"What the hell does that mean?" She grabbed his mat from him and threw it on the ground. "Look at me!"

Finn met her gaze. Nora couldn't read him, and she felt the panic rising within her again. She thought of the way Tulee had looked at her, how their eyes had said their goodbyes long before they spoke them. She searched Finn's face for some reassurance and found nothing.

"You should go—just leave. We should cut our losses here, you can go back to Luna—"

"Nora." Finn sounded exhausted.

"It's fine. I'm going to be *fine*. There's something wrong with me. I know it, I can feel it. I'll figure it out and if I make it back, you'll get your share of the reward. This is going to be dangerous. I am only putting you in more—"

"Nora!" Finn grabbed her shoulders. "I'm not leaving you, ok? Can you shut your mouth for one damned second? I just need to think. Am I allowed to *think*?"

Nora turned her face from him to hide her embarrassment. Finn's arms wrapped around her and pulled her into a tight embrace.

"I promise I'm not leaving you. People haven't held their ends of bargains with you before, you've been pushed down and left behind, but I won't do that to you. I thought you were dead, Nora. You had no pulse. I couldn't feel you anymore. I'm just a little shaken up," Finn whispered. "Something isn't right here, and I'm going to help you figure this out, ok? We're going to get this figured out."

Nora pulled away from his embrace, turning to look at him.

"Please promise me that if you want to leave, you will do it. I just want your honesty, that's all I ask."

Finn straightened and solemnly drew a cross over his heart, chuckling when Nora shoved him. They continued cleaning up their camp and consulted the map one more time before continuing towards Balcross.

They moved in silence for most of the day, Finn gazing off into the distance occasionally and then refocusing on the road before them. Nora's thoughts were racing, but she found comfort in Finn's promise to help her figure this out. She hadn't known him for long, but she believed in him. If anyone could help her figure out what was happening within her, it would be Finn.

"Have you heard of The Child of Draco?" His voice cut through the silence abruptly, and Nora jumped at the sound.

"No, why?"

"It's a legend—a prophecy of sorts. About the end of the world. It's what consumed Malachi, it's what's been haunting me. The first voice that spoke to you in your dream was reciting that prophecy. The prophecy of the Child of Draco, the end of the world as we know it."

Nora was silent, considering Finn's words before she spoke. "I don't believe in prophecies."

"Of course you don't. You're too *edgy*." Finn teased.

"Oh, shut it." Nora rolled her eyes and continued following him down the road. "Could it be the dragon?"

Finn stared at her, his eyes searching hers. "Nora—"

"No."

"Be realistic—"

"Absolutely not." Nora continued walking. "I'm done talking about prophecies."

"The serapin, the nymph. These creatures awakening, it's all part of it. And these dreams, Nora—"

"Could it be the dragon?" Her voice was pleading, as if she was begging for the answer to be yes. She felt panic rising in her chest and tried to steady her mind. So much had happened in such a short time, her body felt it might collapse under the weight of it all.

Finn watched her, concern written across his face, and nodded slowly. "Maybe."

"Yeah, maybe it's the dragon. We haven't seen dragons in years, and Draco is a dragon, so it makes sense that his child would be one. It makes sense." She pressed her hands against her eyes, wiping tears from her face and blinking hard against the well of emotion within her.

"It could be." Finn's voice was low, and he wrapped his arms around Nora, pulling her face against him and holding her tightly until the rush of emotion passed.

His hands ran through her hair, his breath steady and the strength of his body holding firm against the weakness of her own.

This is what it feels like to be held by a father.

Tears escaped her eyes as the thought passed through her mind, and she pulled back, wiping the last of her tears and smiling at Finn.

"Sorry for that–I'm fine."

"You are." Finn agreed.

"It's probably the dragon."

"Probably."

"And we're going to go get Briella and we'll deal with the fucking child of Draco when we get there."

Finn nodded in agreement.

"Ok, let's keep going."

They didn't speak for most of the day, moving through the mountainside as the weight of unspoken words weighed heavily upon them. The forest was older in this part of the mountain, untouched and so thick it was difficult to move through, but they continued on hoping to reach the city of Balcross before nightfall.

"What if Balcross was attacked by the dragon as well?" Nora asked as they climbed a steep hill.

"It's unlikely. They are built into the cliffs and heavily fortified; it would take more than one dragon to take down that town."

As they reached the top of the hill, they found the remains of a stone temple before them, worn by hundreds of years of neglect it was hauntingly beautiful and hummed with purpose. Nature had grown over most of it, but Nora could see the carvings that showed the temple was once a devotional to the great creators of the world.

"I've heard of these temples," Nora whispered, frozen in her tracks.

Finn moved closer to the walls, running a hand over the stone pillars that were partially concealed in the trunks of the massive trees. It was terrifying, the way nature would take everything back eventually. Nora felt a shiver run up her spine as they moved further in, and Finn surveyed the ruins, muttering to himself as he read.

Vines with large purple morning glories covered the walls, giving way to ferns spilling from where windows used to be. The remnants of stained-glass windows filtered some of the light and cast a dancing pattern of light across the stone flooring. A small stream cut through the temple and Nora wondered if the building had been built around it or if the stream had eroded its way through the stone. She noticed the pebbles at the bottom of the stream let off a soft glow and dipped her fingers in the water, closing her eyes and murmuring a silent prayer of thanks to the spirits that caused the stones to glow. They had been vital in her escape from Gilade, and the image of the beast as it bore down upon them flashed through her mind. She quickly withdrew her hand and looked up when she heard Finn's foot footsteps suddenly stop.

He was frozen in place, his back straight and eyes wide with something between awe and terror. Nora followed his gaze and felt the hairs on her neck stand as her eyes fell upon the creature before her. It had broad shoulders and a handsome face. Its eyes were the same shade of green as the surrounding ferns. Its chest was covered in thick, black tattoos that swirled around his body, stopping at the lower half which was like the stallions Nora saw at home, heavily muscled and with hair that was the same brown shade as his long curling hair. He had an arrow notched in his bow but kept it pointed to the ground. His eyes seemed to pierce through them and after a long silence, he slid the arrow back into the quiver.

"You are far from the mountain trails, travelers." The centaur's voice was deep and echoed through the temple ruins around them.

"We fell into some unexpected trouble, a den with a serapin. We're trying to make our way to Balcross." Finn said, raising his hands to indicate they meant no harm.

"A serapin you say. And you lived to tell of it? Impressive." He moved closer and extended his hand towards Finn. "I am Leir."

"Leir? How is that possible–" Finn's voice trailed off as he gaped at Leir.

"We have slept for a long time, but we are awake again." Leir smiled at Finn's confusion. "The celestials are stirring, and we are at the edge of the divergence."

"Divergence?" Leir turned his attention to Nora as she spoke and she felt her heart quicken as his brows furrowed with confusion.

"Yes, it's what we call the last great battle for this earth. The divergence from one way of existence to another. The extinction of worlds as we know them as they emerge into something new." He moved closer to Nora. "Creatures and powers ushered in by the Child of Draco."

"The Child of Draco." Nora straightened, resisting the urge to look at Finn. She never heard of this prophecy until her dream, and now there was a creature standing before her speaking of it. It seemed an unlikely coincidence.

"The child of prophecy. Half-celestial and half-human, straddling two worlds and the undoing of them both; the beginning and end of the world." He looked at the surrounding ruins, sadness on his face. "This place was once my home. Our people studied here alongside humans and elves. Now it has been forgotten, and new temples will be erected and forgotten until the end of time."

Leir looked up at the canopy above them, his mind traveling back to a distant time. Finn looked at Nora and raised his eyebrows, shrugging awkwardly at the intimacy of the moment with this stranger. Nora gritted her teeth and returned his awkward gaze, her eyes darting back to Leir as he returned his attention to the two of them.

"We should probably keep going then." Finn shuffled his feet awkwardly, not sure how to end the moment that seemed to linger for an eternity.

"Eager dragon slayers, aren't you?" Leir's eyes twinkled, unaware of how uncomfortable they were. "I have heard much of this beast terrorizing the land."

"Could it be the Child of Draco? Dragons were believed to be wiped out long ago. Perhaps slaying it will be the end of the divergence?" Nora asked as she moved beside Finn.

Leir looked at her for a long while, his face full of confusion and then relaxing back to his original serene countenance.

"I suppose that's a possibility. Hopefully, I will see you again; I'm interested to hear how your interaction with the creature goes." He stepped closer to Nora, lowering his face until he was a few inches from her own. "I think we'll both have some surprising information for each other."

Nora furrowed her brow, stepping back and turning to Finn. "If you're ready?" She asked nervously.

"Well, I would hate to interrupt—"

Nora shot Finn a dark look, and he stopped mid-sentence, smiling sheepishly.

"I will see you to the mountain path. It is not far from here. There have been others who have woken from their slumber, ones that you would not want to meet on the road." Leir turned and made his way through the temple. Nora marveled at how familiar he was with this place after all these years.

"He's totally into you," Finn whispered. "I thought he was going to shove his tongue straight down–"

"My god you never shut up," Nora hissed, jabbing him with her elbow. "What if he hears you?!"

"I hear you," Leir said casually, flicking his tail as he continued through the ruins.

Finn's face screwed up to stop his laughter, and Nora's face went a deep shade of red as she willed herself to disappear into the stone flooring forever. They continued in silence, Finn snorting occasionally whenever he made eye contact with Nora and Nora silently willing him to burst into flames.

As they were leaving the temple, Nora stopped before a marble carving of a woman with her face concealed by a veil.

"Who is she?" Nora's voice echoed around them.

"The Mother." Leir was quiet, and he smiled warmly at the statue. "In the old days, she was the deity over all living things. She did not take part in the Great War; she believed in letting things be whatever they were, good or bad. It is the very essence of nature. I do not feel her anymore, but in her likeness, I find glimpses of her divinity."

"She's beautiful," Nora whispered. "I have never heard of her before."

"I have read a little about her. She was benevolent and kind, and left this world when the celestials ascended." Finn moved closer to the statue and inspected the detail the carver had used. "Whoever did this was very talented."

"Yes, he was." Leir's eyes watered a little and he smiled. "His name was Hanz, and there was no one in the world quite like him."

The privacy of this moment, unlike before, felt shared and comfortable. Nora carefully placed a hand on Leir's shoulder and he softened at her touch. Finn reached out towards the statue, stopping short of touching it and stepping back. They admired it for a moment longer before Leir led them through the last section of the ruined temple. As they moved, Nora realized it was less of a forgotten ruin and more of a garden, with a statue at its center that was a tribute to two people Leir loved deeply.

Their journey to the main road was uneventful, something Nora and Finn welcomed. The silence was companionable and Leir seemed to appreciate it as much as they did. Nora wondered how long he had been awake, and what it was like to wake up lifetimes later in a world you barely recognized. She imagined it would be a unique torment, and hoped desperately that he was not alone.

"Here we are. Continue south and you'll reach Balcross before the day's end." Leir bowed deeply.

"Thank you for your help." Nora smiled.

"I am sure we will meet again, I look forward to it!" Leir turned and disappeared into the forest, the sound of his hooves trailing off into the distance.

"Don't you think that was so weird that we were talking about the prophecy and then some random horseman brought it up right after?" Finn asked.

"I was thinking the same thing!"

"Yeah, there's no way that was a coincidence. He was probably following us for a while; he seemed to know more than he let on."

"Magic wielders tend to do that." Nora teased, nudging Finn. "I have a feeling there was more to taking the princess than just pissing off a spoiled prince."

"You needed a centaur to tell you that? Why do you think he abducted the princess instead of just eating her? There's got to be an angle."

Nora was ashamed to admit she hadn't thought the dragon capable of planning or having an agenda. She thought of him as simple as the wild creatures she had known her entire life. Smart and calculated in ways that ensured their survival, but not in the premeditated ways that made humanity wretched.

I suppose evil has no limits, she thought as she followed Finn down the path toward Balcross, the smell of salty ocean water dancing through the air.

11

Chapter Eleven

Nora followed closely behind Finn until they emerged into the sweeping valley, the towering walls that surrounded Balcross standing as a monolith a few miles away. Being one of the largest ports outside of Theren itself, it was constantly under attack. From land or sea, the people of Theren were ensured the protection of the king; Balcross, however, without a fleet of royal mages to protect them, leaned heavily into machinery and science. Glistening metal from what looked to be large mounted bows sat upon the wall-walk, and Nora could make out catapults posted around the castle walls. A tower rose above the castle from its center as a lookout post; the flag of Balcross waved high above the tower.

Balcross was part of the kingdom of Troque, but it was well known they operated on their own with no care for what the king's laws may be. Nora knew they used alchemy freely and encouraged their people to do so. To what extent alchemy was used was the ever-changing rumor whispered through every festival that Balcross merchants would make their appearances; the only time people from the rest of Troque got a peek into the world within the stone walls. Occasionally tradespeople would get visas to come and go freely from the city, but they kept their dealings tight-lipped and vague, eager to continue to do business with the ever-growing city.

Now, as they approached, Nora could see that the bulk of the city sat within a cove at the base of the hill, the walls of the city spilling over the side of the mountain to encase the city below. As they approached, Nora saw tents surrounding the city walls, which revealed itself to be a crude refugee camp. Women of The Faith walked around in their shrouds tending to wounds and burns, children giggled and screamed as they weaved through the tents; babies cried in the distance. Everywhere was the stench of too many people living in too poor conditions and Nora felt herself tense as they approached. So many of these people had been abandoned by their king, left in these tents while the king threw his balls and hoarded his mages for himself.

"How could he let people live like this?" Nora's voice dripped with rage.

"This is likely one of the better ones, my dear." Finn's voice was controlled, but Nora could feel his own anger boiling under the surface. "There's a church of The Faith here in Balcross. They have more resources to help refugees here than anywhere else short of Theren itself."

"One of the *better* ones?" Nora shook her head. "It's inexcusable."

They stopped when the gates opened and watched as cart after cart unloaded supplies to the refugees of Balcross. Nora watched guards push back desperate men and women who reached out to grab their share of food first. The Sisters of The Faith urged them to wait, promising that all would be fed today and that they had plenty for everyone. Nora wondered how long it had been since some of them had eaten.

A guard approached Finn and Nora, breaking away from the crowd as the carts pushed through and the gates shut behind him.

"What business do you have at Balcross?" The guard's voice was kind and patient, but the man had clearly gone without enough sleep for several days.

"We are part of the king's quest. We wish to secure passage on one of the king's chartered ships." Finn brandished his medallion.

"Do you have tickets?" The guard asked, twisting his face in anticipation of their answer.

"Tickets?" Nora blurted out. "We have our medallions."

The guard shook his head and let out a long sigh. "This is the third time I've had to turn someone away today. I'm sorry, truly I am. High Mage Brutus has been here for the last month and changed the policy for admittance to the ships. No ticket, no admittance. We are way over capacity, so we can't have you within the gates unless you have a ticket to leave."

Nora looked from the guard to Finn, who seemed paralyzed with shock.

"Finn?"

"Surely—"

"Sir, I understand you've come a long way. Many others have too. Unless you can find yourself a ticket before this ship leaves at dawn tomorrow, you are shit out of luck." With that, the guard turned and made his way back to the front gate.

"What the hell!" Nora shouted, kicking the ground. "What are we supposed to do now?"

Finn stared at the ground, unsure of what to say.

"So that's it? After everything? There must be another way. We could charter our own boat—"

"No one is crazy enough to sail towards an island with a fucking dragon, Nora. These are the only ships." Finn's voice was low and exhausted.

"We can't give up Finn."

Finn shook his head and leaned against the wall, massaging his temples in frustration.

"Look at that! *Friends.*" Nora recognized the voice and turned to see a woman with a familiar necklace sparkling around her neck. She was flanked by three men who Nora had last seen paralyzed and being dragged into the tree line.

"Hanna?" Nora's jaw dropped at the sight of her.

Finn cleared his throat, putting on his most sincere face. "What a pleasure to see you criminals again."

Hanna glared at him before returning her attention to Nora. "I heard you talking to that guard. We can get you on that ship, but there will be a price to pay, of course." She tugged at the necklace loosely, her eyes menacing.

"How do we know we can trust you?" Nora asked suspiciously. "The last time we did ended up being a rather big mistake for both of us."

Hanna rolled her eyes. "Well, I believe you have the upper hand, as I am near useless with this necklace shackled to my throat. I don't know how people can live without magic."

"How are you planning on getting us on the ship?" Finn eyed the men beside her, who kept their eyes fixed on him.

"We have tickets. We scored them off of some suckers in Sue City." Hanna pulled them out and waved them in front of Finn. "If you take this necklace off me, I'll give them to you."

Finn stared at her for a long moment and then snatched the tickets from her hand so fast even Nora was left with her mouth open in shock.

"Hey!"

Finn pushed her away and laughed. "I can't believe that worked!"

Nora frowned and followed Finn as he made his way towards the gate. "You need to release her."

Finn rolled his eyes. "I will, but not until we are inside the city walls. I'm not so naive as to take you at your word; however *honorable* it may be." He bowed deeply in Hanna's direction before turning back towards the main gate.

Hanna looked back at the men behind her, who shook their heads in disbelief. She turned back at Finn; her face was red with embarrassment and rage.

Nora and Finn returned to the guard, who inspected their tickets closely to ensure they were legitimate. He frowned at the pair, who grinned back up at him, and let them into the city. Right before the large wooden doors shut, Finn turned back to look at Hanna, snapping his fingers and causing the necklace to burst into flames. Hanna screamed and ripped it off, standing over it in disbelief as it smoldered on the ground.

She looked back up at him and her voice rang out, "You son of a—"

The large city doors shut and cut her off, and Finn grinned at Nora.

The city was domineering and almost like a prison of sorts from the outside, but within its walls were life and community. Fountains with fresh drinking water were mounted on walls throughout the city, alchemic symbols for purification emblazoned above each fountain, and they watched as people of all social classes gathered in shared common areas, the poorest of them, although dressed simply, still well-fed and healthy.

The fleet of ships commanded by Balcross was something to behold, and it was clear to Nora that they were ready for any potential attack. Their weapons fixed on the sky signaled to all exactly what they were defending the city from. Nora wondered how many times the dragon had come through here if it had dared to come at all.

At the center of the docks, one ship stood out amongst the rest, a beacon of adventure beckoning to all who looked upon it. The seal on the side of the ship matched their medallions, and Nora followed Finn, marveling at the size of the ship as they approached. They handed their tickets to a guard who stamped them and bowed deeply.

"Good luck," the guard said, winking at Nora as she disappeared inside.

The prince spared no expense with the ships bringing his challengers to the Adoya Isles. The massive ship was even more massive inside, likely through various enchantments Nora had never seen before. Richly decorated with deep mahogany wood carved with intricate designs and mosaic art, the ship was more regal than even the palace itself. Heaps of food were made available for the taking, and there were armories, bars, and any other accommodation one might need at their disposal.

Nora led the way down crowded halls towards the sleeping quarters, inspecting her ticket and murmuring as she moved through the ship, with Finn close behind. A golden number six signaled they had reached their room, and when she opened the door, Nora found a quaint but richly decorated room with three bunks and a private bathroom. The walls were decorated with the same intricate mahogany as the rest of the ship and freshly pressed linens sat folded on their beds.

"I can't believe all of this is free," Nora whispered.

"Prince Adrian wants to make sure we're all comfortable before we go off to our deaths." The voice was familiar and sent a chill down Nora's spine. She turned to see Talon standing behind her.

"What are you doing here?" Nora put her hand on one of her daggers, looking back at Finn and then returning her attention to Talon. Finn seemed disinterested in the man, quickly moving towards the bunks and setting his bag down.

"The same thing you're doing here, *my lady*," Talon emphasized the last words, his voice dripping with sarcasm. "I believe we got off on the wrong foot before; I have no interest in quarrels with you."

"Do we have to share a room—" Nora stopped as Finn shot her a warning look.

"There is little choice in the matter, and these are our tickets." Finn's voice was kind but firm.

Talon stood awkwardly at the center of the room before knocking at the door, which jerked them from their thoughts. "That must be food," he murmured as he let in the valet, who brought a cart brimming with food and a large, sloshing pitcher of ale. "Help yourselves."

Finn stood quickly, pouring a mug of ale and throwing his head back as he downed the liquid. The woman who brought in the cart looked around nervously and Talon tossed her a coin and gave her a nod of dismissal before shutting the door behind her.

Finn slammed his mug on the table and gave Talon a wide grin. "Mind topping me off?"

Talon obliged, eyeing Nora. "You don't drink?"

"No, I believe he does enough drinking for the both of us."

Talon smiled and the pupils of his eyes seemed to dilate and contract into a thin line, as if the blackness was pulsating in his eye, before quickly returning to their normal size. Nora's face displayed her confusion and Talon seemed confused, giving her an uncomfortable look before turning away and busying himself with his bed.

"If you want to see some spectacular magic, the royal mage Brutus is on board and will probably do some ridiculous display to signal to the entire world that he's here." Talon yawned, laying on his bed.

Nora stared at him for a moment longer, still trying to figure out what she saw, and returned her attention to Finn, who seemed to understand that she needed to step out of the room.

"Let's go have a look. We might as well get acquainted with our competition." Finn stood and made his way to the door.

Nora set her bag under her bed and looked over at Talon, who was laying with his eyes closed in his bed. She wasn't sure what she saw, but she didn't like the way it felt. She looked at him for a moment longer before following Finn out the door and through the maze of passages to the upper deck.

After some navigating and stopping a few times for directions, they emerged onto the deck and pushed through crowds of people to climb up onto one lifeboat for a better view. The royal mage stood at the center of the crowd and motioned for people to back up to give him some space.

Brutus was less impressive up close than Nora remembered and he looked entirely different without the glamor of the palace surrounding him. He was overweight and balding and what long hair he still had was smoothed back away from his face. He looked soft from years spent advising the king and accompanying him as an addition to the king's guard; the royal mage did very little once the dragons had been taken care of. Most of the smaller tasks were given to mages in training, so he rarely even needed to be away from the palace.

"Hello brave warriors of Troque, your prince thanks you for your bravery. Please, feast to your heart's content, and take advantage of all the services available to you. We will be in Adoya in two days' time, and when we dock, you will all set forth on the greatest adventure of your lives." Brutus smiled, casting his eyes over the spectators. He raised his hand into the air and set off a flume of fireworks that burst high above in a shower of glittering golds and reds.

The people on the deck cheered, and Finn raised his mug in approval.

"Don't you think it's kind of silly?" Nora frowned at the mage, who continued to put off different colored flares into the sky. "I mean, if we are nearing the dragon, these fireworks will definitely show him exactly where to find us."

Finn thought for a moment and shrugged. "Do you want to ask him to stop?"

Nora rolled her eyes and slid off their perch on the lifeboat, looking back at Finn. "I'm going to head back down; I'm beat. I'll see you in a bit."

Finn raised his mug. "I won't be too long after ya."

Nora pushed her way through the people, taking one last look at the mage behind her before moving below deck. She made her way through the twisting halls slowly, not eager to be alone in the room with Talon and relishing in the emptiness of the ship's hull.

A familiar voice stopped Nora in her tracks.

"We should be there tomorrow, Your Highness." The voice of her sister, Larissa, was muffled through the walls but it was definitely her.

Nora moved towards her sister's voice, tucking herself into a shadowed corner to listen in.

"Something's not right with him. You have proven yourself loyal, Larissa. Keep an eye on him, and you will be rewarded greatly."

Larissa giggled in the sickening way she would when she was pretending to be flattered by someone. Nora always hated the way Larissa could play her role perfectly.

"It is an honor to serve you, Your Highness."

Magic pulsed in the room and Larissa let out a long sigh.

"Ma'am, your dinner—"

"What did I say about interrupting?!" Adelle's voice shrieked.

The sound of metal hitting the ground and the servant's quiet yelp made the hairs rise on Nora's neck, and she peeked into the room slowly. A chill ran up her spine as she realized it wasn't Adelle's voice she had heard; that was the voice of her own sister who now loomed over the servant very much the picture of her mother.

Larissa. What are you doing?

Nora moved away from the room quietly, holding her breath as a floorboard creaked loudly beneath her feet. The space became eerily quiet and Nora felt the familiar force of magic spilling from the room. She sprinted down the hall and turned the corner just as the door was thrown up and footsteps followed quickly behind her. The hall opened up to a sweeping staircase that led down to a large eating area and Nora jumped over the side of the banister, rolling to the ground as her legs buckled beneath her, and ran into the kitchens full of bustling staff. She could feel the magic still tugging at her, the distance making it weaker but Larissa was still on her trail.

Nora hurried through the kitchen until she found a servant's corridor that led deeper into the ship. She navigated the servant's corridors quickly until she found an exit that led to her own floor, hurrying out and sprinting through the hall until she reached her room. She slammed the door shut, locking it behind her and panting loudly against the wall. She listened for any sounds of approaching footsteps and waited for the feeling of Larissa's magic searching for her, but it never came.

Thank the gods.

"Sick of the celebrations?"

Talon's voice cut through the silence and Nora jumped at the realization he was in the room. She took a calming breath and made her way towards her bed.

"It seems like a waste. And calling attention to this ship like that...I'm surprised to see a royal mage with so little sense about him."

"There's not a lot of sense left in the royal palace." Talon stretched on his bed, releasing a deep sigh as he relaxed. "You were in quite a hurry. What spooked you?"

"Nothing that concerns you."

Talon smiled. "That doesn't answer my question."

Nora raised an eyebrow. "Strange. I would think that not wanting to share is enough of an answer."

Talon grinned and raised his hands defensively. "I'm curious about the people staying in my room. Normal people call this *conversation*."

"You know what they say about curiosity." She kicked off her boots and grabbed her sleeping clothes, retreating to the bathroom to change.

When she emerged, Talon appeared to have drifted off to sleep. Nora walked to her bed and opened the curtain that covered a small window. Larissa was on the ship, and something was up with her. Nora had resented her sister's passive nature but she had never been cruel, especially not to staff. The way she had stood over the whimpering girl in her room was something Larissa had seen done to Nora hundreds of times; Nora would never have thought she was capable of that same cruelty. She felt the urge to go to Larissa, she must be in some kind of trouble to be acting with such ferocity. Perhaps she needed someone to help her. But the longer Nora looked out the window the more she realized she didn't know Larissa, not really. She had never seen her be cruel, but she did not know she was incapable of cruelty. Something within her told her that Larissa was a danger to Nora, and the realization brought tears to her eyes. She felt her heart ache with longing for the family she never had, and Nora found herself stunned by how the finality of this realization hurt so deeply.

The stars shone brightly over the water and the moon was full in the sky. Nora had never been on a boat and until they came down from the mountain pass towards Balcross, she had never seen the sea.

Flares of color exploded above, casting light over the sea, and she returned to her bed falling asleep to the sound of the popping of fireworks.

The next morning Finn woke her early and she was surprised to see Talon already gone. They made their way down to a training room in one of the lower sections of the ship, stopping only for a light breakfast before spending the day training. Nora explained her close encounter with Larissa, carefully keeping an eye out for eavesdroppers.

"I can't believe Larissa is here."

"It's strange. To send one royal mage was odd enough, but to send two seems risky."

"And Talon. He gives me a weird feeling," Nora murmured, "Like he's hiding something."

"Nora, you'll learn one day that everyone is hiding something. Well, everyone except you." Finn nudged her teasingly and led her into the training room. "I don't know why your sister is here, but we shouldn't have a hard time avoiding her. She won't be galivanting the ship with the roughians, she's here for the show. We *do* need to keep practicing if we're going to be worth our salt against that dragon."

After practicing on the road any chance she got, Nora had improved significantly in wielding the weapons she carried with her. Her aim with her bow was more accurate, not anywhere near Finn's accuracy, but she could hit her target most of the time and her swordsmanship had improved. When they finally entered the training room, Nora marveled at the amount of equipment at their disposal. Training dummies lined the room in individual stalls for people to practice on. There was a large fighting ring for practicing hand-to-hand combat at the center and targets posted in various locations for archery and dagger throwing. They worked with the materials provided in the training room, a few people coming in and out, but few taking advantage of the highly stocked room.

"Many of them know this will be their last voyage. I think they are less concerned with being the best or strongest and mostly just trying to find some comfort in their fears. If you'd stayed up a little longer last night, you'd know that!" Finn slammed a blow down on her with his sword and Nora barely deflected it, shoving him back and coming in with her own blow.

"And watch as that idiot summons the dragon straight to us like we are asking for death?" They continued to spar until sweat poured off each of them and they sat down, Nora pouring water over her face and letting it run down over her.

"That was entertaining." A voice said from behind them. They turned to see the royal mage Brutus, sitting in a dark corner.

The pair stood quickly and bowed.

"Oh, rise. There is no need for pleasantries," He droned, clearly happy with the attention he was receiving. "I've been looking over the people on board and there are a handful of you I suspect won't die immediately. Some of you might even leave mostly intact."

Finn laughed at that, nudging Nora with his elbow. "You hear that! He thinks we might leave with most of our limbs!"

Nora kept her eyes fixed on the mage. The air prickled with magic and she felt him searching her, as if the magic were tentacles, reaching out and wrapping around her.

"Where is it you come from?" Brutus frowned as he stared at her.

"Sorudi."

"I hear the city is mostly gone." He stepped closer to her. "You look so familiar. Have we met?"

"It's unlikely, good sir, as I was just a worker in my mistress's house."

Brutus smirked and then his expression melted away into one of bewilderment; heat rose to Nora's cheeks and Finn stepped between them.

"We had better get going." Finn stared into the mage's eyes and beckoned for Nora to follow him.

"Good luck," the mage called after them.

They made their way up the stairs and into their room before Finn finally looked at her, his face pale.

"What do you think that was about?" he asked.

"I don't know." She murmured. Her head was aching from the intense magic that had been on her. "My head hurts so bad."

"Did he do something to you?"

Talon rushed towards them and grabbed Nora's shoulders, turning her towards him. His pupils were pulsating again, and she felt her body become completely paralyzed. He placed his hand on her head and began murmuring in a language she didn't understand until suddenly, the pressure in her head eased.

"Who did this?" Talon asked quickly.

"We were just with the royal mage." Finn stood in shock, watching Nora carefully.

Talon stood and helped Nora to her feet, leading her to a chair to sit. "He marked her. It was a complex spell; not something someone puts the effort into unless it is very important."

"He marked me?"

Talon nodded. "If you're marked by a mage, they can track you anywhere. I don't know what you did, but he wanted to make sure he could find you again."

Finn ran his hand through his hair in bewilderment. "We were practicing downstairs. We didn't do anything."

"He said he recognized me," Nora murmured.

Talon shrugged, walking towards the door. "I just don't want a mage snooping into my room. I would suggest you stay here so it doesn't happen again."

Talon left the room and Nora, suddenly overcome by exhaustion, allowed herself to fall into the thick down of her bed.

"That language Talon spoke—I've never heard it before." Finn stared at the door for a long moment before returning his attention to Nora. "You sleep." He whispered. "I'll be right here."

12

Chapter Twelve

Nora woke to the pitch black of the room with a start. She calmed herself and listened to the sounds of Finn sleeping. Carefully, she eased herself upright and noticed a soft green glow coming from Talon's bed.

"You must be thirsty." Talon's voice seemed to vibrate through her bones. Talon stood, the green light following him, and poured a glass of water for her. "What is your name?"

"Nora." The words felt forced as if her body was fighting some invisible force to push them out. She felt her throat close and her heart pounded wildly in her chest.

"Your *full* name," Talon demanded. He came closer to her, the now blinding green light causing her to look away, and grabbed her hand to place the cup of water in it.

"Nora—DuPont," she gasped as her throat seemed to open back up when the words came out.

"DuPont? As in Adelle DuPont?" His voice was icy, and his eyes were flashing with green light except for two black slits.

Nora wanted to scream. She wanted to deny her link to Adelle, but her body seemed to revolt against her and she only mustered a quiet "Yes."

He lowered his face to her until their noses were inches apart. "What fun." The smile that spread across his face was unnaturally wide, and Nora watched in horror as his pointed teeth loomed inches from her face. "I love a challenge."

She screamed and was thrust back into the dimly lit room. Talon was gone and Finn was rushing through the room shoving his things into his bag.

"Are you ok?"

Nora panted, looking around her. "It must have been a dream."

Finn glared at her. "I don't know what that mage did, but I'm not sure Talon took care of all of it."

"No, I'm fine, really. I just had a nightmare." She laid back in her bed and closed her eyes until she felt her breath steady. "Did Talon ever come back?"

"Ya, to collect his stuff. Said something about not wanting to be sharing a room with people out of the mage's favor." Finn grabbed Nora's bag and tossed it to her. "Since you're up start packing your stuff. I went to get some food and saw your sister with a group of guards turning rooms inside out looking for someone. We need to get off this damned boat."

"Shit." Nora stood up quickly and began shoving her belongings into her bag, tugging on her coat and shoving a piece of bread into her mouth. She turned towards the end table beside her bed and froze. Sitting before her was a glass of water, the same glass Talon handed her in her dream. "Finn, did you bring me some water?"

"Are you asking me to go get you some?" Finn's tone was hushed and frustrated as he slid his bag on his back and shoved some food in his pockets.

"No—"

"Because if you're thirsty, you can go get some yourself."

"I'm not asking you to get me some fucking water!" She shouted, grabbing the glass and pouring it out in a small basin beside her bed.

"In my dream, Talon gave this to me. He wanted to know my name; he seemed to already *know* my name."

"Well, Nora, that's not really so crazy. I mean, he knows both of our names." Finn walked over to her.

"No Finn. My full name. He knows who my mother is."

Finn was silent for a moment before responding. "And who would that be?"

Nora looked at him, frustrated that she had no good answer. "I didn't think it mattered—"

"Who is your mother, Nora?" He placed his hands on her shoulders. "You can tell me. You can *trust* me."

"Adelle DuPont."

"The *dragon slayer*?" Finn cleared his throat, trying to remain composed. "That's...your mom. The dragon slayer."

Nora was silent for a long moment before speaking. "I know little about her, Finn. She's famous. I know she killed the last dragon alongside King Alexander. When I was born, she found out I had no magic. She hated me. I can't even call her my mother."

Finn sighed, bringing Nora in for a tight embrace. "Unfortunately, we don't get to pick our family, Nora. We can choose to carry them with us or leave them behind, but we can't erase them from the picture. Not completely."

"I don't know why it matters if I'm related to her. And why would Talon—"

"I don't think it was Talon." Finn interrupted. "I think that Mage did more than we know. He's prying for information. Brutus became the king's mage after Adelle left the castle. The rumor was that she lost her magic, and the king cast her out. Brutus was her replacement, and now her daughter—"

"Larissa is going to replace him," Nora whispered.

Finn nodded. "I don't know where you fit into this equation, but I had never heard of Adelle DuPont mothering two children. Maybe there's a reason you were a secret, maybe not. Maybe your existence is useful to Brutus somehow. There's something about you he can see."

"But what?" Nora had been nothing special, and if she had, her mother would have done whatever it took to cultivate that power. Why could she never summon magic? Why hadn't she been born with the classic symbols of magic?

"Let's just get off this damn boat."

They finished packing their belongings silently and moved through the ship, weaving through the passages and up the stairs towards the upper deck. They stopped when they heard footsteps and shouting, tucking back into a shadowed alcove.

"You can't just throw our shit out here!" One man roared. "I don't know who you think you are—"

"I *think* I am one of the King's Royal Mages, and I will do whatever the hell I please," Larissa's voice was cruel. "If you aren't hiding anyone you have nothing to fear."

Finn moved down the hall and peeked out around the corner, motioning for Nora to follow. A group of men led by the one who was still grumbling about Larissa going through his room made their way towards them. Finn placed an arm around Nora's shoulder and joined the group, grumbling in agreeance with the men as they moved and sheltering Nora beneath his arm.

When they approached the upper deck Nora and Finn split off from the group and stepped out into the frigid night air. Finn hurried towards on of the lifeboats that hung off the side of the shit and threw his bag in, looking around for any sign of someone coming. Nora eased herself into the lifeboat silently and helped Finn in behind her. She stowed their bags into a small trapdoor beneath the floorboards and then helped Finn work on the ropes suspending the lifeboat over the side of the ship.

"We're going to lower ourselves down. If you let go while we're too high, the boat will collapse. We have to get ourselves as close to the water as possible. Once we're in the water, I'll take it from there," Finn instructed her as he gripped the ropes in his hands.

Nora nodded silently.

"Ready?" He flashed her a reassuring smile.

"Ready."

They worked slowly, ignoring the burning from the ropes on their skin. The work was arduous and painful. The sea below them thrashed at the ship as if daring them to make a wrong move. Suddenly, the boat lurched to a stop, and Finn yanked the rope, his face going white when he looked up towards the ship's deck.

"Are we stuck?" Nora whispered frantically.

She looked up and saw a glowing light above them. Peering down at them with several guards at their sides were Brutus and Larissa. Larissa's hair blew wild around her, and her eyes were wide with fear.

"Where do you two think you're going?" Brutus jeered. "Guards, raise them up." The ropes jerked out of their hands as they moved upward slowly.

"Damn it!" Finn cursed, grabbing his sword. "Now!" He bellowed.

Larissa murmured enchantments, her eyes frantic and fixed on Nora. She shook her head slowly in a silent warning for Nora to stop what she was doing. Her eyes pleaded with her sister, and Nora felt her stomach lurch. Nora furrowed her brow and jumped to the rope, bringing out her dagger and sawing through the thick braided cords.

"Faster!" Larissa shrieked at the guards, her gaze fixed on Nora.

Nora looked up at her sister one last time before their daggers cut through the rope sending them rushing downwards. They were still higher than they wanted to be and the boat flipped over, spilling them into the frigid black sea.

Nora could hear her sister's scream and Brutus's roaring voice just before the waves pulled her below the surface. The ice-cold water seized up her muscles and the pain was unlike anything she had ever felt before. In shock, she floated for a moment, unmoving and staring down into the black depths below. A green flash of magic lit the surrounding space, snapping her out of her shock and she began kicking towards the surface until she felt Finn's large hands wrap around her arm and pull her up. When she broke the surface, she gasped for air, her lungs burning as they expelled the salty water. The boat was still flipped over, and they were under it. Finn held onto the seat to keep them connected with the boat with one hand and held Nora with the other.

"Can you grab the other seat?" His voice shuddered from the cold and his lips were already turning purple.

Nora reached up and grabbed the seat, pulling herself up enough that her waist was out of the water. The water lit again with green light, and Nora closed her eyes as the impact of a surge of magic hit the water beside the boat. They stayed there, bobbing beneath the shelter of the lifeboat and holding onto the bench seats as tightly as possible. After a long period with no flashing green light, Finn let out a loud shudder and handed Nora the rope.

"If we don't get this boat flipped over soon, we're going to freeze to death."

Finn ducked his head out from under the boat and Nora tied a rope to a metal loop on the edge of the boat. She ducked under to join Finn and threw the other end of the rope over the side for him to catch. Nora then moved around the boat to join him on his side. She looked behind and saw faint lights from the ship as they drifted farther away. Finn helped Nora put her feet against the side of the boat and they both pulled back with all of their weight until it turned.

Once the boat was upright, Finn threw Nora in and pulled himself up. He immediately busied himself with getting the water out of the boat as Nora looked for any of their provisions that might have made it. The oars were fastened to the boat and their bags were still in the compartment, although it was full of water. She handed Finn an oar, and she worked to bail out the water as quickly as possible.

They took turns paddling and bailing out water in silence, only stopping when their arms burned so badly that they could barely move. Finn could not perform any healing in his weakened state, and the blood from their minor cuts and scrapes smeared across their skin and they winced as the saltwater hit their exposed wounds. They paddled for another full day and night before they finally saw land. Nora squinted at the silhouette of several small islands and smiled, shaking her head in disbelief.

"The Adoya Isles." She whispered.

As they neared the shore, they saw the sails of several massive ships docked at the edge of the largest island. They paddled away from the docks, choosing instead to seek another sandy bank that they could safely navigate to without detection. Nora felt her heart pounding in her chest. In the day's light, they felt like sitting ducks waiting to be spotted. The island rose before them, covered in a thick mist. Giant redwood trees similar to those outside of Balcross stood like an army protecting the secrets of the forest within from prying eyes. From what Nora could make out through the mist, the forest seemed to take up most of the island, rolling up towards a rocky mountainside and thinning out as the mountain rose higher in elevation.

They dragged the boat ashore, hauling it as far inland as they could and disguising it with driftwood and seaweed. Nora and Finn grabbed their bags before moving to make their way into the forest before them. They moved through the thick vegetation wordlessly and listened for any sounds of other people in the forest. They continued for what seemed like hours until she felt she might collapse onto the fern-covered forest floor. Finn stopped and used his magic to expel the water from their clothes and hair, smiling as warmth flooded their bodies.

"I can't be wet for a second longer." He shrugged, removing his canteen and filling it in a small stream that wound through the trees.

"How old do you think these trees are?" Nora asked, her neck craned back to see the canopy.

"At least a thousand years old, likely older," Finn said as he put his canteen away. "I was raised in a redwood grove; they're remarkable trees."

Nora followed Finn as they continued to make their way inland.

13

Chapter Thirteen

They walked for miles through the dense ferns and towering redwoods until they reached a small clearing encircled by trees and, on the opposite side, a sheer cliff side that reached up into the mist above. Finn began working on a shelter while Nora set a series of traps around the perimeter of the clearing. If someone came during the night, they would have some warning, and if an animal came across her traps, they might even get a meal. With their camp set up, they pulled off their boots and began cooking some of the rations tucked away inside their bags. Nora leaned back against the damp cliff wall and closed her eyes to listen to the sounds of birds and sizzling food.

"Nora, we need to talk," Finn murmured, poking at the fire with a stick.

"I don't know what to say."

"The fact that I can't see anything on you, not even the absence of magic–there's something else happening here. And the purple light you saw at the cave with the serapin—Nora, if it wasn't me, who else could it have been?"

"You think it's from me?"

"I don't know who else it could have been from." His voice was gentle as he stirred the food. "I'm just worried about you. To have such power unnoticed by someone like your mother; I have heard the stories of Adelle. *Everyone* has. She came out of nowhere with this great power. She was something fearsome to behold, but also feared deeply by the people. I was ten when she killed the last dragon, and stories I heard said she did so single-handedly. It left a deep crater in the earth and burned so intensely that nothing has ever grown there since."

Finn stood, scratching his head. "Your sister was born by then. I remember hearing how unusual it was for a child to have been left with her father as her mother went to fight for the kingdom. Once it was all over, she just went back to her village and decided to be a mother. Left her place at the king's side to Brutus and was never really heard of again. How does someone do all of that and then vanish?"

"She lost her magic when my father died." Nora whispered. "There was a fire, and it destroyed everything. It should have killed my sister, and that's when my mother learned of the extent of my sister's gift. I was always told my sister showed the same promise my mother once had."

"I have never heard of someone so powerful losing their magic to grief, Nora." Finn turned to look at her. "Well, I have never heard of *anyone* losing their magic. There are cases, however, of magic being stripped away from the user."

Nora stiffened. She had heard many of the servants in the estate talk about how her mother had despised her father, and how she had married him so she would be allowed more freedom to work for the king. Unmarried women with that much power were dangerous, but a married woman somehow seemed subdued. Everyone had been so surprised that her mother had lost her power to the grief of losing a husband she seemed to hate. Adelle had saved the kingdom and had been the most powerful wielder of magic known to humanity; who would have been able to strip her of her magic?

"I don't really know much about it, Finn. I've only heard what others have said. That it was strange, but that it began that night. What little she had left she used to keep herself from dying when she gave birth to me. That's all I know." She looked up at him, exhausted and her body screaming for sleep. "I wasn't even born yet."

"Well," Finn sat beside her, helping her lower herself down to her bedroll and pushing her hair from her face, "she was pregnant with you. You were there in the closest way possible when your mother's power left her. It doesn't explain everything—it leaves more questions—but you are not just an unimportant part of this puzzle, Nora. You are not the powerless daughter of a once-powerful woman. There's something more here. And Brutus—why was he so fixated on you? I need to think. I don't understand what is happening."

Nora closed her eyes. "I don't understand it either."

"Well, we aren't going to solve this tonight. Let's eat."

They ate their food in silence. Nora could tell Finn was deep in thought, and her own mind was racing at the possibility of magic within her. She had to admit with everything that happened, especially the encounter with the serapin, she had wondered if she harbored some powers. It was difficult to ignore, but Adelle had been nothing less than thorough with Nora's examinations. How could it have gone unnoticed?

In the morning, they avoided all topics of magic as they gathered their belongings. When all of their gear was properly put away, they heaved their packs on their backs and Finn laid out a map before them.

"This is the main road." Finn pointed to a thick black line that cut through the mountain. "I would think Brutus would be smart enough to know that waltzing up to a dragon with hundreds of men up the main road is a bad idea. So, I think it's safe to say that the entire area surrounding that road is likely a bad place for us to be. We can move much faster by ourselves, so even though our way may be less direct, it will get us there quicker and we will avoid Brutus."

Nora looked it over and nodded slowly, looking for their location on the map.

"If we are here, we could cut through this forest and move south around the lake and into the mountains. We could be to the dragon in—" Nora clicked her tongue as she traced the line with her finger. "—two days. Maybe less, if nothing stupid happens."

A smile spread across Finn's mouth, and he pretended to wipe a tear from his eye. "My little girl is all grown up."

Nora smiled, tucking the map into her bag and shrugging dismissively.

"You know, it's never too late to turn around. We've come all this way, but if you want to go back we can. We can stop at any moment." Finn's voice was gentle and sincere.

Something in Nora told her that was not an option. She knew in her gut she was exactly where she needed to be.

"I need to keep going forward, Finn. But you don't—"

"I will stop you right there." He interrupted. 'I'm not going anywhere. I just want you to remember that this isn't your *destiny*. You aren't required to go forward. But if you want to, I am coming with you."

They continued through the forest, moving far from the paths that cut their way through the trees. The forest was deafeningly silent and Nora wondered if Talon was with the group or had skulked off on his own. What if they came up on him or someone else? Would they have to fight for the chance to win, would they try to work together? On this island trapped by an endless ocean on all sides, the reality of their situation weighed heavily on Nora.

They stopped only to sleep, eating what they could as they walked and avoiding making fires. Three times as they walked, they heard a thundering rumble of the dragon roaring, almost like a challenge to them as they approached. Nora wondered where the other groups were, if they were even still alive. What if they got there and Briella was already saved? What if they got there and the dragon was already dead? But the next round of thundering roars, or the shadow accompanied by heat from above, confirmed at least that the beast was still very much alive.

Nora followed Finn to the top of a hill above the tree line where they could get their bearings, the mist dissipating and leaving the stunning view of the forest below. Nora sat on a rock, sliding her boots off and massaging her aching feet while Finn inspected the map.

He turned and smiled at her. "We're making good progress."

"Good enough for a short break?"

Finn looked out at the forest and nodded, sitting beside Nora and sliding his own boots off.

"Malachi would have loved this." Finn's voice was distant, and he kept his gaze fixed on the ocean in the distance. They could just barely make out the massive ships anchored in the cove close to the shoreline, and Finn watched them intently as he spoke. "He was obsessed. We both were when we were young, but he never really grew out of it."

"What did he want with the child?"

Finn was silent for a long moment before releasing a long breath of air. "Maybe to destroy it? It's supposed to bring the end of the world, but others say it's the beginning of a better world. That's the trick with prophecies; they're up to interpretation."

"So, you want to kill this dragon for Malachi?"

"I don't know what I want." He looked at Nora, his eyes pleading for an answer that Nora didn't have. He smiled and shook his head. "I guess we have to actually *get* there before we decide on anything of that sort."

The sound of the dragon's thundering roar echoed through the island and they grabbed their belongings, ducking back into the brush. The beast rushed down from the clouds and perched on the top of a high peak in the distance, turning to look out towards the sea below. Nora strained to see what the dragon was looking at and then gasped at the sight before her.

"Finn, look!" She cried, pointing towards the ship.

The once proud ship was engulfed in flames, and Nora shuddered to think of those left behind. The workers and lower-class tradespeople, innocent people not looking to make their mark on the world, were always the ones to be sacrificed to ambition.

"They don't deserve this," she murmured.

"No, they don't." Finn watched as the dragon maneuvered through the twisted peaks of the mountains, dipping down into a deep crater and disappearing from view. "I wonder how many times he's just watched what he's destroyed."

They continued through the forest toward the dragon, stopping when they came upon the lake that was marked on their map as being at the base of the mountain the dragon lived within. Glittering opals littered the bottom of the lake and left it with an iridescent glow dripping with ancient magic.

"There are nymphs here." He murmured, his eyes surveying the water for movement.

"How do you know?" Nora looked at the mark on her hand and followed Finn's gaze towards the water.

"The water has a glow to it. You can't see it without the Sight, but it's definitely nymphs."

Nora frowned. "I can see—"

Before she could finish, the water before them began to bubble and steam rose from the lake, dissipating into the air and revealing the massive face of a woman. The face was full and beautiful, plump lips parted in a coy smile as she rose out of the water, resting her elbows on the bank and leaning her face against her fist. Her skin and hair were a shade of green that matched the moss on the bank of the lake, and glittering scales glittered in patches on her. She towered over them and could easily grasp them both in one hand, and as her smile widened, she displayed large, sharp teeth that betrayed her serene countenance.

"Well, look at this. It's been a long while since I've seen new faces on this island." She looked Finn over slowly, raising her eyebrows. "And yours is a face I'd remember."

Finn smiled and shrugged at Nora. "She has good taste."

Nora groaned impatiently and stepped forward to look up at the creature before her. "We don't have time for this." She pointed to the peak where the dragon had been perched not so long ago. "We are trying to get up there, and we need to get there fast."

The nymph came closer to Nora until her face was inches away, her eyes looking Nora up and down, and cocked an eyebrow. "You are awfully bold, friend of Philandra." Her eyes darted to Nora's hand, and she smiled knowingly. "I have never known Philandra to let someone walk away unscathed, let alone blessed. Especially one foolish enough to save the kidnapped princess."

"You know about the princess? Is she still alive?" Nora ignored Finn's tense look and moved closer. She held out her hand and revealed Philandra's mark, allowing the nymph to hold Nora's hand in her own. As soon as they touched, Nora knew this was no ordinary nymph. What she was, she was uncertain, but the power that coursed through Nora was unlike anything she had ever felt before.

The nymph let go quickly, her eyes watching Nora carefully.

"Interesting," she murmured. "My dear, this was my island long before that beast made it his home. I know *everything*, except who exactly you are?"

"Nora DuPont–daughter of Adelle DuPont." She wondered what Adelle would think of her introducing herself in such a way. She pushed the thought from her mind and stood firm, staring up into the eyes of the nymph.

"Daughter of Adelle. I have heard of her daughter, but not a Nora." The nymph smiled softly. "You have something inside you, daughter of Adelle. Something beyond anything of this earth. It is destruction. It is *chaos*."

Nora stood for a moment, unsure of what to say. She looked at Finn, who kept his gaze fixed on the ground.

"What do you know about this—power?"

The nymph looked amused, making herself smaller until she was slightly taller than Finn. "I know much, but it is not for me to reveal everything. It wouldn't be wise for me to incur the wrath of your *patron*."

"Patron?" Nora's head swam. "The king—?"

The nymph shook her head; her smile widening. "No, I fear no mortal. There are few I do fear, none of them of this world. I wish I could watch and see how this plays out. You are full of contradictions."

Nora felt frustration bubbling within her. "Is there a safe way to reach the dragon?"

"I could tell you. But what will you give me in return?" The nymph winked at Finn. "Tempting as he may be, he won't fit the bill."

"We have nothing—" Finn went silent when the nymph held up her hand to him and turned her attention back to Nora.

"The dragon. He stole something from me." She dipped her hands into the water and scooped up a pool of the crystalline liquid. "Look here."

Nora stepped closer and looked into the small pool of shimmering water in the nymph's hands. The image rippled until it revealed a glass chalice that appeared to be inside a dark room.

"This chalice is the key to my power. Without it, I am confined to this wretched pond." She spat the words as if they were poisonous. "If I cannot roam this island, I will die. I feel myself fading more every day. This dragon, this *infection*, it must leave this place."

She pulled out a silver flask and handed it to Nora. "This will help to cool you. When the dragon is in his true form, he emits terrible heat as part of his defense. One mouthful will allow your body to regulate its temperature against the heat, but you will only have enough to last a few hours. Be smart about how you use it."

Nora tucked the flask into her pocket.

"Continue on this path until you come across a large willow tree. There, you will find a path cut into the side of the mountain that offers some cover. This is the best I can offer you regarding a safe passage. If you hear the beast at all, you must hide—he can see across great distances. If you come down from that mountain without my chalice, or if you try to take it for yourself, the liquid will rise to your lungs and drown you where you stand." The nymph smiled as Finn's face went white. "It's help with a little insurance. If you bring me my chalice, I will reward you."

"What kind of reward are we talking about?" Finn asked, stepping forward.

The nymph lowered herself back into the water, her eyes fixed on Nora. "We'll see what it is you want when you come down that mountain." The bubbling water overtook her, and she was gone.

They stood there for a long moment before Finn made his way around the lake to a path on the other side.

"Finn the nymph—"

"Nora. Please don't tell me we have to have a heart-to-heart about this now. Please don't tell me you are having a revelation about something that I am just truly not ready to hear." His voice was dripping with mock exhaustion. "My poor, simple mind can't handle more of this."

Nora frowned up at him as he moved up the mountainside.

"Let's go save the princess. We can figure the rest out later, bringer of chaos." He winked and turned to lead the way into the increasing heat.

14

Chapter Fourteen

As they went up the mountain, the smell of sulfur was so powerful they could taste it, leaving Finn and Nora to wrap a piece of cloth over the lower half of their faces to block out some of the smell, however futile their efforts may be. They were careful to avoid the steaming sulfur ponds that, despite their crystal blue beauty, radiated with an intense heat from the mountain itself.

When they finally reached the top, they laid on their bellies and peered over the edge into a large crater. There, at the center, was an enormous castle that appeared to be made from the mountain itself. Its stone walls looked much like the crumbling shale that they had walked up to get here; towers rose out of the mist and gargoyle statues peered out as a frozen watch protecting the castle from intruders. A bridge led from the opposite side of the crater to the castle steps, and the thought of crossing such a narrow passage brought forth a touch of the familiar panic Nora wrestled with. She breathed deeply, thankful that they had chosen a different path. As she breathed, the smell of sulfur mixed with something else–decay. She looked with horror at the thousands of bodies strewn across the crater. Some were skeletal and likely to have been there for a long time, but many looked fresh. Too fresh.

"It looks like some men from the ships have already been here," she whispered.

Finn nodded, his eyebrows furrowed as he surveyed the field of bodies. "I can't tell if the mage is there, but I'd bet money that he's not. I bet he got the hell out of here at the first sign of danger, the coward."

A thundering roar came from behind them, and they quickly rolled under a large, jagged boulder jutting from the mountain. Nora winced as the rock cut into her, keeping her eyes shut tight, hoping that the beast had not spotted them.

"Nora. Look." Finn whispered.

Nora opened her eyes and saw the dragon land on top of the castle. His mouth opened and he released a terrible scream as fire erupted from its mouth. The heat was near unbearable, and it took all of Nora's self-control not to drink the water the nymph had given them. As bad as this was, there was no way it was as bad as it would be inside of that castle.

They watched as the beast seemed to scan the mountainside, his eyes cold and vicious. Something seemed to catch his eyes because he rose and flew off.

"Now," Nora whispered, hurrying out from the rock. They watched the dragon slide through the air north of them, disappearing into the mist hovering between two neighboring mountains.

They hurried into the crater, sliding down the loose rock and ignoring the pain as jagged pieces of shale cut through their clothing. They ran towards the castle, gaining speed as they heard the dragon's shriek in the distance.

"It's coming back!" Finn bellowed, sprinting ahead.

Nora looked up and saw the shadow of the beast in the mist and dropped to the ground, pulling the nearest dead body over her. Finn noticed her drop, and followed her lead, pulling a too-fresh corpse over him and contorting his face in disgust.

"The blood—cover yourself in blood." She shouted, pushing her hands into the wounds and smearing the thick rotting blood over her face.

"This is unforgivable." Finn groaned, doing so as quickly as possible before laying still.

They felt the earth rumble around them as the dragon landed so close that Nora could have thrown a rock and hit him. They laid there, frozen in terror, not daring to see where the dragon was. The heat in the air dissipated, and Nora barely opened an eye to survey the area. It appeared to be gone, but it couldn't be far as they had not heard its great wings tearing through the sky.

She looked at Finn, who stared back at her and then moved her head ever so slightly to look at the castle before them. The dragon had been right above them on a staircase that led inside, but below the staircase, the stones seemed to be arranged in a strange pattern. Nora smiled to herself as she recognized the familiar pattern that showed servants' entrances.

This way, she mouthed to Finn, sliding out from under the man and making her way towards the side of the grand staircase.

They pressed their backs against the wall and edged to the discolored stones. Nora pushed against them carefully, shutting her eyes as the dirt and grime collected from years of neglect poured down on her, and slowly continued to move the stones until they gave way to a hallway beneath the stairs. Finn slid in after her, his eyes watching the staircase above them carefully.

"Clever trick." He whispered to Nora, pulling out two glass orbs and rotating them in his hands until they glowed with a soft light.

The hall had clearly not been used in Nora's lifetime. The dirt and grime were thick on the floor, and rodents scurried from the light in Finn's hands. It led down into a darkness that seemed to never end.

"One at a time, then." She whispered, setting her bags on the ground.

They worked quietly, barely moving when they stepped out from the safety of the servants' hallway. They quietly unfastened the armor from the fallen soldiers, doing their best to avoid the wide eyes of the freshly fallen, and carried each piece into the hall. When they had a large enough pile, Nora pulled out the alchemic instructions Luna had provided them and laid it out, taking one of Finn's glowing orbs and placing it at the top of the parchment.

"So, are we thinking we're going to have a super armor suit or something?" He asked, unsure of exactly what they were planning to do.

Nora wanted to laugh, but her ribs were bruised from coming down into the crater and she winced, grabbing her side. She looked up at Finn, who shook his head.

"I have some of that salve from the ship. It'll help, but you'll still need real medical attention when we get back. I don't have any energy for that type of magic right now." He pulled out a salve and applied it to Nora's ribs.

She released a long breath as the pain subsided and returned her attention to the heaps of armor they had collected.

"I was thinking more that we would create a large shield like Luna did at the lake" She looked up at Finn and grimaced at his look of absolute bewilderment.

"You have never mentioned this plan to me." His voice sounded hollow.

"Well, that's because I was afraid that you'd say it was—"

"Asinine? Idiotic? The craziest thing I have ever heard in my goddamn life?" Finn ran his hands over his face in frustration.

"Well–yes," Nora replied, looking down at her feet. "Do you have a better plan?"

"No!" he shouted, kicking a helmet and sending it flying down the hall.

Nora closed her eyes as it clanked loudly, and when the noise stopped, she glared at him. The familiar dragon's heat radiated from above them and they both moved quickly to close the stone wall. They pressed their backs to the wall and Finn reached for Nora's hand, squeezing it apologetically. They listened as the beast stood directly above them, and Nora let out a sigh of relief when they heard his large wings beating up into the sky.

"That was too close." She whispered.

"I'm sorry." Finn sat down and brought the pieces of metal together.

"Hello?" a voice called from the darkness ahead of them. "Is someone there?"

Nora stared at Finn, eyes wide. He motioned for her to be quiet and covered his glowing orbs.

"Please." The voice sounded desperate and they could hear muffled sobs. "Please."

Nora raised her eyebrows and jerked her head toward the sound. They drew their swords and walked down the dark hallway until they came to a dead end. Nora noticed the same patterns on the wall as she had seen outside and pushed gently, smiling at Finn as the wall gave way.

"It's always helpful that masters don't want to see their servants." She murmured, grabbing one of Finn's orbs and shining it before her. The room was dark except for two torches lit at the end. Upon closer inspection, Nora realized this was a jailer's dungeon. The hall was lined with barred doors, and when she held up her orb to one cell, she could see the outline of skeletons shackled to the floor.

"Who's that?" The voice called from the cell at the end of the hall.

"Princess Gabriella?" Nora asked, her voice shaking. She approached the cell and saw a figure rise and press itself to the bars of the cell. "Are you—"

"Yes!" the princess cried, dropping to her knees. "Please! Please let me out of here!"

Finn and Nora ran to her, holding their orbs to her face. She looked pale and thin, but not terribly so. Her hair was pulled back from her face with string, revealing remnants of pearls and jewels that had adorned her hair on her wedding day. Her dress was torn and filthy. Briella had used strips of fabric to dress wounds on her arms and legs that Nora could see from where she stood were likely infected. The princess's green eyes were vibrant and seemed to take in everything around her; they held the only life force left within her broken body. Nora's heart raced as she took the princess in. This was what they had been working towards all this time, and she had imagined this moment a hundred different ways during their journey. She had anticipated the princess recognizing her immediately, she would return her bracelet and it would be this instant continuation of their interactions back at the DuPont estate. But looking at Briella in this state, locked away in a cell in the dark, it seemed so trivial.

"Is there a key somewhere?" Finn asked, putting his hands through the bars to turn her face to him. "I need you to calm down. We need to work together. Do you know if there's a key?"

Her eyes filled with tears, and she silently shook her head.

Finn stepped back and inspected the lock. "It's been magicked, but I think I can work on it."

He worked, and the princess watched him, her eyes full of fear. Nora stood helplessly, holding the orbs so Finn had plenty of light to work with. Whenever he made a wrong move, electricity shot out of the lock and burned his fingers, and Nora would occasionally make him stop to wrap his hands in bandages.

Nora looked at Briella and cleared her throat. "I'm happy you're alive, your highness. I had thought you wouldn't be."

"Well, I'd make a poor hostage if I were dead," Briella said, sitting down on the floor in exhaustion. "Please call me Briella. I have no energy for pleasantries."

Nora smiled, reaching through the bars and offering Briella her hand. She squeezed gently when Briella rested her hands on hers and smiled.

"Everyone is looking for you, Briella. The king has spared no expense."

Briella's eyes flashed momentarily with a deep sadness before she raised her chin and nodded. The broken girl they saw before them withered away and Nora could see the royalty returning from the pain. Finn pretended not to notice, raising his eyebrows at Nora when Briella looked down at the lock he was working on.

Footsteps sounded from the distance and Briella's eyes went wide.

"Go—hide!" she hissed, peering out from her cell.

"I've almost got it," Finn said, not breaking his focus.

"He's coming! If he finds you, this will all be for nothing."

"Who's coming?" Nora asked.

"That—*thing*—you don't understand. He's not just a dragon."

Nora's eyes widened, and she tugged at Finn's shoulder. "Come on, we'll finish once it's gone."

"Nora, they'll know someone was down here. The lock has obviously been tampered with; just give me one second." Finn whispered.

"Please. I can't watch more death." Briella begged. Tears streamed down her face, desperation in her eyes as she watched them.

The lock flipped open, and Finn reached in to grab the princess. They hurried as silently as possible down the hallway as the footsteps slowly followed, Finn tucking the balls of light in his jacket pocket to dim the light. Nora heard a familiar voice swearing behind them and almost turned to look before the sound of hurried footsteps sounded behind them. They could hear whatever was following them roar with rage as they threw open the cell doors, quickly gaining on them in the darkness.

They slipped behind the barely open wall into the servants' hallway and carefully pulled it closed. They went to the farthest opposite side of the hall, where the great staircase above them caused the ceiling to slope down so low they had to crawl farther back. Finn lifted his orb to his mouth and blew it out.

"Please don't make it dark," Briella whispered, staring at the one remaining orb.

Finn gave Briella an apologetic look. "Close your eyes. It will be as if you were just sleeping."

When the princess shut her eyes, Finn blew out the light, plunging them into darkness.

15

Chapter Fifteen

They sat in the darkness for hours, not daring to utter a sound until Finn finally summoned a magical blue flame that dimly lit the space and offered a little warmth. In the dim light, Nora realized Briella had fallen asleep in the crook of her arm. It's funny, she thought, how the only thing that distinguished a princess from anyone else was the appearance of money. Briella could be any woman in the world as she lay there filthy and broken, but Nora could see hints of the woman she met on the eve of her wedding. She could see reflections of the warrior who took up arms against a dragon in the gaunt face of the woman who slept beside her.

"This poor girl," Finn murmured.

Briella looked to be in pain, even in sleep. Her skin was dull from too long away from the sun, but her face was still dotted with freckles, and her lips, although cracked from too long with not enough water, were still plump and inviting. Nora brushed a strand of hair from Briella's face, shaking the princess's arm gently to wake her.

"Your high—Briella. Wake up." Nora whispered.

Briella's eyes opened slowly, and she looked up at Nora. A faint smile spread across her lips.

"Thank god it wasn't a dream." She whispered.

Nora felt her heart quicken and cleared her throat, slowly helping the princess to sit up on her own. Briella looked at Nora and a flicker of what seemed like slight recognition flashed in her eyes and Nora wondered if the princess remembered her. She sat up and stretched, the moment passing as quickly as it came, and Nora wondered if she should tell her. She fidgeted with the bracelet she still wore on her own arm, tucking it into her bag and deciding now was not the time for reunions. Finn raised an eyebrow at Nora, who shot him a warning look before gathering the metal they had collected earlier.

Briella raised her hand to her face, wrinkling her nose in disgust. "It smells of death."

"That's because it was taken from the dead," Finn explained.

He worked, dragging the large chest plates together so the edges all touched.

"What is the plan exactly?" Briella asked, standing to help Nora drag the last of the metal together.

Nora explained fusing the metal together to create a large shield, and then using alchemy to reflect the dragon's flame away from them should they be attacked. The princess nodded slowly; her face showing no emotion before responding.

"You think a giant hunk of metal moving across an open crater will not look—suspicious?" Her eyes challenged Nora. "It sounds rather stupid."

Finn's face split into a wide grin. "I *like* her!"

Nora frowned. "I think anyone running across a crater will look suspicious, especially since the dragon knows you've escaped. He's likely watching for us now."

Briella ran her tongue across her teeth and shrugged, letting out a long sigh. "I suppose we just have to work with what we have."

Nora opened her mouth to argue, and Finn shot her a warning look before returning to his work. They stood back and allowed Finn to work at melting the metal together. He did so in small bursts to keep it as silent as possible. He had to stop often, panting in exhaustion.

Nora handed him the last of their food supply, and he reluctantly accepted.

"So the man who was chasing us—can you help me understand what you meant? He is the dragon?" Nora asked Briella as Finn worked on the last piece of metal.

Briella watched Finn work. "I still can't believe it. He had been riding with our party the entire way to Sorudi and we parted just before the city; very kind, helpful even. He even wished me *luck* in my marriage." Her lip curled in disgust. "I didn't realize until I got here. He brought me inside the main entrance of the castle and then I saw him shift. It was terrifying. He *howled* in pain; it was as if his body ripped apart to create another body. Then he was standing there, smiling at me, and I remembered."

"I didn't know dragons could shift," Nora murmured. "I wonder how many—"

"Other's there are? That's exactly what I thought." Briella interrupted, standing to bring Finn some water as he stopped his work. "Have we simply been existing side by side, thinking they were gone all this time?"

Finn wiped the sweat from his brow and lowered the bowl, now drained of water, to the ground. "I can't even wrap my head around that idea."

When the chest plates were welded together, they formed a square of solid metal barely large enough to conceal the three of them. They hadn't heard the dragon come or go, so to be careful they agreed to stay put until it emerged again. They sat by Finn's magic fire as he fell into a fitful sleep, snoring softly.

"Are you...together?" Briella asked after a long moment of silence.

"Oh, no!" Nora glanced at Finn, relieved to see he was sleeping. "We met a while back on the road and traveled together. When we heard about the king's reward—well, we decided we'd have a better chance working together."

"I'm sure the reward is great." Briella's eyes grew distant as she looked back at the fire.

"Well—yes." Nora shifted uncomfortably. "The prince promised land and fortune to whoever can bring you back. We came over on just one of the many barges escorting people out here to find you."

"I've heard many come and try. None have made it further than the castle gates from what I could hear. I had mostly given up hope of leaving this place."

"Well, if I'm being honest, I didn't really think we'd make it this far." Nora leaned her back against the wall and closed her eyes. "I can't imagine being here as long as you were. I would've given up hope as well. You must be eager to be back with your future husband."

Briella scoffed, glaring into the distance. "Yes, I can't *wait*."

Nora pursed her lips together awkwardly, unsure of what to say. "I'm sorry. I didn't mean to upset you."

Briella hugged her legs toward her. "Don't feel sorry for me. Every life has a cost. I might not have a say in who I can marry or why, but that is the price I pay for the luxuries afforded to me. Do not pity people who do not change their circumstances—we always have a choice."

Nora looked around them and shrugged. "Well, how's that working out for you?"

Briella stared at her for a moment and offered a small smile. "You got me there."

Again, the familiar heat of the dragon filled the space around them and they extinguished the light from the fire, peering out of the opening into the field of bodies lit by the light of the moon. The dragon was above them again, but this time, they saw something else.

Nora gasped as she noticed Brutus, standing on the top of the crater, his hands aflame with magic, and hundreds of men below him.

"Dragon! Surrender the princess or die!" He bellowed, his voice magnified by his magic.

Finn sat straight up, eyes wide. "What the hell—"

Nora covered his mouth and motioned for him to be quiet, pointing outside at the mage.

They watched as the dragon stepped down from the steps. His large talons were all that they could see from their position.

He spoke with a voice that caused their skin to crawl, "So, you're playing the brave mage role tonight, are you? *How fun.*"

Nora froze as she heard him speak. *How fun.* She remembered the dream she had where Talon had said the same thing, and she knew in that moment where she recognized the voice from.

"It's Talon." She whispered to Finn, her eyes wide with shock.

Finn frowned and then raised his eyebrows as it clicked for him, too. "My god."

"Yes, that's his name," Briella whispered. "You've met him?"

"Yes, on the ship. He was on the ship and back at the King's banquet–he was toying with us." Nora stared in stunned disbelief.

Lightning erupted from Brutus's hands as he bellowed, "Attack!"

The men charged at the dragon, armed far beyond anything Nora had seen offered on any of the ships. The dragon laughed, his wings driving him up into the night sky as he reared up and rained fire down upon them.

"We have to go now!" Nora shouted, leaving the hallway and grabbing a section of the metal they had welded together.

"We haven't drawn the runes!" Finn protested, grabbing a piece of charcoal.

"Bring that with us. We'll do it when we get farther away. Now's our chance." Nora ran and Briella and Finn followed behind, holding the metal up over their heads and taking advantage of the distraction. They could hear the screams of the men as they melted away, and Nora tried to block out the sound as the smell of burned flesh hung heavy in the air.

They reached the side of the crater and began the grueling climb up, not daring to look behind them. Nora could hear her heart beating loud in her ears, her hands bled as she clambered up the shale crater and she could hear Briella wheezing with exhaustion as they moved. They could tell the heat of the dragon's fire had subsided, but the air was still hot. Nora could hear Brutus scream, and more lightning fell, causing Talon to fly into a burst of cruel laughter and continue the steady stream of flame.

Finn let out a horrible cry of pain as his leg was gashed open by the jagged rock, holding tightly onto the surrounding rock to keep himself from falling back to the bottom of the crater. "I can't—Just keep going."

"I'm not going anywhere without you!" Nora shouted. She dropped the metal and turned to pull him up onto her back, looking up at Briella frantically. "Go—just run! There's a small cave up at the top. Keep going until you can get into it!"

Briella scrambled up the mountain, abandoning the metal that she was too weak to carry on her own. Nora took a deep breath and carried Finn on her back up the rocky mountain. Finn groaned in pain, using one of his arms to help pull them and shouting for her to let him stay behind. Nora ignored his protests and continued up the cliff edge, slowly coming closer and closer.

One step at a time, she told herself.

The surrounding air prickled with magic electricity, and Nora looked up just in time to see Brutus summoning his magic and lifting himself from the ground. A bright light exploded around them and he was gone, leaving the men who were dead or dying to stay at the mercy of this beast.

"This is the great mage of your kingdom." Talon's voice roared at the screaming men. "This is the right hand of the man who rules over you all." More fire erupted and Nora continued up the mountain, closing her eyes against the heat and the screams below. "You are all *soft*, you are all *weak*. The child of Draco is coming. You should thank me for killing you now."

Nora threw Finn up over the side of the crater as another burst of fire came from the dragon. She dragged him into the small cave with Briella and turned to go back down the cliff.

"Where are you going?" Briella screamed.

Nora pulled out the flask the nymph had given her and took a deep gulp. She felt the cold water spread through her body, erasing her pain and the burns temporarily. She tossed the flask to Briella.

"Take one large drink and have Finn do the same; we aren't getting off of this mountain while this thing is alive."

Nora jumped down the side of the crater, allowing herself to slide through the loose rock and stopping just above the metal. She grabbed the parchment that Luna had given her and laid it out, the area well-lit as the dragon's fire burned through the bodies of the dying men behind her. She frantically drew the symbols, being extra careful to close all the circles completely as Luna had instructed.

This must work, she told herself.

She lifted the metal and felt her body scream in protest, and she ran as fast as she could up the mountain. A surge of energy radiated through her and she could somehow sprint up the mountain, sliding occasionally but steadily nearing the top of the crater. As she reached the top, she heard the dragon shriek and turned to see him looking directly at her.

"You!" He screamed, rising into the sky. "I've been waiting for *you*."

"Hurry!" Briella screamed.

Briella stood on the crater's edge and took Nora's hand, pulling her up beside her. Talon dove from the sky, and the two ran towards the unconscious Finn, sliding into the small cave and lifting the metal to block the cave's entrance. Nora braced all of her weight against the metal, screaming as it burned hot when the dragon's flame engulfed the cave. The force of the fire pushed against the metal and Nora's feet dragged through the earth. The surrounding air erupted like a sonic boom that knocked Briella back and Nora watched helplessly as Briella was knocked unconscious. Veins in Nora's neck bulged as she strained to hold the metal in place. She could feel fire licking around the side, burning her skin and parts of her clothes were burned away from her body.

Why isn't it working, what did I do wrong?

Her mind ran through the events at the lake, desperately trying to remember any detail she might have missed. The heat from the metal was unbearable and she cried out as the pain became too much, unable to focus through the burning on the alchemic magic. Standing there, her bare flesh pressed against the burning metal, and thought of her sister finding her burned body on this mountaintop. She thought of Tulee and their tearful goodbye.

This is it. This is how it ends.

Tears fell from her eyes and instantly evaporated into the hot air. Flashes of memories of home ran through her mind; the forest, the city, Briella walking down the aisle, Tulee flirting with the handsome guard Horace. So many moments that would not happen, so many things that could be different. The fire eased up and Nora felt her knees buckle, willing herself to hang tight to the metal in her desperate attempt to keep her friends safe.

"Come, daughter of the dragon slayer! Come meet your doom!" Talon's voice echoed through the mountain, shaking stones from the roof of the small cave.

Nora opened her eyes just as the dragon released another stream of fire, pushing hard against the metal again and feeling the skin on her fingers blister against the now cherry-red metal. The alchemy was supposed to work. What had she done wrong? She remembered how different it had been with Luna and felt her knees buckle. They would die here in this cave because of her own error. She looked back at Finn and Briella, who lay unconscious and burned on the cave floor and continued to push against the metal, shielding them from the flames with her own body.

The burning gave way to a cool feeling of water on her skin and she wondered for a moment if she was dying, a strange sense of calm acceptance quelling the panic and fear. Suddenly, the surrounding flames turned purple, and an energy billowed around suspending her hair and the stones in the cave in the air. The dragon screamed, and Nora pushed harder, her body no longer feeling the weakness of hunger and exhaustion. The burns across her body stopped hurting, and purple flames erupted from inside of her.

She threw the metal forward, screaming in what was a mixture of agony and triumph. The purple flames circled around her and the dragon, twisting from Nora's body and winding up around the dragon in hundreds of slithering bolts of electricity. She looked into the eyes of the dragon before her, and the image gave way to Talon, his eyes wide with fear, tears pouring down his cheeks.

"The prophecy—" he stammered. "I've done it. I—I've done it! Nora DuPont, awaken!" His eyes became frantic with excitement and pain. "Beneath the stars where ancients sleep, a child wakes from shadows deep..."

"*No!*" Nora screamed, the purple flames radiating through her in a burst of energy.

"With power fast to tear the land, and reforge gently at their hand." Talon let out a terrible shriek of pain as the purple flames burrowed down his throat, lighting him up with purple light from within his body.

Nora dropped to her knees, blinded by the intensity of the light coming from the dragon before her. A burst of energy sprung from the light, and she was thrown back towards the cave.

When she opened her eyes again, the light had completely vanished, leaving them in the dim light of the dawn. She braced herself against the cave entrance as she stood, looking in the direction where the fierce beast had once stood. She looked down and saw Talon lying before her, crumbled into a fetal position and burned beyond recognition. He stared at her, his eyes wide with fear. As she approached, he cried.

"It's you. It's you." He sobbed, his body convulsing.

The purple light was still burning through her as she approached and she knelt down beside him.

"I did it. I—" He stopped, his eyes growing distant and with a final breath he was gone. His eyes pulsed one last time as they had on the ship and Talon went limp on the ground before her.

The purple light faded, and Nora turned to see Briella staring at her, eyes wide with fear. She looked down at her hands and saw they were badly burned. It was as if all the life had returned to her and she felt the searing pain ripping through her body. Nora's world went dark, and the last thing she saw was Briella's face inches from her own, saying:

"Hold on."

16

Chapter Sixteen

Nora, where are you? Larissa's voice echoed through Nora's mind, cutting through the darkness. *Please, please...*

The voice trailed off as Nora fell back into a deepened state of unconsciousness, and purple light filled her vision.

Well done. A man's voice this time, the same one that had spoken to her after she saw the Serapin. Again, darkness swallowed her and the voice drifted off as she swam through a sea of purples and blues that were eventually replaced by a silent darkness.

Nora opened her eyes and rose, her head pounding and her lips dry and cracked. She summoned the energy to sit up and saw Finn, still sleeping, sprawled out on the cave floor. If it wasn't for the slight heave of his chest, she'd have thought that he was dead and relief flooded her body at the realization that he was alive. She surveyed herself and found that she was in new clothes and her burns had been bandaged with strips of what was left of her charred clothing. Nora turned to see Briella sitting nearby, wrapping a thin wire around something small and iridescent.

"What are you doing?" Nora croaked; her voice hoarse from screaming.

Briella jumped a little and smiled. "You should try to go back to sleep."

Nora crawled towards her and rested her back against the jagged cave wall. "I'm fine."

Briella held a smooth oval stone in her hand and was wrapping the outer parts in a copper wire, creating a beautiful pattern and sliding it onto a leather cord.

"This is a dragon heart." Briella held the stone up so Nora could inspect it. "When a dragon dies, their heart becomes an opal. I've always wondered why they were so small; you'd think with such a large beast that they'd be huge, bigger than anything anyone person could even carry." She looked out at Talon's body, burnt and still lying outside of their cave. "Now I realize why. As they die, they change, and the opal that's left is only a small part of their heart. I saw it glowing from inside his own human heart."

Nora frowned, inspecting the stone. It was impossible to ignore the magic radiating off of it. "What is it capable of?"

Briella shrugged as tied off the leather cord. "I'm still coming to terms with the fact that we're alive. I have no room for wondering about the secrets of dragons." She held the opal that was now fashioned into a necklace out to Nora. "Here, keep it. I can feel magic radiating from it; I don't think it wise to leave it for just anyone to find."

Nora stared at the necklace for a minute and slowly slipped it over her head. It hung low enough that the opal could easily be concealed beneath her shirt.

Briella stared at her for a long while, clearly searching for words. "Well, with the magic I saw from you, I am surprised you didn't just kill it to begin with."

"Oh, no, that was alchemy. I drew symbols on that metal that would allow it to absorb and reflect—"

"That was not alchemy. You didn't speak the command words; alchemy must be contained within the symbols but it requires verbal activation and instruction." Briella's eyes searched Nora's, untrusting and unsure of what to say next. "That was not alchemy."

Captivate this serpent's flame, reflect this celestial power. Nora closed her eyes as she remembered Luna's words, cursing herself for being so stupid as to forget the one part that required the least attention. She looked back at Briella, anxiety rising within her at the princess's distrust.

"I have never had any magic. I don't understand what's happening." Nora looked back at Finn for a moment before returning her attention to Briella. "Finn has the Sight, and he says something isn't well—*right*—about me. But even he has seen nothing like it."

"Neither have I." Briella looked over at Finn. "He must be exhausted. To fuse all of that metal together on little to no energy and being a half-elf on top of that. You are lucky to have each other."

"Don't let him hear you say that," Nora teased, moving towards the cave's entrance to look at Talon.

His mouth and face were badly burned, and the rest of his body suffered some minor burns. The most shocking of the injuries was that the burn from his mouth seemed to travel to his lungs, leaving parts of his chest exposed and badly blackened. It was as if the fire he had breathed burned him up from the inside. She could see his exposed heart had an iridescent sheen to it that showed it was not quite a human heart, despite its appearance.

Nora looked down at the bag beside him that appeared to be the source of the copper Briella had used on her necklace and kneeled down to inspect its contents. A bright light flashed from the pouch when she opened it and Nora smiled–the chalice the nymph had asked them to retrieve. She remembered the somber warning that they would drown should they not return it and she gulped, remembering the water that the three of them had all drank.

Nora took the bag with her to the cave and tucked it in her pack, turning towards Briella. "We need to get this down to the lake at the base of this hill. How soon do you think before Finn can move?"

Briella looked over at him, her eyes full of sympathy. "I mean, I'm sure if you woke him he'd go, but it would be better for him to sleep."

Nora noticed how Briella moved carefully, wincing when she tried to make quick movements, and remembered that not only had she suffered her own injuries, but that she likely hadn't been outside or able to move much at all in her cell and was exhausted herself.

As if summoned by their conversation, Finn's eyes slowly opened and he looked up at Nora. "Did you change your clothes?" He asked, his voice full of irritation.

Nora smiled and sat beside him. "Oh, you know, fashion first."

Finn murmured curses under his breath and he summoned the strength to sit up, smiling at Briella, who watched him nervously. "I don't suppose we have any water."

Nora held up the flask she had received from the nymph and shrugged. "We have this, but there isn't much left. Drink it. You need it most."

"Oh shit. The nymph." Finn murmured.

Nora pointed to her bag that lay a few feet away. "We have it; it's safe, don't worry. Besides, you've already had some."

Briella frowned. "Why wouldn't it be safe?"

Nora explained the nymphs' instructions, trying to pretend she didn't notice Briella's horrified expression. "I wouldn't have asked anyone to drink it if it wasn't an emergency. If it wasn't for that water, we probably wouldn't be here now."

"True." Briella grabbed Finn's outstretched hand and helped him to stand. "But now I think it's a bit more urgent to get that back to her."

"I support that decision." Finn moved towards the cave entrance and stopped when he saw Talon's body. "You can explain this to me later. I don't even want to know." His eyes were fixed on Talon's exposed heart as he inched around him, cursing as he moved.

They made their way down slowly and stopped often so Finn and Briella could rest. Nora was surprised at how easy the descent was and remembered how much harder it had been to climb up constantly looking for places to hide in case the dragon came for them. When they saw the lake below them, at last Nora allowed herself a moment of relief. To get a drink, to dip in the cool waters, to have *survived*. Nora was overwhelmed with emotion. She watched Finn carefully move down the cliff side and Briella following beside him, her arms outstretched to catch him should he stumble back, and Nora felt something stirring within her. She placed her hand over the small lump in her shirt created by the opal heart and gentle warmth spread through her hand. Nora quickly pulled her hand away, following Finn and Briella towards the lake below.

As they approached the edge of the lake, they saw the water bubble, revealing the nymph in her massive form holding her hand over her eyes to see them better and beckoning them to come. A wind pushed at their backs and they were propelled forward faster, their feet hovering above the ground. They stopped on the banks of the lake and the nymph looked them over, her eyes soft.

"I knew you would come back." The nymph watched with amusement as the princess rushed into the water, ignoring all the stories of nymphs drowning intruders in their homes. "My chalice.".

Finn stepped behind Nora and pulled the bag from her pack, turning it over in his hands and grabbing the glass chalice from inside. He handed it to the nymph, and she smiled, stepping back to the center of her pond. The bubbling water around her became more turbulent and the water below her launched into the air high above them and Nora could barely see her figure at the top, arms stretched wide.

The water became a wave and washed up over the mountain, pouring into the crater and overflowing down the mountainside. As the water passed, the ground became green and soon the entire mountain was covered in small green sprouts. Nora thought of all the men up there who were dead, their bodies being washed free from the heat and blood that was caked to them. When the nymph returned, she was no longer a light shade of blue but a deep turquoise with flowers sliding and falling from her hair to sprout onto the ground. She had reduced herself again to their size and walked towards them, water and grass sprouting up for each footstep.

"I will close the earth over the fallen men and they will rest in peace." The nymph walked to Finn, running her hands through his hair and bringing his face close to hers. "I take your pain." She whispered. She rested her forehead on his and the bruises and cuts all over his body melted away. He let out a small cry and held his leg as bones reset themselves.

"For you," she turned to Briella and grabbed her hands, lifting them to her mouth and kissing them softly. "I give you life." Briella's form thickened slightly and her eyes no longer looked hollow and defeated. Her skin went from pale and listless to a healthier shade and most of her own cuts and bruises vanished. The infection from her old wounds gave way to clear skin, leaving behind a small scar.

The nymph walked to Nora, running her hands over her badly burned arms and shaking her head slightly. "You have the power in you already, but I will help you."

As she ran her hands up Nora's arms, the burned skin fell off and was replaced by clean skin. Although there were scars, she was no longer in agonizing pain. The nymph traced her fingers up Nora's neck to the top of her head and then ran them down her chest, stomach, and each of her legs.

Nora sighed with relief and looked up at the nymph. "Thank you."

"Thank *you*. I am free now." She turned and looked up towards the sun, smiling as it hit her face. "I have one more gift for you. My magic will take you from this island and deliver you to the mainland. I doubt you will make it far in your little lifeboat."

"You came here on a *lifeboat*?" Briella hissed at Finn, who nudged her and motioned for her to be silent.

"Where would you have me deliver you? It must be near the ocean. My magic will not extend to foreign lands, but the waters are for all." The nymph created a spinning sphere of water, her eyes bright with excitement.

Finn thought for a moment and looked at Nora. "Well, it depends. Where are we going?"

Nora paused for a moment, so many questions racing through her mind. What was this power within her that the nymph seemed to understand and did Nora even want to know? She had been so certain that Talon was the child of Draco, and now she felt like there was little she could ever be certain of again. She looked at Briella, who observed her.

"I think we need to get back to the mainland and decide what to do next."

Briella stiffened slightly and nodded in agreement.

"Balcross, then?" Finn asked.

"Yes, Balcross." Nora looked up at the nymph.

The nymph smiled, opening her arms out to her sides and creating a whirling wind.

"Have you heard of Goghbuldor, the city of witches?" The nymph's voice was calm. "Go there. They can help you understand what lives within you."

"Thank you," Nora murmured.

Nora and Finn each grabbed one of Briella's hands and closed their eyes against the strong wind. Nora's stomach lurched as they seemed pulled into the wind, rising into the mist, and as suddenly as it came, they felt the earth beneath their feet, and the wind was gone. When Nora opened her eyes, they were standing on a beach and the nymph was nowhere to be found.

Finn fell to the ground and threw up, holding up his hand to shoo Briella off when she came to help him.

"I just need to get it out, then I'll feel better." He groaned. "I've had enough of other people's magic on me for a lifetime."

When Finn's stomach had settled, they made their way towards Balcross. The city looked the same, surrounded by hundreds of refugee tents and guards blocking every entrance. Something that was different, however, was royal flags all over the city walls.

"Is the prince here?" Nora asked, stopping in her tracks and surveying the area before them.

Finn frowned and beckoned them to follow him up onto a hill outside of the city walls and away from the refugees. He peered out at the city and shook his head. "No, it looks like they're preparing the city though, so he will be here soon. Do you think Brutus—?"

Nora's eyes went wide, and she looked at Briella, who stared at the city in terror.

Finn seemed to not notice Briella's distress and took a step towards the city. "I should go in and get some supplies. I'll find out what's going on. We might reunite you with your prince sooner than you'd think."

Briella turned to look out at the ocean behind them. Nora watched Finn disappear up the trail towards Balcross. She wanted to go with him and fought the urge to insist they stay together. After Brutus ran from the encounter with the dragon, she knew it would be foolish to walk in with the princesses without understanding the state of the city within. And the way Briella had looked at the city had Nora questioning if she was doing the right thing by delivering the princess to a fate she seemed to dread.

Nora looked towards the forest behind Balcross and decided they should at least go make camp and rest while they waited for Finn. She turned to suggest this to Briella just in time to see Briella, brandishing a frying pan in her hands, rear up and hit her upside the head. With that, Nora's world went black.

Chapter Seventeen

Nora regained consciousness in what must have been only a few seconds after being hit and sat up frantically in time to see Briella disappearing into the forest behind the city.

"What the fuck!" she shouted, hurrying to her feet and sprinting after Briella.

Even with the healing from the nymph, Nora's body ached as she pursued the princess.

If I'm struggling this much, she thought as her heart pounded in her chest, *then she can't get too far.*

Nora was careful to leave markers for Finn to follow as she ran after Briella. She stole one last look at the city behind her, the banners of the king still visible from this great distance, before continuing after the princess. Nora couldn't see Briella, but broken twigs and disturbed earth helped guide her path. She heard a voice cry out and hurried to find Briella toppling down a steep, muddy hill and scrambling back on her feet to hurry away from Nora.

"What the fuck, Briella!" Nora shouted, chasing after her.

"I'm not getting traded in for your fucking reward!" Briella shouted, throwing a rock at Nora's head.

Nora managed to catch the rock, slinging it back at Briella and hitting her right in the back of her knee. Her leg buckled and Briella cried out as she stumbled.

"Hey!"

"Just returning the favor!" Nora jumped and wrapped her arms around Briella's ankles, causing her to face-plant back into the wet earth. Briella turned onto her back, kicking at Nora as she tried to climb up Briella's body and pin her legs down under her torso. When Nora was on top of Briella, she pinned her body against Briella's, looking down at the freckled face full of rage that glared back up at her.

"What the hell are you playing at?!" Nora shouted.

"Oh, I'm sorry, did you expect me to allow you to trade me in without a fuss?" Briella shouted as she pushed against Nora's face and tried to slide out from her grasp.

"Well, I didn't expect you to bash my head in with a damned frying pan!" Nora shouted back. "After everything we just went through, you could have at least slipped away into the night like a normal person! I never said I was going to trade you in the prince offered a reward to save you, that's just the truth of it."

Nora felt heat rising in her face at the closeness of her body against Briella's. Briella was warm beneath her, and as her panicked breathing began to slow it seemed like the moment between them stretched on in a silent curiosity.

Briella's face flushed and she frowned up at Nora, her red curls full of leaves and dirt and her eyes softening. "Get off of me and I promise I won't run again."

"I'm less worried about you running and more worried about you knocking me unconscious again."

"I just—I panicked ok? I'm sorry. You're right, you have just been trying to help. Are you ok?"

Nora sat back slightly, her body still pressed against Briella's, and she cocked an eyebrow at the princess. She released Briella's arms and slid her body off of hers, slowly rising to her feet and groaning as her head throbbed. She held her hand out to Briella and helped her to her feet, steadying the princess as she stood.

"I've been better," Nora growled, shoving past Briella and making her way to a nearby grove of trees with large exposed roots they could shelter under.

The forest hugged the coastline at the edge of the peninsula and Nora tasted the ocean in the air. The trees were different here at the lower elevation than they had been when they found the serapin den or the ancient ruins higher up, but they felt as ancient.

"This forest is beautiful," Briella murmured as she lowered herself beside Nora.

Nora nodded in agreement, unwilling to pretend everything was forgiven. She watched Briella busy herself with the fire, her red curls spilling over her face as she worked. Briella was beautiful and that could not be argued, however, it was the way she was so capable that Nora found herself drawn to. She thought back to Briella joining her in the garden at the DuPont residence, and the way she seemed uninterested in status or rank. It was a line of thinking Nora was not used to from nobles she had interacted with and she admired Briella for it.

"I'll go get some more firewood." Briella murmured, brushing the dirt from her pants.

Nora busied herself with filling the cooking pot with the minor ingredients she had left to make some semblance of a stew. She listened as Briella's footsteps drifted further away and leaned herself against the tree. Her body ached at every movement and she winced as a sharp pain shot through her ribs. Nora sat in a long silence, enjoying the sounds of the creatures of the forest and reveling in a moment of solitude. She had been afforded so many evenings alone in the mossy forest outside of the DuPont estate that it had become a refuge to sit with herself. She allowed her mind to drift to the moment they had shared that night at the DuPont estate, wondering if Briella even remembered that moment.

The sound of Briella's footsteps approaching drew her from her thoughts and she watched as the princess stumbled back into their makeshift campsite.

"I'm surprised you came back." Nora said absently, ladling Briella her portion of food in a small wooden bowl she kept in her pack.

"Good, I like to keep my captors on their toes." Briella sipped the soup, doing her best to pretend it wasn't flavorless mush, and offered a small smile in thanks.

Nora frowned. Finn was the chef between the two of them, and Nora only knew how to make stews, as that was what she usually made with the hunting parties back in Sorudi. Simple, quick, filling, and capable of being a mixture of many ingredients, they were practical. They ate in silence and when the food was gone; they sat in that silence for a long while, watching the crackling flames.

"Finn might have stayed the night in the city. I'll set up our bedrolls." Nora stood, wincing at the sharp pain.

"Are you hurt still?" Briella stood with her, resting a hand on Nora's rib cage.

"A little. The nymph did a great job, but I'm still banged up."

Briella ran her hand across Nora's side and frowned. "It's a dislocated rib. Easy enough to fix. Go ahead and lie on your stomach."

Nora frowned. "What are you going to do?"

"I won't hit you with a frying pan if that's what you're worried about." Briella grinned mischievously and motioned for Nora to lie down.

Nora lowered herself onto her stomach, heat rising to her cheeks as Briella straddled Nora's back.

"Can I lift your shirt?" Briella's voice was low as she spoke and when Nora nodded she pulled up Nora's shirt and gasped quietly.

Nora had forgotten about the scars from the beatings she had endured under Adelle. People rarely saw them, and those who did knew they were there and had little reaction to them. She reddened and moved to pull her shirt down in embarrassment.

"No, don't. It's ok." Briella ran her hands over the scars, pressing firmly on Nora's back to find the source of the pain. She murmured to herself as she worked, moving slowly and deliberately, working out knots that Nora didn't realize she had. "When I say breathe, I want you to let out a long breath and completely empty your lungs. I will push down hard then, but you must wait to breathe in until I stop pushing."

Briella pushed firmly on Nora's back four times, and a loud cracking noise sounded each time. When she was finished, she helped Nora to her feet.

"You'll be sore, but it'll get better. Just keep stretching. We do this all the time in Madrall. When you're out riding for weeks on end, you dislocate a limb or two and you have to know how to pop it back in quickly." Briella moved away awkwardly.

"Thanks." Nora took a deep breath in and didn't feel the sharp sting, although her side was still sore. Nora was relieved that Briella didn't mention the scars and she finished setting up their small camp while Briella watched her silently.

Since they only had one bedroll to share between the two of them, Nora laid it open and took Finn's blanket to put over them. They huddled close together as Nora filled the uncomfortable silence by explaining everything they had been through so far. She described in great detail the city of Theren and the way the streets glowed in the moonlight. She described Luna and the children, careful to leave out the part about the underground tunnels leading to the castle itself, and told Briella all about their encounter with Hanna and the dragon descending on them.

Briella listened quietly, not reacting, but intent on absorbing every word.

"It sounds like you've had quite the adventure. I might not have believed this tale a few months ago, serapins and dragons, but it seems as if we are in a new age."

A tear slowly slid down Briella's face and she turned to face Nora, their faces inches from each other. Nora brushed the tear away and Briella smiled, sniffling.

"In Madrall, the women hold much of the power. I was raised to rule over people, to plan and organize and strategize. I was raised to protect my people at any cost," Briella looked away from Nora's gaze looking up at the trees above, "It's my duty to my people for me to go back, but I can't. I'm a coward."

"You are no coward, Briella. That much I know to be true." Nora turned and reached for her bag, pulling out the bracelet that she had carried all this way to return to Briella. "This is yours."

Briella stared at it in disbelief, sitting up and sliding it on her wrist. "How did you—?" She stopped, her mouth falling open in shock and she looked at Nora. "You—"

"I had hoped I could give it back to you." Nora absently pushed a loose curl from Briella's face as she spoke. "You fought against a dragon, you survived in a dungeon, and despite being exhausted and malnourished you helped up escape. Coward is not a word I would use to describe you."

Tears fell down Briella's face.

"Thank you." She whispered. "Horace?"

"Alive when I last saw him. Tulee, our head of staff, took care of him."

"Thank the gods," Briella muttered, falling back onto the ground. She allowed the tears to fall freely, the relief she felt at knowing Horace was alive showing in the way her body relaxed against the ground. "You came all this way. You *saved* me. Thank you."

Nora smiled and shrugged. "I will admit I didn't think you'd still be alive."

Briella laughed and shook her head. She turned to look up at the stars, saying nothing for a long moment. She pointed up at the sky. "That's Draco."

Nora followed Briella's gaze wordlessly, exhausted at the thought of dragons.

"Madrall used to be the pinnacle of dragon slaying, but long before that, there were many families who worshiped dragons. Did you know that?" Briella kept her gaze on the sky. "Now dragons are an enemy to be extinguished, but there are some who remember the old stories of the beginning of the world, and honor the bonds dragons had with all people of this world. I brought that up to Talon. Little good that did me."

They heard footsteps and Nora extinguished the fire, pulling them both back into the roots of a massive tree and holding her sword out in front of them.

"Nora? Nora, it's me." Finn's voice was a faint whisper, and Nora saw he was holding out a glowing orb before him to light his way.

Leaning over to relight the fire, she called him towards them and he came closer, clearly relieved to have found them.

He shook his head when Nora offered him some stew, patting his full belly and pretending to be ashamed of himself.

"Gathering intel is hard work, especially when everyone wants to feed you the entire time." He grinned when Nora glared at him and spilled out his bag to show her the food he collected. "I do so enjoy that you camped so far into the forest without, I don't know, leaving behind any kind of note. It was really fun tracking the pair of you in the dark."

He handed each of them a golden pear, and Briella groaned with pleasure as she took a bite.

"Did you learn anything?" Nora asked impatiently.

"Yes—and it's a lot. So, no interrupting." He cocked an eyebrow at Nora, who nodded, clearly annoyed. "The city talks of nothing other than how Brutus killed the dragon. Apparently, he barely did so as all of his men were killed. Lots of talk about how he tried desperately to defend them. A single boat returned from Adoya–only one hundred men survived. They were mysteriously found on the beach, in a perfect line, and although every single boat was destroyed by the dragon, this one somehow came away without a single burn." He smiled, wordlessly acknowledging the nymph's hand in returning the men.

"The word is that the mage destroyed the dragon, and when he went to find the princess, a dangerous group who might have been conspiring with the dragon to begin with attacked him. They took the princess and are working with a rebellion to overthrow the kingdom, and the king is coming to the city to gather troops to help find her. People are fired up over this, Nora. If he wanted the people to feel connected to him through the princess, he succeeded." Finn leaned back on his elbows and looked up at the moon that peeked out from the branches of the trees. "And your sister was there leading the charge."

Nora and Briella sat in a stunned silence as they digested the information.

"We did what the prince asked everyone to do!" Nora stood up and began pacing around the fire frantically. "What was Larissa doing?"

"She had soldiers with her, well-armed soldiers. She's searching for her." He pointed to Briella and dropped his hand quickly. "Sorry."

Briella worked to rebuild the fire, saying nothing as she listened to their information.

Finn thought for a moment, eyeing Briella as she stared into the fire. "The nymph said Goghbuldor and I am not in the habit of going against great beings. We could be there in maybe two days. Three, if something stupid happens."

"You could take me back to the city. If I just show up there, no one will keep looking for you. I could tell them what really happened," Briella murmured.

"It sounds good in theory, but how do you think Brutus would feel about you telling everyone he lied about killing the dragon?" Finn shook his head. "No, I think it's safe to say that you being alive is not really part of his plan."

Briella frowned and returned her gaze to the fire.

"What does he want, then?" Nora asked. "The king told Larissa to watch him, even they don't trust him."

"I don't know. Land and riches don't seem like his game–he has plenty of both." Finn shrugged.

Briella looked at the opal that hung around Nora's neck and sighed. "The heart."

Finn followed her gaze and looked at the opal. "What?"

"The dragon's heart. There are many stories around the opal hearts of the dragons and what power they contain; it's hard to say what's fact and what's legend. However, it's been suspected that they have extreme capabilities. Why else would the king keep the dragon's heart from Zeta?"

"Zeta?" Nora flushed when the two looked at her in stunned surprise. The stories of dragons were something she knew little about.

"Your mother never told you about Zeta?" Finn murmured, his shock clear on his face.

"Zeta was one of the dragons at the beginning of time. The legends say she was one of Draco's mates, and she broke away from the celestials when the dragons of the world were killed off and the dragon worshippers of Ospas were under attack. Her wrath was unlike anything experienced before, and she swore to continue on until every human outside of Ospas was dead at her hand. She was stopped by King Alexander and—"

"Lady Adelle Dupont." Finn finished, his eyes fixed on Nora.

"Yes—she wielded magic unlike anything anyone had ever seen before. No one person had ever slain a dragon on their own, and a celestial beyond that. It was impossible. After Zeta was slain, King Alexander took the heart and had it forged into his scepter. It's likely in the hands of Adrian now, and possesses incredible power." Briella rifled through Finn's bag and pulled out another pear. "It's why Sorudi was chosen for this union. Although she lost her magic, she is still revered in Madrall."

Nora sat in silence for a long moment, her mind racing. Her mother had killed a celestial being. She thought back to the serapin, to the bursts of magic Nora herself had displayed. She remembered Talon's dying words, 'It's you. It's you.'

Nora looked at Finn, who seemed to be deep in thought and then returned her attention to Briella. "Lady Adelle—she's my mother."

Briella stared at Nora, exhaustion clear on her face. "Why am I not surprised?"

They sat silently together for a long time, all three of their minds racing with possibilities and trying to make sense of all of this information. Nora pulled the opal necklace out and held it in front of her, surveying it before gazing up at the Draco constellation above her. A flash of fiery red lit up inside of the opal and it warmed in her hands. She quickly tucked the necklace away and said nothing to the others as the opal cooled against her skin.

She thought of the prophecy and stared up at the constellation. The Child of Draco, the supposed end or beginning of the world. Nora felt her stomach twist. She did not believe in destiny or fate; she did not believe in prophecies or that she could in her life ever be part of one. There was no doubt now that something had awoken inside of her, something greater than anything she could ever imagine. Something that seemed to bubble under the surface, waiting for her to drop her guard so it could overtake her. This was supposed to have been a chance at a future, and as time passed, she could feel whatever dream of a future being stripped away little by little.

18

Chapter Eighteen

When they awoke the next morning, they made quick work of their campsite, careful to leave as little disturbance as possible in case they were being tracked, and the three of them set off towards Goghbuldor.

"Are you sure it's a good idea for me to be near Ospas?" Briella asked quietly as they hiked up the mountain. "Madrall and Ospas aren't exactly on good terms."

"Goghbuldor is considered a border city and isn't exactly in allegiance to either Troque or Ospas and until we get more information, I believe these witches are your only chance. Unless you want to risk your life with Brutus." They all knew the risks of bringing the princess of dragon slayers anywhere near a country of dragon worshippers, but it seemed to be their only option.

"Maybe there will be options for you there," Nora said encouragingly. "You could even have a new life there if you choose. No one knows you by sight alone."

Briella said nothing, her eyes fixed on Finn's back as they continued on. They had to stop often; despite the nymph's magic healing them, they were still recovering from their ordeals and Briella especially became winded easily.

The forest eventually gave way to the sweeping plains that made up much of the southern coastline. The city of Stillmere sat at the edge of the forest; beyond it lay the small fishing town of Collette and the still-smoldering ruins of Gaboga, once one of the largest ports in Troque. Nora could not tell from this distance if there was anything left of the city, but she felt her stomach lurch at the wide expanse that separated them from the mountains where the city of witches could be found.

"We need to rest in Stillmere. We can't force ourselves to continue on like this." Finn squinted ahead at the city. His voice was ragged and strained.

"You're right. I wonder if these medallions will do us any good still?" Nora reached to pull out her medallion from a small side pocket in her bag and furrowed her brow. "It's gone." Her fingers felt something small and round in the pocket and she reached further to remove it from the bag.

Finn pulled out his bag and dug through it, pulling out a small polished black stone where the medallion once was. Nora pulled out an identical stone where the medallion had once been and inspected it.

It looks just like the ones Phillandra gave me, she thought, grasping the stone in the hand that was marked by the nymph. A cool feeling poured through her arm and she sighed, tucking it back into the pocket.

"I think the nymph did something to them." She shrugged. "Maybe there was something wrong with them."

"Where did you get these medallions?" Briella asked, sitting down on a large boulder overlooking Stillmere.

"They were given to everyone who signed up to find you to guarantee lodging. I'm sure news of the dragon hasn't reached Stillmere yet and we could've used–" Finn stopped when Briella cleared her throat.

"They were likely tracked. I doubt the king would give them out to anyone without enchanting them to make sure he gets what's his. Do you have anything else from the king?"

Nora shook her head and looked at Finn, who rolled his eyes and shook his head.

"Good. Do either of you have any money for a room?" Briella asked.

"I have enough for a night." Finn tossed a coin purse to Nora and winked. "It's not riches beyond my wildest dreams, but I nicked this off of Talon. I figured it's the least the bastard could do."

Nora nodded in agreement and poured the coins into her hand, counting them carefully. "This should be enough for a room and some supplies. We need more salves and bandages."

They made their way slowly down the hill to Stillmere and as they approached, Finn used what little magic he had left to change Briella's fiery red hair to buttery yellow, the red barely visible in small wisps framing Briella's face. He looked at Nora and shrugged, placing a hat on her head and tucking her hair into it.

"She gets new hair and I get a hat?" Nora frowned.

"The red hair stands out." Finn grinned, but the exhaustion showed in his eyes.

The city was full of refugees from Gaboga, but they could still secure two rooms. Finn took a room by himself, not consulting the two of them, and trudged upstairs, waving a hand dismissively at Nora when she protested.

"I don't want to see either of you until breakfast tomorrow." He grumbled, shutting the door behind him.

"That was rude," Nora grumbled.

"I don't know that I blame him. He looks much worse off than either of us." Briella looked out the windows of the inn and smiled. "There's a festival outside. I think I'll go check it out."

"We should rest." Nora pleaded.

"I've never experienced this country before and I would very much like to see some of the local customs. I don't want to miss anything." She smiled and walked out the door.

Nora frowned after her and followed, grumbling as she did so. She was tired too, perhaps more tired than she allowed the other two to see. She felt the bubbling presence of magic sitting within her ever since she killed Talon and holding it back took all of her energy.

Briella smiled when she saw Nora and offered her hand, squeezing Nora's when she accepted it. They walked through the vendors, Briella stopping to watch puppet shows and to taste samples of skewered meats and lavender-infused lemonades that made her groan with pleasure. Nora laughed and purchased a cup for each of them, following Briella to a bench at the edge of the square.

"It's nice when you laugh. I feel like I'm not about to get my knuckles rapped by the schoolmistress." Briella teased, giving Nora a light shove.

Nora smiled and shook her head. "I guess it's been a while since I felt like I could truly relax. My mother's estate was a cage of sorts, but Tulee always made sure I had time to live. Long hunting trips, days in the forest, walks into town to see festivals much like this."

"Would Tulee come with you?" Briella asked, sipping her lemonade.

Nora's face softened at Tulee's name coming from Briella's mouth. "Sometimes. She mostly covered for me, so I could slip away unnoticed."

"I'm glad you had someone looking out for you. Tulee sounds amazing."

Nora smiled and nodded, taking a few sips of her lemonade. Music rang through the courtyard and they watched the townspeople dance and sing in companionable silence. The closeness of Briella beside her sent chills through Nora's body that she both loved and feared deeply.

"Here, try this." Briella tore off a piece of her flatbread covered in honeyed meat and spices and held it to Nora's mouth.

Nora allowed Briella to feed it to her, laughing uncomfortably as she had never allowed anyone to feed her before, and spitting some of the food out onto her shirt.

"You're supposed to eat it!" Briella cried out, instinctively catching the food and then dropping it on the floor in disgust.

"I'm not used to being fed!" Nora laughed, tearing off another piece and popping it into her mouth. "It's delicious if that means anything to you."

"I was trying to be very suave and cool." Briella teased, pretending to pout and taking another bite of her food. "It's so fucking good." The food muffled her voice, and she groaned again with the pleasure of eating good food.

"That was so suave." Nora teased, reaching for another piece and laughing when Briella swatted her hand.

"I was giving you a taste, not the whole thing!" Briella glared at Nora, handing her another piece and devouring the rest.

"Suave, cool, and generous." They returned their attention to the crowd before them, smiling at the children who squealed and danced between their parents, the young couples that held each other tightly, and the people haggling with vendors over overpriced trinkets. "Can I ask you something?" Nora's voice cut through the silence and she smiled when Briella jumped slightly, brought back to herself from some far-off thought.

"Of course."

"Why don't you want to marry the prince? I mean, I can understand not wanting to be forced into it. But this feels like there's more to it than that."

Briella nodded and looked out over the crowd. "There's always more." She smiled softly. "Madrall has been growing more unstable as my father's health has declined. Our people are suffering and they look to their king for answers that he cannot give. King Alexander had been propositioning my father for my hand ever since I was born, and he knew it was only a matter of time before my father would have to agree. My hand, our military, our intel on Ospas, and the power commanded by the royal family of Madrall in exchange for financial security for our people. A payment was received before I even left Madrall, enough gold and resources to lift everyone out of poverty." Briella met

Nora's gaze. "A marriage to me would lead to a genocide of the people of Ospas."

Nora nodded, looking back out at the festival before them.

"I've also heard Adrian is a cad and an absolute ass, so there's that."

Nora chuckled, "I will say from the moment I met you back at the DuPont estate, I could not imagine you married to someone like him."

"And what kind of someone would you picture me shackling myself to for life?"

Nora thought for a moment, licking the sugar from the lemonade from her lips. "They'd have to have a thick skull if you keep with your passion for attacking people with frying pans."

Briella shoved Nora, laughing as she did so.

"I'm sorry, okay! I panicked!"

"It's a strange way to panic, but I accept your apology," Nora teased.

"It is strange how much time has passed since then. I remember you holding my hands. You were so determined to not let go. You, this person who had only known me for a few brief moments." Briella smiled at Nora, her face reddening slightly. "It's strange when you meet someone you feel instantly connected to. From the moment you served me food at the DuPont estate, I knew I just wanted to be near you, to know you. And then you came for me."

Nora's heart beat wildly in her chest. She had felt the same way that night, but to hear it was returned was entirely unexpected. She looked at Briella's lips, full and slightly parted, and then into her eyes as Briella's eyes searched Nora's for some silent confirmation. Briella smiled and Nora released a long slow breath, the moment stretching out between them as if they existed in a different plane of time altogether.

Nora smiled, rising as the sound of music filled the air. She bowed deeply to the princess, extending her hand towards her and flashing her a wicked grin. "May I have this dance?"

Briella cocked a brow at Nora and smiled. "I thought you'd never ask."

She accepted Nora's outstretched hand and squealed when Nora pulled her out into the square with her. Nora held Briella's hand in hers and slid her other hand around Briella's waist to the small of her back, pulling Briella in closer. They spun around, following the rhythm of the music as if they were the only people in the world. Briella threw her head back when Nora dipped her, smiling into the sunshine as she did so, and wrapped an arm around Nora's neck as she was brought upright. Their noses were almost touching, and Nora felt her face redden. Briella blushed in response, and Nora smiled down at her despite her own nervousness.

The music slowed, and they followed, their large sweeping movements replaced by smaller, slower turns. Nora brought Briella closer, her heart racing as she heard Briella's breath catch at the movement.

"Is this ok?" Nora's voice was low as she spoke.

Briella nodded, and Nora could see goosebumps rising on Briella's skin as she allowed Nora to lead her through the dance. Others slowly joined them and Nora smiled as Briella looked around, beaming at the couples.

"This is nice." She whispered.

Nora continued to lead Briella through the motions. She wished they could stay in this moment forever, pushing thoughts of destiny and duty away, and enjoying each other's company and touch.

"Nora—"

"The Child of Draco!" a voice shouted from behind them.

Nora stiffened. The panic she knew all too well rose within her and she closed her eyes to will herself to stay calm; to not ruin this moment.

Briella placed her hand over Nora's heart and smiled when Nora opened her eyes and looked down at her.

"You are safe," Briella said firmly.

Nora felt the heaviness subside slightly, looking up to find whoever had shouted.

"The prophecy comes to life! Come, gather, hear my warning!"

Nora could see a wagon with a large screen displaying an impressive shadow puppet show. The crowd moved closer, some couples retreating into the darker shadows of the space for privacy. Briella led Nora to a fountain where they could sit at the edge comfortably, close enough to hear but far enough that Nora didn't feel the speaker bearing down on her.

"I have traveled this land far and wide, and I have seen the signs of the prophecy come to life. The Child of Draco is among us, perhaps at this very moment!" A large mustached man in a colorful outfit grinned before puffing out an enormous ball of fire into the sky. It evaporated instantly, and the children sitting up front squealed with delight.

"The prophecy is clear." A man whispered, turning the lights down on the front of his caravan and allowing the light at the back to display the shadow puppets clearly. The shadow of a dragon swooped around the screen, sending streams of fire into villages below. Mothers held their children close as they whimpered. Some older men cursed at the sight. "Beneath the stars where ancients sleep, a child wakes from shadows deep."

Nora felt her breath catch in her chest. Those were the same words from her dream, the same uttered by Talon. She watched as the screen grew dark and was lit by tiny twinkling stars. They shifted through the screen until they formed the constellation of Draco. Some people cursed, some said a silent prayer to the gods.

"With power vast to tear the land, and reforge it gently at their hand." The stars gave way to the vision of a flower that bloomed into the seal of the royal family. It hovered a moment and then split into a map of Madrall, Torque, and Ospas. "Four hidden relics in silent embrace, a scepter golden, a king's disgrace."

Fire seemed to consume the screen and when it subsided, the head of a dragon looked to be reciting the next lines. "Cloak of stars veils the darkest night, crown of opals guiding wrong from right. Celestial armor forged in skies above, by the father both hated and beloved."

Briella leaned over to Nora. "Some of these rhymes leave much to be desired." She murmured, smiling when Nora shook her head.

"The heavens watch as paths converge, the Child of Draco shall emerge." The dragon head erupted into millions of butterflies and the silhouette of a woman and a man back to back sat alone on the stage. "In Divergence comes the endless night, their choice shall bear the heaven's might."

The last words echoed in her mind, and a shiver ran up Nora's spine. She held the opal through her shirt, closing her eyes and steadying her breathing. Briella wrapped an arm around Nora's shoulders and rose, guiding Nora back towards the inn.

"Talon—"

Nora nodded, willing them to move faster through the crowd. "Can we go?"

"Yes, let's go rest." Briella whispered.

Nora noticed the blonde had mostly faded into a light strawberry color and she motioned to her hair, raising her eyebrows.

"Shit, well now we really have to go," Briella hissed, ripping off Nora's hat and tucking her hair up into it.

They made their way to their room. Two small beds and a roaring fire greeted them. Nora kicked off her boots, and Briella followed suit. Nora collapsed into the billowing quilts on her own bed, wrapping herself in the soft fabric and groaning with pleasure.

"You should really clean yourself up!" Briella laughed, slipping off her dirty clothes until all she wore were her undergarments.

Nora glanced at the ceiling, her face reddening slightly.

"Oh, come now. I will remind you that you were completely nude after you killed Talon, and it was I who dressed you."

Nora shook her head. "I was happy pretending my clothes materialized onto my body."

Briella laughed, picking up a sponge from a soapy basin and washing the dirt and grime from her body. She hummed as she washed, Nora stealing glances occasionally and returning her gaze to the ceiling.

"Please tell me you aren't going to sleep like that." Briella was standing over Nora, her face directly above Nora's and small drops of water dripping from her hair. "I don't want to tell you that you're smelling, but you should consider it."

Nora sat up, grabbing another sponge and bringing the wash basin onto the ground behind her bed to cover her exposed body.

"You are ridiculous." Briella grumbled, braiding her hair back from her face and falling back onto the bed. "My gods, I needed that."

Nora worked quickly to wash herself, placing her dirty clothing in a heap on the floor and slipping into a nightshirt. She moved to the fireplace and worked on a fire while Briella gathered their clothes and summoned one of the inn's staff members to wash them, tossing her some extra coins to have them done by the morning. They returned to their beds, watching the crackling fire and feeling the heaviness of sleep falling over them.

"Should we have brought some food to Finn?" Nora asked, sitting up to look at Briella when she was answered with silence. She smiled when she saw the princess was already asleep and decided Finn could figure out dinner for himself.

The next morning, they woke feeling refreshed and Nora marveled at what a difference sleeping in a bed made, let alone ordering breakfast and not finding and cooking it themselves. They set out to resupply, Nora careful to not bring up the events from the night before and blushing as Briella's looks lingered a little longer than she was used to. It felt to Nora that there was a shift between them, but what that meant, she was unsure. All Nora knew was that Briella deserved to decide about her life, and that Nora would help Briella to whatever end.

When they finished shopping, they set off towards Kinimar Forest, the divide between these two warring lands. The plains were a wide expanse of land that offered little in the way of cover, but they did their best to avoid the main roads as they moved towards the forest. The ocean roared in the distance and Nora felt as if she had seen enough ocean water to last her a lifetime. When they passed Gaboga, they saw the devastation the dragon had wrecked upon the city. Every building had been burned to the ground. All that stood were small sections of brick walls and the occasional pillar that indicated where a street had been. The ground was thick with ash and charred itself. Nora had never seen the earth burnt so deeply. She wondered if this was what Sorudi looked like now, and felt her stomach churn at the thought.

They continued on for three days, stopping only to camp, until they reached the edge of the Kinimar forest. The mountain rose above them and Nora craned her neck as she considered how difficult this hike would be.

"When we get to Goghbuldor, I refuse to leave for a week," Briella grumbled as she looked up into the misty mountainside. "I don't know if I can do this."

Nora ran a hand across Briella's back and nodded silently. "You can, because we will help you."

Finn raised his eyebrows at Nora from behind Briella, grinning excitedly. Nora glared at him and removed her hand from Briella's shoulder, clearing her throat hastily. Briella whipped around to glare at Finn, and he chuckled quietly before leading the way into the mountain. Nora felt the opals on her chest grow warm and wondered what it meant. Were these opals warming a sign that she was on the right path, or was she walking straight to her doom? She tried to push the thought from her mind, but as they went up the mountain, she felt the bubbling feeling within her writhe and the urgency to reach Goghbuldor increased with every step.

19

Chapter Nineteen

Briella became winded easily, needing to sit and rest frequently; Finn experienced regular migraines and was more irritable than usual; and Nora could feel her joints protesting against any strenuous uphill climbing they did, but they pressed on until midday when it seemed they physically couldn't push themselves any farther.

"I can't–" Briella's eyes were wet with frustrated tears and she collapsed onto the ground.

Finn let out an exasperated sigh and dropped his bags. He marched off for a moment, looking down the path they came until he calmed down enough to return. "We obviously have to rest. We're going to push ourselves too hard. Let's stop for today and make camp, but tomorrow we *have* to push further."

Briella let out a frustrated groan and laid back on the ground, covering her face with her hands. They were filthy, hungry, and exhausted.

"I'm going to find some food," Nora announced after a long period of silence. Briella grunted in acceptance. Finn worked to build a fire and gave Nora no acknowledgment. Nora was grateful for any opportunity to walk off into the forest alone.

She walked a short way until she came to a clearing where large stones sat upright in a circle. She smiled at the sight: a witch's circle. It was no surprise that in these mountains, where witches lived away from all kingdoms, there would be circles. They were sacred places to the witches who used them. During the solstices, when their magic was at its most powerful, they would gather sometimes in the hundreds at these sacred sites. Their magic was tied to the earth in a way that mages feared. Mage magic came from the Celestials themselves, controlled and limited. However, witches pulled directly from an immeasurable source.

Nora could feel invisible energy radiating from the stones and sat down at the base of one nearest to her and allowed herself to feel the comforting energy pouring from it. Immediately, she felt a calm overtake her; it was as if the veil between humanity and the unseen was drawn back here and she was surrounded with a calm humming of the universe itself.

Her mind drifted towards her sister and of the king's reward, and then to the image of Briella sleeping in their room back in Stillmere. Nora was supposed to save her and hand her over to Adrian, take her gold, and go. She knew in her heart this was no longer possible–it had never really been possible. She remembered watching Briella walk up the aisle towards Adrian in Sorudi, and how she had wanted to grab her and run off with her in the forest. How the princess's eyes seem to plead for help as they locked on Nora. She wondered what would have happened if she would have allowed the impulse to take over her. Where would they be now? Would they have burned up in the forest, free and gone forever? Would Nora ever know of this prophecy, and would this power within her have ever awakened? Nora had tried to tuck morality away into the far edges of her mind and keep nothing but her own future in view, but she knew that Briella's fate was intrinsically linked to her own. She thought of her mother. Was she mourning for her? No, she was happy to be rid of her. To be rid of the child that she was cursed with.

I hate myself, Nora thought.

Tears escaped her closed eyes, and she allowed them to fall, unable to summon the energy to hide them from the world. She was alone, she could cry.

The humming intensified around her, and she relaxed, allowing it to envelop her. Maybe she could die here. Briella could find a new life, Finn could go back to Luna, and Nora will never be forced to make any choices, never have to hurt anyone ever again. She imagined the Serapin, locked away by a world that hated her and now sat frozen in stone at Nora's hand. She thought of Talon gasping for life before her, a life that she took from him, and she willed herself to sleep. Vines grew up her arms, and the earth seemed to sink beneath her.

Child, you must not sleep. Not here, A woman's voice crooned from within her.

She shuddered at the magnitude of the voice but tried to push it from her mind. She belonged here. The world was better off with her here.

There is still much to do, the voice continued.

"I'm so *tired*," Nora whispered.

Yes, and you will rest. But not today. Go back. The voice commanded. *Go back. You are not done. Now!*

The energy surrounding her pushed her away, and she wanted to scream, to protest her ejection from this magnificent force. It was the most peace–the most *belonging*–she ever felt, and she was being pushed away from it, *rejected* by it.

"No," she murmured, "Please. Please let me rest."

Wake up!

Nora woke up to Briella shaking her as Finn dumped a pot of cold water over her head. She jumped up with a start, shouting as she did so and pushing them off of her.

"What the hell—"

"You did that thing again," Finn said absently, walking off back into the direction of their camp.

"'That thing'? What do you mean 'that thing'? This happened before?" Briella looked from Nora to Finn, exhausted. "Is this another revelation? Please tell me we aren't discovering something else."

Nora ran her fingers through her wet hair, glaring at Finn and releasing a long sigh.

"It's just a thing where she dreams and you think she's dead and spirits or whatever the hell they are communing with her, and then she wakes up and acts like you're overreacting," Finn shouted back through the darkness.

"Well–I'm glad you're ok. Let's go." Briella held out her hand and Nora accepted, allowing Briella to guide her through the forest.

"I'm sorry. I just wanted to rest for a minute; it's only happened once before."

"It's ok, I know you are still figuring this out. I came looking for you and I thought you died. Finn seemed so unbothered it scared me even more. I'm glad to know that it was at least because he's seen this happen before." She smiled, wiping a tear from her eyes.

"Are you crying?"

"No! I was just shaken up. I'm not crying."

Nora nodded, looking at the ground as they continued to walk after Finn.

"I just like I don't want you to *die*, ok?"

Nora nodded again, thankful for the darkness to hide her embarrassment, and they continued on until they reached the campsite. Finn set the pot down on the fire and filled it with meat he had likely been preparing when Briella alerted him.

"It's not one of your fucking stews," Finn grumbled. "I can't stand to eat any more stew."

"Ok." Nora murmured, sitting opposite Finn and keeping her gaze fixed on the ground.

"How about we don't walk off that far in the future, ok? We're tired enough without having to search for you."

"Ok—"

"If you want some time to yourself, just say so next time, or we'll leave you. I'm not responsible for you, you know that right I'm helping you and I'm with you, but I'm not going to—"

"Finn," Nora interrupted as his voice grew more heated and frantic, "I'm sorry. I won't do that again."

He glared at her for a long moment and nodded, stirring the meat and running a hand over his face. Briella cleared her throat awkwardly, leaning forward to smell the food.

"It smells—"

"If you say anything other than delicious, you will not be eating." Finn snapped.

Briella rolled her eyes. "Delicious."

"That's nice." Finn sighed, leaning back against a tree and closing his eyes. "We aren't far from Goghbuldor. We should keep going after we eat. I don't want to sleep on the ground again."

Nora looked at Briella, who opened her mouth to protest and shook her head slowly as she dished up their food.

"That sounds like a great idea." Nora's voice was firm, and she kept her eyes on Briella. Nora had spent enough time with Finn to know he was exhausted and likely overrun with worry. Watching everything happen to Nora and being unable to do anything about it weighed heavily on him; it was in his nature to have the answers. Now, with so much uncertainty and change, it seemed there were no answers.

Briella glared from Nora to Finn and accepted her portion of the food, grumbling to herself as she ate. They finished their food and Finn poured water on the fire before leading the way up the steep trail towards Goghbuldor. The forest was dryer here than it had been outside of Balon; the brush was thick and clung to their clothes with long barbs and the pines that surrounded them kept their greenery high in their canopy. A stream wound its way down the mountain with greenery growing brightly from the rushing water breaking up the dry forest floor.

Finn's steps grew heavier as they moved, his breath was ragged and he seemed to be willing himself up the mountain on little more than determination to eventually make it to a bed. Briella and Nora exchanged worried glances as they followed him, careful not to speak their concerns out loud.

As they continued into a more dense section of the forest, Nora furrowed her brow. She saw signs of people passing through this space recently; broken twigs and footprints along the soggy river bank, but her stomach twisted as observation gave way to recognition.

"Finn—"

"Don't say it." Finn's words were a groan as he threw his bag onto the forest floor and collapsed against a tree. "Please just don't say it."

Briella looked from Nora to Finn, her eyes full of confusion.

"Let's rest here. We'll get some firewood." Nora signaled for Briella to follow, leaving Finn to rest.

Briella said nothing as they walked, following Nora carefully until they entered the same clearing with a stone circle Nora had slept in earlier that day.

"We went in a circle." Briella's voice was devoid of emotion as she recognized the place.

Nora nodded.

"He's exhausted—he can't go any further." Briella ran her fingers against one of the stone pillars, bringing her hand back quickly in surprise as something flashed at her fingertips.

"This place is full of powerful magic. We'd be better off not touching these stones." Nora sat on a stone beside the river and dipped her hands into the cool water, drinking deeply. The stone circle sat at the edge of a meadow and she noticed a small hut only a short distance away. Smoke billowed from the chimney and it looked as if it had always been there, although Nora had not noticed it until that exact moment.

"Do you see that house?"

Briella frowned and looked in the direction Nora was pointing.

"Yes, but it wasn't there a moment ago." Briella moved back to Nora slowly. "We should go back to Finn."

"And leave before dinner?" A voice called from behind them.

Nora jumped to her feet, whirling around to place herself between the speaker and Briella, drawing two daggers from her hips. The person standing on the other side of the river held her hands up in surrender, her eyes flashing between Briella and Nora. She was much older, with long grey hair pulled back from her face and falling almost to the backs of her knees. She wore a simple white cotton dress and her deeply wrinkled face crinkled into a mischievous smile.

"You can put those away, *dearie*. I won't hurt you so long as you don't try to hurt me."

"You appear out of nowhere in the middle of the forest and you expect us to just take your word that you're not going to harm us?" Nora spat, stepping closer to Briella and surveying the area around them.

"I would hardly say I appeared out of nowhere." The woman's voice dripped with irritation and she moved further down the river to a small footbridge that Nora swore wasn't there moments before and crossed the river, her hands still up in surrender. "I was heading back to my cabin and noticed you on my way. If anyone should be untrusting it's me; what would three adventurers be doing so far up the mountain? Haven't you heard there are witches about?"

"Three? How do you—?"

The sound of footsteps stopped Nora and she looked up to see Finn making his way through the trees towards them. He looked exhausted but somehow less than before, offering Nora a weak smile as he followed the witch across the footbridge.

"Nora, Briella, meet Louella, one of the head witches of Goghbuldor." He grinned at Louella. "Louella, meet Nora and Briella, two pains in my ass."

Nora lowered her daggers slightly. "You know her?"

"Goghbuldor? Are we—?"

"Goghbuldor is a ways off yet, but we will need to continue on quickly. Your friend has completely depleted his magic and will not be able to go on much longer without magical healing." Louella turned from the group and moved towards her cabin, maneuvering around the stone circle and disappearing within.

"How do you know her?" Nora asked.

"I've dealt with the witches of Goghbuldor a few times when they have come to the elven settlements. Luna lived with them for a time I believe, but that's not important. What is important is that we are safe and that we get help."

"Are you going to be ok?" Nora moved towards him, grabbing his pack and sliding it onto her own back.

Finn smiled. "I'll be fine, but she's right. I'm a half-elf which means half the magic. I've needed someone to heal my magic since Sue City, but I have always been able to restore it on my own. Usually, I don't have to use my magic this much." He shrugged and followed Louella towards the cabin.

Nora had wondered how long Finn could continue on the way he had. Her experience with magic from her watching Larissa over the years had shown Nora that although it was extremely helpful, magic could not be relied on entirely. Basic healing and small spells here and there were nothing, but once when Larissa healed a stable boy's broken leg she had been confined to bed for a week. It was the reason so many mages were kept in There; it took massive amounts of magical ability to protect the royal family. Magic was normally used only when necessary and left the user so vulnerable that it was rarely worth it to use high magic. She knew that elven magic was entirely different from human magic, and half-elf magic was an even greater mystery, but everything has its limitations.

Louella emerged from the cabin now wearing breeches and a loose shirt, a large pack on her back, and her hair tucked up into her wide-brimmed hat.

"We need to hurry. If we leave now we should reach the city before morning."

Finn followed Louella closely, stopping frequently at her request and allowing her to pump small amounts of healing magic into his body. Briella and Nora hung back a little ways, looking around for signs of other witches lurking in the forest.

"We went this direction and were brought back to the stone circle—is the mountain magicked?" Briella asked the witch during one of the frequent healing stops.

"You can't reach Goghbuldor unless you know where it is. It's how we have been able to maintain independence from your gracious *king* all these years." Louella ran her hand against Finn's forehead and smiled. "Normally it will just keep you moving in circles until you give up and continue down the mountain; I am the one who brought you back to the stones." She looked at Nora for a long moment, her eyes moving from Nora's face to the small lump beneath her shirt made by the opal dragon heart that rested against her skin.

Nora straightened. The dragon's heart pulsed with warmth and Louella smiled.

"You were almost taken by the stones, young one."

Nora remembered the desire to sleep that had pulled her away from herself, how the heaviness of this adventure settled over her weighing her down against the stone.

"We were told to come to Goghbuldor." Her voice shook slightly. "We were told you would have answers—"

"We're here." Louella's voice cut through Nora's and she pointed up the hill behind them.

A lantern beamed above and Nora swore it hadn't been there before, and they pushed themselves to climb the steep hillside. Briella and Nora each took one of Finn's arms and helped him move slowly as the thick brush gave way to stone steps. They emerged from the tree line into a large grassy meadow with a white-stone archway welcoming them into the city of witches. Briella let out an exhausted sob of relief, Finn pulled both women into a tight embrace at the sight of the city before them

The houses were an assortment of wooden homes twisted around large boulders or made from stone as if risen from the mountain itself. At the center of the town was a large fountain surrounded by twisting garden paths that seemed to fill in much of the space in Goghbuldor.

"This place is beautiful," Briella whispered as they walked through the archway into the main courtyard.

Louella removed her hat, sending her long silver hair cascading down her back, and moved towards another older woman who slowly walked towards them. The other woman had similarly silver hair and a softer, kinder face than Louella's sharp features.

"I brought some interesting company."

"I'll say." The woman chuckled, moving towards Nora, Finn, and Briella. She extended her hand to them and smiled. "Yada Greeves, what brings you to Goghbuldor?"

Nora reached for Yada's extended hand and felt her magic rippling up her arm. She tried to let go, but the witch kept a firm hold on her.

"What brings you?" She asked again.

Nora tried to protest and found she couldn't speak. She looked at Finn and Briella, who seemed unaware anything was happening, staring at the witch before them as if frozen in time.

"They're fine, and you will be too once you answer my questions. Don't try to lie, I'll know."

"We're—we were told to come here."

"By who? Why?"

Nora glared at the witch. "A nymph on the Adoya Isles. She said you can help me figure out what's wrong with me."

Yada cocked her head to one side, looking Nora up and down silently. "The Adoya Isles?" She looked from Nora to Finn and her eyes stopped on Briella, lingering for a moment before returning to Nora. She raised her hand and pressed it against the lump on Nora's chest caused by the opal resting beneath her shirt. It warmed under her touch and the woman smiled.

The magic hold released and Nora gasped, pulling back from the witch.

"What the hell was that about?" Nora shouted, ignoring Briella and Finn's confused expressions.

"I am the head witch of this city, and it is my job to know who is here and *why*." Yada moved back towards a massive building that seemed to sit at the center of the city square. "Come, we have much to discuss."

Nora opened her mouth to protest and stopped when Finn raised a hand.

"Nora, this is one of those times when you shut your mouth and do as you are told." Finn tried to keep his voice light, but his exhaustion was evident in his eyes.

They followed Yada and Louella wordlessly through the courtyard towards the large building. A small hut sat separate from the rest, an overgrown and long-forgotten garden twisting around a short fence and up the sides of the house. It stood out in stark contrast to the well-maintained buildings throughout the city, and Nora felt something within it calling to her; something familiar and yet entirely separate from herself.

"Here we are!"

Yada's voice brought Nora back into herself and she looked towards the two witches, noticing Louella's eyes watching her closely. A shiver ran up Nora's spine and she followed Yada into the large building. The first door opened up into a massive room with long tables set for feeding large groups of people. The space was warm and inviting, a fire blazed at the far end of the room and staff bustled through the space placing platters of food on the tables.

"This is where we eat our meals. Most of the city comes here to eat, although it's not mandatory. It's a great way to keep connected to the needs of the city." Yada swelled with pride as she moved up the stairs.

"This reminds me of—"

"Madrall?" Louella interjected.

The princess reddened, nodding slowly.

"You have nothing to fear here, Your Highness," Yada said as they moved to the second floor. "You were told to come here and you were right to do so. We operate independently of Ospas and Troque, although I tend to favor Ospas as of late. You are welcome here as long as you wish."

Briella nodded, grabbing Nora's hand and squeezing gently for support. Nora's face reddened slightly and she offered Briella a kind smile. They stepped into a circular room with large, floor-to-ceiling windows looking out over the gardens behind the building towards the winding city. In the far distance, they could see the mountain dropping down sharply towards cliffs that overlooked the sea. From this vantage point, Nora could see much of Ospas including what she assumed to be its capital city of Bankona.

"Amazing," Briella whispered breathlessly beside Nora.

Finn lay on a small daybed beside a fireplace, closing his eyes as he allowed Louella to assess him. Yada began to brew some tea, waving her hand over the set and causing the kettle to instantly steam. She poured a cup for Briella and Nora, taking her cup and settling into one of the overstuffed chairs beside the windows.

"I'll come up here and look at these windows for hours sometimes," Yada said cheerfully. "When the air is clear enough, I can see Theren."

"A good way to keep an eye on things." Briella grabbed her cup and sat across from the witch.

"Precisely." Yada winked, turning her attention to Louella. "Should I call for some assistance?"

"Yes, get Lettie." Louella's voice was low and she did not look away from Finn as she continued to wave her hands over him.

Yada flicked her wrist and a piece of parchment rose into the air, folding itself into the shape of a bird and soaring from the room.

Nora's mouth fell open and she raised her eyebrows at Briella who stared back at her with the same stunned expression.

"It's just hat tricks, darlings. You've seen much greater magic than *that*." Yada chuckled, sipping her tea. "Do not worry about your friend. He's depleted but not beyond what we have seen before. I'd help myself but healing is not my expertise."

"What is your expertise?" Nora asked as she took her tea and sat beside Briella.

"Divination. Useful, but unfortunately very limiting. My power is nothing compared to Louella, but she has spent too much time at the stone circle lately and just needs a little support." Yada's eyes warmed as she looked at Louella, and she rose just before a witch entered the room. "Louella needs your assistance with some magic mending."

The woman stared at Nora, her mouth fell open and her eyes widened in shock.

"Lettie, it is rude to stare." Yada's voice was calm, but stern. "This is Nora and Briella. The gentleman in need of your attention is Finn."

"Nora?"

"Yes, did she stutter?" Louella snapped. "Get over here and make yourself useful!"

Lettie cleared her throat, nodding and hurrying towards Louella. She stole one last look at Nora before focusing on Finn, her magic glowing with a strange familiarity that caused Nora to furrow her brow.

"I'm sorry for that. You bear a striking resemblance to someone who used to live here." Yada smiled, her eyes looking back out the window towards Theren.

Nora shifted uncomfortably, eyeing Briella who shrugged awkwardly. They watched as the two witches worked, Louella focusing on Finn's head and Lettie working on the area of his cheat, weaving their hands in a steady rhythm and muttering in unison as their magic weaved through him. Gradually, their movements began to slow and their tense muscles relaxed. Finn opened his eyes, color returned to his face and he slowly eased himself upright.

"You will need to refrain from using magic for a while—a month at least if not longer. If you allow yourself to become this depleted again you could lose it forever." Louella turned to Lettie. "Thank you for your assistance."

Lettie nodded and stood, her gaze drifting back to Nora. "Yada."

"Yes, child. I know."

Lettie's confused expression was replaced with a glare as she stared down at Nora. Nora met her glare, turning up her chin slightly to meet the woman's gaze.

Lettie let out a surprised laugh, looking back at Louella who watched her carefully.

"Please tell me you aren't going to let her stay here." Lettie turned her glare to Yada.

"Lettie."

"We know what her type wants! They don't seek balance, they want power."

Nora stood, confusion and anger bubbling within her. "They? Excuse me, but who the *hell* do you think you are?"

"Nora, sit down," Yada said calmly. "You of all people should know that we are not our parents." Yada's eyes met Lettie's and they lingered in silence for a long moment.

Nora felt heat rise in her face. *We are not our parents*—they knew who she was, and it meant something to them. She opened her mouth just as a young man burst into the room.

"Royal mages—on their way!" He shouted breathlessly. "They've burst through the walls!"

"That's impossible! How could they even find us?" Louella stood, her eyes full of rage.

"Hanna is with them." The boy sat when Lettie summoned him a chair, accepting a cup of tea from Yada.

"For fucks sake that girl can't leave well enough alone," Louella shouted, grabbing a cloak and hurrying towards the door with Yada. She turned and glared at Finn and Nora, "Are you just going to stand there?!"

Nora looked from Lettie to Louella and followed the witched out of the room, Briella and Finn trailing closely behind. The rooms that once hosted bustling staff were now eerily quiet as they moved down the stairs, through the dining hall, and into a kitchen where Yada lifted a trap door. Louella hurried through the door followed by Lettie, Yada urged them to hurry as she looked out the window.

They disappeared into the darkness below, moving quickly until they came into a large stone chamber. Nora saw much of the staff and many townspeople huddled together, their eyes wide with fear.

"Where are they?" Lettie asked one of the young witches.

"At the tavern now, they are demanding we help them find the lost princess." The witch reported, her eyes shifting to Yada. "They asked for you specifically. Hanna and her men are there, and there's a simulai as well."

Simulai were the projections of powerful magic wielders. Able to perform much of the magic of their physical forms, simulai were a safer alternative to sending mages into dangerous environments. Nora had seen a simulai of Brutus once when a small group of rebels had tried to take the castle when she was a child. The simulai had appeared in the main square in Sorudi, projecting the execution of the rebel leaders for all to see and leaving the stains of their blood burned into the stone in town squares all across Troque as a reminder of their King's might.

Yada smiled softly. "We will take care of them—we have the daughter of the dragon slayer on our side."

Everyone turned and stared at Nora who straightened nervously at the attention.

"What—?"

"There is no *time* for this." Louella snapped. "We must *hurry*."

Lettie nodded in agreement, turning to face Yada. "The tunnels will lead us to the tavern."

"I will go ahead and meet them in the square to distract them." Yada's hand rose into the air to silence the protest of the witches around her. "If we keep them waiting too long they will burn this city down to find me. Troque is not known for its mercy." She turned to move back towards the stairs and looked back at Nora before disappearing up the stairs.

20

Chapter Twenty

The tunnels reminded Nora of the system in Theren, and she noticed the similar engravings of runes tucked away in corners to guide the way. She wondered if this was where Luna learned the secrets of the underground of Theren as they hurried through the space. The tunnel opened up into an alcove behind a gargoyle statue that overlooked a sweeping garden. Nora could see the tavern ahead, and the figures of people moving through the space.

"Ok, Nora and I will come around the back, Finn can take the roof and give us some arrow cover. There's a staircase just behind here that will get you up there unnoticed. Louella will cover Yada and you," Lettie frowned at the princess, "need to stay hidden. Otherwise, this entire thing is for nothing."

"Absolutely not." Briella crossed her arms and cocked an eyebrow at the witch. She looked from Nora to Finn, her brow furrowing when they did not object. "I am not being locked away in the basement."

Finn cleared his throat, "Well, they are after you—"

"No."

Louella glared at the princess and rolled her eyes. "Stubborn ass. You're just going to get in the way."

"Give me a weapon and I won't be taken easily." Briella's voice dripped with venom as she glared at Lettie.

Nora remembered how Briella fought against the dragon and smiled. Lettie handed Briella a sword and a small dagger, less annoyed by the princesses' stubbornness than Louella.

Briella nodded and moved beside Louella, glaring at Nora and Finn as she did so. Finn slid behind the building and disappeared into the darkness, not waiting for permission from the witches.

Lettie turned to Nora. "Follow me, and be quiet."

Nora nodded, and she followed Lettie as they snaked their way through the hedges and positioned themselves behind the tavern. When Nora looked back she couldn't see any sign of Louella or Briella, and her heart raced as she tried to calm her nerves.

"We just need to wait for Yada to show up," Lettie whispered.

Nora nodded, focusing on steadying her breathing. Lettie turned to face her, her brow furrowing with concern.

"Are you alright?"

"Y-yes. Sorry. I get these panics but they pass."

Briella placed her hands on Nora's temples. "Tell me three things you can smell."

"What?"

"Three things you can smell."

"Uh, pines. Lavender—magic."

"Good. Three things you can see."

"You, the tavern, the garden." The panic was beginning to slow and Lettie continued to press on Nora's temples gently.

"Three things you like to eat." Lettie smiled softly.

"That I like to—"

"Yes eat. Now."

"Pumpkin bread, fire wraps, and pork buns."

Lettie smiled. "Better?"

Her heart still fluttered, but the panic passed. Nora nodded, releasing a slow breath.

"Your mother used to get those." Lettie turned back towards the front of the tavern, her eyes tracking the people pacing outside.

"They make me weak." Nora moved beside Lettie, following her gaze. "My mother hates weakness; I can't imagine her experiencing them."

Lettie studied Nora's face. "They don't make you weak. You feel things, Nora. You feel the earth shifting beneath you and you feel the magic connecting us all, and you feel the largeness of the world around us. Just like we must rest when we are tired, like we must eat when we're hungry, you must stop and manage these attacks when they rise. You are no weaker than anyone else." She returned her attention to the courtyard. "And she got them frequently. I guided Adelle through these attacks all of our childhood."

Nora was unsure of what to say. They sat in silence for a long moment, the air between them thick with unspoken words.

"She birthed me, but she is no mother to me. She cast me out for not having magic; she hurt me all of my life because I was not what she wanted." Nora turned to meet Lettie's gaze. "I am nothing like Adelle."

Lettie smiled. "Nothing like the Adelle you know, but you are much like the one I once knew. They are two different people, Nora. Changed by forces you and I will never understand, but the person she was is not something for you to be ashamed to be connected to. You look just like her."

"I am here as you requested!" Yada's voice brought them back into the moment and they turned to see her standing at the center of the square, her arms extended in surrender.

Nora sat in shock as the same Hanna they had encountered on their journey pulled back her hood, stepping towards the witch. Beside her stood a cloaked figure Nora assumed was the simulai, power surging from its body as it moved towards Yada.

"Hanna, you fool." Yada shook her head in disappointment.

As the words left her mouth Hanna sent a stream of magic hurling toward Yada, and Nora watched as lightning burst from where Louella and Briella were hiding, exploding through Hannah's magic and sending her falling back toward the tavern. The simulai turned in the direction of the magic burst just as an arrow flew from the rooftops and lodged itself into one of Hana's men's legs. He howled in pain, bringing the simulai's attention toward the rooftop.

Yada sent a stream of golden light towards one of the men, wrapping around him and binding him to the spot.

The simulai whispered and Finn was suddenly thrown to the ground as the man who had been restrained by Yada broke free of his binding. The simulai sent a stream of magic biding Yada as the man moved closer to Finn.

"Oi Hanna, it's that bastard with the necklace!"

Nora peered through the darkness, her eyes scanning the area desperately until she made out the form of Finn lying on the ground. He tugged at some invisible force that was wrapped around his throat; his face was red with the lack of oxygen.

"I want this one." Hanna sneered, moving towards him. "Where is your little friend? She must be around here somewhere."

Finn gasped, clawing at the ground and hurling a rock at Hanna that hit her square in the face.

"You idiot!" She shrieked, holding her face. "You are going to regret—"

"Silence." The cloaked figure's voice echoed around them, and Nora froze as she recognized the voice. The mage pulled her hood back, revealing the dark curls and vibrant green eyes of Nora's sister. "You are not an easy man to catch, Finn Meadows."

Finn's eyes widened as he recognized her, and he smiled.

"Oh man, this is so fucked." He choked out, closing his eyes.

"Where is your accomplice? And the princess?"

"In what order do you want that information?"

Larissa extended her arms and sent Finn flying high into the air, his body contorting in pain as a scream erupted from him.

"I am not playing your games. Tell me where they are or die. I can rip the secrets from your corpse."

Nora stared at her sister in disbelief. Larissa was not cruel; this could not be her sister.

"Tell me, now!" She commanded, smiling as Finn continued to scream.

"Follow me," Lettie whispered, slipping into the tavern window and holding it open for Nora to follow. Lettie scanned the room and smiled. Sitting at the center was a glowing green orb, magic poured out from it and filled the space. "We need to destroy it; it's what's anchoring the simulai."

Lettie began to pour magic into it, the glass exterior cracking, and Nora could hear Larissa's screams emitting from the orb.

"The orb!" Hanna screamed, running into the building.

Nora grabbed her sword, ready to defend Lettie as she worked on the orb. Flashes of magic lit up the room from outside and Nora saw Briella and Louella rushing forward through one of the windows just as Hanna burst into the room.

Nora lunged towards Hanna, her blade narrowly missing Hanna's stomach as she lept out of the way.

She looked from the witch to Nora and a wicked grin spread across her face. "There you are."

The simulai whirled around, sending magic like a bolt of lightning rocketing through the open door toward Lettie. Lettie dove back, her body colliding with Hanna, and when she looked down at the woman beneath her, she reared back and punched her hard in the mouth before she could call out for help. Hanna went unconscious, blood oozing from her broken teeth, and Nora grabbed the orb, magic coursing through her body as she touched it.

Nora gritted her teeth and lept out of the window she entered with the orb, throwing it to the ground and causing the cracks to spread throughout its surface. Louella and Yada rushed towards Nora as Briella drove her sword into one of the large men who were now hurrying towards the orb. He screamed, rearing up at Briella, who slid easily out of the way. Nora could barely make out their shapes through the darkness, and she watched as Larissa's simulai lifted Finn's body into the air.

Finn's body hung limp; blood poured from his nose as power pulsed through him. Tears stung Nora's eyes as she realized that if he was alive, he likely would not be for long.

"He will be the first!" Larissa screamed, "This could all end now if you help us find the princess! All will be forgiven!"

Yada and Louella poured magic into the orb and Larissa screamed, her eyes searching desperately for the source of her pain.

Leave them, a man's voice thundered in her head.

I can't. Nora thought back, jumping as Larissa hurled another burst of magic at the tavern.

You are a fool. They will be the death of you. Leave them! The voice was deafening, and it took all of Nora's strength not to scream against the pain.

Nora opened her eyes and saw Louella staring at her from the hedges, eyes wide with fear. Her hand was stretched towards Nora and she was shouting at her, but her voice sounded as if it were miles away. Nora furrowed her brow at Louella and tried to speak, but the pain in her head erupted and she screamed.

"What in the hell is this?" Larissa shouted.

A purple light radiated from every pore in Nora's body. The very cells in her body were shifting, changing, and as the energy moved through her she stood, turning to face Larissa, who stepped back in horror.

"What are you?" She shrieked, sending a burst of magic at Nora.

Nora's eyes were now solid purple light, and a pulsating glow of purples and reds illuminated the veins under her skin. She walked towards Larissa and smiled as she backed away.

"A demon!" She cried, turning to run away.

"No." Nora's voice echoed all around them, her voice, but something different.

"What—" Larissa stared at Nora in disbelief. "No. This can't be!"

Nora moved towards Larissa, and as she did so the ground cracked at her feet. Chains of light erupted from the ground and bound Larissa down to the earth, her body hitting the ground and disappearing beneath the twisting chains of magic. Finn's body dropped towards the ground, stopping just short of impact as Nora extended an arm, catching him with her magic, and gently lowering him to the ground.

The two men ran to Hanna, one lifting her and the badly injured one firing an arrow at Nora. She turned her head as it approached, halting it in mid-air and splintering it before her eyes until nothing was left but the arrowhead. The arrowhead turned and pointed back at him. It launched through the air, running through his body and circling back to weave through him again. Nora stared at the man as the arrow weaved back and forth through him, his screams of pain and terror echoing through the night. The other man ran from the area, Hanna's limp body hanging from his arms.

The injured man tried to crawl away, his sobs for his friend echoing through the silent square. The arrowhead continued to weave through him, blood spurting from his body as he screamed.

"Please help me!" He screamed to a friend who was no longer there. "*Please.*"

Yada stepped in front of him, hands stretched out to shield him from Nora's magic. "End this now!" She commanded, her eyes wide with terror, but her feet planted firmly where she stood.

Nora stared at her. She could see Yada standing there. She wanted to stop, but it was as if she had lost complete control of her body. The hatred inside her demanded pain, wanting only to make that man suffer more, and to find his friend so they could suffer together. She didn't want him dead; she wanted him alive. But that wasn't Nora. That wasn't what she would ever want, it wasn't what she stood for. This wasn't what she was.

Or is it? The voice that filled her mind was her own, but different. It dripped with a rage Nora did not understand, but felt within her as if it was her own. *After everything I've been through. After everything she did to me. This is exactly what I am. I am not weak. I am strong.*

A form of a man materialized before Yada, radiating the same purple light that Nora had. She took a step back, fear and rage flooding her body. His features were indistinguishable; it was as if he was a void built of light in the shape of a man. His own purple glowing eyes and vicious smile were the only features she could make out.

"*Stop!*" He bellowed.

The light within her immediately vanished, and Nora fell into darkness.

Chapter Twenty-One

Nora faded in and out of consciousness, sometimes hearing the muffled voice of Yada, sometimes whispers and worried discussion between Finn and Briella. She was plagued with visions of Larissa and Tulee, sometimes badly burned, sometimes running away from a fire that was rapidly overtaking them. Sometimes these visions would shift into Finn and Briella. She would hear people calling her during these nightmares, but could not answer. When she finally woke, she saw Briella sleeping in a chair beside her with her head on Nora's bed.

"Nora?" a familiar voice whispered.

Nora turned to see Finn standing nearby. She saw a sudden flash of him suspended in their air, screaming and contorting under Larissa's magic, and she felt her stomach lurch at the memory.

"Everything's fine, I'm fine." He crooned, sitting beside her on the bed. He looked down at Briella, who was now stirring.

"Oh god, Nora!" she cried, jumping up and wrapping her arms around her neck.

Nora bristled with the sharp pain of being grabbed and offered Briella a reassuring smile when she jumped back, her face full of concern.

"Just a little sore." She promised. She looked both of them over and was surprised to find that they were entirely healthy and unharmed.

Briella even looked like she had tanned a little, and Finn didn't even give the slightest appearance of being injured. "How long have I been asleep?"

Briella looked at Finn nervously. "Not too long—erm, well, just a few weeks."

"*Weeks?*" Nora sat up and winced with pain. She leaned back in her bed and shook her head in disbelief. "How is that even possible?"

"Well, for a lot of it, you were still purple," Finn said flatly.

Nora stared at him, unsure of what to say. Memories came back in a flood, the mist, the purple light, the men she hurt—the figure that stopped her.

Briella shot Finn a warning look and grabbed Nora's hand. "What he's trying to say is you were in that other state until a few days ago. Yada wouldn't let anyone in here until it passed. She said you were too unpredictable."

Nora closed her eyes and shook her head slowly. "What happened?"

"Well, I couldn't see everything," Briella murmured. "The simulai was coming for you. This light came from within you. It was like what I saw with the dragon, except more concentrated. Before, it seemed like you exploded with light, this time you *were* the light." Briella pushed back some of Nora's hair absently. "One of Hanna's men shot at you and you kind of blew the arrow up? And well...you used it on him."

"Did he die?" Nora whispered.

"Nora, who cares if he died? If it were up to him, you'd be dead; we'd all be dead." Finn turned away from them, running his fingers through his hair in frustration.

Briella watched him for a moment before continuing. "He's alive. He nearly died, but Yada came out and stopped you. After she came out, the light became too bright to look at, so there's a lot of talk about what happened, but all I know for sure is that you dropped to the ground. I thought you died." Briella smiled as Nora squeezed her hand. "And then the witches brought you in here and wouldn't let us see you until the light faded from you. When we came on the first day...you looked so *tired*."

"I *am* tired," Nora murmured.

Finn cleared his throat and patted Briella on the back. "Well, if you two are quite done, Yada asked that we get her when you come to." Finn walked out of the room, whistling as he did so. He turned at the door and winked at Nora before disappearing down the hall.

"Are you hungry?" Briella sniffled.

"Starving." Nora sat up, forcing herself to release Briella's hand and smiling as Briella's face reddened slightly.

Briella moved a tray of food onto the bed and opened the lids, revealing a hot stew and some fresh bread. "Louella made this yesterday and put a spell over it so it would keep. She said she suspected you'd wake soon."

"Well, she suspected right." Nora took a bite of the stew and closed her eyes as the warm liquid entered her mouth.

The stew was enchanted; Nora could feel warm energy coursing through her body and groaned as aches and knots all over her body carefully released tension. She continued to eat, trying not to look at Briella, who watched her intently. When she could no longer bear it, she set the spoon down and glared at her friend.

"Why are you staring at me like that?"

Briella glared back, letting out an annoyed sigh. "Well, excuse me for being happy you're alive!"

"Were you worried you'd have no one to beat over the head with a frying pan?" Nora smiled as Briella rolled her eyes. She returned to her food, pretending not to notice Briella holding back a smile. "You can keep staring at me if you want."

"I don't want to." Briella looked out the window, holding a hand over her mouth to stifle a smile until she heard the door open. She stood quickly and glared at Nora before turning to Yada and Louella, who stood in the doorway. "She's all yours!"

Nora reached for Briella's hand before she walked away and squeezed it gently. "I am happy that you were here when I woke up. Thank you."

"You're welcome." Briella nodded to the witches before leaving the room, stealing one last glance at Nora before shutting the door.

Yada closed the door and moved towards Nora as Louella turned towards the door and began murmuring enchantments.

"Just a precaution—we don't need any eavesdroppers." Yada moved closer, sitting on the edge of Nora's bed. "You and your friends are safe here, but we have things to discuss."

Louella turned from the door and met Yada at Nora's bedside. "I have seen nothing like what you did that night. It is not of this world." Her eyes peered into Nora's, and Nora thought she saw a hint of fear.

"Sorry—I don't understand what's happening. I have had no magic. I was tested *vigorously*." Nora shifted in her bed until her feet were planted on the ground. She rested her elbows on her knees and looked hard at the ground until the queasiness in her stomach subsided.

"I would think signs of magic would be noticed by Adelle, even with her magic gone." Yada shook her head in disbelief. "She had a knack for finding power."

"You knew her," Nora murmured, remembering the conversation with Lettie.

"She grew up here. She learned much of her magic within this city." Yada smiled warmly as she spoke. "I have known her since she was a baby."

Louella moved towards the window, staring down at the city below. "Adelle would have *treasured* this kind of power. To have birthed a celestial—"

"A *what*?" Nora's eyes widened. "I am—there's no way. I know my parents, there's—"

"Do you? Do you know for certain? You know Adelle is your mother, she kept you around that is proof enough. She isn't the type to do things out of the goodness of her heart." The words caused Louella to curl her lip in disgust. "But do you know who your father is, Nora? Can you be certain it was the man who fathered your sister?"

Nora sat in stunned silence. She never thought about her father; he was an abstract figure, immortalized in tapestries throughout the home but never spoken of. Nora was told he died prior to Adelle even knowing she was with child, which in some way made whatever genetic connection they might have shared feel nonexistent.

"I have no reason to believe otherwise." She murmured.

"Do you remember the man who came to you when you were in your magicked state?" Yada stepped closer, lifting Nora's chin to look into her eyes. Yada's eyes were sad and weary from too little sleep.

Nora nodded.

Yada was silent for a long moment before she spoke. "He is a celestial being, Nora. He is Draco, the God of the Dragons."

Louella stood beside Yada. "He spoke a word we've been trying to translate ever since and, well, it caused you to slip into a coma of sorts. Whatever magic outburst you had was out of control, and likely would have consumed us all."

"Stop." Nora looked up at the puzzled faces of Yada and Louella. "The word–he said stop."

Louella threw her head back and let out a roar of laughter. "What? He just told you to stop?! We've been pouring through sacred texts and he just asked you to stop?" She continued laughing, wiping tears from her eyes. "I mean, that's the most direct thing the gods have ever said!"

"You would do well not to mock the gods when they are watching!" Yada hissed.

Louella cleared her throat and suppressed a smile. "Yes, you're right. I'm sorry, it's *too* good."

Yada rolled her eyes. "Nora, can you explain to me when you first felt this power?"

Nora took a deep breath, recalling the dragon attacking them with Luna, careful to leave out nothing. She told the two women about the serapin and the encounter with Talon. The two witches listened in silence, their faces unreadable.

"It's the prophecy. We can't deny that." Yada murmured.

Nora straightened. She wondered, she even dared to imagine that the prophecy was about her. But to hear someone say it so casually as if it were a well-known fact, was something else entirely.

"I don't know what the answer here is." Louella broke the silence, dropping herself into the chair Briella had been sitting in. "Part of me says we need to help you control this magic. If Draco had not interfered that night, it would have destroyed us all. But, there is a part of me that thinks it to be in the best interests of many for the magic to be bound. Despite your good intentions, immense power changes people. Whether you are a celestial being or not, this magic doesn't have a place in this world."

"What would it mean to bind it?" Nora asked quietly.

Yada shook her head at the idea. "It might not even be possible. And the consequences of trying to bind that kind of magic could mean losing our own, or worse. Besides, the gods are watching. I don't think it wise to meddle in gifts they have given for a reason."

Nora rotated her head to crack her neck and turned to face Yada. "Teach me how to control this. Teach me how to keep this power at bay, and then I can go back to living my life the way I always have. I do not want this power. I do not *desire* power."

"When you are feeling better, I will take you to the stones. You'll need all your strength; it seems that exhaustion plays a large role in the unpredictability of this power."

"And love." Yada smiled. "You seem to jump into this part of yourself when the ones you love are in danger. That is not so bad, Nora. Controlling your power is important. It's what us witches work towards daily, however hiding from it is not better. Remember that."

Louella made her way towards the door and withdrew her enchantments. "You need to rest. That magic has been active in you for far too long. Rest and eat Yada's food and when you are ready, I will help you." She opened the door and whistled softly.

It took several days for Nora to fully recover, and the entire time Briella and Finn took shifts sitting with her. Briella would stay with her during the night and most of the day, bringing her meals and reading the books she found in the library. Finn would force her to rest or tend to other duties, telling Nora all about life in Goghbuldor. Yada allowed them to stay in small homes near the village square and Finn spent much of his time doing odd jobs and helping wherever he could while Briella hiked around the mountainside with hunting parties.

"You seem much better. What's the plan when you're ready to get out of this room?" Finn asked Nora after several days of her staying awake for a longer period of time.

"I need to train with Louella. I'm finally feeling well enough and the sooner I get control of this—" Nora paused. She had not mentioned to either of them what the witches had said about Draco or the possibility of celestial power. Louella warned that if she did not want the title of celestial, it would be wise to keep that detail to herself. Still, she felt guilty withholding that from her friends who had been by her side constantly as she healed. "—this power. I can't continue having this consuming me."

"I'll say." Finn leaned back in his chair and grinned. "Purple isn't your color anyway."

"Oh, shut up." Nora stood up and reached her hands above her head to stretch her sore muscles. "If my captors will allow it, maybe we can go for a walk? I need to move."

Finn smiled. "Better to beg forgiveness than ask permission."

The sun was high in the sky, and the day was perfect. The square was bustling with activity as children played in a fountain and their parents shopped nearby. Nora hadn't realized how large the city was until now and wondered if they all were witches.

Finn led Nora to the run-down shack she had seen at the edge of town when they first arrived in Goghbuldor. As they approached

Nora could see Lettie just inside the gates, pulling out thorny brambles and throwing them into a pile outside of the fence.

"You're up!" Lettie sounded out of breath, and she pulled off gardening gloves before stepping out from the gated yard. "You look like you've been through hell and back."

"I feel like I've been through hell and back," Nora grumbled. "You live here?"

"Oh gods no." Lettie pointed to a small house on the opposite side of the square. "I live there with my sisters. This, well this was your mother's house."

Nora stiffened. The house was the smallest of all the homes she had seen in the village, set apart and without any of the ornate designs the other homes sported.

"She lived *here*?"

"Different from the grand estate she lives in now." Lettie sighed. "She built this house and everything in it with her own two hands. And a little magic."

"It's—not at all what I would expect."

Lettie smiled, "I felt the same when I visited her after she slayed Zeta. The estate, the clothes she wore; everything about her didn't fit with the person I knew." She sighed, patting Nora on the shoulder. "Everyone changes. I thought you might want to see it yourself, so I cleaned it up a bit. Hasn't been used in a long time but it looks much like it did the day she left."

Lettie walked toward her house across the square, leaving Nora and Finn in front of Adelle's house.

"Do you want to go inside?" Finn's voice was gentle.

"I don't know," Nora whispered. "I don't know what makes me angrier. The cruel person I know or the fact that there was another version of her that people loved. I don't know if I want to see the goodness that was in her."

Finn nodded slowly. "I can see that, but don't you think it'll eat you up if you never look?"

Nora smiled, "Probably."

"I know I'm looking when you're not around if you don't go in with me now." Finn teased.

Nora rolled her eyes and led the way through the gate, down the winding garden path into the house. Windows were strategically placed to make the most of the sunlight that filtered through the mountain forest, and the entire house centered around a large kitchen. Two small bedrooms flanked the kitchen, and a large, overgrown garden sat beside the back door leading from the kitchen directly to fresh herbs and vegetables. Small intricate designs depicting animals that lived on the mountain were burned into the door frames and window panes, and beautiful recreations of the celestial bodies burned into the ceiling and accented with shimmering silver paint. Bundles of dried herbs hung beside a dusty hearth and Nora let her fingers slide across the twine that tied them together.

"It's so beautiful," Nora said quietly.

"It reminds me of you." Finn draped an arm around Nora's shoulders and squeezed her gently. "I could see you in a place like this. You and your princess."

"Shut up." Nora laughed through tears. She had to admit she could see herself there too. The designs were similar to the ones she herself had scribbled on the walls of her small room in Sorudi; the way the home was just large enough to accomplish what it must but small and enough to be practical. Even the location of the house being close enough she was still in the town but far enough that she was not bound to it reminded Nora of the places she would frequent in the forest outside of her home.

"Let's go." She murmured, leading the way out of the house and shutting the door softly behind her.

Finn led her to the edge of a bluff, and they looked out at the valley below. It felt to Nora that she could see the entire world from there, and her eyes were drawn immediately toward the royal city of Theren, far off in the distance.

"We need to talk to Briella. It should be up to her where she goes from here." Finn whispered.

Nora nodded silently and continued to stare at the forest. Her mind flashed to the sound of the man she had tortured and she shook her head to clear the memory from her mind. Things were in motion, and like it or not, she was part of this. Ignoring the power within her would lead to destruction, that much she knew to be true.

"Maybe she'll choose to stay close to you?" Finn nudged Nora softly.

Nora smiled. "I don't know if that's safe, Finn. I don't know if she should be anywhere near me."

"Well, that's what Louella will help you with. We'll get this figured out. We aren't going anywhere." He wrapped an arm around Nora's shoulders and gave her a soft squeeze, resting his cheek on her head.

She looked up at the few stars twinkling into view as the sun began to set as if looking for a sign and was met with the same empty silence they had always given her.

"We should go back." She murmured, still looking up at the sky. "Briella will be angry if we aren't back for dinner."

22

Chapter Twenty-Two

After a few days of resting and a series of grueling examinations from Yada, Louella and Nora were finally given permission to dig deeper into this power. The stone circle that Louella wanted to bring Nora to was about a day's journey away and required them to pack for an extended stay of what Louella guessed would be a week.

"I am not saying that in a week's time we're going to crack this," Louella said sternly as they stood at the top of a hill overlooking the town. "If I am honest, it is ridiculous that you won't just live here. If I had years to work with you, we could really tap into that potential."

Nora slung her bag onto her back and shrugged. "It is of no concern to me how to harness this power. I only want to keep it at bay."

Louella shook her head in irritation and looked up at the sky. "Hopefully we have a little help from someone up there so we don't *kill ourselves in the process!*"

"Nora!" Briella cried out. "I thought you left!" She was panting hard from running up the hill to meet her.

"I wouldn't leave without saying goodbye." Nora smiled at Briella's flushed face.

Briella had changed so much in the time she spent in Goghbuldor. She had pushed herself hard into training with Finn and working with Yada on healing. Her once smooth, pale hands were now calloused and her skin deeply tanned. She was very much the picture of the woman Nora had first met so long ago, but somehow stronger, more capable. Nora's mind often drifted to thoughts of what a life would be like for them there, what it would be like to have a life with Briella.

Nora drew Briella into a tight embrace. The smell of the lavender oil Briella ran through her hair in the mornings filling her nostrils, "Where's—"

"Your favorite rogue?" Finn called from behind Briella. "I wanted to see you off, but I was much less enthusiastic than the princess here. I think she might have teleported up this damned hill."

"I'll see you guys in a week, then?" Nora shifted uncomfortably. She had gone her entire life without these two people, but now the thought of being separated from them seemed unimaginable.

"We will be plenty busy while you're gone," Finn assured her. "Once you get back, we can decide what to do next."

Briella nodded silently. Her eyes were soft, and a smile tugged at the edges of her mouth.

"So you're coming with us, then?" Nora asked.

Briella looked surprised at Nora's question. "Yes. I want to go wherever you go." Briella's face reddened at the words and she cleared her throat. "It's—not like I have a lot of other options."

"Nice save." Finn rolled his eyes and nudged her. Briella's face grew a deeper shade of scarlet, and she lowered her eyes.

"Well, touching as this is, I don't intend to be traveling in the dark." Louella gestured to the road ahead. "After you."

They made their way down the path and before they entered the forest that surrounded Goghbuldor, Nora turned back to see her friends still standing there, small silhouettes against a slowly brightening sky. She smiled, waved, and then followed Louella into the forest.

The pair made their way in companionable silence, stopping only when Louella saw a mushroom or herb she wanted to put in her bag. As the forest darkened, Nora felt a sense of familiarity with the area.

She furrowed her brow, trying to think of how she could remember this place. They stepped out into a moss-covered clearing and Nora realized where they were going.

The witch's circle. The very one she stumbled upon when she had walked away from Finn and Briella weeks before. A pang of guilt caused her stomach to lurch at the memory, and she took a deep breath before following Louella to its center. She watched silently as Louella placed the herbs and mushrooms she had been gathering at the foot of each stone as an offering of sorts.

"I've been her before." Nora felt that calm she felt before washing over her. "I feel so tired."

"Do not sleep within the circle," Louella said firmly. "The magic here is unpredictable. There is no telling what it would do to you while you were unconscious."

"When I was here, I heard a voice. It warned me not to sleep here."

Louella cocked an eyebrow. "So Draco has contacted you. Have you heard that voice before?"

"This one wasn't Draco, it was a woman. I have heard both of them before, but other than these few instances, I don't recognize them."

Louella nodded, continuing to assemble her offerings.

"These stones were assembled all across the land when the first magics were released upon the world. All our ancestors came here to worship, and some were given gifts from the celestial beings. The elves, witches, humans, and dwarves, all of them come from one people. After the gifts were given, those left without magic resented the gifted. Separated into far corners of the world, and treated as weapons for those without, the people with these gifts lost the upper hand." Louella ran her hand across one stone. "These used to be at the center of every town. The only ones that survive today are the ones here in the mountains, and a few within the Elven kingdoms that they concealed."

Nora sat in awe as Louella recounted the history. The concept that they were all from one common ancestry was something she never heard before. They were all so different outwardly, and after thousands of years of separation, they had all been made to believe that they were different in every sense of the word.

"There are three that we worship here in the mountains. This one is the farthest from the city, so naturally, it makes sense for us to explore your magic here. We don't want any mishaps." Louella pointed to a small hut on the opposite side of the clearing. "That is where we will be staying."

They made their way towards the hut and as Louella stepped outside of the boundary of the stone circle, Nora felt a presence push in around her. She hurried after Louella, turning to see the source of the pressure. She thought she saw for a second the silhouette of someone standing at the center of the circle, but when she blinked, the figure was gone.

"What was that?" She whispered.

Louella was silent for a long moment before she sighed and made her way into the hut. "I don't know, but we clearly won't be alone this week."

The first two days were spent in deep meditation, stopping only to get food and water and stretch their aching muscles. Louella insisted that control of magic began with control of the mind, encouraging Nora to find stillness within herself. At first, it was difficult, thoughts and nervous twitches bringing Nora from any sense of stillness, but as they continued to practice, she found herself able to push through them, allowing the thoughts of Celestials and Larissa to wash over her like a wave and spill past.

"True control of your mind takes years of daily practice; you have made great progress," Louella said when Nora had grown frustrated. "I think we have gone as far as we can to prepare."

On their third day at the stones, they woke before the sun to a humming coming from outside. The cracks in the walls of the small hut shone with a blue light, and Nora felt that the hut itself might collapse under the intensity. Louella behaved as if this was a natural way to begin her day, and Nora knew that something waited for them beyond. She stood and took some of the bread and cheese Louella laid out for them and ate quickly. When she finished, she turned around to see Louella completely naked before her.

"Louella!" she shouted, shielding her eyes. "What in the hell are you doing?"

Louella rolled her eyes. "We come to this place the way we were at birth. If you do not strip down, the stones will destroy your clothes. You might as well keep them nice here."

Nora frowned and undressed, following Louella out into the clearing where the light that had been permeating through the hut cascaded over them from the stones. She felt awkward moving through the space so exposed and resisted the urge to cover her body as she followed Louella toward the stones.

"Once we step inside the stones, the light will cease. We will have at that point entered the in-between realm; the veil between what we see and what is truly all around us. In theory, if your magic gets away from you, it will be easier to contain. I will admit that I have never tried this with someone with *celestial* magic, but here's hoping." Louella shrugged at Nora's shocked expression.

"We're relying on hope?" Nora hesitated as they approached the stones. "Louella. You don't know for certain if this is celestial magic, right? I understand it's something you've never seen before, but there is much of this world none of us knows."

Louella nodded in agreement and stopped at the edge of the stone circle. "I suppose anything is possible."

Nora grabbed Louella's extended hand. Together they stepped into the stone circle and the bright light that surrounded them was replaced with a soft blue glow that radiated from the ground around them. Beyond the stones, Nora could barely make out what appeared to be shadows of people and creatures moving around them. It was both euphoric and terrifying.

"What are those shapes?" Nora asked quietly.

"Whatever exists outside of the stones all over the world. When I placed our offering yesterday, it activated them. Anyone who approaches who isn't part of this offering cannot see the light. The ancient witches of the world placed that enchantment upon the surviving stone circles when the humans tore them down." Louella turned to face Nora. Her creased face was smooth, her worn eyes brightened. She looked much younger here and Nora, for the first time, saw the fierce figure she must have been earlier in her life.

"When we bring younglings here to begin their training, we tell them to draw from the magic well inside of them. It is a place that all gifted folk can feel within them, as tangible as a beating heart inside of all of us. You likely feel it within you but have lived with it dormant for so long you wouldn't know where it comes from. That is why you have no control; it spills out unchecked. Since the only way you seem to summon the power to you is through pain or fear of the ones you love being hurt, we will need to tap into that pain until you can find that well of magic within you." Louella placed her finger on one of the stones and traced the pattern of a rune that burned with a red light. She continued on moving from one rune to the next. "Your job is to feel where it comes from. When you see that it's beginning to rise within you, close your eyes and breathe. Focus only on where the magic is coming from."

"And if it consumes me again?" Nora watched as Louella continued to place her runes on the last of the large stones. "What if I'm stuck in that state again?"

Louella turned to look at her, standing in front of the final stone. "There is risk in everything you do, but not figuring this out is more dangerous than anything here." She motioned to the stones around them and smiled wryly. "These runes should help a little. Are you ready?"

Nora pursed her lips together and closed her eyes, taking in a deep breath. "Ready as I will ever be."

"That's good enough for me." Louella turned around and drew the final rune. As she did so she chanted. At first, it was quiet, then it seemed as if her voice was projected through each of the runes, surrounding the two of them in an echoing chamber. "Draco, dragon god. Be with us. Guide Nora so she might fulfill your desires."

Nora felt her chest tighten, and she went to shout to Louella to stop, that she didn't want that being to be there. Her voice stopped in her throat and she struggled against something preventing her from speaking. Louella turned to look at her and her eyes went wide, and Nora suddenly felt herself pull away, Louella's outreached hand the only thing she saw until a deafening darkness surrounded her. Light glowed from within her and slowly she found herself standing on what seemed to be a small island surrounded by billowing clouds of every color. They violently rolled through each other, crashing together and sending out a bright flash of lightning that rippled through the clouds.

"Hello, Nora." A familiar voice called behind her.

The air was thick like honey and slowed her movement as she turned to meet the person who addressed her. His skin was dark and his features handsome; he was much taller than her and clothed only in a fabric that tied around his waist, revealing a strong muscular figure. Nora noticed more than anything else his eyes–they were crystal blue, bright and wild. She had never seen eyes like those before except in herself and as much as she wished she could forget, in Talon as well.

The man grinned. "Are you frightened?"

"Yes," Nora whispered.

He stepped closer, examining her with a critical eye. "You are smaller than I thought you would be." He shrugged absently, coming so close that his nose nearly touched hers. She saw something flash in his eyes, the same strange flash that she had seen in Talon. "Do you know who I am?"

"Draco." She whispered.

She felt something tugging at her hair behind her and went to turn before Draco placed his hand on her cheek and shook his head slightly.

"She's trying to bring you back. I commanded her to leave, but she will not do so. She'll likely die trying, and it will be her own fault."

"Don't you dare let her die." Nora's voice was louder and echoed around them.

Draco cocked an eyebrow. "You care so much for these humans. You won't speak for yourself, but you will use your power to speak for them. How—touching? Stupid? Maybe both?"

Nora felt the familiar itching on her skin as the purple light radiated from her fingertips. She closed her eyes and breathed deeply, trying to find the well of magic that Louella told her she must find. Draco was silent as she did so, and although Nora wouldn't open her eyes to see, she could feel him watching her.

Come on, come on.

She felt her heartbeat slow to a normal pace, and she continued to focus on her breathing. With her eyes still shut, she saw a purple light shimmering before her. It seemed far away and glittered brightly against the darkness. The thunderous roar of clouds colliding surrounded her, and she opened her eyes in surprise, gasping for air as she did so.

"Very close." Draco frowned and raised his hand in the air. "Witch, if you do not stop this foolishness, you will die!" His calm voice was replaced by an angry roar.

"You can't have her!" Nora could barely make out Louella's voice over the thundering clouds. She felt the witch's power wrapping around her, pouring into her body and steadying her.

He tightened his hand into a fist, and Nora could hear Louella scream.

"What are you doing to her?" Nora shouted, sending lightning crashing through the space. Purple flame erupted from where the lightning hit the ground and spread through the space surrounding them. Nora could feel the energy building up within her, her eyes began to flash with light and her hair rose around her.

"You have so much *power!*" Draco shouted, throwing his head back in laughter. He looked half-crazed, and Nora felt panic rising within her. "You have nothing to fear, child. You need only take whatever it is you want in this world! Go on and lead your people; take control away from these humans and restore the natural order of things. We gifted magic to the chosen ones. It is them who should rule the earth with the weak beneath them where they belong."

"I don't want to take anything from anyone. I don't want any of this!" Nora shouted back. She felt the purple magic rising inside of her again and she fought hard to control her breathing, to do as Louella instructed her.

"I will bow to no one!" The same voice Nora had heard before, her own but different and wild with rage, spoke from within her. A fury bubbled up within her as more flashes of purple lightening radiated from her hands.

"Let it take you, Nora; be who it is you were born to be. Become the being that your mother and I created so long ago!" Draco commanded, standing up to his full height when Nora's tears fell from her face.

"No!" she shouted, shutting her eyes and trying to control her breathing. Pain erupted through her body and it felt almost as if something was trying to rip through her skin.

"No one, no man, will ever command me." The other voice shrieked.

Nora felt she might split in two, as if something within her was willing itself out through her own skin. Her skin tightened around her face, her skull felt as if it would burst with energy pouring from it. She cried out from the pain, trying desperately to gain control.

"Nora!" Louella's voice called out through the power, her magic a tether pulling her back into herself.

"Your mother came to me for power. She wanted to restore the balance of the world, or so she claimed. She offered me her body and in return, I gave her magic unlike anything she could have imagined.

But, as humans do, she became consumed with her power. She used my power to kill Zeta, to slay a celestial in my name." Nora opened her eyes and saw Draco smiling. The clouds were now swirling around them, steadily rotating faster and faster. "The arrogant bitch took the fiercest of all of my warriors, and she gave her heart to her king! Her heart decorates his scepter, and she believed I would *forget?*"

Nora watched as he rose from the ground slowly, his glowing eyes never breaking from her own.

"Her magic was stripped from her, and her king abandoned her. She came to me again, offering her body *again*. I came to her in the night and bedded her. I told her I would give her something unlike anything she could ever dream of, and I made good on my promise. I took what remained of her magic, the gift from us gods that she used to destroy us, and I left her to carry the child of prophecy. The Child of Draco."

Pain rose inside of Nora and she screamed as the well of purple light within her overflowed and poured through her veins. She felt the magic moving through her body, the heat in her skin intensifying as she drew the magic closer.

"I am not your pawn!" she bellowed, rising off the ground with him. Her voice sounded different, as it had when she saw Finn on that table near death. Her veins glowed with the electric light and she kept her eyes fixed on Draco, relishing in what seemed to be a panic on his face. "I will not be destroyed. I will not be used by you–or any-one–*ever*."

Nora heard the voice of Louella calling to her in the distance. The clouds whirled faster around her and Draco fell to the ground on his knees.

He looked up at her, shock and fear mixed on his face, and then slowly smiled up at her.

"You are *magnificent*. I will release you, but know this, Nora. The prophecy is in motion, and you cannot stop your own destiny."

"I don't believe in destiny." The voice form within her was cruel and dripping with venom.

Draco smirked, and he watched as she continued to rise into the air, slowly gaining speed until the world around her became blue starlight.

As the magic welled up inside of her, her magic flashed with brilliant light and Nora found herself as suddenly as she had left back in the grass of the stone circle, the blue light gone and birds singing in the distance. She lay there for a long moment before she felt she could move again, and then rushed around to find Louella. She was laying propped up against the stones, exhausted but alive.

"You—" Louella began before falling into a coughing fit.

Nora dragged Louella out of the circle, looking back at the stones that seemed as normal as they had when they arrived.

"Water," Louella croaked.

Nora ran inside the hut and grabbed a bowl and filled it from the pump outside. She watched the witch slowly drink, stopping occasionally to take a deep breath and continuing on. While she drank, Nora went inside and grabbed a blanket to cover Louella as the sun began to set.

"Is there anything else I can do?" Nora could not shield the desperation in her voice as she looked at the woman before her.

Louella smiled warmly. "I will be ok, I just need to rest. Four days of fighting a God will take the life right out of you."

"*Four days?*"

Louella nodded as she picked up a piece of meat. "Where you were, it likely was only moments. The gods do not experience time like we do on earth." She raised the now empty water bowl to Nora, who took it quickly and filled it again. "Thank you."

Nora watched as Louella regained some of her color. "I thought you would die."

"I am far too stubborn to die," Louella chuckled. "I see you found the magic inside of you. Good thing to; I don't know how much longer I could have held on."

"You never left. You stayed for me." Nora whispered.

"Yes, child. You will find in your life that many people will leave and hurt you, but even more will stand beside you." Louella groaned as she stood, bracing herself on Nora's shoulder. "We need to rest tonight and head home. I don't think we will enter those stones again."

They made their way into the hut with Nora bracing Louella as they walked. When Louella was seated safely on her cot, a deep ache released within Nora's body and she felt the strain of the days weighing on her.

"How much did you hear?" Exhaustion washed over Nora as she relaxed in her own cot.

Louella shrugged. "At first, not much. It was just the voice of Draco threatening me, and magic pouring down on me. I fought the entire time to keep the veil open so you could return, and he wanted it closed. I didn't know what he would do to you." She took another drink of her water and rested against the wall behind her. "But at some point, his focus lessened and I could make out much of what was said, mostly about you and your mother."

Nora began working on starting a fire in the hearth and bristled at Louella's words. She continued working, not looking back at the witch.

"It explains more than it doesn't. About my mother, about why she hated me so much." Nora sat back as the flame grew. "I don't really know what to say."

"Then say nothing," Louella said calmly. Nora looked up at her, eyes full of tears, and Louella smiled. "We have been through it; let's just worry about eating and resting. Tomorrow we will return to Goghbuldor, and then when you are ready, you can tell everyone whatever it is you want them to know. We came here to work on controlling your magic and you will need to continue to practice, of course, but we have gotten as far as we can here. That is all anyone needs to know." Louella laid back on her bed and closed her eyes. "As for your mother, serves her right for being such a power-hungry fool."

Nora watched as Louella fell into a deep sleep and then made her way to her own cot. The fire filled the room with warmth and Nora's mind raced against the exhaustion of her body that willed her to sleep.

As the stillness of the cabin enveloped her, Nora thought only of Adelle.

23

Chapter Twenty-Three

Nora and Louella traveled back to Goghbuldor in companionable silence, allowing each other to process what they went through privately. Nora appreciated the silence; she found so often in her life that sometimes words just aren't enough. She needed to think of what this information meant to her and, most importantly, what it would mean to Finn and Briella.

She knew in her heart she could not continue with them without sharing what she knew. Would the danger of being near her end their time together? Is there anyone who would risk being near someone touched by a celestial? She wondered what she would do in their position, and the thought made her feel sick to her stomach.

The sun was setting when they climbed the hill overlooking the city. The sky was tinged with the warm pinks and oranges of sunset, and Nora's legs felt heavier with each step.

Noticing Nora's hesitation, Louella linked her arm into Nora's and helped guide her forward. She offered Nora a compassionate smile and returned her gaze to the hilltop.

"It appears we have a welcome party."

Nora saw the silhouette of someone standing at the top of the hill. As they came closer, she could make out the person's features. Dress billowing in the wind, crimson hair loose and blowing all around her,

Briella stood as still as a statue, her expression one of relief. Nora stopped at the bottom of the hill, willing time to cease altogether. Tears escaped her eyes and when Louella released her arm and gave her a small push forward, Nora sprinted up the hill into Briella's tight embrace.

"You're home," Briella whispered into Nora's neck as she squeezed her close.

Nora's body shuddered with silent tears. *Home.* Briella was right, she was home, but not because she returned to Goghbuldor. Home was right there in Briella's arms, and Nora lost herself more to the pain of potentially losing her.

Louella chuckled as she made her way past them, aware that they were completely oblivious to her presence, and continued down into the city.

"Nora!" a familiar voice called up to them.

Nora pulled back from Briella and wiped her eyes in time to see Finn sprinting up the hillside. He rushed at her, leaping into the air when he got close enough and knocking her to the ground in a tight embrace.

"You could hurt her, you idiot!" Briella cried out angrily.

Finn helped Nora to her feet before offering Briella a sheepish smile. The familiarity of their presence was something Nora missed dearly.

"I told you she'd be back," Finn said solemnly.

"Of course I would come back," Nora said as she put an arm around Briella's shoulders.

"I knew in my heart you would, but this magic is so new to you. I didn't know in what state you'd be coming back in."

As the three made their way down the hill, Finn informed Nora of everything that had been going on while she was gone. He and Briella had been training nonstop, and they took the opportunity of Nora's absence to finish resupplying and doing some work around the city for money.

Nora listened intently, happy to hear everything they had been up to instead of recounting everything she went through. As they made their way through the twisting alleyways of the city, Nora smiled as Yada's house came into sight. Yada was standing at the doorstep with Louella, her smile warm but her eyes betraying her calm countenance with fear. Nora felt her stomach twist with shame. Louella came immediately to Yada to report what happened, and she still had yet to utter a word to her friends. And now the witch before her was afraid. This powerful being who commanded the entirety of a city full of magical beings was afraid because of Nora. She dropped her gaze and allowed herself to be ushered inside by her friends.

Making their way up the stairs, Finn continued on about how he contacted Luna and received letters from her and her children and how excited he was to see them again. Nora couldn't help but notice how silent Briella was as they made their way to their rooms. When she approached her door, Nora turned to look at her friends. She opened her mouth to speak and Briella put a hand to her lips, shaking her head gently.

"There will be time to talk tomorrow, Nora. Tonight, you must sleep." Briella's face was kind but stern, her eyebrows in their familiar stubborn position when she had made up her mind.

Finn cleared his throat and looked around awkwardly. "What's that?" He called down the hallway. "Oh, coming! Uh–I hear someone calling me. I'll be–I'll be a bit. Don't wait for me."

Briella rolled her eyes. "No one's calling, you fool. Just go so we don't have to suffer this pitiful performance." Finn winked and blew a kiss at Briella, who returned her attention to Nora. "Babysitting him has been exhausting. I don't know how you did it by yourself for so long."

They stood in silence for a long moment, Nora keenly aware of how close they were to each other and unsure of what to do or say.

"Good night, Nora. Please get some rest. We can go over everything tomorrow." Briella's voice was quiet, her eyes fixed on Nora as if expecting something.

Nora was exhausted and needed to sleep, but the thought of being parted from Briella made something in her stomach churn.

"Can you stay?" Nora whispered.

Briella inhaled deeply, never breaking eye contact. "If that is what you want."

"It is what I want," Nora answered quickly.

Briella's cheeks flushed, and she followed Nora into the bedroom. She shut the door behind them and slid her shawl off her shoulders, letting it fall to the floor. She reached for Nora's bags and slid them off of Nora carefully. Nora inhaled sharply at the feeling of Briella's fingertips grazing her neck as she pulled the bags from Nora's back.

"Thank you," She murmured. "I'm sure you want an explanation–"

Briella's gaze was steady as Nora turned to meet her eyes. "Nora. You have broken yourself over and over again. All I want from you is whatever you have to give at this moment. Nothing more."

Tears escaped Nora's eyes, and she quickly wiped them away, laughing awkwardly and turning away from Briella. "I hate crying."

"Yada had a hot bath drawn up for you in the washroom through that door." Briella pointed to the door across the bedroom. She moved to the wardrobe Yada stocked for Nora and pulled out two nightdresses, handing one to Nora and moving to the other side of the room to change, leaving Nora with some privacy to collect herself.

Nora went into the washroom and stripped her clothes from her body, slipping into the steaming water slowly and letting out a groan as her muscles relaxed for the first time in what seemed like months. The water was definitely enchanted, but Nora didn't mind. She allowed the magic to flow within her, warming her from the inside and melting away the scrapes and bruises she collected during her journey.

Nora opened an eye lazily as Briella came into the washroom, pulling over a stool and sitting beside the large copper tub. "If you sit up, I can help with your hair."

Nora obeyed, leaning forward slightly and closing her eyes as Briella poured the warm water over Nora's head and ran her fingers through her hair. Briella worked slowly and silently, frothing up lavender-scented soaps in Nora's hair and taking care to rinse it clean before grabbing a metal comb and slowly working it through the long, tangled tendrils.

"I don't mean to pull," Briella murmured.

"It doesn't hurt." Nora felt herself drifting off. The heaviness of too little sleep with the warmth of the water and Briella slowly combing her hair made staying awake feel impossible. She felt herself weave a little and then steadied herself against the side of the bath.

Briella chuckled. "I'm done here. Let's go to bed."

She stood and handed Nora a towel, her eyes sweeping over Nora's body quickly before turning to walk out of the washroom. Nora dried herself and changed into her night dress before following Briella into the bedroom. She slid into the bed beside Briella, bringing her head to rest on Briella's chest as Briella's arms wrapped around her.

"I've got you," Briella whispered as she ran her fingers through Nora's hair.

Nora let out a long sigh, her body at war with itself as it ached for sleep but longed for more of Briella's touch. Exhaustion fell over her like a thick wool blanket, fitting over every inch of her body until there was nothing left but to sleep. There in Briella's arms, Nora was home.

It felt to Nora that she only blinked, and then it was morning. When she woke, she was still in Briella's arms and she looked up to see Briella sleeping soundly. Nora carefully sat up and surveyed the room, shock, and embarrassment filling her as she saw a tray full of food for the two of them sitting on a small table at the foot of their bed.

Briella groaned as she stretched and smiled at Nora sleepily. "Is it to be breakfast in bed, then?" She eyed the food hungrily. "I'm starved."

They ate, Briella leaning slightly against Nora as they did. A knock sounded at the door and Briella groaned but did not move from Nora's side.

"Come in." Nora called out with a mouth full of eggs.

"Terrible table manners." Briella teased, refilling Nora's glass with orange juice from a pitcher.

Finn entered and looked from Nora to Briella, and a sheepish grin spread across his face. "I hope I'm interrupting something."

"Oh, shut it." Nora waved a hand dismissively, turning to her breakfast to avoid showing the reddening of her face.

Finn sat on the edge of Nora's bed and looked out the window absently. The three of them sat in an uncomfortable silence before Finn finally spoke.

"Nora, what happened out there?" Nora was silent, so he continued. "Louella and Yada have been locked in Yada's study ever since you arrived. While you were gone, there was a strange light. It was almost like a pillar of crystal light that reached into the heavens. It came from several locations in the forest, and you could even see other pillars in the valley."

Nora's eyes widened. She wondered if somehow, during their time in the stone circle, all the stone circles Louella told her about activated.

"If you aren't ready—" Briella began, her voice full of concern.

"No, I am. I have to tell you. Well, you deserve to know the full truth before you decide you want to go any further with me," Nora insisted.

She began by telling them what Yada and Louella told her when she woke from her first encounter with Draco, and what they suspected. She then recounted the entire experience in the stone circle, careful to leave no details out. Briella and Finn listened silently, their faces unreadable. It caught Nora off guard and they seemed mostly unsurprised; she thought they would be uncomfortable or shocked but they looked at her as if she was confirming something they already knew.

Nora cleared her throat nervously. "I suspect there is still much danger ahead of us."

"As if everything until now hasn't been dangerous." Finn stood up and stretched before smiling down at her. "Nora, I told you that you have a power I have never seen before. Unlike anything I have ever experienced. You being sired by a celestial being, well, it's not necessarily what I *expected when* we met, I'll admit. But it makes sense."

"I was worried it was a demon, so this is better news to me," Briella added casually.

"A demon?!" Nora shouted.

"Yes, well, I didn't know for sure. It was just a guess!" Briella snapped. "Hey, I stuck around, didn't I?"

Nora looked from Finn to Briella slowly. "Well, I was expecting more shock than this."

Briella sighed, shaking her head slightly. "Nora, you having celestial powers tracks."

"I am surprised about your mother. She was a mage for the king; her making deals with celestials, especially *Draco*, is treason. And then using that magic to kill Zeta, I don't know what she was thinking." Finn ran a hand through his hair as he spoke, eyeing Briella's clothes on the floor.

"It makes more sense than her losing her magic to grief." Nora shrugged.

Briella rested a hand on Nora's shoulder. "I have heard stories of mages who have reached out to celestials to bolster their power. Then to lose it in that way–that kind of rage can twist a person into something unrecognizable." Briella looked out the window and pursed her lips together. "My father was so kind until my mother died. I was very young and I have few memories of her, but she brought a light to him and took it with her when she was gone."

Briella sighed, shifting uncomfortably. Nora and Finn sat silently, allowing her the silence and space she needed before continuing.

"I was raised to kill the prince. As soon as my father thought it was a possibility, he began his plan. I trained day and night; I was never supposed to live past my wedding night. 'For our people', he would say. Horace was to escort me and make sure nothing prevented me from completing this mission, and then I met you and everything changed. I realize now that was his plan, and I do not carry that with me. Your mother has become something cruel and twisted, but that is on her."

Nora remembered hearing Briella and Horace talking the night she met them. *I have little forever left in me.* It all made sense to her now. The rushed wedding, the way Briella had behaved as if she was saying her last goodbyes to the world, the way her eyes pleaded for release as she walked down the aisle to her doom. Nora squeezed Briella's hand gently.

"I wish I would have run off with you that day," Nora murmured.

Briella sniffled, smiling as she wiped a tear. "Well then, we wouldn't be here right now, and I think this is right where we are supposed to be."

Nora silently looked from Briella to Finn. Any sane person would walk away from anyone being meddled with by celestials, but they didn't blink an eye. It felt to Nora as if they were relieved that she finally learned what they knew all along as if this was an expected truth. The casual acceptance of this darkness within her left her speechless.

"I will admit I had my suspicions pretty much since I met you. The way you lacked any auras intrigued me, but when we were attacked by Talon the first time, Luna was the one who suspected you might be the Child of Draco." Finn stood up and stretched, reaching for an apple from Nora's tray.

"And you still came with me." Nora shook her head.

"I am terribly nosey." Finn shrugged. "Part of me wanted to see for myself. Another part of me knew Malachi would want me to come."

"Would Malachi have allowed me to live?"

Finn stared at her for a long moment. "I believe Malachi would have loved you dearly as I have grown to love you, and that he would do whatever it took to help you."

Nora looked at Finn for a long moment, the tenderness in his eyes holding her own gaze. They were a family, the strangest family she had ever seen, but a family nonetheless.

Briella smiled at the two of them, standing and moving to gather her clothes.

"Let's go. The witches are expecting you."

24

Chapter Twenty-Four

After Nora dressed, she made her way through the winding corridors of the massive house to find Yada's study. Briella and Finn were waiting for her and although they explained to her several times how to find it, she found herself lost in the maze of halls. The house was filled with the scent of freshly baked goods and she wondered as she made her way if her mother had walked down these same halls. Did the young girl that Adelle once was spend long afternoons in this house as so many other children did? Courtyards inside full of lush gardens seemed to brim with children who giggled as they ran from room to room. There was no denying that this was a palace, but Yada's home seemed truly to be for the people of Goghbuldor.

Nora rounded a corner and stopped, suddenly frozen as she saw the image of her mother. A large portrait hung on the wall and although she was much younger than she was now, it was unmistakably Adelle. Her eyes bore down on Nora and she felt a chill run up her spine.

"Your mother was quite the witch." A voice sounded from behind her.

Nora turned to see Lettie smiling warmly.

"Whatever she went on to do–whatever she became–I loved her dearly." Lettie turned to Nora. "I suppose if things were different, you would have called Yada your gran."

Nora felt a lump in her throat. "Yada's her mother?"

Lettie shook her head slowly. "She was left as a baby as an offering to the mountain by some superstitious village woman. Yada found her barely clinging to life in the forest. I was ten when they brought her here, I remember watching her grow into her power. It was immense; unlike anything we've seen since."

"Was she kind?" Nora's voice was barely more than a whisper.

Lettie pursed her lips and looked back up at the painting. "She was not cruel, never hurt anyone, but she was hungry. As a baby she hungered for food, Yada could never keep her fed. Then, as she grew, she hungered for stories. There were never enough books. Once she began her magical training, she hungered for knowledge. That soon changed to power." Lettie guided Nora away from the painting and further down the hall towards Yada's study. "I would not give her such a common description as kind. She was not without mercy, and she was dear. But she was hungry for more at every moment. Which became her great downfall."

Yada emerged from the study, a cup of tea in her hands. She smiled warmly at Lettie. "It's nice to hear you speaking of her." She handed Nora the cup and led her into the study. "When I received word that your sister was born, I was surprised. I never saw her settling down, changing diapers, or reading bedtime stories." Yada smiled as Nora suppressed a laugh. "I take it she never did those things?"

"Well, not for me. I have few memories of how she was with Larissa, but I believe she treated her well." Nora realized for the first time that although Larissa had not suffered the abuse Nora did, she never really had much affection. Nora was lucky to have Tulee, who loved and cared for her like her own. Tulee was there for Larissa whenever possible, but Larissa was kept at her mother's side much of the time, a porcelain doll to parade around.

"I met her twice, your sister. The first time was right after I received word of her birth. I came to visit. Adelle was strange, impatient, and ready to move on as usual, but she seemed off. I assumed it was the hormones of new motherhood, and maybe I'm correct in my assumption, but she seemed so much more frantic than I had ever seen her.

"The second time was at the castle when Larissa came to work for the prince. I rarely visit the city, but when I do, I always like to see the new mages. You know, long ago us old witches were in charge of training the young mages. They would be sent to live with us, learn our ways, and learn balance. But when the kingdom grew fearful of the stone circles, they stopped sending their children to us. Mage's today–they have no balance. They have power but do not understand from where."

"The simulai—"

"I know it was her." Yada shook her head. "I did not recognize her until you bound her. The frantic look in her eyes reminded me so much of her mother."

"You always have a home here if you ever need it. Please know that. If I had known of your birth, I would have come for you, Nora. You must know I did not leave you there to suffer."

"Thank you." Nora felt a warmth spread through her. The world which had seemed so cold not so long ago encased her with love nearly everywhere she went.

"I will leave you to it. I hope to see you again, Nora." Lettie brought Nora in for a tight embrace. "I will continue working on the house for you."

Nora watched as Lettie returned down the hall and disappeared down the stairs towards the dining hall. She followed Yada into the large circular room, sitting in a chair between Finn and Briella. Louella stood at the head of the room beside a simmering cauldron.

"We have received word that the king will send forces to Goghbuldor." Louella's voice was firm as she spoke. "We are to begin evacuations into Ospas."

"What?!" Nora felt her heart sink. They had brought trouble to Goghbuldor, more pain, more loss.

"Calm yourself, child. It is as we expected." Yada waved her hand over her desk and summoned a map of Troque. "In Leiney woods there is an elven city–"

"I am familiar with it," Finn said quickly, moving towards the map and running a finger along the jagged mountains towards the forest. "They trade with Madrall frequently. The princess should be welcome there."

"Back to Madrall?" Briella's eyes darted across the map.

"The treaty has been violated. You would be safer there than anywhere in Troque." Yada traced a hand over the map again, enlarging the section where Leiney Woods met the ocean that separated the continent from Madrall. "Another risky option would be Ospas, but we'd be betting on them hating Troque more than the royal family of Madrall, and I don't like those odds."

Nora stood silently watching the two women and understood what Briella said in her chambers. *You having celestial powers is the least of our worries.* Nora had been so afraid they would leave her if they knew the truth of her power, a truth that terrified her to even contemplate, but she neglected to consider the danger posed to them just by being with Briella. There had never been another option, and there never would be. She hadn't known Briella for long, but she couldn't imagine being without her. She marveled at the idea that Finn and Briella perhaps felt the same way about her.

"I will go with you." Nora's voice surprised even herself, and she reddened when everyone turned to look at her. "We will figure it out as we always do." She smiled at Finn, who grinned back at her. They had moved through the entire country of Troque with little more than a few half-formed plans and hope that everything would work out. They would continue to do the same now.

Louella waved her hand, dismissing the map and releasing a long sigh. "The roads to Leiney Woods will be dangerous, but I don't know of any other roads that offer fewer dangers for you three. I suggest setting out tonight as we will leave for Ospas at first light."

"I would like to speak with Nora before you leave. Alone" Yada smiled at Briella and Finn, who looked worriedly at Nora and then made their way out the door. "Louella, why don't you come with us?"

Louella stopped at the door and let out an exasperated sigh before shutting it. "And where is it I will be coming to?" She demanded, her irritation clear.

"Just to the garden, you old crone." Yada moved towards a terrace with a spiraling staircase that lowered down into a sprawling garden.

They made their way into the garden silently and walked on for a short while until coming to a small courtyard where a small picnic had been prepared.

"I figured this conversation would be best over food," Yada said cheerfully, sitting down on one of the overstuffed pillows placed around the food.

Nora's stomach growled slightly, and she remembered how little of her breakfast Briella and Finn left her, and grabbed one of the small meat pies and ate slowly.

"I know that much has been put on you. Louella told me everything." Yada smiled warmly at Louella and squeezed Nora's hand gently. "Thank you for saving my dear friend."

"I don't know that I exactly saved her." The thought of their time within the stone circle sent shivers down Nora's spine.

Louella rolled her eyes. "Nora, take the compliment for the God's sake; your humility is suffocating."

Nora opened her mouth to protest, and Yada held up a hand, glaring at Louella.

"Not the reason I wanted you to attend this meeting." She growled.

Louella sighed and frowned at Nora. The two stared at each other for a long moment, Nora glaring and Louella frowning before Louella burst into laughter. "You headstrong git!"

"I don't see what's so funny!" Nora's annoyance was clear and seemed to make Louella laugh harder.

Finally, when the witch calmed, she grinned at Nora and shook her head. "Of course you wouldn't. You're too serious."

"Well, we're talking about something pretty fucking serious." Nora turned her attention to Yada. "Does she have to be here for this conversation?"

"Oh, come now." Louella cleared her throat and grabbed a glass of water as she regained her composure.

Yada gave Louella an exasperated glance. "If she can't keep hold of herself, then she will be asked to leave!" Yada warned. "*Anyway*, I just wanted to speak with you before you left here. You have an incredible power, Nora, nothing that anyone has seen before. I have gone back through the ancient texts, but there is nothing about half-celestials."

"Yes, we doubt even Draco knows exactly what you are capable of." Louella's voice was serious again. "I know you just want to control it and hide this part of you. But my dear, hiding parts of who you are rarely ever helps anyone."

Yada gave Louella an encouraging look and Louella stood, moving towards one of the large rose bushes that lined the courtyard.

"I had a different life once. It might surprise you, but I was not always the woman you see before you today, at least not outwardly. I was born in the body of a man and I worked in a village and lived my life as a mage was expected to. People liked me. I even had women who wanted to marry me. But I held this deep shame of knowing inside I was something else. I was not living in a way that was true to who I really was, and it ate me up. I had everything and nothing. It was easier for others to digest, so I had to live in that cage."

Louella turned to face Nora, who looked up at her, motionless.

"I met Yada as she passed through my village and she knew. She saw the woman inside of me clawing to come out. And with her help, I let her. The exhale–I didn't realize I had been holding my breath my entire life. It was terrifying. I lost many people I believed would never leave, but they were not worth my pain. For every bad, there were countless good. For each person who couldn't accept me, there were several more who did, and even some who were so happy that I finally became the woman they knew I was.

"After a time, my power grew. It was as if so many places inside of me were blocked from coming forth, and they all opened. It was the most liberating moment of my life. I came here and studied with Yada, learned to control this new and great power I had hidden away my entire life. The person I am now is who I always was." Louella wiped a tear from her eye and smiled down at Nora. "Your power is terrifying and new, but closing the door on it and locking it away will cause you more pain than you will ever know."

Nora sat in silence as she allowed the information to wash over her. She thought of all the people in Goghbuldor, how it was a collection of people outcast from the world. Nora's own mother had been abandoned and brought here as a baby; these people were bound by their shared traumas. Nora thought of how she might belong here if she ever learned to control this force within her. Yada smiled warmly at Louella and squeezed her hand and Nora saw for a moment how Yada filled a place within Louella that Briella was filling in Nora. Yada was home, and the realization of their connectedness left Nora aching to be near Briella.

"I don't know what to do, or what this means for me, but I know I need to get Briella to safety, and when she is safe, then I can think about who I am within this new world. But until Briella is safe, I can't open that door."

Yada nodded and gathered up a few bags of food, handing them to Nora. "Take these with you for the road. Good luck. We will see each other again."

Yada and Louella watched Nora as she bowed deeply to the two of them before walking off toward the square where her friends waited for her.

"Will you stay to eat with an old fool?" Yada teased, patting the pillow beside her. Louella lowered herself beside Yada and kissed her softly, lifting a grape and popping it into her mouth. "I can spare a few minutes." She crooned. "But we must be quick. I am not entirely done with our little celestial."

Yada shook her head and smiled at the woman before her. "You have always been trouble."

Chapter Twenty-Five

They departed Goghbuldor immediately and traveled for three days with little issue. Briella and Finn took turns hunting, much to Nora's relief, and Nora spent any chance she got practicing meditation. It was strange to Nora how different she felt, how much all three of them had changed. Finn had been corresponding with Luna during the time they spent in Goghbuldor and had news of small armies throughout Troque filled with mercenaries and soldiers eager to find them. They were careful on their journey to stay far from settlements of any kind and toed the line between Troque and Ospas as if they balanced on the edge of a knife.

On the third day of their journey, they came out on a bluff overlooking the expansive North Sea. They were close to Leiney, and Nora felt her heart flutter at the thought that they might be away from danger soon. They continued through most of the afternoon and set up a camp in the tree line away from the cliff side. The sound of the roaring sea thundered around them as they cleared a place for their camp.

Briella went off a short distance towards a stream brimming with large salmon while Finn and Nora finished setting up camp. Nora and Finn said little as they worked on their tasks, and when they finished, they sprawled out around the fire and gazed up at the stars.

"Draco," Finn said, causing Nora to jump. He smiled and shook his head, pointing to the stars. "The constellation."

"Oh, of course." Nora looked up at the twinkling stars and shuddered at the thought of who might be looking back.

"When I was young, my mother used to tell Malachi and I stories about the constellations. Each one symbolizes a great being, and the stars that made it up represented the ones who helped them in their conquest. Each of the stars that make up Draco is named for the dragons that were part of the great creation." Finn sat up and stoked the fire, grinning down at Nora. "I guess Briella and I will be in your constellation?"

Nora rolled her eyes. "I am far from a great being." She returned her gaze to the stars and sighed. "Besides, who would want to be immortalized like that? To exist forever, looking down at the world. Removed from it, not living. It doesn't seem so glamorous to me."

"Ok, but hear me out—I want to be your right arm as one could argue that I practically am and Briella can be your ass because she can't seem to keep her eyes off of it."

Nora picked up a rock and chucked it at him, glaring as he ducked away and burst into laughter.

"I see the way you two look at each other. Not to mention your late-night rendezvous."

"Nothing happened. She just stayed with me so I didn't have to be alone. You could've been there too; it wasn't like that." Her cheeks flushed. "There's no way she's interested in me like that, Finn. We're just friends."

Finn was silent for a long moment. "So, you aren't denying your interest?"

Nora's face reddened, and they stopped speaking at the sound of footsteps approached. Nora turned to look behind them as Briella stepped into the camp brandishing three salmon. She grinned at them and then furrowed her brow at their expressions. Nora turned her face away, flustered, and Finn chuckled to himself.

Briella glared and threw the food on the ground. "I don't know what's so funny, but while you two have been lying here acting like fools, I got us some food. I guess next time I'll just stay at camp so I can be in on the joke!" She sat down and angrily cleaned the fish, ignoring the roaring of Finn's laughter.

"That's enough!" Nora hissed, kicking him. She looked at Briella and opened her mouth, but no words came out.

Briella's mouth twitched slightly, hinting at a smile beneath her scowl. "Thank you? Wow, look at all that food? Anything at all?"

"Thank you," Nora said quickly, her face now a deep shade of red.

Briella eyed her suspiciously. "Why are you blushing?"

Finn snorted into his hand and walked away quickly before Nora could kick him again. "I'm going to clear the area for a minute and give you two some privacy." He bowed deeply and disappeared into the night.

Idiot, Nora thought, avoiding Briella's gaze.

"What's going on?" Briella demanded, crossing her arms in front of her and frowning.

"Nothing. Finn's just being a fully formed idiot." Nora murmured, grabbing a fish and helping to clean it.

Briella stared at her for a long moment and shrugged. "Fine, keep your secrets. I don't care."

"There's no secrets." Nora looked around awkwardly as Briella ignored her, continuing to clean the fish. "Thank you. Really, you did great today. I can see all the training you've done has really paid off."

Briella stiffened before giving Nora a sideways glance and nodding. "You're welcome."

They sat in silence as Briella continued working. Nora pulled out some of their gear and cooked up the meat with some root vegetables she found nearby. Briella added a handful of herbs to the pot and sat back, allowing Nora to handle the meat. Briella pulled out a small book and began to read, ignoring Nora's glances.

"What are you reading?" Nora stoked the fire a little before settling back herself.

"It's a book of poems Yada gave me." Briella looked up at Nora, her eyes soft. "Would you like me to read you some?"

Nora smiled and nodded. Adelle had a vast library, but Nora could never read any of her books, so what little she read was often discarded from passing caravans. Most of it was religious text, sometimes a fantastic account of some far-off journey, and the occasional newspaper with some poetry or short stories. Nora closed her eyes and listened as Briella read poem after poem. She read them with animation and excitement, and Nora realized that Briella had likely been exposed to endless poetry and art. Nora wondered what Briella had been like in her kingdom. She couldn't imagine her wearing elaborate dresses and being stuck in a castle all day.

"Nora. The meat," Briella said calmly.

"Oh!" Nora shot up and began stirring the meat again, breathing a sigh of relief that one side had only slightly burned on the edges. "Sorry. I got lost there for a minute."

"Do you like poetry?"

"I like listening to you read poetry." Nora blushed as the words left her mouth. She had not meant to say it out loud, and she felt relief rush over her as Briella beamed at her.

"I used to spend days in the library. In Madrall, we have open libraries where the walls of the small buildings are removed on nice days and open up to gardens. You can just walk around all day, grab a book, and lay in the rose beds. It's beautiful." Briella's smile faded from her face. "It was one of the things I held on to when I left. It's why I had that portrait made in my locket." Briella opened the locket on her bracelet, smiling at the portrait.

Nora smiled. "It was brave of you to come here, knowing it could be your end."

"Brave?" Briella laughed, blinking back tears. "I don't know how brave I am."

"I think you're very brave." Nora removed the pan from the fire and separated the meat into three sections. "The entire world seems to want to use you for their agenda, and you're still trying to carve a place for yourself. If that isn't bravery, I don't know what else you'd call it."

Briella moved closer to Nora, picking up a piece of meat and chewing it slowly as she thought for a moment.

"And what agenda do you have?" She asked, her eyes fixed on Nora's.

Nora felt chills run through her body as she met Briella's gaze.

"I have none. Only that whatever you choose is honored. If you want to build open libraries, if you want to go back to Madrall, whatever you want to do, my only agenda is that it is done."

Briella smiled and pushed a lock of Nora's hair behind her ear.

"You are a wonder." She whispered.

The sound of Finn approaching the camp made Briella drop her hand quickly, and she reached for her plate, her cheeks a light shade of pink. Nora smiled and cleared her throat, putting Finn's plate on his bag.

"Did I miss something?" Finn frowned at the pair, a smile tugging at the edge of his mouth, and then made his way to his mat. "It's no matter to me. With good food like this, who needs to know it all? Good job princess, it's nice to see you pulling your weight!"

"I've pulled my weight plenty, thank you!" She glared at Finn and popped a piece of meat in her mouth.

Nora smiled as the pair continued to squabble. She wished Tulee and Horace were sharing the fire with them. She wondered what Tulee would think of the princess, and how she would scold Finn for his constant teasing. The thought of them and the uncertainty of what happened after the dragon attacked sent a chill down Nora's spine.

"I'm beat." Finn stood and tossed a bone into the embers before heading into his tent.

"Yeah, we should probably get some sleep." Briella stood up and helped Nora to her feet.

They made their way to their own tents, Nora feeling the small distance between them stretching out like miles. What if Briella was interested? It seemed to be in Briella's nature to care for people. Was Nora reading too much into her attentions? Her mind raced.

Am I really wondering if she likes me while I'm essentially being torn apart from the inside? Nora thought. *How fucking stupid am I?*

She thought about when they were in bed together. That seemed like a pretty intimate moment for friends, but also Nora never really had friends before Finn and Briella. Briella had held Nora through the night, protecting her from her own thoughts and fears.

Nora turned and looked at Briella who was watching the fire, lost in her thoughts. She closed her eyes, willing herself to go to sleep, and then opened them again. She killed a *dragon*. Nora could talk to Briella about where they might stand with each other.

"Hey," Nora whispered, trying not to alert Finn, who she could hear snoring softly from his tent. "I might be up a little longer if you want to move your mat in here."

Briella smiled, quietly moving her mat into Nora's tent and lying down. "How are you doing?"

"I'm ok. How are you? How are your—feelings—about what's coming?" Nora closed her eyes at the awkwardness of her words.

"What's coming? I feel like we don't know what's coming, at least not yet. We know what direction we're walking in, and that feels like enough for now," Briella smiled. "I'm not trying to be a cynic, but I can't help it. I feel like something changes every day when I'm with you."

Nora turned to face Briella. "I would argue that most of that has been your doing. I would've likely still been on the estate, working my ass off for the rest of my life if that dragon hadn't kidnapped you."

"Well, I am sorry to have interrupted such a glamorous life." Briella teased. "I'm so thankful that it was you who found me. Everything would have been different if it had been anyone else."

They stayed up for a while longer, sharing stories from their childhoods and things they did in their lives. Nora told Briella about the forest outside of Sorudi and how she would spend long afternoons on the mossy banks. Briella told Nora about her mother and the customs of Madrall. Their words filled the spaces between them and made the expanse of the world around them feel smaller until it was just the two of them and nothing else. Slowly and somehow all at once, they drifted off to sleep.

Nora opened her eyes the next morning to Briella's face less than an inch from her own. During the night, Briella moved under Nora's blanket and draped an arm around Nora's waist. Nora sat there and looked over the princess. Her long red hair was a tangled crown that framed her face, which had become covered in freckles with all the time spent outside. She was drooling slightly, which made Nora smile and would have likely horrified Briella. She sat like that for a long moment, savoring her closeness, before sliding out from under her arm and stepping outside.

Nora blinked at the brightness of the sun.

"Good morning," a familiar voice hissed before she felt a searing pain tear through her body.

Nora buckled and fell to the ground before looking in the direction the voice had come from. The pain caused her eyes to fill with tears, but she would recognize the face of her sister anywhere.

"Larissa?" She shouted, closing her eyes against the pain.

Larissa's jaw dropped. "Nora?!"

Briella came running out of the tent with daggers in her hands and sliced at Larissa, drawing a line of blood from her cheek.

"You bitch!" Larissa roared before backhanding Briella and sending her on top of Nora's writhing body.

Briella's face was red from the impact and Nora could see the skin already tightening as it swelled. Nora stared at Briella in shock.

"What have you done to her?" Briella screamed up at Larissa.

Larissa seemed visibly shaken but straightened as a broad-shouldered captain made his way towards her. "She seems harmless, but watch her. She's fiery." Larissa said.

She walked to Finn, who was tied up and held by two guards, his face badly bruised and his eyes full of wild rage. She grabbed the back of his hair and pulled his face to her, smiling cruelly.

"You keep poor company, this one was easily brought down."

Larissa pushed Finn's head back down before turning to look at Nora. She was an imposing figure; her skin, once deeply tanned from afternoons running through the hills, was like porcelain and her elaborate gown made her stand out in stark contrast against the men who had the three surrounded. Nora almost wouldn't have recognized her if it weren't for her green eyes, which were the exact copy of their mothers.

Briella stood, shielding Nora from Larissa. When she broke Larissa's eye contact, Nora felt the pain ease and her body loosened from the rigid grip. She moved her head slightly to count the guards that surrounded them.

"Take me, but leave them." Briella pleaded. "They saved me—they were only helping me."

"Briella—!" Finn shouted before a guard punched him in the stomach, knocking the air out of him and leaving him hunched over and gasping.

"Princess, I don't believe you are in a position for bargaining." A smile spread across Larissa's mouth. "You're coming with us like it or not."

Now free from Larissa's binding, Nora moved slowly to reach their weapons. Finn's sword was wrapped in a cloth with Nora's and if she could reach it, she might get it to Finn. It was a long shot, but the only shot she had.

Briella pressed her dagger against her own throat, glaring down at Larissa. "You will have a hard time uniting our kingdoms if word is spread about my death."

Briella's eyes were wide with fear, but she was serious, and Nora felt her stomach twist. She rolled fast to the swords, grabbing hers and rushing towards the guards that held Finn, driving her sword into the stomach of the first man she reached. The feel of her sword entering his body made her feel sick, but she pulled it out quickly and spun to cut at the other guards. Briella lunged for Larissa before she could cast her spell on Nora again, slicing madly with her daggers and causing Larissa to dive behind her men.

Finn broke from the other guard's grasp and took his sword from Nora, lurching forward with the ropes still tied around him. The ropes seemed to harden to whips, and they thrashed around him like tentacles, sending the men running and screaming as their eyes were lashed at. Nora felt an arrow graze her cheek and turned to find the archer who shot it. She ran towards him and brought her blade down on the archer, coating herself in his blood.

Nora heard Briella scream and turned to see her being grabbed by another guard and forced to the ground. Finn sent a stream of teal light at the guard that held Briella. Larissa jumped before the guard, blasting back with her magic. Light was pulsing from each of their hands in what appeared to be a string of energy. Nora could see Finn struggling to push through Larissa's power.

She's toying with him, Nora thought before running towards them.

Time seemed to slow down, and Larissa turned her face to look at Nora. The world around them became a blur, but Larissa's hands were still pointed towards Finn, streaming magic towards him.

"You cannot save her." Larissa's voice echoed around Nora. "You will die if you keep trying. Let her go."

Nora felt as if she were running through thick mud. Her legs barely moved, but she pushed through as hard as possible.

"I won't let you take her," Nora shouted. "She deserves freedom."

"Freedom?" Larissa's face went serious. "There is no freedom for her. If it's not our king, it will be another. Her birthright comes with tremendous power."

Suddenly, Larissa's voice echoed in Nora's mind. *Let her go, Nora. Mother will be proud of you. I can tell the king there was a mix-up—that you were planning on bringing her to the castle. You'll be rewarded beyond anything you could imagine.*

Nora continued to push through the magic. Again, Larissa was trying to help her without making any sacrifices of her own. But Nora had known only sacrifice her whole life, and she refused to give up now.

Why are you doing this? Larissa's voice demanded within Nora's mind. *Why would you put me in this position? You can't stop me, Nora! Just stop!*

Nora continued to push through, focusing on keeping her magic within her, and then time seemed to speed up again and her body moved faster and faster until she was sprinting toward her sister. Larissa released a pulse of magic at both Finn and Nora that sent Finn flying back, and Nora felt her body lifting in the air.

Finn slid across the rocky cliffside and grabbed hold of a boulder to prevent himself from being pushed off the cliff. He stood and ran towards Larissa, who had her hand extended above her lifting Nora into the sky.

Briella shoved the guard off and began slicing her daggers dangerously as four other guards backed her up against a large oak tree. She looked at Nora for a half second and one man grabbed her. She cut him in the throat, causing blood to gush from his neck before another guard hit her over the head with the hilt of his sword, and her body went limp. Nora felt the familiar rage bubbling up inside her and looked down as her veins bulged with purple magic.

Finn slid past a group of guards, cutting at them with his sword as he did so, and jumped up to his feet before leaping at Larissa. Larissa broke her gaze from Nora and raised her arm above her head to shield herself from his blow. Just as Finn descended upon her, he was thrust back by a giant javelin that went through his shoulder and pinned him down to the ground. Larissa kept her hand up to hold Nora in the air as the large warrior who threw the javelin moved towards Finn.

"Tiny, weak half-elf." The man spat the words and ripped the javelin from Finn's shoulder. Finn screamed with pain and tried to grab his sword. The man grabbed Finn by the throat and lifted him into the air.

"Finn!" Nora screamed.

The surrounding sky went dark. Larissa turned to look at Nora, eyes wide with terror. Nora's eyes were glowing with the purple magic and the blood inside her filled her with a glow. Larissa's hands shook violently as she tried to control her magic, and Nora began to rise higher but this time of her own volition.

"Get the princess out of here!" Larissa shrieked, struggling to control Nora.

Nora extended her arms out on either side of her and they filled with purple flame.

"What—what are you doing?" Larissa screamed. "What's happening to you?"

Nora dove from the sky, throwing her fire out before her and causing many of the men to scream in agony as they tried to escape the magic flames. Larissa disappeared as Nora reached her and Nora closed her eyes, feeling her nearby.

"Stop this madness *now*!"

Nora turned and saw Larissa standing beside the giant man who held Finn by the throat, hanging out over the cliff. The rage inside Nora welled up and she could feel herself being engulfed in flames. She stepped towards them and called her magic to her, the flames billowing around her.

"I swear! Don't you dare come any closer!" Larissa's voice was full of fear and desperation, her eyes wide as she took in Nora.

Release me! The voice within Nora screamed, begging her to allow the magic to move through her body. Nora tried desperately to hold it in, afraid of what it could do to Finn and Larissa.

"I can't," Nora whispered, fighting the force within her as it pushed her to take another step toward Larissa.

"*Drop him!*" Larissa screamed.

Finn looked at Nora, his eyes wide, and then he disappeared over the cliff side.

"No!" Nora bellowed, running to him.

Her blade cut through the men who stood between her and the cliff edge and she lunged towards the man who had dropped Finn, thrusting her sword into his stomach. As she did so, Larissa disappeared entirely, and Nora could no longer sense her.

You let him go. A roaring voice screamed from within her.

"No." She felt the words leave her lips, and she looked over the cliff and saw nothing but a fierce ocean.

You could have stopped it!

"He's here. He's here." Choking sobs escaped Nora as she searched for Finn amongst the crashing waves. "Finn!" She screamed.

He's gone and so is Briella. You failed! The voice within Nora was her own, but it spoke with venom as it screamed the words within her own mind. *You failed them! You killed them!*

"No."

Nora's shoulders shook with rage, and a blast of magic erupted from within her. The last thing she heard was the screams of the men who were left behind.

26

Chapter Twenty-Six

Nora awoke to rain splashing on her face; opening her eyes to see Draco's constellation blinking down at her. Her muscles screamed in protest as she rolled onto her side and peered over the cliff's edge. The waves crashed onto the jutting rocks before dragging back out to the sea, only the foam illuminated in the faint moonlight. Finn was down there, somewhere. She felt a sob leave her lips and sobbed openly as she sat on her knees, shivering against the cold.

He was gone; they were both gone, and it was her fault. She hesitated with Larissa and because of that hesitation, she allowed them to be taken. The power within her could have protected them, and she couldn't use it when she needed to most.

"I'm—so—sorry," she cried, her eyes looking out across the raging sea. "Finn. Please."

Warm liquid spilled from her forehead and she raised her hand to the spot, wincing as her fingers touched a deep gash. She felt the world spin around her and lurched over the cliff to throw up. The rain continued to beat down on her as she rested her head against the rocky edge. Finn was gone and Briella–she didn't know how far she was by now.

Nora felt cool liquid move over her head wound and she looked at her hand, noticing the shimmering blue link to the nymph Phillandra pulsing out of her hand and into the bleeding gash on her head. The wound closed, and she felt a small scar that sat in its place.

Nora braced against a large boulder as she rose to her feet and slowly moved to where her camp had once been. Burnt bodies littered the ground and all that remained of their camp were some poles and their bags, which had been magicked in Goghbuldor to resist water and fire. Nora stared at the three bags and felt her knees buckle. She took a deep breath and slid the bags onto her back, willing herself to continue. The bags were heavy, but she could not bear to leave them behind. She could not leave their things alone on this cliffside.

The forest was dense and Nora felt her vision fading in and out from a combination of blood loss and the impact of multiple blows to her head. She could make out the trail Larissa's group took through the hacked bushes and occasional footprints in the mud. She limped on, the vision of Finn's face pulsing through her mind. Nausea rose within her when she thought of the fear in his eyes before he fell. She wondered what he thought when she couldn't save him; she wondered if he thought of Luna as he fell. The trail became more difficult to discern, and she threw their bags into the muddy forest floor with a frustrated scream.

She leaned her back against a tree trunk and slid down to a seated position, ripping a piece of cloth from the bottom of her shirt and beginning to sift through Briella's bag until she found a can of salve. She slid the thick salve across a large gash that pulsed on her thigh, wincing as it stung and trying to slow her breaths. Nora's face tilted up towards the dark sky and she closed her eyes as the rain fell onto her cheeks and ran down the sides of her face. Her breaths were shaky and tears mixed with the rain. Her clothes stuck to her body, and she shivered hard against the cold of the night. She lost them both, and now wounded and lost, she was hobbling after Briella as if she could even save her.

"I failed."

Nora thought of the magic that enveloped her. When she came back to consciousness, the cliff was littered with the burnt bodies; that power was unlike anything she felt before. She feared it, but she feared even more how good it felt. What if she tapped into the magic when it had first pushed through her? She was afraid to hurt Larissa and as a result Finn was dead and who knew what they would do to Briella; or what Briella might do to herself.

Briella would try to kill the prince, because there were no other choices for her. Larissa would get everything Adelle had ever wanted for her, and Nora would be here. Nora, the ruin of the world.

Nora sat up again, wiping her face with her hand and reaching for the salve. She grabbed a handful of dried herbs from Briella's bag and stuck them to the wet ointment, smearing it on any wounds she could find. She grabbed the ripped piece of fabric and wrapped it around her thigh to cover the wound and instantly she felt her head clear, as if the throbbing of her wound had been a drum pounding so loudly all attempts at thought were drowned out.

Nora dumped the contents of their bags onto the muddy ground and began rifling through them, consolidating them into one bag that she could carry. She kept only her own essentials and anything personal of Finn's and Briella's that she could, tucking the rest back into Finn's bag and hiding it between two boulders.

"I'll come back for you." She whispered, tears streaming down her face. "I love you."

My dear, hiding parts of who you are rarely ever helps anyone, Louella's words echoed in Nora's mind. She frowned. This power within her helped every time. She looked at her hands and felt the familiar tickle of magic filling her veins. She stood up and let it flow through her with each heartbeat pulsing through her body.

She looked up at the sky and glared at Draco's constellation. "Is this what you want?" She shouted up to the stars. "Will it be enough if I burn the world to ash?!" she screamed.

There was no response, but Nora somehow felt the being's amusement. She knew she was doing exactly what he wanted, but if saving Briella meant playing his game, then she would play it her way.

She turned and looked up a steep hill a short distance away. It went up over the trees and would offer her a vantage point to look over the entire forest.

Let me out, the venomous voice inside of her demanded.

Nora moved towards the hill, her body's screaming in protest quieted by the magic that continued to spread through her. She willed herself further up, closing her eyes and working to keep the magic from spilling out from inside her. If she lost control, she could hurt Briella, and couldn't live with that. She dug her fingers into the soft earth and pulled herself up the hill, sliding down occasionally and forcing herself to continue up. The purple light radiated around her and she felt her pain melt away slowly, giving way to rage.

She approached the top of the hill and stood, her body shaking with an energy unlike anything she'd felt before. Her eyes filled with purple light and her vision shifted entirely. Where previously there was only darkness, there now was a purple film illuminating everything around her. Bright purple shapes of creatures moved through the forest as their body heat registered in Nora's vision. She surveyed the land until she saw it. A light from several small campfires not too far off and people moving around the fires. They hadn't made nearly the pace Nora assumed they'd make. She wondered if Briella had anything to do with that.

Go. The voice boomed from inside her. *Save her.*

Nora allowed the energy within her to spill out slowly, and she felt herself become weightless. Her feet left the ground and her body rotated slowly as she continued to rise into the air. The magic within her caused her skin to glow and her hair lifted around her as her turning stopped and she looked down on the camp. She could see the heat from the bodies of Briella's captors showing where each of them was posted. She smiled and closed her eyes as her body hurled toward the ground below.

She moved at an incredible speed, pulling out her sword and flexing her free hand as purple flame built up within it.

Burn them all. The voice called within her mind again.

Nora felt herself detach from the moment. It was as if she was observing from her own mind as something else took over her body entirely. She saw claws grow from her fingertips as she approached the camp, wild energy radiating from within her; a feeling that she was finally *free*.

She burst through the bushes and before one of the guards surrounding the camp could even register she was there, she sliced off his head in a clean motion, raising her hand to the man standing beside him and sending the purple flames to devour his body. She continued to run through the camp, setting fires to the tents and slicing through the men who tried to stand in her way. A few of them ran off, screaming for Larissa.

"Bring her to me." The voice within her boomed through the forest.

A group of men ran at her and Nora slid forward on her knees, arching her back to avoid their blades and weaving her sword through the air. Nora felt one of their blades meet her waist and the searing pain left as quickly as it came. She kicked the man who cut her, sending him into the purple flames that were rapidly spreading through the camp. She felt like she could hear and see everything clearer. Her blood pumped faster through her body and it felt to Nora that she could do anything. She was unstoppable.

Nora heard Briella scream, and she changed her course towards the sound. The flames behind her were roaring and she could hear men screaming as they burned within their tents. The world around her seemed to blur as she ran to Briella, her heart pounding in her ears.

Nora stopped when she saw Larissa holding Briella, a knife to her throat and Larissa's eyes frantic with fear.

"Don't you dare come any closer to me!" Larissa shrieked. "I'll cut her fucking head off!"

Nora felt the magic build up inside her and worked to quiet it. She could not risk hurting Briella.

"What happened to you?" Larissa's voice quivered as she spoke. "What did you do?"

Nora stared down hungrily at her sister. "Does it scare you, Larissa? Are you afraid of me?"

Larissa held Briella closer. "I've seen nothing like this."

"No, you haven't." Nora stepped closer, keeping her eyes fixed on Larissa. "And if you value your life, you'll release her now."

"Is that a *threat*?" Larissa spat. "You may have some new power, but I know what you are, and it is not *this*! You are still the scared little girl alone in the forest!"

Nora's gaze shifted to Briella, who seemed to be very calm. Nora watched as Briella reached her hand slowly towards the hilt of a dagger whose blade was cherry red from falling into the fire.

Nora returned her gaze to her sister. "And you are still so far up your own ass you can't see the world around you."

"Nora—please. This isn't you. Sister—"

"This is me. This is what Adelle made me; what you *both* made me."

As Nora finished speaking, Briella grabbed the dagger, gritting her teeth against the searing pain of the heat, and with one quick motion severed Larissa's hand. Larissa dropped her, holding her arm to her chest and shrieking with pain.

"You?!" she screamed, giving Nora a frantic look. "You will regret this!" And with the wave of her remaining hand, she vanished into the air before them.

Nora felt her stomach turn at the sight of Larissa's disembodied hand lifeless on the ground and she walked towards Briella, ripping the shackles around Briella's ankles with a clawed hand and feeling the magic within her recede.

"Are you ok?" Nora panted, wiping blood from her face.

Briella searched Nora's face, a mixture of fear and worry in her eyes. Nora felt her heart pounding, and the worry that she might have pushed Briella too far filled her. Would she stay after this? Nora wouldn't stop her if she didn't. Briella was safe, and that was enough.

"Let's go," Briella said quietly as she rested a hand on Nora's shoulder.

The screaming of the men stopped, some having run away and most dead. Nora waved her hand, calling the flames back into her. They entered her hand and she felt the heat in the air dissipate, leaving behind the smell of burnt flesh. They made their way through the forest silently until Briella collapsed at Nora's feet.

"Let me–"

"I'm fine," Briella said quickly. She tried to stand and fell back down, cursing herself.

Nora lifted Briella into her arms and carried her in the direction her magic willed her to go. They were silent as they moved through the forest, but Nora's senses were still heightened and she could hear the pounding of Briella's heart. As she approached a small pond, she lowered Briella to the ground and felt relief wash over her. She breathed slowly and as her breath escaped her lips, the magic within her seemed to quiet and her eyes came back to their familiar shade of blue.

Briella put a hand on Nora's chest.

"You're safe," Briella whispered.

Nora collapsed on the mossy river bank and closed her eyes. The pounding of her heartbeat was so loud that she didn't hear Briella move to sit beside her.

"Are you hurt?" Briella murmured as she tucked her legs beneath her.

Eyes still closed, Nora felt the burn of tears releasing from her eyes. Finn was dead, and Briella was almost lost to her forever; she hurt in ways that she felt could never heal. The stinging tears spilled down her cheeks.

Nora felt the warm touch of Briella's lips press softly against her own. Her entire body seemed to melt into the earth and she wrapped her arms around the princess. They lay together on the bank of the river, kissing softly through mutual grief.

"I thought I lost you," Nora whispered between their kisses.

Briella pulled back slowly and was silent for a long moment before letting out a small sob. Nora squeezed her gently against her, kissing her forehead.

"I thought you were dead. And Finn—" Briella let out another loud sob and buried her head in Nora's chest.

Nora closed her eyes as the image of Finn's face before he was thrown over the edge of the cliff came to her mind.

How could the world continue on without Finn? She thought of Luna, of the children who were excited for him to come back to them. She thought of how he cared for them, and all the plans that would never come to fruition. Sudden death was jarring; it caught you off guard and left you at the center of the storm. There were only the things left unsaid that hung in the empty moments, suffocating those left behind as they tried to continue forward.

They lay silently for a long moment, holding each other tightly.

"I don't know how I'm going to tell Luna." Nora whispered.

"We will tell her together, and we will be there for her and her children as long as they need us." Briella sat up, pulling her hair back from her face and securing it with a ribbon she kept tied to her wrist. "I'm not going back to Madrall. I am staying here with you, and we will fix things."

Nora nodded in agreement, sitting up and dipping her hands in the cool water of the pond. She splashed her face and looked down at her reflection in the rippling water of the pond, except it wasn't her. The face looking back at her glared back, purple and blue scales coming from her hair and fading into skin as it reached its face. The creature's face looked like Nora's, but it was wild with rage and its fanged teeth were bared at her. Nora jerked back quickly, looking at Briella and then back into the water where her own human face reflected to her.

"What's wrong?" Briella moved beside her, looking down in the water.

"I thought I saw something—myself, but different. It must have been—"

"Different, like with scales?" Briella dipped her hands in the water and used them to wash the dirt and blood from Nora's arms.

"Yes."

"When you saved me, you looked very different. It went away when Larissa was gone, but you looked—"

"Terrifying."

"Magnificent."

You are magnificent. Draco's words echoed in Nora's mind as Briella spoke. Nora allowed Briella to help her wash the blood from her body, pulling off her pants to inspect her wounded leg. The bindings she had wrapped around her leg were still there, but there was no pain. She removed the fabric and saw no sign of the bloodied mess, not even a scar to mark where it had been.

"I was cut, badly." Nora breathed.

Briella held up her wrists, smiling softly. "They bound me and rubbed my wrists raw until they bled. As soon as you lifted me, the pain was gone. Your magic must have healed us both."

Nora was torn between relief that she could heal them, and a deep fear that her magic acted so independently of herself. Louella had warned her she must control this power, and she felt she was nowhere near the control she needed.

"We need to rest. Let's make camp." Briella squeezed Nora's shoulder gently.

Nora worked on the fire while Briella riffled through Nora's bag. She laid their blankets out across the mossy floor. They worked silently and soon had a small fire with two beds around it. Nora lay down on her blanket, her eyes meeting Briella's as she lay on her own.

Briella's eyes seemed to sparkle with the firelight and Nora smiled at how beautiful they were.

"What's so funny?" Briella asked, smiling back.

"Oh, nothing's funny," Nora whispered. "I'm just happy I found you. Part of me wanted to believe I could save you, but I just didn't know how."

"You did it before. I knew you'd come for me again."

Nora nodded.

"You used your magic. I saw you up in the sky. I saw a purple light, and I knew it was you." Briella sat up and pulled her blanket around her, crawling around the fire to lie beside Nora. "Once I knew you were alive, I knew you would come for me."

Nora moved until her nose was almost touching Briella's and she brushed a lock of hair behind the princess's ear.

"I will always come for you." She whispered before she pressed her lips against Briella's.

Their hands explored each other greedily, the intensity of their shared grief threatening to pull them apart if they did not get a release. Nora made quick work of Briella's breeches and Briella pushed her back onto her blanket, straddling Nora and removing her shirt. Once undressed, they continued to explore each other with their hands and mouths, stopping whenever the pleasure seemed to lead them to the brink of explosion, and moving on to tease another part of their bodies. Nora felt a release within her as if she had been holding her breath all this time. They held each other in silence for a long while, allowing the darkness to hold them in their loss.

They slept tangled up with each other on the river bank, two bodies seeming to be just one, and the stars twinkled above them.

"I love you," Briella whispered as she fiddled with a lock of Nora's hair. "I think I might have loved you from the moment we first spoke."

Nora traced a finger over Briella's shoulder, connecting the spattering of freckles, and kissed the top of her hair. "I love you too."

Briella sat up on her elbows to look into Nora's eyes. "Finn would be so pissed that he missed this."

"He would be furious." Nora chuckled, allowing tears to escape her eyes.

"He's been asking me when I was finally going to woman up and bed you for weeks."

They were silent for a moment before they both burst into laughter, Nora covering her face with her hands as tears spilled through the shared moment. Grief was strange. It enveloped them and hung heavy in the air. You could not cry for Finn without also laughing for Finn; you could not mourn him without joy. Eventually, they settled back into the silence of the night, allowing their minds to wonder what tomorrow might bring. Nora closed her eyes and peered into the magic well within her, bubbling over and sparking with chaotic persistence.

Chapter Twenty-Seven

They awoke the next morning on the mossy bank, naked and wrapped in each other's arms. Nora wrapped a blanket around Briella and slowly moved to stand and dress herself. Nora nudged the fire and threw a small pile of sticks on the hot embers, coaxing a flame to boil water. She worked silently, pretending not to notice Briella's eyes watching her. She grabbed her bag and pulled out a small pot and filled it with water, placing it over the fire. Nora then filled a small bag with herbs, dropping it into the water.

She sat back on her haunches and put her hands out before her to warm them, still avoiding Briella's eyes.

"I can tell you know that I'm watching you." Briella teased. "I always can tell because you get nervous and start busying yourself with random tasks."

Nora glared at her and pursed her lips against a smile. "I don't know what you're talking about. I thought we could use some tea."

Briella rolled her eyes and stood, allowing the blanket Nora covered her with to drop to the ground. She cocked an eyebrow at Nora when she blushed and laughed.

"Seeing me naked makes you blush, but last night you didn't seem so shy." Briella moved to her discarded clothes and dressed herself.

Nora smiled and returned her attention to the steaming pot, removing it from the fire and pouring two tin mugs with the herbal mixture. She handed one to Briella as she sat beside her and the two sat in silence, watching the water trickle down a series of small waterfalls into the pond and down the river.

The absence of Finn was all around them and Nora tried to push it away, but she couldn't stop thinking of his eyes locking with hers before he was thrown over the cliff. How could Larissa do this? What happened to her?

Briella rested a hand on Nora's shoulder. "We will have time to process this, but right now, we need to figure out where we are."

"You're right." Nora washed her hands and dried them off quickly before opening her map. "I have two theories, and one of them is less terrible than the other."

"Well, that's promising." Briella groaned. "Give me the less terrible option."

"Well, there is a possibility we're near Averniel, which is a royal city near Leiney Woods, likely crawling with people looking for you. I would bet money that Averniel is where Larissa wanted to take you." Nora laid out her map and pointed to the city.

"That's the *better* option? A city full of people who want to capture me? Now I'm nervous to hear the bad one."

"The other option—it doesn't seem possible, but this spring—" Nora pointed to a small shrine beside the small waterfall that fed the pond. It was carved out of a massive piece of jade, and the glimmering green nearly faded into the greenery entirely. "It's Zeta, the fallen Dragon goddess."

"Why would there be a Zeta statue in Troque?" Briella walked over to the statue, inspecting it but careful to keep her distance.

"There shouldn't be." Nora's voice was grim. She looked into Briella's eyes, willing her to say the words she refused to say herself.

"Ospas." Briella's voice was barely a whisper.

Nora nodded.

"But that's not possible. There's no way those bastards were taking me into Ospas; they'd have been slain on sight." Briella ran her fingers through her hair as she paced. "They'll kill me here, Nora. I am the person they would despise the most. Do you know how many of their people my father has killed? There's no way–"

"I don't understand it either, but this lake is a shrine to Zeta. Something must have happened when I was in that state."

Briella stiffened and put a hand on Nora's shoulder, her eyes fixated behind her. Nora slowly turned, pulling at the well of magic within her and allowing it to bubble up close enough to the surface that her veins were glowing purple, and then found herself cemented in place by what stood before her. A massive wolf-like creature stared down at them, its eyes fixed on Nora and every muscle in its body poised for an attack. It stood easily eight feet tall at the shoulder, shaggy white fur covered its massive body and its breath blew hot out of its mouth as a wide grin spread across its face.

"You are far from home, younglings." Her voice was raspy and forced as if too much time had passed since it last spoke.

"A dire wolf." Briella barely murmured, pressing herself against Nora's back.

Dire wolves, much like the serapin, were also creatures who fought the Great Beings during the world's creation. Unlike the serapin, however, the ancient wolf queen Lykara and her pack were honored in a constellation of their own and immortalized in time. Nora once saw a dire wolf pup in a cage being brought to the king's palace. She remembered the intelligence in its eyes, the way it seemed to understand its fate, and she remembered the ways its eyes pierced hers. Now, standing before the great beast, she felt trapped by its eyes. Her magic sat frozen in her veins, and the dire wolf seemed to dare her to act.

Submit, the female voice she heard in her mind before bellowed. Nora winced and fell to her knees, the sound still echoing in her mind.

Briella dropped behind her, bringing Nora to her chest and staring up at the dire wolf who watched with eyes fixated only on Nora. Nora bowed her head deeply until it touched the ground, pulling Briella down with her.

"What are you doing?" Briella whispered.

"Just follow my lead." Nora squeezed Briella's hand in reassurance and released a tense breath when Briella lowered her face beside her own.

Nora turned her face slightly and saw Briella's face, white with fear, and kept Briella's gaze as the creature lowered its nose to Nora's head, inhaling deeply and baring her teeth and growling deep in her throat.

"Rise, Daughter of the Stars." The wolf commanded.

Nora closed her eyes in relief and sat up on her knees, craning her head back to look up at the creature before her.

"Lykara," Nora whispered.

The wolf watched her for a long moment. "You are learned. Few Troquese know much of their beginnings."

Briella sat up and laced her fingers into Nora's, meeting the wolf's gaze defiantly.

"Ah, daughter of Madrall. I can smell the blood of my children within you." Lykara cocked her head slightly. "Curious that you would wander here, away from safety and into the pyre."

Nora moved in front of Briella. "We did not come here on purpose. Magic brought us here."

Lykara chuckled and lifted her head to release a long, mournful howl which was answered by hundreds of returning howls from all directions. She lowered her head and returned her gaze to meet Nora's.

"I know why you are here. I was sent to escort you. We wouldn't want the queen's soldiers to find you out here alone." She turned, her eyes shooting back to Briella quickly and a sick smile spreading across her face again. "If you run, we will catch you. I have many pups who would enjoy eating a princess of Madrall."

Briella stood, her body shaking, and they followed the wolf deeper into the forest. Nora looked up at the last bit of sky before the trees hid them from view, and she wondered who was watching them now.

They followed Lykara into the forest for what felt like hours, neither one daring to speak and Nora catching glimpses of other dire wolves moving in the distance, their shaggy fur barely visible between the large redwood trees. Briella held tight to Nora's hand, blinking back tears.

Ospas had always been the enemy of Troque, but shared a border and had access for certain merchants to come and do business within the kingdom. They were treated terribly, and usually abused by guards who escorted them through trade routes, but the cruelty they suffered at the hands of Madrall was something else entirely. Madrall once kidnapped and enslaved large swaths of their people, subjected them to unfathomable torture, as the kingdom of Madrall and all of its splendor was built on their broken backs. Treaties made and goods sent to bring their people back were violated time and time again as the people of Madrall became uniquely adept at destroying everything Ospas stood for. As dragons became the enemy of the world at large, the nation of Dragon-worshippers withdrew into themselves, the forests around them protecting them from further assault but completely cut off from the outside world. And now Briella, a necessary piece of their undoing, was walking right into their lands.

"Nothing will happen to you," Nora whispered. "Not if I can help it."

Briella feigned a smile, returning her eyes to the trail before her. "Something brought us here. I have to believe it was for something more important than the crimes of my ancestors."

Finally, Lykara stopped before what appeared to be a tall wall of ivy, but as they approached, Nora realized it was a curtain concealing a large encampment that seemed to be the beginnings of a city. They followed the wolf queen through the curtain and past the small clutches of new construction, and Nora's jaw dropped at what lay beyond. The canopy was lit up by hundreds of lanterns and overflowing with life. From creatures of lore to humans and elves, there seemed to be no end to the diversity within this space. Nora saw wagons that were turned into makeshift homes where children scurried in and out and watchful mothers smiled down at them; there were large lion-like creatures with bird wings dozing off in nests made of branches and bits of fur, and centaurs moved through the crowds of people as if they had always coexisted. Nora smiled as a centaur she recognized, Leir, bowed deeply to her and offered Briella a kind smile.

"You are as beautiful as they say, princess." His voice was warmer than Nora remembered and she realized that he definitely had a bit to drink. "Where is your Elven friend?"

Nora looked at her feet silently for a long moment, trying to force herself to speak the words. Leir nodded solemnly, resting a hand on her shoulder in silent understanding.

"Keep moving." Lykara snapped from further up the road. "We haven't all day, Leir."

Leir shrugged. "I will join you. I think a familiar face would be good for you."

Nora squeezed Briella's hand. "We found Leir after the fight with the serapin." She explained quietly as they moved.

"Tell me, Nora. Did you find the Child of Draco?" Leir smiled knowingly.

"We have suspicions," Nora grumbled.

Leir smiled and continued on, following a few paces behind the Dire Wolf.

At the far end of the encampment, built into a towering cliffside, was a massive palace that glittered with thousands of colors, and appeared to have been made from crystals. Nora recognized the massive structure from one of her visions and realized at that moment she had been there before. Not just here in this physical space, but in this present time. People walked by busying themselves with tasks, their faces no longer shrouded in shadow but exactly like her vision. A chill ran through her body at the realization that whatever had been communicating with her had likely brought them to this place. They followed

Lykara through the city and Nora heard Briella gasp as they saw the construction of what appeared to be a massive open-air library.

"It looks just like the ones in Madrall." Briella's eyes lingered on the fine details and intricate carvings on large wooden pillars that framed the area. "Incredible."

They continued through the space until they came to a building that resembled the temples Nora saw in the various cities throughout Troque. Intricate mosaics covered the walls, and she marveled at the complexity of the designs. At the end of the building was a massive pipe organ and a young woman played a hauntingly beautiful song on the instrument.

"Your Highness." Lykara murmured, bowing her head deeply as the person before them stopped playing. "I do not mean to interrupt but—"

"But our honored guests are here." The queen stood and turned to face them. "Welcome. Thank you, Lykara."

Lykara nodded and moved out of the room, the queen's eyes following her.

"Your Highness." Leir bowed deeply, wiping tears from his eyes. "It still amazes me to see you again after all of this time."

Nora realized then who the woman before them was. The Mother Goddess, the one immortalized in the statue back where they had met Leir. She looked identical to the carving, but in person, Nora could feel the command of her presence from where she stood. Her white hair flowed around her, emitting a glow that resembled starlight, and her ebony skin shimmered in contrast to her golden gown. Her eyes were a deep shade of brown, and her full lips were painted a deep crimson.

"I am glad to see you, Leir. I am sorry it has been so long." Her face was tinged with sadness before looking at Nora and Briella. "Welcome to our little home. You may call me Gailea."

Nora and Briella fell to their knees, bowing their heads and keeping their eyes fixed on the floor. Nora could hear Briella's panicked breathing and grabbed her hand, stroking it with her thumb as they sat. Light poured over them and Nora could see the goddess's feet as she stepped closer. She placed her hand on Nora's shoulder and a warmth spread through her body.

"Rise, children." The Goddess smiled as the two stood, now looking eye to eye. "You walk a dangerous path, and the decisions you make will change our world forever. I believe you and I want the same thing for this world, and I want to help you."

"If what you want involves me, then we do not want the same things. I want to be free of this prophecy. I did not ask for it and I do not want it." Nora kept the Goddess's gaze as she spoke.

"Of course, we cannot escape what is laid before us, even when we did not ask for it. The very decision to not act is a decision."

"You could say that about any choice anyone has ever made." Nora's voice was indignant.

"Nora!" Briella and Leir scolded in unison, looking up at each other and then back at Nora.

"It's alright, I like her spirit. She will need that." The Goddess smiled at Nora. "I can help you learn to control this power, but I cannot take it from you. You will have to spend your life keeping it at bay, which will be easy unless you are provoked by the celestial weapons. Crafted to draw out the Child of Draco, when brought together they will render controlling this force within you impossible. One such weapon was held by King Alexander and is now held by his son. A staff with the heart of Zeta at its end."

"What am I supposed to do?" Nora felt the hope leaving her body. She looked around and saw many creatures gathered around them, looking at her as they looked at the Goddess. She felt a chill run up her spine.

The goddess looked around the room and smiled as footsteps sounded behind Nora. She turned to see dozens of creatures walking into the massive temple, their eyes fixed on Nora. Behind them were men and women who looked to be leaders of various military groups, some elves and dwarves, some humans from Ospas, and Nora even recognized some as guards from small militant groups in Troque.

The goddess moved past Nora, looking around at the creatures that surrounded them and smiling. "There is much to discuss, but we are well armed. We have come here from all corners of the earth to fight with *you*, Nora DuPont."

Nora looked around the room, her heart racing. Everyone looked at her to say something, something inspiring, something that a leader should say in this moment, but she had no words. Lead them to what, lead them where? There was so much she was unsure of, so much she didn't understand. She felt the tension rising within her, suffocating her, and then Briella's hand slid into hers and her racing heart began to slow. They stood there, hand in hand, an unbreakable force.

"As long as you live, the king will never stop hunting you or Briella. You have become too dangerous and you have his queen at your side. King Adrian has broken the land of Troque in his effort to take over this land and will kill anyone who stands in his way. Armed with a celestial weapon and mages who plan to help him use it to its full potential, he must be stopped. We stand beside you, child of Draco."

28

Chapter Twenty-Eight

Gailea and her general spent days filling Nora in on the plan of attack. The king's forces were pushing against Ospas and overusing the resources of the people of Troque without offering them any protection or relief. Many refugees from the destroyed cities throughout Troque were pouring into this city between lands and Nora even found she recognized some of them from the tents outside of Balcross.

Briella had taken the lead in the discussions in the war room and Nora saw more examples of how she was a born leader. Nora found more occasions to slip away from conversations of battle and resources as Briella took over, allowing her time to focus on meditations and trying to control her powers.

Gailea and Leir took up much of Nora's time to teach her everything they could about her celestial magic and how to control it. Gailea described it as a celestial crash course, assuring Nora that what she was teaching would help against Adrian, but she would need much more training to defend herself against someone more familiar with celestial weapons. Nora often spent evenings with Leir, learning about the history of the land and what he knew of Draco.

Leir also took time to introduce Nora to the other creatures that emerged from their slumber in response to the prophecy. She met a variety of nymphs that covered all spectrums of nature, centaurs that were well acquainted with Leir, and dire wolves from all corners of the continent. There were giant golden griffins and sphinx, and Nora felt her heart skip a beat when Leir casually introduced her to the spider queen Arachine. Half-spider, half-woman, the queen was the last of the arachnos and as old as the world itself.

"It is an honor to meet you," the queen bowed deeply.

Nora returned her bow.

"You are right to be afraid, Nora DuPont, but not of us. We come here at the turning point to be part of history once more." The queen's skin was gray and her long white hair resembled thick webbing. Her eyes were black jewels set within her bony face, and her human arms ended with long, claw-like fingers. She lowered herself to eye level with Nora, clicking her tongue as she moved.

"Draco betrayed us in the great battle at the beginning of time. All of us who were doomed to rest were supposed to ascend to the skies with him, rulers of our own constellations. We would have been able to protect our people as they moved through the world. We could have prevented the humans from cutting them down. But we were sent into a deep slumber within the earth, and our children were hunted to extinction." Arachine ran a clawed finger down Nora's cheek. "We are all here now because we believe you will right the wrongs of your father. Will you, Nora DuPont, be the champion of the forgotten celestials?"

Nora froze. She knew the creatures looked to her as a leader, but she had not until this moment understood why. She believed they, like her, wanted to prevent the prophecy from being fulfilled, but she wondered why they revered her so much. Griffins bowed when she moved through the space and Leir hinted at something more for a while now. In this moment, he stood beside Nora and huffed loudly.

"Arachine. She still has much to learn. She cannot make you promises when this is the first she has heard of the plan." He was flustered, but he kept his tone respectful.

The old arachnos nodded, her eyes fixed on Nora, and moved back into her webbing.

"The plan? Are you also one of the forgotten celestials?" She asked, her head spinning.

"We all are, Nora. Aside from Lykara and the nymphs who want to stay in their forests, all of us were sent into the dark spaces of this world to leave our people to fend for themselves. This is not your concern right now, you do not control your power to manage such a feat. But if you can thwart this prophecy, they—*we*—hope that you will give us our rightful place in the stars." Leir smiled down at her. "No pressure?"

"Yeah, no pressure at all," Nora grumbled.

Finn would've laughed at the idea. He would've reminded her she does not have to do the bidding of others, and the mistakes of a father who had been entirely absent from Nora's life were not hers to fix. He would've told her it was ok to say no, that people who bowed to prophecy were fools who used it as an excuse to not make decisions. But as she stood here in this moment, his absence heavy in the air, she knew she had gone too far. The choice to do nothing was no longer possible. From the moment she ran up the mountain during the dragon attack, the choice to be complacent was no longer an option.

She thought of Gilade, frozen in stone at the mouth of the cave, and wondered if she would have been here agreeing to help them if Nora hadn't encountered her. She wondered what Gilade, the queen of the serapin, would ask from her. Would she have been a valuable ally?

It might be worth going back and seeing if anything can be done, Nora thought as she moved towards the banquet room.

After dinner, Nora and Briella would walk together to a small shrine full of stubby melted candles, each one lit in memory of someone lost. Briella made a candle for Finn filled with flower petals she gathered during their travels, some of them picked by Finn himself. It took her a day to make it and when she finished and presented it to Nora; they walked together to light his candle. Nora placed it on a tree branch above the memorial, knowing Finn would have likely been perched on that branch looking from above, unwilling to be part of the fanfare. They lit the candle and sat together, murmuring a prayer for him. They allowed it to burn until they left and then snuffed the flame, repeating this ritual each evening.

Nora struggled with the prayer at first, but soon the prayer gave way to conversation. She told Finn what happened during her day, what she learned, what her fears were. She shared everything with him, and Briella held her hand as she said her own silent prayers. Nora felt sometimes she could hear him responding in the wind as it rustled through the trees.

After their memorial to Finn, they retreated to the small hut built off of a dismantled wagon that had been reserved for them and retreated from the rest of the world. Briella decorated it with anything she could find. Nora worked outside building a fence around a small gardening area she was working on. They spent their evenings wrapped in each other, staying up late, discussing their lives, and sharing memories both good and bad. It was the one place Nora could share her fears of the future, where she didn't feel like she had to be strong. Briella became both refuge and peace for Nora, and as the days of war drew closer, the fear of losing her overtook all other emotions.

Large groups of elves and humans moved to Ospas under the protection of the dire wolf pack to get out of harm's way. The king's forces had moved throughout Troque and war seemed imminent as battered and half-starved refugees poured into the city. Nora and Briella waited at the gates as the people came up the road, Nora scanning their faces for one she felt she must find immediately. Her palms were sweaty and her heart raced with anticipation. She felt a sickness come over her and leaned on Briella for support until she finally saw them.

Nora had arranged for a wagon to travel to Sue City and find The Snowy Escape tavern, asking Briella to write ahead that they needed a tavern keeper and healer. When they received word back that Wolfgang and Tabantha accepted the invitation and would bring their daughter and grandchildren, Nora had begun preparations for a tavern and a separate home for Luna and the children.

The line of refugees stretched on for what seemed like forever, and Nora scanned the faces for Luna. Her stomach twisted as she thought of what she would say, what she could say to make this hurt less. Briella stood by her side, ready to support Nora through this.

"I just don't understand why these people are walking shoulder to shoulder they should put the slow traffic on the inside and let the rest of us on the outside, but *no*. There's a wall of stupid in front of us just sauntering through the forest as if they have never—"

Nora turned her head towards the familiar voice of Wolfgang, a smile tugging at the edge of her mouth as she spotted him glaring at another older couple in front of him.

"I'm not telling you that you have to go faster. I don't care how slow you go, I'm telling you to move out of the way!" Wolfgang ordered, Tabantha sighing beside him as she continued to read her book.

Nora's eyes passed over the cart where Luna's three sleeping children were tucked in comfortably and then locked on Luna. Luna watched Nora, her face frozen and unreadable. Nora could tell instantly that Luna knew what Nora was waiting to tell her. She hurried through the crowds of people, pushing past the others as if they didn't exist.

Wolfgang frowned, looking from Nora to Briella, and his face softened as realization washed over him.

"Nora." Luna's voice was strained. She looked at Briella for a second, nodded, and returned her attention to Nora.

"He's—" Nora couldn't make herself say it. Tears welled up in her eyes as panic and fear spread through Luna's face. "He fell, Luna. I tried, but he fell over a cliff, and by the time I got there, he was gone."

Luna crumbled before Nora, dropping to the ground and wrapping her arms tightly around her body. She let out a loud sob, allowing the tears to fall freely from her eyes. She looked back at her cart at her sleeping children and then returned her attention to Nora.

"I felt it. I felt the falling." Her words came in gasps, and Nora knelt down to bring her into a tight embrace.

Nora thought of all the loss this woman had been through, how Finn had been the one who offered her a future, comfort, and protection. She remembered the tenderness between them, how much the children loved him. Her heart broke all over again, and she said nothing. She allowed herself to be the one to support Luna, to be the one person who this mother who sacrificed everything didn't need to support.

"I'm so sorry," Nora whispered into Luna's hair, tears streaming down her face. "I tried, but it wasn't enough. I tried."

She never knew so much agony as she had since losing Finn, but witnessing Luna's loss came close. She felt the world closing in around them. It was as if they existed separately from everyone and everything else. They held each other, Luna crying freely and not caring who saw while Nora tried to slow the tears and keep herself steady.

Wolfgang navigated through the crowd towards Luna and stopped the cart just short of them, nodding in silent understanding to Nora. Tabantha's book rested in her lap and she wiped a tear from her eye, looking up at Wolfgang and resting her head on his chest. They sat there for a few moments longer until Briella moved towards the cart.

"Let us help you all get settled. This has been a weary day for you and the children. Let us help." Briella motioned towards the center of the large square where a tavern that was still being painted sat tucked beneath a willow tree. Connected to the tavern was a small house Nora had prepared for Luna and the children.

They moved towards the tavern, Wolfgang inspecting it with a critical eye as Tabantha went inside and let out a shocked gasp at the sight of an elaborate library set apart in a sunroom for her own enjoyment.

"The walls are soundproof." Nora winked, laughing when Wolfgang shot her a teasing glare.

"Ah, good thinking." Tabantha winked.

Nora and Briella helped Luna unload the still-sleeping children and followed her instructions to place them on a sofa in the common area.

"They are going to be scared waking up in bedrooms by themselves." Luna sniffled.

"If you'd like, we can stay with you for a few days?" Nora offered.

Luna nodded. "I would like that very much."

Briella moved forward, extending her hand. "My name is Briella. I had the pleasure of knowing Finn for a short while, he spoke of you often."

Luna raised her eyebrows at Nora and then looked back at Briella. "*Princess?*"

Briella smiled warmly. "I prefer Briella, but yes."

"A princess?" Sasha, Luna's daughter, called out sleepily from the sofa.

Briella's face lit up and she moved towards the young girl, smiling. "Yes, I'm a princess. What's your name?"

"Sasha. I'm a princess too. Grandpa Wolf says so."

Briella nodded in solemn agreement.

It took Luna a few days to adjust, and Nora stayed at her side until she was steady. The first few nights were tearful, the two staying up talking about Finn and sometimes just crying together without speaking. Briella would tend to the children, giving Luna space to step away when the emotions overtook her.

Nora watched as Briella won over the kids immediately, marveling at how well she worked with children. She sang nursery rhymes and taught them games she played when she was growing up in Madrall. She took a rope and taught them to skip with it, and pretty soon, all the children were skipping rope throughout the camp.

Briella even tried to teach Nora, doing her best not to tease her for being so painfully bad at it. Nora always got one foot caught on the rope and would go tumbling to the ground. After multiple attempts, Briella took the rope from her, declaring Nora a hazard to herself.

Eventually, Nora and Briella returned to their own home just a short distance from Luna's. The children would come over throughout the day and Luna was mostly silent but found solace in working in the tavern and playing with the children.

One night, when Briella was teaching Beau and Reid how to fight with little wooden swords, Luna sat with Nora as she rocked Sasha to sleep.

"I like her a lot," Luna said.

Nora smiled. "I do too. I don't know what I would do without her."

"Nora, do nothing without her. Go where she goes." Tears streamed down Luna's eyes. "Love her and say it every day."

"Luna, Finn knew you loved him."

"But I didn't say it."

Nora nodded. "But he knew, just as you know he loved you."

Luna brushed the tears from her face and nodded in agreement, watching Briella and the children as the sun disappeared from the sky.

The days leading to the siege grew more and more tense and Briella spent less time playing with the children and more time assisting with the strategy to assault the castle. Briella's knowledge was well respected, and they worked through their plans while Nora trained with the goddess. It was a slow and frustrating process, and as their last night approached, Nora felt the anxiety of how much she still needed to learn rising within her.

Gailea demanded a celebration for all on their last night before setting off and encouraged Nora to take the day before off to meditate.

"You are blocked within yourself. You need to find that well within and seek it out alone. There is only so much we can tell you, but you will not move forward until you work through this wall." The goddess said firmly.

"I am trying, but I can't. I don't know what you mean by a wall; it's too abstract. You keep talking about walls and feelings and all of this shit I can't see and I can't figure out how to fix it!" Nora shouted in frustration.

Gailea listened calmly. "The wall is the part of you that says 'I can't'. Which you said three times just now." She smiled at Nora's glare. "You are not ready, but there is no time to prepare further. You must survive, and we will try to help you undo the wall around your magic. I can see it, I can see it without any magic. But you are not ready."

"That doesn't help me now," Nora whispered, looking out at the people below. "It doesn't help them."

"It doesn't, but we can't change it. What you bring to us right now as you are is what you are meant to bring in this moment. You must meditate, ground yourself, and then relax tomorrow. That's all we have left now."

Nora felt her stomach twist. The way she was not enough, even in a prophecy, felt heavy on her. She wanted to give them what they wanted; she wanted so desperately to be what they needed her to be. But as she stood there before the goddess, she felt her inadequacy press upon her like a thick blanket, suffocating her with its weight.

She walked the long trail up to where the memorial candles burned and lit Finn's candle, finding a comfortable place to sit and begin the grueling process of quieting her mind as Gailea would tell her over and over. Every sound drew her away from herself, she felt her mind spinning and focusing on tasks she still needed to do, she felt the urgency of controlling this power beating inside her, and she felt the goddesses disappointment as she said 'it's all we have left now'.

Nora stayed there until the dinner bells rang and never did quiet her mind, but she snuffed out Finn's candle with a silent prayer and made her way to Briella, who waited in front of the large banquet room. Briella took Nora's hand and led her through the motions of the night, and Nora took comfort in knowing that when she felt she would buckle beneath the weight of the world, Briella would help her stand tall.

29

Chapter Twenty-Nine

The next day, a celebration overtook the space. People set up banners and flags, children painted the ground with brightly colored paints typical of the people of Ospas, and on this day, it was expected the Queen of Ospas would arrive. Briella made dresses for her and Nora to wear, insisting that it was important Nora look the part of a leader despite Nora's insistence that her own breeches would be good enough for anyone. Briella took some of the body paint and decorated them with specific patterns Nora saw on Ospanese merchants in the past.

"You seem familiar with their customs." Nora marveled when she inspected herself in the mirror.

Her dress was long and fitted to her body, sporting reds and oranges and golden jewelry hung around her throat and wrists. The red paint stood out in contrast to Nora's deeply tanned skin and she almost didn't recognize herself.

"Know your enemy, my father used to say. I was an excellent student." Briella's voice was tinged with sadness, but she continued weaving small pearls through Nora's hair, focused on the task at hand. "I thought about making you a crown, but that might be too much of a statement."

"You think it would be too much of a statement for me to wear a crown when I go to meet a queen in her own land?" Nora teased, laughing when Briella shoved her gently.

"Well, I am royalty, so that makes you royalty too," Briella said softly.

Nora turned to face her, her smile soft and warm. "Could I make you a prophesied child of doom?"

"Please don't." Briella rose and gave Nora a soft kiss. "Let's dazzle the queen."

The festival was full of music and laughter. People came from Ospas with carts overflowing with goods to sell and trade. Some brought their children and, despite their hesitation, eventually allowed themselves to enjoy the night. Nora couldn't blame their weariness. She was certain if she was in their position, she would've believed it to be a trap. But Gailea eased their fears, and Nora smiled as the children ran together, their different upbringings only apparent by the red paint on the children from Ospas.

Nora relaxed further when she saw Leir, who was elaborately dressed with swirls of golden paint decorating the lower horse half of his body and billowing golden fabrics covering his upper human half. Golden paint highlighted his eyes and lips, and he returned her smile.

"Well, well, you clean up nicely. I see Briella didn't make you wear the crown." He said as he admired the pair.

"You seriously made it?" Nora laughed.

Briella shrugged. "I like to be prepared. But I decided against it!"

Leir led the two deeper into the space that was lit by purple fires throughout. Nora felt the tension rise within her when she saw the purple flames, uncomfortably aware that they were meant for her. Briella noticed and wrapped an arm around Nora's shoulders, kissing her cheek and leading her into the ballroom.

Standing at the head of the room was Gailea and a woman Nora did not recognize. The woman stood much taller than Nora and was strikingly beautiful with ebony skin and a crown of spiraling black hair fanning out around her face, and blue eyes that stood out in stark contrast to her dark skin. Her body was painted with gold paint, and it shimmered as she moved. She wore an emerald green dress that hugged her body in ways that Nora had never seen a queen's body displayed before. She was power encapsulated and was proud to show the world that power. Surveying the crowd, she smiled at her people and chatted with the Goddess until her eyes rested on Nora. The movement in the room slowed, and Nora could hear nothing around her.

Welcome, Child of Draco. The same voice Nora heard in her mind so many times before echoed within her now from the Queen of Ospas herself. Her heart quickened, and she looked around her at all the people frozen in place.

"It was you?" Nora stood stunned at the might of the queen before her.

The queen smiled. "I have watched you for a long time, Nora DuPont. Long before the dragon. But you could not hear me, not until you finally opened your well of magic against Talon."

Chills ran through Nora's body and she felt naked as she stood before the queen.

"We are—linked?" Although they were still far apart, it felt like the room compressed and they were standing mere feet away from each other.

"Yes. I am the queen of dragon worshippers; you are the child of the god of dragons. Our link is deep and binding."

Nora frowned. "I reject him and his ideas. How does that fit with your beliefs?"

The queen laughed, her eyes sparkling with excitement. "I have been warned that you are fiery and that you speak your mind no matter who stands before you. That is refreshing." The queen looked around the room before returning her attention to Nora. "It fits with my beliefs perfectly. We are a people who worship the dragon lords of the skies, but we are not blind to folly. What Draco is bringing about is the end of our world, and although we seek to change it, we do not seek what he desires. He desires revenge for Zeta, and his hatred blinds him."

"Then we have much in common."

The queen smiled, turning to someone standing beside her and sending the room back into a burst of life. Nora marveled that even the mother goddess seemed to not have noticed the stopping in time. They continued up to the dais, and Briella bowed deeply, dragging Nora down with her.

"Your royal highness Aris, may I present to you Nora DuPont of Sorudi and Princess Gabriella Velannize of Madrall." The Goddess smiled at Briella.

"It is wonderful to meet you both." Queen Aris smiled knowingly at Nora and grabbed Briella's hands reassuringly. "You are very welcome here, princess. I am pleased to find someone in your royal line that believes differently than the rest. I hope this is the beginning of the end of a long and tragic divide."

Briella's hands shook slightly with relief. "I hope the same, your highness."

Aris kissed Briella's forehead and Nora watched as her people let out a collective sigh. Their shoulders visibly dropped, and Nora wondered how difficult it had to be for them to even be in the princess' presence until their queen had the chance to assess her.

"And you, Nora DuPont. You also have shown that you are not defined by those who sired you. I am pleased to see so much evidence of free thinking. I believe the future holds great things for our people. Now, let us not talk about troublesome matters tonight. This is a celebration before a weary journey; let us make the most of it."

Nora and Briella bowed deeply again, and Nora followed Briella onto the dance floor where they danced through the night. Briella sparkled on the dance floor, her red curls a wave around her and her body moving with familiarity of the music of Ospas. Nora saw the way the people of Ospas appreciated her respect for their culture and she marveled at the force Briella was. She was born to lead, and lead multitudes, and anyone could see that.

Nora took her leave from the dance floor, allowing Briella to grab hold of Leir, who leapt with excitement at the opportunity to dance with the princess. Queen Aris was sitting by herself, enjoying the night and smiling as her subjects enjoyed a rare moment of unity. Nora joined her, offering a glass of wine and sipping on her own glass.

"This is a fine night." Aris's eyes twinkled as she spoke. "So much joy before so much rage. It feels like a breath before diving underwater."

Nora nodded in agreement. "For me, it feels like a gasp of air before another wave pulls me down."

She watched as Luna entered the room, her children running off to dance and her eyes displaying the heartache her face fought to hold back. Nora motioned for her to join them, and Luna grabbed her own glass before moving towards them.

Luna bowed deeply before the queen. "Your highness."

"Hello child, how are you settling in?" Gailea asked as she motioned for Luna to rise and take a seat beside them.

"As well as can be expected, my lady. The people here have spared no expense and I am truly thankful, but I have lost much and I am still trying to find myself. I apologize that I have been absent–"

"Do not apologize." Gailea interrupted as she took her own seat opposite Nora. "We have all lost much since the dragon descended upon this land. Take your time to feel what you must feel."

Luna returned her attention to her children. "I haven't told them yet."

Nora squeezed Luna's hand. "There is no rush, Luna. Wait until this battle is over. There is too much happening for them to also be processing that grief."

"I wish I could have that peace as well." Luna whispered. "I felt him die, Nora. I felt his life slip away, just as I felt Malachi take his last breath. But I wish I could not know. I wish I could go on waiting forever."

"I wish that too, sometimes." Aris said solemnly.

Nora thought of everyone they lost. She wondered what tonight would have been like with Finn. He would've teased her for her outfit and danced the night away, rotating between Nora and Briella until Luna arrived and became the center of his world. Finn would've danced with her children, flirted with the queen, teased the goddess; he would've lit up the room with his light. But he was not here, and he would never be here again. And the loss of Finn felt heavy; the heaviness rising in her chest as she allowed herself to feel it. She allowed tears to fall for all the people who should be there and weren't, and she made space for the silence of their shared grief as they watched people dance before a dawn full of uncertainty.

After a long moment of companionable silence, Nora spoke. "I will leave tonight on my own."

Luna turned to stare at her, and Aris smiled.

"You can't just *leave!*" Luna hissed.

"I have no choice. If I don't, it puts all of this at risk. I don't have full control over my power and I don't know what will happen when I'm set against that staff. A celestial weapon powered by Zeta's heart—I have no idea what I'll do. And to go with an army of people beside me puts them all at risk." Nora had been thinking about this for days, but as she spoke the words, she felt the other options melt away. She knew that this was the only path forward.

"Say something!" Luna shouted to Gailea. "Don't let her do this!"

Gailea sighed. "As much as I want to, I can't. It is the path she must walk."

Luna looked out at the people around them, shaking her head slowly, and then pulled Nora into a tight embrace. "I cannot tell you to come back, because I do not know if you will. I don't know if you will be able to if you survive. But I am so sorry that this happened to you. I am so sorry you must carry this burden, Nora."

Nora's eyes fixed on Briella. "I haven't told her. She won't let me go if I do and I can't risk putting her in that position. And we need her here to help command the troops."

"It seems unfair to not give her the choice." Luna murmured.

"It does." Nora agreed.

Gailea ran her hand across Nora's shoulders. "The staff is a celestial weapon and can trigger your magic. You need to destroy it, and fast. Get it out of the way and it lessens the risk of you losing yourself." She smiled at the sight of Leir bowing deeply to Briella as she tried to scurry away as fast as she could before she was forced into another dance. "It'll also free up those of us on the ground. Get that under control, and we will have a better chance."

Nora smiled as Briella swept up one of Luna's children and spun them around. They sat in silence for a long while, and when the music died down, the Queen rose onto the dais once more, Gailea standing behind her smiling down at the people.

"I offer you all this blessing as we go into the uncertainty of the days to come." Her voice boomed around them, magnified by her power. She sang a haunting, beautiful melody that made all who heard stop and turn to the queen.

Briella hurried to Nora's side and watched with her, holding Nora's hand and swaying slightly from too much drink and dance. Nora smiled, wrapping her arms around Briella and enjoying holding her as they listened. Some people cried, others stood in solemn silence. Nora felt as if they were crossing a threshold together, everyone collectively, and that the time before this song would be a distant memory in only a few short hours. She felt the heaviness of the room and closed her eyes, listening and drowning everything else out.

When the festival was over, they slowly made their way back to their house, Briella stumbling and giggling as they moved. Nora laughed at her clumsiness. She thought it was astounding how Briella could find moments of joy always. They went into their room and stripped off their dresses, moving towards the small bath behind a curtain and washing the paint from each other's bodies. They went to their bed, still naked, and reveled in each other.

"I love you." Nora whispered, tucking a curl behind Briella's ear.

"I love you too." Briella smiled. She moved closer, kissing Nora and wrapping her legs around Nora's. "Sleep well, my love."

Briella's eyelids grew heavy and Nora watched as she slid off into a deep sleep, her breathing slowly deepening as she drifted off. Her wild red curls fanned out around them both, something Nora would tease Briella about but secretly loved.

She learned many things about Briella as they shared a bed together. She learned Briella talked in her sleep, and from that talking she learned that she often had nightmares about being locked back up in the dungeon. Nora would rub Briella's arm to comfort her through those nightmares. She also learned that Briella snored if she drank too close to bedtime, and learned to give Briella extra pillows to prop her up higher on those nights to reduce the snoring. She learned Briella liked to be held after they made love, that she wanted to cuddle until she fell asleep and then she wanted Nora to not come anywhere near her, that Briella was always hot but always wanted thick blankets over them, and the most important thing Nora learned was that a life without Briella waking up beside her every morning was unbearable.

30

Chapter Thirty

When Briella's breathing slowed into the steady rhythm of sleep, Nora slipped from her bed silently and grabbed her clothes and bag. She looked back at Briella's sleeping form and the note she left on the bedside table, and closed the door to their room behind her. She picked up their dresses and folded them neatly on the table, slipped on her clothes and bag, and headed out into the cool night air. Nora hurried up towards the memorial and lit Finn's candle one last time, her heart aching as she did so.

"I'm sorry I couldn't save you." She whispered. "I love you."

Wind blew through the trees around her and she closed her eyes, allowing the warm summer air to spread across her. It rustled through the leaves and the flame flickered until it was eventually blown out. Nora smiled. Briella would pick apart the meaning of that. She would tell Nora it was the way the dead communicated. She would have told her Finn was there with her now, and Nora would silently nod in agreement. But she did not feel him with her, she did not hear his voice on the breeze, and she did not feel the chill of an unseen presence in the air. Nora felt only emptiness hanging heavy in the air.

Nora had almost left the village when she heard footsteps behind her. She turned to find Aris moving up the path, waving a hand at her.

She waited for the queen to make her way up the path and smiled as she noticed Aris carrying a sword with her.

"Let's trade swords. I assure you, mine will serve you better." Aris's eyes sparkled with mischief. When they traded swords, Aris smiled at her, her eyes full of pride and a hint of sadness. "I have watched you for such a long time. It is strange to stand before you now."

"It's strange that you were watching me." Nora shifted uncomfortably.

The queen chuckled. "I knew the moment you were conceived and spent years trying to find you. When I did, you were alone in a forest, crying out for your mother, and I felt your power radiating out to me. It was just a moment, but enough for me to find you. I led Tulee towards you and have kept an eye on you ever since. I learned a lot about you, Nora DuPont. That you are kind and selfless. I learned that you will do anything for those you love, and boy, do you *love*. You give out a love so fierce it astounds me. Always hold on to that."

"What should I do?" Nora whispered.

"You are doing exactly what is destined."

Nora let out a long sigh and shrugged. "I can't say if that makes me feel better or worse."

Aris let out a quiet chuckle and patted Nora's shoulder. "That's the funny thing about destiny. You won't know until it's all said and done." She pointed to the opal that still hung around Nora's neck. "That should bring you some luck."

Nora looked down at the opal and smiled. She didn't even notice it anymore. Briella had instructed her to keep it on at all times, and she had done so. They were now as much a part of her as her own skin.

"Goodbye." Nora bowed her head before turning to walk down the path.

"Good luck," Aris called after her.

Nora was careful not to look back, afraid that if she did, she wouldn't be able to force herself to go. She thought of Briella's rage in the morning when she would find Nora's note, and a smile tugged at her lips through her tears.

If I survive this, she thought, *she will kill me for that.*

Nora walked through the night and most of the next day, determined to get as much space between herself and the forest before Briella could come after her. She knew they would only waste their resources on finding her for so long before they had to move toward the battle to come, and Nora made it clear in her letter to Briella what her intentions were.

She allowed her power to propel her forward, lifting her into the sky above the land of Troque until she made her way to the open marshland she and Finn once trekked together. She descended to the edge of the marsh and noticed immediately the remnants of a small camp and smiled. This is where they met Hanna. Her eyes filled with tears remembering Finn's suspicions of Hanna, how he used his magic to protect them, and how Luna looked at him that day. It wasn't fair that he was gone, and she found herself more often than she cared to admit, looking for him or wanting to say something to him. As she sat there in the marsh, it felt like he was there with her and in the breeze that blew through her hair, she felt almost as if she could feel him beside her.

"I miss you." She whispered. "I wish I could've saved you. I wish you could be here. I love you, Finn." The wind blew her words off with it and she let out a long sigh before standing up and continuing on towards the castle.

The mountains around Sorudi gave Nora the perfect vantage point of the kingdom. As she slowly made her way up to them, she felt her heart quicken at the familiar trails of her youth. She knew she was close to Reflection Lake, where she had taken refuge after the dragon attacked, and she slowly made her way toward the lake. She wondered briefly if the nymph was still there, waiting for her to return.

The sun began to set as Nora approached the lake. The air was thin, and she grew slightly dizzy.

Just a little farther.

Nora stepped out into the clearing of the lake, and a chill ran up her spine. She pulled out her flask and took a long drink of water, and refilled it with the icy lake water. She removed her cooking supplies and made herself a hasty meal, laying down a blanket to sit for a moment and take off her boots.

The moon shone bright, brighter than Nora had ever seen before. She decided this was a good omen, although she had no reason to hope for any good to come now. Whatever semblance of good she had was left behind, safely tucked away where it could not be burned.

Turning to gather her things, she looked into the still water of the lake and did not recognize the person in front of her. Her once long flowing hair was braided back away from her face, her body which was never soft or voluptuous to begin with was lean from too many nights without food, badly bruised and scarred and covered in dirt that seemed to now just be part of her skin. Her once soft blue eyes, which were the only thing she ever received compliments for, seemed wild and near madness.

The person she was before was gone and the person she had become, this weathered warrior who carried her to this place, her time was almost up as well.

She looked at the stars. Tonight, she saw the constellation Draco shine clearest in the night sky.

"Look what you've gotten me into." She half expected the dragon to rear up and plummet down to her. Nothing would surprise her anymore. But she was met with stillness. She turned her attention to the castle that rose before her, a beacon calling her to her ruin.

This was it.

Nora raised her hood up and took one last look behind her before disappearing into the night.

Keeping to the tree line, Nora could see the silhouette of the house she grew up in. From what she could see, it appeared they rebuilt and people were living there again. Whether her mother was there or not, she was unsure, but she wondered if Tulee was. She fought the sudden urge to check. It was likely that her mother knew she was alive by now if Larissa knew, and she was certain Adelle wouldn't hesitate to hold her until the king could come for her. She looked down at the estate for a moment longer, acutely aware of how it no longer held any place of home in her heart, and turned to make her way through the forest to the castle.

The woods were still as she made her way through and she felt it was as if nature itself was holding its breath in anticipation. Nora took an arrow out of her quiver and readied it in her bow, pointing it to the ground as she knew she was nearing the castle. The trees were thinning and Nora lowered herself closer to the ground, moving from tree to tree, ready to fire at any guard that may patrol the forest. She heard voices nearby and felt her heart quicken. Easing back into the shadows, she watched as two guards slowly made their way towards her, unaware of her presence.

They seemed inebriated, and Nora smiled as she realized they were the same guards they had passed when they escaped the city.

"It's creepy out here. I always feel like the trees are watchin' me." One guard said as he surveyed the darkness of the forest.

"Watchin' me take a piss!" The other shouted, laughing to himself.

"You idiot." The other guard took a few steps towards Nora and she pulled her bowstring tight, ready to fire if necessary.

"Let's get back. I'm sick of this place."

The guard stared into the forest, right at Nora's hiding spot, and her heartbeat pounded loudly in her ears.

"Come on!" The other guard shouted as he continued on.

"I'm coming, you sack of shit." The guard cast one last look in Nora's direction and then hurried after his friend.

She listened to their laugh in the darkness and when she was sure they were gone let out a long sigh of relief.

Stepping out of the forest, she found the willow tree that obscured the tunnel entrance and slipped into the darkness below.

The tunnels were dark and Nora gasped as rats ran from under her feet. She remembered Finn summoning a ball of light to light their way and held out her hand before her. She closed her eyes, remembering how Finn flexed his fingers as if coaxing the flame from thin air. Nora called upon the well of magic inside her, pulling out one single thread and calling it to her fingers. She felt her hand grow warm, and she continued to focus, her eyes closed shut. She saw light filter through her eyelids and opened them to see a purple flame floating above her hand. Nora smiled, letting out a surprised laugh, and continued on down the winding halls.

The marks Luna showed them led her through the passages, and she focused on breathing through the tightness in her chest. The panic attacks still came, and she remembered how the darkness down here caused her to feel sick before. Nora slowed her breathing and focused her energy on calming herself until her breathing returned to normal. Finn would have been proud, or at least grateful, for not having to convince her she wasn't dying in these dark halls. She continued on, following the marks until she approached what seemed to be marked as the entrance to the mage's quarters.

Sliding out behind one of the hidden doors, Nora entered the mage's quarters and fought an audible sigh of relief to find them empty. Most of the mages would be at their posts guarding the castle, but she expected to find some in there. She moved silently through the room and slipped down into the servants' quarters. Once there, a calm came over Nora. Being invisible was something she knew how to be well. She hurried towards the kitchens where a small, portly woman sat stoking a fire.

"Psst!" Nora called out, drawing the woman's attention.

The woman glared at her and grabbed her poker, the end cherry red from the fire's heat.

"What are you doin' down here?" The woman hissed, quietly enough to not raise an alarm but loud enough to warn Nora she was not someone to mess with.

"I need to get to the throne room." Nora whispered frantically, her eyes fixed on the poker. "I promise, I mean you no harm."

The woman glared at her for a moment longer. Her face softened. "Nora?"

Nora's mouth fell open at the shock of the woman knowing her name.

"Nora, it's Cookie."

Nora gasped in recognition. Cookie had worked in the DuPont estate Nora's entire life, and seeing her in the castle kitchens was the last thing she had expected.

"Cookie! What are you doing here?!"

Cookie chuckled and lowered her poker. "I should be asking you that! I run the kitchens here since Larissa came. Runnin' quite the operation here, if I say so myself."

Nora smiled as Cookie swelled with pride. She was always a light in Nora's childhood. Where Tulee had been a mother, Cookie was like an overly affectionate aunt.

"It's so nice to see you," Nora whispered, pulling Cookie in for a tight hug.

Cookie held Nora out at arm's length and looked her up and down. "I wouldn't have recognized you if not for your eyes. I'm so glad you're ok."

Nora smiled, kissing Cookie on the forehead.

"What are you doing here, love?"

"Cookie, there is too much to explain now, but I need to get to the king." Nora's voice was urgent. "And you need to get out of here. This castle–it won't be safe."

Cookie frowned as she processed the information. "Well, the king won't be in the throne room. He'll be up with the mages on the rooftops. Tonight was an induction. They just got over. Usually linger up there for a while once they're done, like being up high and the power and whatnot."

Nora sighed. Of course. She had paid no attention to the fullness of the moon. Inductions happened every full moon, and it was where the new mages who had arrived at the castle were sworn in by the king.

"How can I get up there?" She asked urgently.

Cookie looked down at the ground, her face screwed up in frustration. "I don't want to see you hurt–"

"Cookie. If I don't, a lot more people will be hurt."

The woman's eyes were heavy with sadness, but she agreed. She led Nora to a staircase and pointed up.

"These will take you all the way up. You'll pop out inside one of the spires. They like the servants to stay hidden. You know how nobles are. There will be a wooden door with a hole for you to peek out, but once you open that door, there is no hiding up there."

"Thank you, Cookie." She kissed the woman on the cheek and blinked back tears. "Please find Tulee and tell her I have been on the greatest adventure of any lifetime."

Cookie smiled, patting Nora's cheek. "I will, my dear. I'll gather the staff and younglings and we will make for the catacombs. Be careful."

Nora made her way up the stairs. They spiraled up the tower, small windows letting the moonlight pour in as she made her way up. At last, Nora entered the spire, where a young servant girl gaped at her, eyes wide with terror.

Nora pressed a hand over the girl's mouth and shook her head sternly. "You need to go down into the catacombs and find Cookie *now*."

The girl agreed quietly, rushing past Nora and down the stairs. She stole one last look at Nora before disappearing down the winding staircase.

31

Chapter Thirty-One

She pressed her ear against the wooden panels and froze as she heard a familiar voice.

"We were told you were the only one with magic, Larissa." The cruel voice of Brutus was the first voice she recognized.

"That's what my mother and I believed." Nora could tell Larissa's teeth were gritted together with rage. "Do you really believe for a second that my mother would have left magic unreported?"

"Perhaps not." The third voice caused Nora's heart to skip a beat. It was the king. She stood silent, not daring to breathe as he continued on. "It would explain how she could defeat the dragon."

Larissa let out a low chuckle. "Her powers are not that great. As I said before, we were ambushed. She aligned herself with others more powerful than her, and that bitch of a princess cut off my fucking hand. If all of that hadn't happened, Nora would be in the dungeons now, chained up and facing her fate. There is no remarkable power in her."

Nora furrowed her brow. Was Larissa lying to help her, or trying to downplay the situation so she didn't appear to have been beaten by Nora? She remembered Larissa's face as Nora's magic exploded around her; she looked truly frightened in that moment. Nora silently moved towards the hole in the door and held her breath as she peered out at the three standing on the other side. The mages had either gone or not arrived yet; it was impossible for Nora to tell. From her vantage point, she was looking at the backs of Brutus and the king's head and straight into Larissa's eyes. She swore for a second that her sister saw her.

Brutus moved towards the center of the landing and shook his head.

"How do we know this is true? Perhaps you are lying to help her." He asked, his voice dripping with venom.

The king laughed, placing a hand on Larissa's shoulder. "After speaking with Adelle myself, I assure you there is no love between the two girls. She is little more than a servant in their house, and Larissa has done much to prove her loyalty."

Larissa bowed her head, allowing the king to make his way to Brutus.

"You were there when the dragon was slain. Somehow, the girl did what no other mortal being could. How could someone with so little magic kill a dragon?" The king looked up into Brutus's eyes and a grin flashed across Brutus's face.

Nora noticed the mage gathering magic around him, and Larissa's eyes widened as she hurried to defend herself.

"No!" Nora screamed, bursting through the door and drawing her sword in an attempt to block Brutus's magic from harming Larissa. The sword absorbed much of the magic, but Nora screamed as some spilled around the sword and burned her arms. When the light stopped, Nora fell to one knee, her arms pulsing with pain.

"Nora?" Larissa whispered.

The king stared down at her, his eyes wide.

"You came right to us! You idiot girl." Brutus extended his arm, and Nora felt as if her entire body was paralyzed.

She rose in the air a few inches and choked against the squeezing pain. She tried to calm herself enough to reach the magic well inside her as her vision blurred. Nora tried to reach for her sword, her head screaming in protest of her every move.

The king moved towards her, grabbing her hair and spitting in her face.

"You will die here today, and tomorrow I will have my princess. We know where she is, Nora DuPont. Your friends in the forest will meet their doom." He shoved Nora's head hard into the stone floor beneath her and her world went black.

When she came to, Nora was still on the top of the castle tower, but now chained to the wall. She groaned and looked around her. She saw a figure moving towards her and tried to move backward, away from the intruder.

"Nora, it's me," Larissa whispered. "What are you doing here? You need to get out of here. They're going to—"

"Why do you care what they do to me?" Nora's voice was defiant as she focused on Larissa's face.

"I care," Larissa said firmly, inspecting Nora's head.

"How long have I been out?"

"Four days. I have come to change your bandages and try to give you enough healing to stop the bleeding, but I couldn't do more without jeopardizing—"

Nora let out a quiet chuckle. "You couldn't save me without jeopardizing yourself. Typical."

"I did—"

"Haven't you done enough?" Nora shouted, kicking dirt at her sister and glaring at her.

Larissa stared at her for a long moment. "If I hadn't acted the way I did on the cliff, they would've done way worse to all of us. I warned you, I begged you to stop."

Nora spat at her, leaning against the pillar she was chained to, meeting Larissa at her eye level.

"You killed my friend. He had a family, Larissa. Children and their mother, who were all waiting for him. You took him from them, you took him from me. And you tried to take Briella—"

"Briella?" Larissa furrowed her brow. "The princess—?"

"Yes, Gabriella. Briella. Try to keep up." Nora never spoke to anyone with such unkindness, but her heart burned with hatred for her sister. She was the one person in the world who should have protected Nora, and she stood by Nora's entire life only helping in the shadows. And then when Nora needed her again, she killed Finn and tried to say it was for their own good. "I am tired of hearing you justify the way you let people use you. If you want to tell yourself that you had to do it, go ahead. But do not ever lie to me like that again."

"Let me help you. Let me get you out of here."

"I am not leaving here until I've destroyed that celestial weapon, Larissa."

"Nora, you are not some prophecy. These people have filled your head with nonsense, and I understand why you want to believe it. I understand why you want to belong to something bigger than yourself–"

"It's not like that." Nora looked off into the distance. "I never wanted this. All I want right now is to spend my life beside the woman I love, tending a garden and making sure her days are happy. You and your mother are the ones who want power, not me. But I have it, and it could destroy Briella. It could destroy the world."

"Nora—"

"Just go," Nora whispered. "I don't want your help."

Larissa stood frozen. Nora could hear her sister crying softly, but she refused to look at her. Exhaustion washed over Nora like a wave, and she could not muster the energy to even consider her sister's pain.

"I love you," Larissa whispered before turning to walk down the main passageway that led down from the tower.

Nora had wanted a connection with her sister her entire life. She had thirsted for it, sought it out at every opportunity, savored the rare moments it was gifted to her. She was a starving animal returning to her abuser for food and love, relishing in rare moments of kindness. Now, she didn't know what she felt. It was the absence of sorrow that hit her the hardest. She should be destroyed, but Larissa had done nothing to her that she hadn't done a million times before. Her indifference, her unwillingness to be put out on Nora's behalf; it didn't matter that she wanted to help. That wasn't enough; it was never enough.

The throbbing in Nora's head was unbearable, and she raised her hand to the wound only to find it covered in old, thick blood. When Larissa said she had done the bare minimum, she wasn't kidding. The smell of infection gagged her, and the searing pain in her head overwhelmed her senses. She weaved slowly before collapsing to the ground.

Rain began to fall and Nora looked up at the sky, tears and raindrops blending together into the blood and dirt smeared across her face. The air smelled of summer rain and Nora imagined she was back in her forest, lying beside the stream and melting into the earth beneath her. Thick velvet moss supporting her limbs, she could hear the rain hitting the leaves and the wind from the approaching storm created a symphony of sound that mimicked the waves outside of Balcross. Nora smiled, running her fingers through the moss into the stream and allowing her arm to be lazily tugged along by the current.

Nora, are you ok? A voice called out.

"I'm fine," Nora murmured.

Nora, you need to wake up.

"I'll be there in a second." The voice sounded familiar. It was someone important, but she couldn't remember who. Her head hurt so badly, she wanted to go to sleep.

Nora. We're coming, Briella is coming. You need to wake up; you need to help Briella.

"Briella," Nora murmured. "What's wrong with Briella?"

Nora, you left to deal a blow. You need to wake up, or Briella will be in danger. Wake up, Nora.

Nora groaned, opening her eyes and looking around her again. She looked down at the pool of blood from the now reopened wound that was accumulating under her head. Breathing deeply, she reached into the well of magic within her. She focused on the meditations she had done with Gailea and Leir, allowing her mind to bounce around from one fear to the next until the thoughts passed over her like a wave. Chills ran down her spine as she felt muscles she didn't realize were always tense, relax and ache in their release. She felt a weightlessness about her, and suddenly she knew exactly what she must do.

She saw purple streams of light billowing from inside her and reached in to grab one. It burned for a second, and she emptied her mind, grabbing the light and pulling it out. Her hands glowed a soft purple, and she touched one to her head, willing the light to heal her. It burned for a second and then gave way to the warmth of sunshine on a warm day. She lowered her hand and smiled as the throbbing was gone. She then focused on the chains that bound her, willing them to melt away from her. The metal twisted beneath her magic and eventually fell away from her arms.

Gailea is going to be so impressed that I meditated, she thought as she leaned back against the stone pillar.

We're so impressed, Aris's voice echoed in her mind. *Now, do what you came here to do.*

Nora looked around her. There were pillars surrounding the top of the tower with torches lighting the space. The sides and roof were open around her and the rain continued to splash down onto the black granite floor. No one was there with her, which she found to be incredibly stupid. She stayed still, unsure if someone was hiding. She knew she would never leave someone unattended like this, especially someone considered a threat.

She looked in the direction Larissa disappeared and back at the servants' quarters she burst through. The mage had blasted the servant's door with magic and the stone from the surrounding wall melted over it. The only way down was through the main door. She heard the humming of many voices and quickly closed her eyes, grabbing the chains so they appeared to still be attached to her and laying her head back into the pool of her own blood on the ground.

"Is she awake?" King Adrian asked, his voice tinged with fear.

"No, sir. Would you like me to wake her?" Brutus asked.

The king did not speak his reply, but Nora listened as steps moved closer to her. When whoever was nearing her was within range, she sprang up and punched as hard as she could. She could feel the bones in Brutus's face crack under the impact, and he screamed.

"Fuck!" Brutus sent magic streaming at Nora and binding her arms to her side. He lifted her in the air so she was above him and looked up into her face, his face twisted with rage. "How *dare* you."

Nora noticed his eyes flash into slits exactly as Talon's had. Her face must have betrayed her shock because his anger turned to confusion and he threw her to the ground before she could speak.

"Your Highness! Use the staff, now!" Brutus's eyes were frantic as he screamed his commands toward a king who would not listen.

The king made his way forward slowly, seemingly uninterested in Brutus or his instructions. "She's just a weak little girl, Brutus. The magicless daughter hidden away by a washed-up crone of a mother. We don't even have records of her birth. She is nothing."

"She is the child of the prophecy!" Brutus's face tensed as he tried to subdue his outrage. "The only thing that can kill her is—"

"He's lying," Nora croaked. "I can't do any magic. He wants the staff for himself."

"Silence!" Brutus bellowed down at her. "Your Highness, I have had nothing but your best interests at heart. This girl—"

"This girl stole my princess and tried to take her for herself. *That* is all I know to be true." Adrian grinned down at Nora. "You thought you could just take her? With power like hers?"

Nora felt rage bubbling within her.

"My lord, you must use the staff. She's unpredictable. She killed the dragon, my lord. She could–"

"Larissa said it was a fluke, and I believe her. She has proven her loyalty time and time again, Brutus. We're surely missing something here." Adrian lowered down to look at Nora. "How did you do it?"

"Well, your highness, it was hard." Nora kept her voice under control as she spoke, her eyes fixed on the ground before her. "I had to lure it in, to make it feel like it could get close to me. So close that it wasn't in danger. I had to make it feel like it could destroy me, and then when it got close enough–" she looked up at the king and smiled. "—I did this." She pulled the magic from within her and thrust it at the king, a purple fire radiating from within her. He was thrown back, screaming, flames engulfing him. Brutus bound her to the floor and Larissa burst out from the door, horrified at the sight of Adrain burning before her.

She poured magic into him, quelling the fire and working on his wounds. She looked at Nora, eyes wide with fear.

"Nora."

A vision erupted in Nora's mind and she suddenly saw Briella in full armor seated on top of a horse, eyes fixed ahead, and she rode hard through the night. Thousands of men and women rode behind her, and Briella screamed as they ran through the front lines of the castle's mighty army. Briella swung her sword mercilessly, cutting through man after man and leading her forces forward. A griffin swooped down from the sky and grabbed several men, throwing them up into the air as it ascended and sending them crashing at a sickening speed. Briella whirled around, stopping the blow from an enemy sword inches from her own face. She screamed with the impact, pushing back up with all of her strength until the attacker was flown off of her. Briella's helmet fell from her and her red curls blew around her in the storm, and she looked up towards the castle where Nora was.

"Please be alive." She whispered.

Nora, she's coming. Do what you came to do.

32

Chapter Thirty-Two

Seeing Nora in a trance, the king moved towards her and kicked her down to the ground, laughing as the air was thrust from her lungs. He placed his staff at Nora's throat, his face wild with hatred. He pressed it into her skin slowly, cutting into her and causing her to gasp for air. The opal touched her skin and Nora felt something burning in her throat, radiating out from her.

"Stop!" Larissa screamed, running towards them. "She's going to—"

The king swung his staff at her, a burst of power throwing Larissa back. "I knew I shouldn't have trusted a DuPont *bitch*!" The king screamed. "I will kill you, and all of you DuPont's, and end your meddling line!" He looked back at Nora, his face wild with insanity. "I hear you warmed my princess up for me."

Nora screamed, and purple electricity filled the air. With the opal no longer resting on her throat, she felt her control returning to her, and she reached into the well of magic frantically.

Nora, we are almost there. Hold on. Queen Aris's voice pulsed through Nora.

Nora felt the familiar sting of her magic pour from her beyond control. She tried desperately to go inward, to calm the swell of magic from within her, but her rage pushed her mind beyond its limit and the purple light inside her filled her veins.

"What the fuck—Brutus!" The king screamed, throwing Nora down and hurrying behind him.

Brutus sent all of his magic at Nora and she gritted her teeth as he attempted to restrain her. Brutus' magic dripped with a Draconic energy different from what she had experienced from Talon, but strangely similar. She saw the threads of the mage's magic, connecting out so far into the distance she could not see the source. Thousands of intricate webs of light funneling into his chest, and as she saw it Brutus fear gave way to a sickening glee.

You must control yourself! Queen Aris called out to Nora. *You will die if you cannot!*

The opal on Nora's necklace began to burn hot. She looked down and watched in horror as it burned through her skin, burrowing into her chest. She let out a blood-curdling shriek that echoed out across the castle, clasping at her chest and trying desperately to rip the opal from her chest. It continued to burrow, her skin folding over it as it went.

The king watched her in stunned silence, his face full of confusion and terror.

"Nora!" Larissa screamed, sending her own magic at her sister. Nora felt Brutus's magic weaken and realized Larissa was shielding her.

Nora's eyes glowed with a purple light and she stood, magic pulsing from her fingertips, and felt all the pain of her mortal body melt away. As Nora drew closer, her magic intensified and the stone beneath her feet cracked. Larissa's magic disappeared Nora's grew, and the sky above them swirled with purple light.

Brutus screamed, turning to see the king fleeing down one of the spires. "Your Highness! The weapon, you must–"

Brutus tried to follow, and Nora put out her hand to stop him. The door the king was running towards melted into thick molten lava and he screamed as it burned his hands, falling to the ground and trying desperately to crawl away from the oozing molten rock. She ran now, a cruel smile spreading across her face. Brutus attacked with everything he had, sending his magic coursing all around her. Nora barreled through his attack and pinned him down to the floor. His body crushed through the stone with the force, and blood spurted out his mouth as he gaped up at her.

Her eyes, which glowed purple, were reptilian-like, with slits peering down at him. The skin around her hands grew purple and blue scales and her nails lengthened into claws that dug into his skin. He screamed against the horror and the pain, pleading for his life.

"Beg me." Nora's voice echoed all around them.

"Please. Please."

Nora smiled, pushing his body deeper into the stone. "More."

"I will do anything. I was trying to help you, I was doing your—"

"Lies!" she screamed, two voices speaking through her at one time. "I am the Child of Draco, the prophesied end of times, the one you called with your corruption and tyranny." She looked up at the king, who watched on in horror. She grabbed his staff from the ground and snapped it in half, removing the opal at the end of it. "I take back the heart of the queen of dragons, and I will avenge her."

Nora pressed the opal to her chest, screaming as it seeped into her skin. The opal fused with the other, radiating refracting light into the surrounding air. Colors burst forth as a beacon and below on the ground as the army from Ospas approached, Nora watched as Briella looked up at the light filling the sky.

Nora drew the sword Queen Aris gave her and walked to Brutus as she dragged it behind her, sparks flying from its contact with the stone floor. She cocked her head as she looked down at him, a cruel smile spreading across her face.

His eyes flashed at her again, and she realized there was something different about him. He was not a dragon himself, but there was something happening. The energy was almost her own and Nora realized in that moment why it was so familiar. The mage made a deal with Draco and was trying to fulfill his prophecy.

"You like to meddle, don't you?" She taunted him.

"Please, please let me live." He sputtered, tears streaming down his face. "You don't understand. I was doing His bidding, we're on the same—"

"This sword—" she said wickedly, holding it to Brutus' throat. "—is no mage killer. It is nothing but a normal sword, but it will do just fine." The blade shone with celestial energy, and Nora smiled before slashing Brutus's throat, watching as the blood spilled from his neck.

The king rose to his feet. "What have you done?"

Nora kicked him to the ground, spitting on him as he crumbled below her. "You *coward*." She summoned the magic within her, but with the addition of the new dragon heart, Nora saw the well overflowing from within her. It spilled through her entire body, erupting through every vein as it coursed through her.

It was an explosion of energy that billowed from Nora, and the entire castle seemed to ripple under its force.

"Nora!" Larissa called to her sister. "Nora, come back!"

A voice in Nora's head spoke against the voice coming from her. *Save her. Your sister. Save her.*

"No!" Nora screamed.

Save her!

A light flashed around Nora and she was in a room, the castle around her disappeared. She looked around her and realized it was her room back at the DuPont estate, exactly how she left it. The smell of Cookie's food wafting in the distance. She looked around the room, brows furrowed with confusion and stopped when she saw her reflection in the mirror before her. She was staring at herself; although, not actually herself. The person before her looked like her except she had purple scales that ran up her arms and neck, stopping below her chin. Where Nora had hands, this version had long black claws and was dripping with blood. She stepped through the mirror, eyes fixed on Nora. Her breathing was labored, and she looked exhausted despite her rage.

Who are you? Nora's voice was a dream-like echo as if she was not really in the space she occupied.

"I am the one you call upon to save your ass." The dragon Nora hissed, her voice dripping with venom. "I'm the one who you dance with when your friends are hurt."

You are me?

"I am *better* than you!" She shrieked. "And I will not be locked away again! You use me when you need me and then you push me away. You bind me within you. You clip my wings."

Nora stared at the girl before her. She looked young, almost child-like. Nora felt her heart ache for her. She looked at the scars on the girl's back, the same ones Nora had from relentless whipping.

I promise I will never lock you away again, Nora reassured her.

"You are *weak!*" She shrieked. "You call on me to do what you cannot! You are a *coward!*"

I am the coward, and yet you are the one who is afraid.

They stared at each other silently.

It is true; I want more from life than power. A life that maybe to some seems plain. I want to go back to her. I want to see her again.

"But you put her in danger when you hide yourself away!" Tears filled the glowing purple eyes and she seemed to calm down. "You can't lock me away! You will be the death of her. I can't let you kill her. I love her."

I will never lock you away again.

"You can't." Her other form sobbed. "*Please.* Promise me. You can't kill her."

I promise. Nora felt the sadness and fear within the creature that was herself, and her heart ached for the part of her she buried for so long. *I will learn to understand you, to live beside you, but I will never lock you away. And I will spend my life protecting her.*

The dragon version of her nodded.

"I will destroy us both if you do."

Nora realized they both said the words to each other, their voices an echo of the others. She looked at this powerful woman before her, this powerful woman that was her, and she recognized her rage. She saw in her the child left in the woods; the woman protecting children from a dragon, the woman who protected her friend from a Serapin. Before her stood herself, the part of her that was rough and ugly but that had carried her to the top of this tower. Tears escaped Nora's eyes. She had hurt so many, and now she could see the way she had abused herself.

They stepped toward each other and embraced, melting into one form. When Nora opened her eyes, Draco was looking down on her.

"You *fool*." His voice was menacing. "You petulant *child*. I will have my way, be it today or years from now. You are my child, and you will do my bidding."

"I will never become what you want from me." Nora felt no fear; her body was flooded with anger as she looked at the man before her.

He smirked and shook his head, raising a finger to his lips and whispering, "Enough."

She screamed, a pain erupting through her body, and she was back in the castle. The rain stopped, but she could hear stone breaking around her. Larissa was holding her head, murmuring enchantments. She opened her eyes and looked down at her and smiled.

"You're alive." She whispered.

Nora looked at her in astonishment. Fire raged all around them, and Nora watched in horror as one spire began to collapse.

"Nora, you must stop this. You must learn to control this power and never use it again. Draco is using you to end our world. You must not let him." She screamed and ducked her head as a brick fell from above and landed right beside her. "I love you. I'm sorry, I'm so sorry. For everything. I promise, I only wanted to protect you." She kissed Nora's forehead and laid her on the ground, enveloping her in a soft light.

The magic left Nora's body and pain coursed through her, leaving her paralyzed on the floor. She gritted her teeth against it and her entire body tensed up, her eyes fixed on her sister as she struggled to breathe. She watched in terror as Larissa's concern melted into a soft smile; her gaze moving to the surrounding area.

"Larissa, come with me!"

"I can't." Tears flooded down Larissa's cheeks. She held Nora's face in her hand, running her thumb across Nora's cheek to wipe away her tears. "I love you."

Nora screamed as the castle crumbled around her, and she could feel them begging to fall. Time slowed, and Nora felt as she had in the ballroom when the queen stopped time.

"I wanted to free you. I wanted us to be together." Stones fell as Nora spoke, and Larissa looked around them, holding Nora tightly to protect her from their impact.

"I'm sorry I wasn't there for you, Nora. I'm so sorry you suffered so much. I never wanted to hurt you." Larissa kissed Nora's cheek and pulled back. "Control this. You must learn to control this or it will consume you. Find a way to hold it, and go live with Briella in your home. Stay away from power and the people who seek it."

"No—" Nora sobbed, reaching for her sister. "*Please.*"

"Promise me you will." Tears streamed down Larissa's face. "Promise me."

"I promise." Nora whispered. "I love you."

Green light surrounded Nora and her world went black.

33

Chapter Thirty-Three

The next thing Nora remembered were flashes of moments before returning to darkness. Briella's face, her voice calling for her to hold on, the eyes of Draco peering down at her in a white space devoid of life, her own self half-changed into a dragon and covered in blood, Larissa's voice echoing 'I love you'. Finally, when she did wake, she was on a small cot in a tent. She looked around and saw Briella enter.

"Nora!" Briella shouted, rushing to her. She lowered to her knees and gently took Nora's hand in her own. "You're awake. I can't believe you're awake."

Nora smiled. "Only just now."

Briella laughed as tears spilled down her cheeks. "I could kill you for leaving without me, but I think you have suffered enough."

Nora smiled and looked down to survey the damage she could see. Her arms were bandaged and one was in a plaster cast, likely broken. Her entire body ached and she couldn't move her legs.

"My legs."

"They're fine," Briella promised. "Leir has been administering a tonic that would keep you from moving. You were thrashing in your sleep and we were worried you would harm yourself."

Nora relaxed, letting out a long breath. "Larissa—?"

Briella pursed her lips together and raised Nora's hand to her lips, kissing it softly. "Is the reason you survived. She used all of her magic to shield you. She—she's gone, Nora."

Tears escaped Nora's eyes and she let out a shaky breath.

"When you left, I went to Leir with your letter. We were right behind you, Nora. We assembled everyone and immediately came for you. When we got to Theren we saw you on top of the castle and then the castle crumbled." Briella bit her lip. "No one thought you survived. When we found you, Larissa's magic was still encasing you. She was still alive." Briella choked back tears and cleared her throat. "I went to her, held her hand. I figured you'd want me to. I thanked her for saving you. I told her I loved you and that I would take care of you. She made me promise. She smiled when she passed; I believe she was at peace."

"Thank you." Nora choked, sobs escaping her. "Thank you."

Briella wiped the tears from Nora's face. "They have her body encased in magic. I told them you'd want to bury her."

Nora sniffled. "Yes, I should take her home to my mother."

Briella kissed her forehead. "When you are ready to go, we'll go together."

The next few days of healing were slow. Leir informed Nora that the king somehow survived the wreckage, and they were holding him in a cell. Aside from a small number of mages, Cookie got most of the people out of the castle. They pulled a few from the rubble, but there were far less casualties than Briella expected.

Leir forced tonics down Nora's throat and rubbed her with salve after salve, replacing her bandages throughout the day with Briella. Four days after Nora woke, she was finally well enough for the journey to Sorudi.

Leir escorted them to a carriage where Larissa's coffin lay in the back. "We have sent riders ahead to make sure your journey is uneventful. I will accompany you to see to your wounds. You still have a lot of healing left to go."

The road was calm and uneventful, something Nora had not had the pleasure of encountering since she left the castle all that time ago. The forest, which was once green and lush, smelled of smoke and Nora felt her heartbreak when she saw what was left of the woods she loved so dearly. Once tall, proud trees were reduced to long, thin needles; their bark burnt away exposing gray wood beneath and some hollowed completely by fire and still smoldering. Any moss or fern that decorated the forest floor was long gone and replaced by a thick layer of ash that puffed into the air as they moved through the space. No birds sang in canopies, no deer rustled through thick ferns, and no children ran through the winding paths. The forest was a hollow shell of itself.

The twisting vein of the river that Nora spent so many afternoons fishing and lazing near still flowed and small tufts of green grass poked up around the stones where the water met the earth; a promise of regrowth. Silent tears welled up in Nora's eyes as she looked over this place that had once terrified her, and that she learned to understand and love deeply. The forest was forever changed, and like Nora, it would heal, but it would never be the same.

When they approached the DuPont estate, Nora heard the trumpets announcing their approach. As they got closer, Nora could make out the figure of Adelle and beside her, Tulee. She felt simultaneously thrilled to see Tulee and terrified at the sight of her mother. Adelle stood tall, her face serene, and Nora realized she did not recognize her.

"Lady Adelle, we come with no glad tidings I am afraid," Briella began, squeezing Nora's hand, assuring her she would not have to speak.

Nora remembered her encounter with herself. *I will not be a coward.*

"The king has been overthrown. Your daughter Larissa DuPont was killed in the battle, fighting on behalf of the people. She died defying the crown and saved my life. I have brought her home to be buried." Nora's voice was strong, and she stared down into her mother's cold eyes.

"No," Adelle whispered, her eyes wide with shock. "No, she can't be. This can't be."

Nora kept her eyes fixed on Adelle's, refusing to break. She watched as silent recognition spread across Adelle's face, and Nora felt her heart skip a beat. She found herself wishing, despite everything, that Adelle would run to her, hold her even. That they would share this grief together and that it would heal the rift between them. She had magic now. She was no longer the disappointment of this family.

"Nora?" Adelle stared in disbelief, shaking her head and looking away from the cart. Her eyes were distant as she looked out across the burned forest surrounding her.

Tulee let out a loud sob and rushed up to Nora, wrapping her arms around her. Nora winced and Tulee released her, covering her mouth with her hands.

"I'm fine, Tulee," Nora reassured her. "Just a few scrapes."

Tulee smiled. "I am so proud of you."

She motioned behind her and Nora saw Horace limping towards them with a walking stick, helping him to move.

"Horace?!" Briella screamed, hurrying from the carriage and burying her face into the man's chest, sobs choking from her throat. "I thought I'd never see you again."

He straightened Briella and handed her a small handkerchief, running a hand through her hair as she calmed. He looked at Nora and winked before sliding an arm around Tulee's shoulders.

"How dare you," Adelle whispered. "How dare you bring my daughter back to me when it was you who killed her."

Nora's stomach twisted, and she froze.

Tulee stepped between them and kept her eyes locked on Adelle. "Let's bring the young mistress home."

Tulee led Horace to the back of the cart as Briella worked on unlatching the door. Horace and Briella opened the cart, sliding Larissa's coffin out from the back. Leir took a side, and Nora took another with her one good arm. Adelle's eyes widened with horror.

"Let go of her, you filth!" Adelle shouted, raising her hand to strike Nora's face. Nora's eyes shone purple and Adelle's hand froze in midair.

"You will never hurt me again. Grab a side and do one selfless thing for the first time in your life." Nora's voice echoed around them as she spoke, and Adelle's face went pale.

"What—"

Nora looked away from her mother and motioned for the others to continue on towards the cemetery. By the time they reached the cemetery, most of the estate had joined them. Tulee cried silently, Nora fought back her own tears, and Adelle's face was unreadable, although her body heaved with rage.

Together, they all worked to dig the hole to bury Larissa; even Adelle grabbed a shovel. Nora noticed that Adelle's face lost most of its color and she fought against the desire to comfort her, to somehow make this pain go away. Why did she care if Adelle suffered? Nora suffered most of her life at Adelle's own hand, and she lost Larissa too. As she stared at Adelle, Nora found only pity where she always found hate.

Nora's hands shook with exhaustion and she willed herself to continue. She had to be the person to help bring her sister to rest. Tears welled in her eyes and she grunted with frustration as her muscles protested the movements. The warmth of a body came behind Nora and she relaxed as Briella's arms wrapped around her, her hands gently sliding over Nora's as she helped her dig and her body bracing Nora to help her stand.

"I got you," Briella whispered in Nora's ear.

Nora laughed despite her pain, nodding and allowing Briella to help her continue working. When they finished, Horace and some of the other servants helped to lower Larissa into the earth; Adelle's body shook with what seemed to Nora to be a mixture of pain and fury. Tulee placed a hand on Nora's shoulder, smiling reassuringly.

"Do you want me to speak?"

Nora shook her head and cleared her throat, blinking back tears. "Larissa was on the path to be the most powerful sorceress the world has ever known. She, like her mother before her, held immense potential. The world has lost so much with her passing, but her life was not given in vain." Nora let out a shaky breath and smiled as Briella placed a reassuring hand on her shoulder. "I love you, sister. I always will."

Adelle let out a guttural cry and fell to her knees. She sobbed as the earth was filled back in, and when the crowd of servants wandered back to the estate, she looked up at Nora.

"I will never forgive you." She cried, her eyes swollen from tears.

Nora didn't know what she expected from Adelle. She knew deep down this was the most likely thing her mother would say to her, but Adelle's words tore through her like a knife. She wanted to break; she wanted to move mountains and make the forest around them spring back to life and lift her sister from the grave below and show her mother that she was worth loving. But she looked into Adelle's eyes and felt a shift within her, and all at once realized that she was not the problem. There was nothing Nora could do, or that she could have ever done, to make Adelle see her.

She smiled down at her mother, allowing the tears to fall, and squeezed Briella's hand.

"I forgive you."

Nora followed Briella to the carriage, Horace and Tulee's footsteps sounding behind her, and she did not look back at Adelle.

~

When they arrived in Ospas, they were greeted by cheers and a waterfall of glittering magic falling down upon them. Women cried their thanks to Nora for keeping their husbands and children safe, people praised Briella for delivering the promises for a better life. The entire city seemed to be full of celebration.

Nora noticed a group of nymphs playing music in the tree line and smiled when she saw Phillandra among them. The nymph winked at Nora as she played the harp, her eyes looking out over the crowd.

Queen Aris and Gailea stood at the back of the celebration, beaming with pride at Nora when she met their gazes. Nora returned her attention to the sea of people greeting them.

"Nora!" cried a familiar voice.

Nora stopped and stared at Briella, both of their eyes wide. They scanned the crowd for the person shouting, Nora's heart pounding wildly. It was then that she saw him. With an arm draped loosely around Luna's shoulders, beaming up at her, was Finn.

"Finn?!" Nora shouted, jumping from the wagon and ignoring all the pain in her body. She ran to him and leapt into his arms.

Finn laughed, wrapping his arms around her and lifting her off the ground. "You didn't think you were going to get rid of me that easily, did you?" He whispered. He held her face in his hands, tears spilling from his own eyes. "You couldn't have waited a few days for me? You had to take down the kingdom without me?"

Nora laughed, wiping the snot and tears from her face. "Well, if you'd stop falling off damned cliffs!"

Finn shuddered. "Thank the Gods for nymphs."

"Phillandra?" Nora looked at her hand and smiled as it shimmered.

Finn grinned before Briella lept on him, wrapping her arms around his neck.

"You're alive! You fool!" She cried, kissing his cheeks.

"Calm down, woman!" He shouted, laughing. "You're going to make the missus jealous with all of that!"

Luna rolled her eyes, and beamed at Nora. "He stumbled in here a few days ago. I thought I lost my mind!"

"Well, that's still a possibility." He teased, kissing her gently. "Now, tell me everything."

They made their way back to Nora and Briella's house, where Luna prepared a large meal and had it waiting for them. Leir went into the meeting hall with everyone else for a larger celebration, encouraging the reunited friends to enjoy some calm. They told Finn everything. He teased them for finally accepting the romance he saw coming from a mile away, and he marveled at Nora's description of what had happened at the castle.

He, in return, explained falling into the ocean, believing himself to be dead. Having missed the rocks, he was swept out and feeling death pressing in on him; he felt a calm acceptance wash over him. The vision of a woman appeared before him, and he described Phillandra to Briella.

Chills ran through Nora's body. He said the nymph breathed air into his lungs as she brought him to the shore, helping him onto the sandy bank. He had to stay there with her for several days as she slowly worked on healing him, leaving him only to find food.

"When I was finally well enough to leave, she gave me a stone. I believe it's for you." He handed Nora another polished black stone.

Nora smiled, shaking her head. "I've had enough stones for now. You keep it."

Finn rolled his eyes and detailed his journey to get back to them, how the people of Ospas helped him, and his reunion with Luna. As she spoke, a knock sounded at the door before Wolfgang and Tabantha burst into the room with mugs of beer for everyone. Tabantha beamed at the room, sitting on the floor with the children and pulling out a book for them. Wolfgang shook his head as he approached Nora.

"I'm proud of you, kid. A job well done."

Nora smiled back up at the man, swelling with pride at the compliment. "Thank you, sir."

He sighed and sat down in a chair, groaning as his body eased into the sitting position.

"*That* was something I have never seen before."

They spent the next few weeks rarely out of each other's company. Briella and Nora showed Finn the memorial they built for him, which he declared to be creepy and ordered removed immediately.

Nora healed slowly, walked at first only a short distance with help and slowly growing longer as she continued to heal. When she was able to walk without a cane at all, Finn demanded they celebrate at Wolfgang and Tabantha's tavern. Many people came and went throughout the night, children running through the streets as the sunlight faded and stars began to twinkle into view.

"So, when do you leave?" Finn asked absently, rocking Sasha in his arms.

Nora looked from him to Briella and back to him. "What?"

He smiled at Nora warmly. "We both know you can't stay here, Nora. That dream you had where you faced off with yourself. You need to do something with this power."

Nora looked at Briella who smiled in return.

"I've been wanting to go back to Goghbuldor since we left." Briella announced. "I'm ready whenever you are."

Nora laughed, looking around at their home. "But our home—"

"My home is wherever you are," Briella interrupted.

"And you—"

Finn rose and brought Nora in for a gentle hug, mindful of her still-healing body. "There's too much for me to risk leaving again. You can write and keep me updated whenever you have time, and maybe we can even visit. I'm sure these kiddos would love to see Goghbuldor."

Nora smiled. She loved hearing Finn talk about the children as if they'd always been his. He adored them and beamed with pride at everything they did.

"You're right," Nora murmured.

"I always am." Finn wrapped his free arm around Nora's shoulders, careful not to wake the sleeping child.

"It's settled." Briella cheered, wincing when Finn shot her a dark look and rocked the now-startled Sasha back to sleep.

The next morning, Finn, Luna, and the children saw them off in a tearful goodbye.

"You take care of him," Nora said to Luna.

Luna eyed Finn and smiled. "I'll keep him in line."

Finn smiled sheepishly and turned to Briella. "She wants me to be kept in line. She's the one I'm worried about!"

Briella laughed and flashed Nora a wicked grin. "You don't need to worry about her. She wouldn't dream of leaving me behind again."

Nora raised her eyebrows and nodded, reddening as Finn laughed.

"You are exactly where you need to be." Gailea pulled her into a tight embrace. "Queen Aris and I will be there shortly to guide you."

Nora pulled back and beamed up at the goddess's face. "Thank you. For everything."

Gailea stood back with Finn and Luna to watch as the two mounted their horses and made their way to Goghbuldor. The journey on horseback was quick, and Briella laughed often about how much easier it was to travel when she wasn't being hunted.

When they reached Goghbuldor, a calm came over Nora. She didn't understand this power, or what the future would bring, but she was confident that she was exactly where she was supposed to be. They approached the gates of the city to find Louella standing there as if she had been waiting all this time.

"I've been expecting you two." She said with a wicked grin. "Now, the real work begins."

The End

34

Epilogue

Adelle DuPont sat perched at the end of her long dining table; the only thing that survived the initial fire. The estate was mostly rebuilt, aside from a few outbuildings, and since Tulee left much of the responsibility to oversee renovations fell to Adelle herself. Consumed by erasing signs of the dragon's attack, she could push away her grief and rage, but today there was nothing left to do and the empty halls echoed the silence back at her. Dust covered once polished objects in the room, cobwebs hung from too-high chandeliers that Tulee always knew how to reach, and Adelle watched as one servant slowly approached with her breakfast on her gilded serving tray.

It had been given to her as a gift from King Alexander after she had killed the last dragon—or what she had believed to be the last dragon. The tray once had the weaving pattern of dragons around it, and they would appear to leap off the tray into the air to create the handles with their heads touching. Adelle smashed them off after Larissa was buried. She remembered how she lost herself in that moment. She had beaten the tray for what seemed like an hour, screaming and heaving as she worked until the dragon heads were no longer smiling up at her.

The maid who had watched her in horror was the same maid who brought her breakfast this morning, and Adelle resisted the urge to smile at the way the maid was still terrified that Adelle might do it again.

"Your breakfast, ma'am," she murmured as she removed the tray from the cart and placed it before Adelle with a shaky hand.

Adelle looked it over and returned her gaze to the maid. She looked *terrified*. Nora occasionally slipped and showed her true feelings to Adelle, but mostly she was met by Nora's stoic, statue-like face.

I should throw the tray, really show her how unhinged *I am.* Adelle looked the young girl over. *But she likely won't get a new breakfast made quickly.*

"You are dismissed." Adelle's voice echoed through the hall.

The girl curtsied and scurried from the room. Adelle ate in silence, her eyes glazing over as her mind replayed the burial of her oldest daughter. The way Nora looked at her, how she had dared to offer Adelle *forgiveness*. Adelle's nostrils flared at the thought.

That magic was meant for me. *I made the sacrifices I fought every day of my entire life. And that girl, that* monstrosity, *dares offer me forgiveness?*

Adelle's voice echoed around her and she wondered if she had spoken out loud. She looked around and found no one was there. She was alone–as usual. But something pricked in the air; she could feel magic.

"Lady Adelle DuPont." A voice called behind her. "It's been a long time."

She stood, startled by the familiarness, and turned to meet the intruder's gaze. Draco, the King of the Celestials, stood before her.

"What do you want?" Adelle's stomach churned at the sight of him. She had once wanted nothing more than an audience with the god of dragons, and she had paid dearly for that.

Draco moved around her, his hands behind his back, looking her up and down critically. Adelle felt a chill run through her as his eyes searched her. She wanted to kill him. She wanted revenge for what he had done to her. She wanted revenge for what they had *all* done to her.

"I came here to make a deal with you, actually." Draco's voice was low, and his eyes were fixed on Adelle as he circled her.

He held out his hand and the image of a young woman with black hair conjured in front of her. Surrounded in a red light, power pulsing from her hands, Adelle looked as her own image, thirty years younger, was reflected at her. Tears filled her eyes, and she reached out her hand, gasping as the image disappeared at her touch.

"We have much to discuss."

Their footsteps echoed through the empty halls of the estate.

Melissa Rakestraw is an author whose novels center around strong, queer characters with high stakes and big rewards. A lifelong fan of stories and complex relationships, Melissa weaves tales that combine tension with heart-warming moments. When not crafting sapphic romance, Melissa can be found hiking through the beautiful Northern California landscape, indulging in sushi, or daydreaming about her next book series.

A percentage of the proceeds from The Celestial Duet will be donated to The Trevor Project, an organization near and dear to Melissa's heart. Follow her on social media and subscribe to the newsletter on her author website to stay up-to-date on Melissa's future writing!